Brides of
GEORGIA

50 States
of *Love*

Brides of GEORGIA

3-in-1 Historical Romance Collection

CONNIE STEVENS

BARBOUR BOOKS
An Imprint of Barbour Publishing, Inc.

Contents

Heart of Honor

To Miss Ann:
You are a living example of what it means
to have a heart of honor.
How blessed I am to call you my friend.

Chapter 1

Fort New Echota, Georgia
May 1837

Abigail, the matter is settled."

Abby Locke drew in a defiant breath at her father's tone and lifted her chin. The soldiers under Colonel Ephraim Locke's command jumped when he spoke, but Abby wasn't one of his troops. Did he think her fragile and defenseless merely because she wore skirts and petticoats instead of a uniform? She was a capable, grown woman, nineteen years of age.

"I still don't understand your reasoning, Father. Why must I leave the fort? You know I despise living in the city. The first thing Aunt Charlotte will do is plan a cotillion to parade me in front of every eligible bachelor she can find within the rolls of Raleigh society." Abby didn't even try to suppress the peevishness in her voice. "She'll drag me to her garden parties and teas so her friends can match me with their sons or nephews."

Her father turned to face her, displeasure forcing his thick eyebrows into a V. "Your aunt has done a great deal for you. You wouldn't have had the opportunity to attend Salem Female Academy were it not for the benefit of her connections. You should be grateful." He clasped his hands behind him and glowered at her.

She bit her lip. Admittedly, she'd resisted going to Salem at first. Some of the friendships she formed there carried her through the lonely times when she longed to be at the fort with her father and couldn't understand his insistence in sending her away. Had he known her best friend at Salem Female Academy had been Jane Ross, daughter of Cherokee chief, John Ross, he wouldn't have been pleased.

His gruff lecture interrupted her reminiscing. "My sister has tried her best to mold you into a proper young lady." He shook his head and took a few steps away from her, reducing his voice to mutter, as though his private thoughts took control of his tongue. "Heaven knows I didn't know what to do with you after your mother died."

Her father's comment, whether meant for her ears or not, seared her heart. Despite longing for his approval and affection, circumstances continually created differing opinions to divide them. Between her disagreement with him over the government's orders to remove the Cherokee from their land and her resistance to travel all the way from Fort New Echota to Raleigh to live with her aunt, she and her father found little common ground on which to agree. Just once, couldn't circumstances offer her a way to make her father love her?

"Why can't I stay here with you?" The words slipped out before she could stop them, but once they were out, she had no desire to snatch them back.

Her father plucked his hat from the rack and straightened the cock's feather on the side. "You know perfectly well why. Couldn't you for once in your life comply with my wishes without an argument? There is no point to this discussion. You know as well as I that tensions between the government and the Cherokee are becoming dangerously strained. I don't feel it's safe for you to stay here. I've made my decision, and I'll not tolerate this debate."

Father placed the hat atop his head and twisted the end of his mustache. He stood with his polished boots spread apart and one hand tucked behind his back. His typical posture gave the appearance of a fortified stone wall. "I've already received a letter from your aunt, and she is expecting you by the middle of June."

Abby itched to stamp her feet in frustration but such action would only strengthen her father's argument. What if she simply refused to go? Surely Father wouldn't bind her and forcibly toss her on the wagon. Would he? No, he'd never do anything so undignified, and the embarrassment she'd cause him with her refusal would only add to the long list of criticisms he kept in his head. She'd exhausted every plea. Nothing would change his mind.

The mantel clock chimed seven times. "Now then, your childish petulance has caused us to be late. Mrs. Cobb was told to expect you at seven sharp." Father hoisted her stuffed satchel and stalked to the door.

Abby snorted, certain Mrs. Cobb knew the colonel's headstrong daughter was digging her heels in, resisting the inevitable. It wasn't as if she wanted to be contrary. If things had been different, if her mother hadn't died, perhaps her father wouldn't have found it necessary to send her to her aunt. Her exasperation melted on a sigh of regret. She draped her light shawl around her shoulders and fussed with the ties of her bonnet.

Father's only response to her sigh was a frown, and he didn't meet her gaze before pushing the door open. His eyes shifted to the empty boardwalk beside the door where Abby's trunks had been sitting. "I see the man came and picked up the rest of your luggage already." He scowled. "I wanted to meet him and speak with him."

A retort made its way to Abby's throat, but she swallowed hard and denied it voice. Father didn't fool her for a minute. What he really wanted was to interrogate the man Mrs. Cobb had hired to guide them on their journey.

"Father, you know Florrie Cobb as well as I do. She wouldn't hire someone if she didn't believe he was capable and trustworthy. And besides, he will no doubt be waiting in front of the sutler's store with the wagon. You'll have ample opportunity to put him through your inquisition."

Father's *harrumph* rumbled back to her ears as he descended the stairs and lengthened his stride. Abby scurried to catch up with him. They crossed the compound and soldiers snapped to attention, cutting their right hands up to their temples in a stiff salute as her father passed. How could Father consider their situation unsafe when they were surrounded by soldiers who jumped at his very presence? Despite his claim of danger, Abby felt his real reason for sending her away was that he considered her a burden, especially when she dared to defy him.

Panting in her effort to keep up with her father, Abby followed on his heels until they came to the sutler's store. A wagon with a brand-new canvas stretched over the bows sat in front of the store waiting to take her where she didn't want to go. The early morning mist created an eerie shroud that encircled a tight cluster of army wives who took turns hugging Florrie Cobb, a gray-haired woman with crinkled lines around her eyes that deepened when she smiled.

One woman dabbed her eyes with the corner of her apron. "Florrie, we're going to miss you so. What if the new sutler doesn't want to carry yard goods or some of the other items you and Dewey always tried to get for us?"

At the mention of her late husband's name, Florrie's eyes glistened. "Now, Mabel, you know I can't run the store by myself. I'm sure the new man will order whatever you request. Besides, my niece in Raleigh is expecting me to come and live with her family." Florrie turned and her face brightened when she caught sight of Abby. She held her hand out and mischief gleamed in her eyes. "Here you are, my dear. I was beginning to think you'd won the argument."

Heat crept into Abby's face. Almost everyone at Fort New Echota knew of her penchant for disagreeing with her father. Florrie's quip, however, hinted the widow's sense of humor hadn't been affected by her recent bereavement. She'd be a pleasant traveling companion.

Father cleared his throat. "Mrs. Cobb, where is this man you've hired? I must satisfy myself that my daughter will be in good hands."

Abby bit her lip to restrain the grin that was tugging the corners of her mouth. "If he doesn't meet with your satisfaction, does that mean I can stay, Father?"

As expected, his jaw muscles twitched and his chin jutted out. Father turned a stern glare in her direction and with a purposeful shove, maneuvered her satchel into the back of the wagon. His lips, pressed into a tight, thin line, almost disappeared under his mustache.

At that moment, a tall, slender young man stepped out the door of the sutler's store, carrying a large crate filled with supplies and foodstuffs. Abby's breath caught. Mesmerizing hazel eyes glanced her way and held her captive for a split second. His sandy brown hair curled over his collar, and the breeze blew one lock in his eye. He stepped around her, carrying the box toward the tailgate.

"Excuse me, Miss."

The intonation of his voice rippled through Abby as she watched him heft the load with ease. Staring was impolite; Aunt Charlotte would cluck her tongue. Abby mentally reprimanded herself, but her gaze refused to listen. The young man stepped to the side of the wagon and checked the lashings securing the water barrel. It wasn't his muscular build that she studied. Abby couldn't take her eyes off his uniform. Darkened areas of material on his shoulders and arms traced the places where epaulets and rank insignias had been removed. Even the brass buttons bearing the army crest were missing, replaced with wooden pegs inserted through the buttonholes to keep his shirt closed. Raised on a dozen different army posts, nobody had to explain to Abby why his shirt was devoid of military displays.

The young man tugged the brim of his hat at Abby. "Miss Locke?"

Before Abby could reply, Father stepped between her and the man. "What is the meaning of this? Mrs. Cobb, do you know who, or should I say *what*, this man is?"

Florrie lifted her skirt as she stepped down from the boardwalk. "Well, of course, I do, Colonel. This is—"

"I know who he is." Father's voice lost its usual bellow. Instead, he lowered it to an ominous cross between a hiss and a growl that raised the hairs on the back of Abby's neck. "His name is Nathaniel Danfield. I had business at Fort Reed the day he was stripped of his commission and dishonorably discharged." Father's back was as rigid as a flagpole. "Mrs. Cobb, surely this isn't the man you've hired to act as an escort for my daughter and yourself all the way to Raleigh."

❧

Nathaniel questioned his choice of wearing the unadorned uniform blouse. He'd purchased two shirts that bore no evidence of his dismissal from the army, but the tenacity in his gut refused to retreat from the truth. Until he could clear his name, he'd encounter many more people like Colonel Locke. He lifted his chin and looked the colonel squarely in the eye. A reflex in the muscles of his right arm twitched with the instinct to salute, but he held his hand stiffly at his side.

"Colonel, I don't believe we've met, but since you seem to know me, we can dispense with the introductions. I'm not going to try to change your opinion of me. All I can offer is my word as a gentleman that I am committed to see the ladies safely to their destination."

An explosion of air burst from Colonel Locke's lips. "*Pfft*. Your word? This is unacceptable. Do you expect me to take the word of a man who defied orders and acted in contempt of the United States Army?"

Nathaniel cut his eyes to the group assembled near the wagon. Several appeared aghast at Locke's announcement, and one of the ladies fanned herself with her apron. Some soldiers crossing the compound stopped and stared. The cool of the morning couldn't prevent the heat that rose up his neck from his gut.

Mrs. Cobb stepped forward. The petite woman with her graying hair wound in a bun at the back of her head planted her fists on her ample hips and frowned at the colonel.

"Colonel Locke, I will ask you to remember that I am entrusting my own well-being to this young man as well as that of your daughter. Lieutenant Danfield and I—"

"He relinquished the privilege of being an officer in the federal army when he acted contrary to orders. Don't refer to him as lieutenant," Colonel Locke blustered.

Nathaniel ground his teeth and refused to recoil in the wake of Locke's bellowing. What was the worst the man could do to him other than public humiliation?

Apparently Mrs. Cobb wasn't intimidated by the colonel. The feisty older woman shook her finger at the pompous man. "Now you wait one minute, Ephraim Locke. I've had a long discussion with Nathaniel, and he has been completely honest with me. As is my practice, I talked over the matter with God. I'd never set out on such a venture without consulting Him first."

"Now, Mrs. Cobb, I didn't—"

"The good Lord has given me peace about hiring this young man to guide me to Raleigh. And furthermore, my niece and her husband, Mr. and Mrs. Jeremiah Barton, have been informed of our traveling schedule as well as Nathaniel's name and background." She turned to look at Nathaniel, and he could have sworn he saw her wink.

His heart smiled to know he had an ally in this spunky widow woman. "Ma'am, all the supplies are loaded. Is there anything else?"

"No, that's everything." Mrs. Cobb cast a glance to the sky. "The fog is lifting, and there is more than enough daylight to get under way. We should be able to leave within a few minutes." She peered into the back of the wagon. "Nathaniel, you'd best remove Miss Locke's belongings from the wagon since she won't be accompanying us."

The colonel's daughter ducked her head, slipping one hand up to cover her mouth before stepping over to the wagon and reaching for her satchel. She gripped the bag and dragged it toward the tailgate. Colonel Locke's face turned purple, and the veins in his neck stood out. The temptation to grin almost got the best of Nathaniel, but he maintained a stoic military bearing as the situation unfolded.

"Now, see here, Mrs. Cobb." The man scowled and reached to take the bag from his daughter's grasp. Miss Locke sent her father a withering look and stepped away from the wagon. "It's imperative that my daughter make this journey to Raleigh, and with the present situation regarding the Cherokee, I can't take the chance on the immediate availability of an escort." He pushed Miss Locke's satchel back into the wagon. Tossing a glare in Nathaniel's direction, he delivered an unmistakable warning, every bit as meticulous as issuing an order to a subordinate.

"I'll expect that my daughter will be delivered safely to her aunt in Raleigh, and I'll hold responsible anyone who impedes her journey in any way."

Nathaniel gave a short nod. "Since you are unwilling to take my word as my bond, sir, I can only state in the presence of these witnesses that I will do everything in my power to ensure the safety of both these women and see them transported to Raleigh as expeditiously as possible."

Colonel Locke took a step closer and lowered his voice to a menacing growl. "You'd better pray that to be the case, because I will hunt you relentlessly if any harm comes to my daughter."

Chapter 2

I f the first day of their journey was any indication, Nathaniel didn't hold out much hope for a pleasant passage through the north Georgia mountains. A soft late-spring breeze stirred the trees, the sun bathed his shoulders in warmth, and the vistas provided a feast for the eyes. But Miss Locke's complaining tongue cast a shadow of gloom over what might otherwise be an enjoyable trip.

"Mr. Danfield, are you aware that you've loaded this wagon incorrectly? The heavy trunks should be over the wheels instead of against the back of the seat."

Nathaniel pressed his lips together. He didn't bother to explain that he'd spent extra time balancing the load for stability. In addition, he'd arranged the cargo with the ladies' comfort in mind, stacking blankets and quilts behind the trunks to provide space for them to sit and read or do needlework. The colonel's daughter made no mention of his efforts.

He turned his head to call over his shoulder. "Are you ladies comfortable back there?"

Mrs. Cobb replied first. "Yes, Nathaniel, we're fine."

Miss Locke's snort of disagreement followed on the heels of the widow's words. "I don't see how you can expect us to be comfortable when you've hit every rock and rut between here and Fort New Echota."

Nathaniel started to offer her the reins but refrained from doing so, afraid she might take him up on it. He tightened his grip.

Mrs. Cobb clucked her tongue. " 'He that refraineth his lips is wise. The tongue of the just is as choice silver.' Abby honey, it's a long way to Raleigh. Criticism will only make the road bumpier."

A grin tipped Nathaniel's lips upward as he snapped the reins to encourage the horses to step up their pace a bit. Stopping the wagon to kiss Mrs. Cobb would likely earn him further scorn from Miss Locke, so he satisfied himself with basking in the silence that resulted from the widow's gentle rebuke.

Growing up in the preacher's house, he was accustomed to hearing scriptures used as a ready answer for any of life's questions. But Nathaniel hadn't bothered to look for a verse that instructed a man who'd been branded with dishonor. Reverend Danfield would be disappointed, more so than he already was. Nathaniel's insistence on joining the army instead of becoming a minister hadn't been well received by the man who raised him. How could he write to the kindly preacher and tell him about the dishonorable discharge? Nathaniel shook off the thought.

ﻝﻪ

Nathaniel traced his finger along the crude map and frowned. According to Rufe, the hostler at Fort New Echota, they should have come to a miner's road by now. Nathaniel had patiently endured the elderly man's ramblings about fighting in the Revolution and being among the first to carve out an existence in the part of Georgia they now navigated. While the old gent spun his stories, he scratched out the markings on a scrap of oilcloth with a piece of charcoal and assured Nathaniel if he followed the miner's road, he'd be in Blairsville in less than a week, cutting a couple of days off their journey. Counting off the sunsets and sunrises in his mind, they should have come upon Blairsville two or three days ago.

When he'd steered the team onto the trail they currently followed, he'd thought this was Rufe's miner's road. By the time they'd made camp last night, the road had narrowed to a path barely wide enough for the wagon. Surely if they pressed on today, they'd come to Blairsville, where they could replenish their supplies.

He leaned to his left and glanced around the corner of the wagon at the women who were engaged in making breakfast. The colonel's daughter had proved her worth at helping with the cooking and setting up camp each evening. She and Mrs. Cobb got along well. All her faultfinding seemed to be reserved for him. His uncertainty about their position would no doubt spur a whole new round of criticism. The relentless rain they'd encountered the past two days had slowed them considerably, and the colonel's daughter had all but accused Nathaniel of causing the inclement weather. If God used each circumstance to teach His children some spiritual truth, Nathaniel hoped he learned it quickly.

Nathaniel grimaced as he recalled the conversation he'd overheard the night before between Mrs. Cobb and Miss Locke. He wanted to resent Miss Locke's attitude, but her lamenting over being sent away struck a nerve. More than most people, Nathaniel understood the sting of rejection. *Felicia's rejection.*

He gritted his teeth against the uninvited memory and stuffed the map into his bedroll. The aroma of fresh coffee and frying fatback drew him to the campfire. Miss Locke glanced up from pouring coffee into a tin cup. She made a lovely picture standing there in the midst of the early morning sun that created planes of ethereal light beaming through the trees. Lovely, as long as she didn't open her mouth.

Mrs. Cobb handed a tin plate to Nathaniel. "There's still some honey in the crock." She tucked an unruly tendril of gray hair into her bonnet. "Do you think perhaps you could snare a rabbit for supper?"

Nathaniel looked past Miss Locke through the trees. Woods should be full of game. He nodded. "We'll stop early this afternoon, and I'll go hunting."

"Stop early?" The disagreement in Miss Locke's voice grated on Nathaniel's nerves like a striated note from an out-of-tune fiddle. "We'll be on this cow path you call a road forever if we stop early. It doesn't look as if it's been traveled in years. Weren't we supposed to arrive in Blairsville before now? You know we're running low on food and other supplies."

"Abby dear, Nathaniel is doing the best he can." Mrs. Cobb patted the younger woman's shoulder and handed him a tin cup of steaming coffee.

The sigh that escaped Miss Locke's lips defined her melancholy mood. "Do you think we'll reach Blairsville today?"

It wasn't a question he wanted to answer. The sinking sensation in his stomach mocked him as he stared at the women over the edge of his coffee cup. He wished he could assure both ladies that they were on course and on schedule. Old Rufe's map and directions were proving as faulty as the man's memory of the battles he'd fought. Other men at the fort could have given him more accurate directions, but none would speak to him. His stigma of dishonor caused doors to slam in his face. Rufe was the only one who talked to him.

Deciding honesty was best, he took a sip of coffee and met the expectant gazes of both women.

"I hope so." He didn't blink as he looked squarely into Miss Locke's eyes and braced himself for her reaction. "This miner's road is not what I expected." He jutted his chin toward the rising sun. "For the most part, this trail is heading straight east. After the rain and clouds cleared last night, I checked the position of the Polaris star to the north and the constellation Orion to the south. I had hoped this miner's road would lead us in a more northeasterly direction."

"You hoped?" Miss Locke sputtered. "Do you mean to tell us we're lost?"

Irritation burned in his chest. "I just told you we can accurately determine our position by the sun during the day and the stars at night." At least that much was true, but he stopped short of telling the women they weren't lost. He stuffed the last bite of corn bread in his mouth and dropped his empty tin plate into the bucket on the tailgate.

"If you ladies will break camp, I'll start harnessing the horses. I want to be ready to roll in twenty minutes."

Miss Locke planted her hands on her hips. "But you just said you don't know where this road leads."

He gave her a hard look. Her dark-brown eyes snapped with tenacity, and the curve of her cheek presented a mighty temptation for a man to forget himself. Mahogany hair pulled back into a single thick braid down her back caught the morning light. But present circumstances carved a chasm between them.

"Twenty minutes, Miss Locke." He strode off to tend to his task wishing they were closer to Raleigh.

≥•

As the lingering raindrops evaporated from the foliage and the sun rose to its zenith, Abby was grateful for the canopy of trees. The ascending terrain most of the morning had hampered their progress. Mr. Danfield pulled back on the lines to bring the team to a halt and glanced over his shoulder at her and Florrie.

"We'll stop here for about thirty minutes to rest the horses. I'll see if I can find a stream to fill the canteens."

Florrie tucked away her knitting. "We'll have some lunch ready for you when you get back."

When Abby slid to the end of the tailgate, Mr. Danfield offered his hand and helped her disembark the wagon. The strength of his hand sent tingles all the way to her elbow. Without a word, he slung the canteens over his shoulder and proceeded up the trail. She followed him with her eyes. Was it her imagination or had the way grown narrower? The ravine to the left plunged several hundred feet and the woods and thick underbrush on the right hemmed them close to the edge.

Abby busied her hands helping Florrie with assembling a lunch of leftovers. Nathaniel returned to the wagon and tossed the canteens inside. He accepted the piece of cold corn bread Florrie handed him and sat on a rock. He appeared troubled, as if he had something he needed to confess.

"Ladies, you aren't going to be happy about this, but I'm afraid the trail up ahead is impassable."

"What do you mean?" Distress filled Abby's chest. With every passing day the knot in her stomach grew. At first the prospect of spending the rest of the year with Aunt Charlotte nurtured resentment, but as she and Florrie talked last night, the widow's gentle understanding caused

Abby to admit regret in forcing her father's hand. Given another chance, she'd repent of her insolence and disrespect, but it was too late. She was already more than a week's journey away from the fort, following a trail on a wooded mountainside that led to who knew where. Needles of panic pricked her. "Are we going to have to cut our way through? I thought this was a miner's road."

Florrie laid a calming hand on Miss Locke's shoulder. "What do you propose, Nathaniel?"

He swallowed the corn bread and took a sip of water from his tin cup. "We have no choice. We'll have to turn around."

"Turn around? And go where?" Abby flung both arms out to her sides. If she could choose, she'd opt to go back to Fort New Echota. But the privilege of choice had been taken out of her hands.

Mr. Danfield gestured in the direction they'd come. "Two days back we passed a trail that branched off to the north. It seemed to be well traveled, but according to the map and directions I was given—"

"What map? Whose directions?" She tried unsuccessfully to keep the petulance from her voice.

The deposed army officer stood and drained the remainder of his water cup. "Miss Locke, we need to turn this wagon around. You can help if you want to, but if not, please do me the favor of staying out of my way."

Mrs. Cobb wrung her hands. "Abby! Nathaniel! Both of you stop this. Squabbling isn't going to get us where we need to go."

"Hmph." Abby crossed her arms and turned her back on him.

Was this a bad joke? As much as Abby dreaded going to Raleigh, being lost in the wilderness didn't hold much appeal either. She watched as Mr. Danfield maneuvered the horses to the side and then guided them to step back, turning the wagon sharply backward. The left rear wheel dug into the soft, rain-soaked dirt. She waved both hands over her head.

"Stop!"

Mr. Danfield threw her a vexed look. "What is it, Miss Locke?"

She pointed to the wheel. "You need to put something under this wheel before it sinks in any deeper."

Mr. Danfield stomped over and scowled at the wheel. "I'll see if I can find some flat rocks."

Florrie bustled over and looked over the situation. "We can help, can't we, Abby?"

Before she could reply, Mr. Danfield held up his hand. "No, no. I don't want you ladies carrying rocks. They're likely to be muddy after two days of rain. Besides, you might find a snake living under a rock."

Abby pondered his last statement. She couldn't dismiss her father's opinion of the man. Disallowing her and Florrie to help him with the rocks might be chivalrous, but dishonor was a designation she couldn't ignore. Sometimes snakes weren't the only things of which to beware.

Once he had a number of rocks in place, he took the reins and waved his hand toward the ladies. "Miss Locke, if you and Mrs. Cobb will please stay over there while I back this wagon up." He whistled to the team and encouraged them into motion.

The rocks worked, and the wagon lurched backward. The instant the left rear wheel cleared the rocks, however, the soft dirt crumbled and collapsed under the weight of the wagon, triggering a small landslide down the ravine. The rear wheel pitched downward, slamming the wooden spokes on an exposed boulder. The wagon tipped precariously.

Abby clapped a hand over her mouth to prevent a scream from escaping. Thumping and scraping noises inside the canvas-covered wagon testified to the shifting of the cargo. She heard the trunks slam against the tailgate.

Mr. Danfield calmed the spooked horses. "Whoa, there." He looked over to where Florrie stood clinging to Abby's hand. "You ladies keep back. That ledge is unstable."

The initial alarm that tightened her throat ripened into anger in the space of a single heartbeat. She crossed her arms over her chest and allowed the sarcasm to spill from her mouth. "Now is a fine time to realize that. Why didn't you check before you began backing the wagon up?" She sent him the hottest glare she could manage.

He didn't give her a glance but instead slowly edged to the back of the wagon to inspect the left rear wheel. She heard him heave a sigh.

"The wheel spokes are broken."

"Oh dear. What will we do, Nathaniel?" Florrie clasped her hands under her chin.

He came around the front of the wagon, patting the horses as he went. "We have a spare wheel tied under the wagon bed, but I'm going to have to use a lever and fulcrum to raise that corner of the wagon up. First, I need to lighten the load."

Heat rose into Abby's face. "This is outrageous. When my father hears of this—"

"Abby, please." Florrie spun and gripped her by the shoulders. The widow spoke as sternly as a schoolmarm. "Your anger isn't helping. Let's give Nathaniel a hand unloading."

Mr. Danfield picked up a large rock and positioned it behind the right rear wheel before reaching in and grabbing two bulging satchels. He tossed them to the ground and eyed Abby. "I'm going to make sure the brake is set. Don't try to climb into the wagon."

He strode to the front of the wagon and set one booted foot on the hub of the wheel to climb to the driver's seat. A gravelly laugh sounded behind her. She whipped around. Two men, the lower half of their faces covered with neckerchiefs, pointed guns at Mr. Danfield.

Chapter 3

Abby's breath caught in her throat. One of the men aimed his gun in her direction. It looked like a cannon. Her heartbeat roared in her ears. Mr. Danfield raised his hands and moved toward Florrie like he was stepping on glass. Abby fought off a wave of dizziness and clenched her fists, forcing air into her lungs. She would *not* swoon.

"You, I said move." The gunman wearing a leather vest and faded red neckerchief waggled his weapon in her face. "Get over there."

"Miss Locke?" Mr. Danfield spoke in a quiet, even voice. "Just do what they say. Come over here with Mrs. Cobb."

"Please, Abby." The quiver in Florrie's voice pierced Abby's heart. How dare these hooligans frighten Florrie. Outrage ignited deep within her chest. "Mr. Danfield, *do* something."

The other man wearing the blue neckerchief over his face cackled. "Sonny boy is doin' just fine, missy. Now do as you're told and you won't get hurt."

She backed up toward Florrie. The poor woman's hands trembled as her fingers clutched Abby's sleeve. Abby cut her eyes toward Mr. Danfield, who reached to push her behind him.

"Take what you want, but leave these women alone."

Abby couldn't believe her ears. "What do you mean, telling them to take what they want?"

The man with the red neckerchief laughed. "She's a spit-fire, ain't she?" Abby shivered under the scrutiny of his cold eyes.

The outlaw glanced over his shoulder. "See what's in them bags there."

"No!" Abby started to take a step forward, but Mr. Danfield grabbed her arm and tugged her back behind him.

"Stay put, and be quiet."

Indignation rankled her as the second man yanked articles of clothing from the satchels and tossed them in the dirt. "I'll not be quiet. He has no right—"

Mr. Danfield spun to face her. His glower froze her words before they could cross her lips. He hissed at her through clenched teeth, "What would you rather lose? Your belongings or your life? Now be quiet, and do what they say."

Abby glared back. Her chest heaved in and out, and her stomach twisted into a knot.

"That's good advice." The man in the vest sent a piercing look in Abby's direction, while the one with the blue neckerchief yanked her reticule from the satchel.

"What have we here?" The thief tugged on the strings holding the purse closed, but the first man stopped him.

"Toss it here. We'll look inside later when we bivouac." He brandished his gun and motioned Mr. Danfield toward the team. "Unhitch them horses and bring 'em over here."

Abby saw the muscles in Mr. Danfield's neck stiffen, and he hesitated for a long moment. When the man pulled back the hammer of his pistol, Mr. Danfield lifted both arms out to his sides.

"All right." He moved toward the horses. "Just leave the ladies alone." He followed the criminal's order with wooden-like movements, continually glancing at Abby and Florrie. Ire curled its claws around Abby's stomach. Her mind raced to remember where Mr. Danfield kept his rifle. *Under the driver's seat.* Could he reach in for the gun while unhitching the horses?

Mr. Danfield loosed the horses from their harnesses and led them where the outlaw directed, looping the reins over a low-hanging branch. He returned and positioned himself in front of Florrie, motioning Abby to stay behind him. The bandit standing before them directed the other to raid the back of the wagon. The second man holstered his gun and climbed up the front wheel, swinging his leg over the driver's seat and into the back of the wagon. The very idea of either one of the malefactors touching her things—especially those things hidden in the bottom of her smaller trunk—sent shafts of revulsion through her. No, they would not put their filthy hands on her precious keepsakes. She lunged forward.

The outlaw in the leather vest startled when she knocked against his arm. His gun fell to the ground. Before she could draw breath, Mr. Danfield dove for the weapon. A tangle of arms and legs ensued as the two men fought for control.

The other man stuck his head out of the wagon when the scuffle started. Abby grabbed a downed tree limb with the intention of using it as a club. The rotten wood broke apart in her hands. She threw the piece she still held at the thief who jumped from the wagon, whacking him full in the face. He reeled for only a moment, but it was long enough for her to lower her head and charge into him like an angry bull. Caught off balance, he fell against the wagon with a grunt of surprise.

"Why, you little she-devil..." He pushed away from the wagon, and it wobbled on the unstable ground at the edge of the ravine. He came at her, growling fiercely. She nimbly jumped beyond his reach, nearly becoming ensnared in the ongoing struggle between Mr. Danfield and the first man as they continued to wrestle for the weapon. A gunshot split the air as Danfield knocked the pistol from the outlaw's hand. Florrie's terrified scream ripped through the trees.

In the space of a heartbeat, Abby glanced in Florrie's direction. The second man grabbed Abby around the middle. His grip forced the air from her lungs. She wrenched one hand free and clawed at the brute, dragging the blue neckerchief away from his unshaven face. His vile breath turned her head, and she saw Mr. Danfield still fighting with the man in the vest. He slammed his fist into the bandit's jaw, sending him sprawling.

With lightning reflexes, Mr. Danfield leaped across the space, his hands outstretched and fingers splayed. The outlaw who held Abby shoved her aside and turned his attention on Danfield. From the corner of her eye, she saw the first man stagger to his feet.

"Watch out!" She and Florrie screamed in unison.

Danfield caught the neck of the man with whom he fought in a headlock and spun him around to meet the other man surging toward him. The man in the vest crashed against the wagon while Danfield continued to fight with the one who'd accosted Abby. Rain-softened soil along the rim of the ravine crumbled and fell as loose rocks gave way from under the two left wheels. The wagon tilted as the unstable ground caved in under the weight.

The outlaw in the blue bandanna reached for his gun, and Danfield lunged for the man's arm, the two of them rolling in the dirt as they wrestled for possession of the weapon. The other man bent and picked up the rock with which Danfield had chocked the rear wheel and raised it over his head, aiming it at Mr. Danfield.

"No!" Abby hurled herself into the man, causing him to drop the rock. He lurched backward at the same time Danfield scrambled to his feet and grabbed his opponent, slinging him into his partner with unexpected strength. Both men slammed against the wagon.

The conveyance teetered as more rocks loosened from the soft earth, tipping the wagon at a perilous angle. Unbalanced and no longer held fast by the team, the wagon pitched to the side and toppled down the ravine.

Abby watched in horror, as trunks and crates entangled with bedding and canvas, all crashed through the labyrinth of saplings and brush on its way down the abyss.

A string of curses blistered her ears. Abby jerked her head to see the bandit in the blue bandanna whip his gun from its holster and point it straight at her. She forgot how to breathe.

"No!" Mr. Danfield's voice rang out, the single syllable elongated in strident discord with the simultaneous explosion of gunfire. His body impacted hers, plowing her to the ground. Somewhere in the midst, Florrie screamed.

Abby lay in the tangle of muddy leaves and vines, unable to move or breathe. Was she shot? No pain ravaged her senses. Numbness overtook her, whether from injury or fear, she couldn't tell. Mr. Danfield lay motionless beside her, facedown in the dirt.

One of the outlaws kicked at Danfield and bellowed at his partner. "You fool! Why'd you have to kill him?"

"I wasn't trying to kill him. You let the girl see you." More vile words contaminated the air. "What about the old lady?"

Florrie! Dear God, please don't let them hurt Florrie.

"Leave her. Grab that purse. C'mon, let's get outta here."

Heavy footsteps ran to the horses, but still Abby didn't move. Not until the hoofbeats faded away behind them did she release her pent-up breath and realize her heart was still beating.

"Abby! Nathaniel!" Florrie fell to her knees beside Abby, sobbing.

The strength that propelled Abby to fight off their attackers evaporated. An avalanche of weariness buried her beneath its smothering folds. Even the energy required to lift her head waned like fading beams of light at sunset, but she managed to open her eyes and turn her face in Florrie's direction.

"Oh, Abby, I thought you were dead." The distraught woman sucked in great gulps of air and wrapped trembling arms around Abby.

Dead. Mr. Danfield remained unmoving. Was he breathing?

Abby found the will to pull herself to her hands and knees. The man her father called dishonorable lay bleeding beside her. The scene that occurred minutes before plowed through her mind again. Had Mr. Danfield really thrown himself in front of that outlaw's gun? Surely she was mistaken. In the heat of the moment, she'd imagined it.

"Help me roll him over, Florrie."

The two women succeeded in turning him to lie on his back. A bloody river ran profusely down his face from a deep gash along his temple. Abby laid her hand on his chest. There. . .his chest rose and fell.

"He doesn't seem to be bleeding from anyplace else." Florrie rose and scurried over to the articles of clothing strewn about, picked up a chemise, and shook it out. With vigor that surprised Abby, the widow tore the garment down the middle. "Here, use this."

Abby took the cloth and began blotting at the wound, but the flow of blood did not abate. Mr. Danfield didn't stir. Abby glanced around.

"Do you have anything in your satchel that will hold water?"

Florrie frowned at the scattered belongings, puzzlement etching her features. After a moment she brightened. "Yes. I have a small leather pouch with a few mending supplies in it." She searched the area, picking up items until she located the tiny sewing case. "Here it is. But we have no water. The canteens were in the back of the wagon."

Abby pointed up the trail, the opposite direction taken by the outlaws. "Mr. Danfield went up that way to fill them. He must have found water somewhere."

"Of course." Florrie dumped out the contents of the pouch and hurried in the direction Abby had pointed.

Left alone on the trail with Mr. Danfield unconscious and wounded, awareness seeped into Abby's brain that the cloth she held refused to be still. She fastened her stare to their guide. It wasn't Mr. Danfield who moved beneath the cloth. Her own hands trembled uncontrollably. Sucking in as deep a breath as she could muster, she willed the involuntary tremors to obey her and cease their shaking. She glanced behind her in the direction she'd heard the horses gallop away. Might the outlaws come back to finish the job?

"Please, God, tell me what to do." She pulled the bloody cloth away from Mr. Danfield's head and refolded it, pressing a fresh layer against the wound. What if Mr. Danfield didn't wake up? What if he bled to death right there in the middle of the woods? "Forgive me, Lord, for complaining and finding fault. Please don't let him die."

"He will not die."

Abby gasped and jumped, her splintered nerves on end. Standing not ten yards away was a Cherokee woman holding an oddly shaped basket.

The small, wiry woman with snapping black eyes moved beside Mr. Danfield. Her simple homespun dress billowed around her when she knelt and set her basket aside. She lifted the wad of bloody cloth from his wound and peered intently at the gash. She looked over at Abby. "Can you make a fire?"

Abby cast a glance around her. "Even if I can find dry wood, I don't have any friction lights or even a tinderbox. All our supplies were in the wagon and—"

The Cherokee woman gave a soft snort. "Plenty of flint rock. Gather wood from places in the sun." She nodded toward a sparsely treed area up on the ridge above them.

Abby hurried to obey, still wondering how this woman had happened upon them. She climbed the hill toward the ridge where the sunlight warmed her. It was only then she realized she shivered. Grabbing downed limbs and branches at the edge of the tree line in full sun, she found them mostly dry. Dead vines and underbrush from last year's vegetation offered a source of fast ignition. She pulled hard at the vines, wincing as they cut into her fingers. When her arms were full, she descended the slope back to the trail where Florrie now knelt beside the Cherokee woman.

"I found a little stream falling over some rocks." She held up the leather pouch. "It's not much."

The Indian woman directed Abby in building the fire. Once the flame caught and hungrily licked at the twigs Abby fed it, the woman pointed toward the edge of the ravine. "I need thin, flat rock. Be careful not to fall like your wagon."

Abby cautiously scavenged until she found a suitable rock and handed it to the woman who reached into her basket and sorted through some leaves and roots. She placed a flowered head of a stem on the rock near the fire and began pulverizing it with a smooth, stained, egg-shaped stone she took from her basket.

Curiosity captured Abby. "What is that?"

"Fleabane." The woman kept working without looking up. "It will stop bleeding."

As the rocking motion turned the cluster of tiny blossoms into mush, the Cherokee woman added selected leaves and a bit of water from Florrie's pouch. The sticky mess grew into a glob. Abby watched in fascination as the woman applied the slimy substance to Mr. Danfield's wound and then held it in place with strips of cloth torn from the destroyed chemise.

The woman sat back, apparently satisfied, and wiped her hands on her skirt. "When night comes I will make a poultice. Stop fever getting into the wound."

Florrie clasped her hands at her waist. "How can we thank you. . .we don't even know your name."

The Cherokee woman did not take her eyes off Mr. Danfield, but merely replied, "I am Wren."

"Wren." Abby stared at the woman. Surely God had sent her as a direct answer to Abby's prayer. "Florrie and I thank you for what you've done for Mr. Danfield. How—" She shook her head trying to make sense of everything. "How did you happen to come along right when we needed help?"

Wren shrugged. "I watch. I see your man try to turn wagon. I see men who steal from you and hurt you."

Abby didn't bother to inform Wren that Mr. Danfield wasn't her man. "You saw what happened?"

Wren nodded silently, staring in rapt attention at Mr. Danfield.

While Florrie added a few more pieces of wood to the fire, Abby peered at the assortment of leaves and petals. "You were out gathering..." She gestured to the contents of Wren's basket. "Do all these leaves and roots and things have a purpose?"

A tiny smile lifted the corners of Wren's mouth. "Everything God gives has purpose." Her fingers plucked several leaves from the assorted plants in her basket. "Need more water."

Florrie hurried to do Wren's bidding, and Abby watched the Cherokee woman crush the leaves against the stone.

"What is that?"

"Pipsissewa leaves. They help heal wound." Wren continued to study Mr. Danfield while she worked.

"Why are you staring at him like that?"

Wren turned her gaze on Abby, and the determination in the Cherokee woman's eyes made Abby catch her breath.

"He is a good man."

Chapter 4

Nathaniel opened his eyes. Dawn streaked the eastern sky pink and gold, and the chilled air permeated his bones. Snips of fragmented memory slid together to form a picture—two outlaws, fighting over the gun, the wagon crashing over the edge of the ravine. And something else. Ragged edges of awareness swirled through his mind. *Miss Locke.* Did she really hold his head in her lap? Was it her voice he heard praying for him?

Had Felicia ever prayed for him?

He turned his head and caught sight of her tending the campfire. What he wouldn't give for a cup of hot coffee. But if the wagon went down the ravine it had taken all their supplies with it. Despite the absence of coffee, however, something smelled wonderful.

He started to sit up and pain knifed through his head. A groan escaped his parched lips. He lifted his hand and touched his temple. A bulky cloth wrapped his head.

"Oh, thank goodness, you're awake." Relief edged Miss Locke's voice. She knelt beside him and peered beneath the bandage. "The bullet grazed your head. Swelling seems to be down, and the bleeding has stopped. Do you think you could eat something?"

Was she joking? He could eat a bear. He managed to pull himself up and lean against a tree trunk.

"I'm starving."

A small smile tweaked Miss Locke's lips. His eyes widened with a startled jolt. A smile? Perhaps the gunshot brought on hallucinations. Warm tingles tiptoed through his stomach at being the beneficiary of such a rare event. Wonderment pricked him. Could he coax another smile from her?

She turned back to the fire and returned a moment later with a piece of roasted meat on a stick. Nathaniel's stomach growled when the aroma of the delicacy teased his nostrils. He gingerly pulled a piece of steaming meat off the spear and slipped the juicy morsel into his mouth. He'd never tasted anything so good. Had Miss Locke or Mrs. Cobb gone hunting?

Miss Locke pointed at the meat. "Grouse. Wren caught it early this morning in a snare."

Grouse he understood, but who was Wren? As he licked juice off his fingers, a Cherokee woman of unidentifiable age approached him.

"You eat. This is good." She bent and gazed unblinking at his face before gently pulling the bandage away from his head, inspecting the wound.

"Mr. Danfield, this is Wren. She has been a great help since yesterday." Miss Locke held out a tin cup. "It's willow bark tea. Wren made it. She says it will help relieve your pain."

Nathaniel gave Wren a slight nod—the smallest movement of his head produced a raging headache. He took the offering and sent Miss Locke a questioning look. "Where did you get the cup? I thought everything was lost with the wagon."

"Before it got dark yesterday, Wren and I climbed down a little way to see if we could find anything."

He took a sip and found the concoction surprisingly sweet. "This isn't too bad. I thought it would taste like—" No, he shouldn't mention anything as indelicate as a stable floor in the presence of ladies.

Miss Locke stooped beside him. "One of the first things we found was the honey crock. The crates of supplies dumped out when the wagon turned over. That's how we found the cup. We have a fork and two plates, a little bit of cornmeal—although most of it spilled—the coffeepot without its lid, and one small pot."

Mrs. Cobb held up Nathaniel's bedroll, still secured with thin strips of leather. "Wren found this and one of the canteens."

Nathaniel listened to the pathetic list and tried to be grateful for the few things they had. But his stomach clenched when he pictured Miss Locke trying to climb down the embankment. "I'm glad you were able to find a few things, but please don't try to go down there again. It's too dangerous."

"I tried to tell her that." Florrie piped up. "But she's hardheaded."

A rosy flush crept into Miss Locke's cheeks, and she ducked her head. "Mr. Danfield knows how stubborn I am. Besides, we didn't go far." She gave the tin cup a nudge. "Drink the rest of that tea. Wren wants to clean your wound."

Something about the Cherokee woman struck a familiar chord, but the effort to recall if he knew her made his head hurt. She scowled at him when he kept turning his head to look at her, but the corners of her mouth twitched with evidence of her amusement. Her fingers moved with deft precision as she cleaned the gash on his head and gently applied some kind of green mush.

"What's that stuff?"

"It is more easy to care for wound when you sleep. Be still," Wren scolded.

A quiet snort reached his ears. Miss Locke put one hand over her mouth while she poked the fire. The young woman was full of surprises. After complaining for an entire week about every aspect of their journey, she risked her neck trying to salvage a few of their supplies, and now she revealed a sense of humor. He'd imagined a number of reactions from her regarding their predicament, but laughter wasn't one of them.

Wren completed her ministrations and pointed to the bedroll Mrs. Cobb had placed beside him. "You rest now. Best medicine."

He shook his head and immediately wished he hadn't. With eyes squeezed shut, he waited for the pain to clear. "We can't stay here. We need to find our way back to that other trail."

Mrs. Cobb sat in front of him. "Nathaniel, we need to talk." Miss Locke knelt beside Mrs. Cobb while the widow continued. "Wren says you need to rest at least another day or two."

"But then what?" The usual belligerence was absent from Miss Locke's tone. "Whether we go on or turn back, either way we'll be on foot."

"I know we passed a trail a couple of days back." Nathaniel dragged his fingers across his forehead. "My first responsibility is to you ladies. We need to find the nearest town." He looked at Wren who appeared to be waiting for an invitation to join the conversation. "Wren, how familiar are you with this area?"

The Cherokee woman cast a heedful glance among the three travelers, as if determining their trustworthiness. "I know the woods."

Nathaniel's vision swam as he leaned forward. "None of us mean you any harm. From the looks of things"—he touched his bandage—"you've been very kind, and we're grateful." He studied her a moment. Her eyes held a wariness that he understood. He'd seen firsthand the abominable treatment many of the Cherokee received during the relocation process. He didn't begrudge Wren her caution.

"Can you direct us to the closest town?"

Wren seemed to weigh his request. Her eyes locked on his, as though searching the depth of his soul for truth. The lines between her brows eased. "I trust you, Danfield. You show you are a good man."

To his surprise, Miss Locke gave a short nod. A tiny flame of hope flickered to life within him. Clearing his name and restoring his honor stretched out before him like an arduous journey of a thousand miles, but

Miss Locke's nod represented the first step forward.

"A small town lies two, maybe three days travel from here." Wren pointed up the trail in the direction they'd been traveling. "I will take you."

"But Mr. Danfield said the trail was impassable." Miss Locke's puzzlement showed in her expression.

"For a wagon, yes." He looked to Wren for confirmation. "I was told this was a miner's road."

Wren nodded. "The men who dig for gold, they travel this way sometimes. They ride horses. Lead mules. They do not drive wagons."

Self-incrimination accused him for not obtaining more accurate information, but he shoved it away. He had a more important job on which to focus, and he didn't need the hindrance of carrying another load of guilt.

"You rest now." Wren repeated her instructions with an edge of insistence.

"All right." He pointed at Miss Locke. "But you have to promise you won't do any more mountain climbing. As soon as I'm able, I'll go and see what I can recover."

Another surprise. She agreed.

≈

Waves of relief washed over Abby. His head obviously pained him, but seeing him awake and speaking eased the constrictions around her heart despite their situation. Her realization carried with it an element of confusion. Her relief at Mr. Danfield's recovery outweighed her concern of their dilemma. A week ago she didn't care a fig about Mr. Danfield, though admitting as much stirred shame in her middle. The Moravian Sisters who ran the Salem Female Academy had taught her to demonstrate God's love and benevolence to all people. Guilt smote her to think she'd so quickly accepted her father's judgment of Mr. Danfield without seeking evidence of his character for herself.

Lying on the ground instead of in the wagon last night resulted in little sleep, affording her ample opportunity to relive the fight with the outlaws. In her mind's eye, she repeatedly pictured Mr. Danfield shoving her aside and throwing himself between her and the outlaw's gun. It wasn't her imagination. He truly had saved her life. The full understanding of what he'd done deepened her regret over the way she'd treated him for the past week. Somehow she must find a way to thank him, because simply speaking the words fell far short.

She hiked up her mud-stained skirt and walked over to the edge of the ravine. Leaning against the rough bark of a pine, she pulled her braid around to the front of her shoulder and unwound her thick hair. Running her fingers through the tangles, she wondered for the thousandth time if her mother's hair had been as dark and thick as hers. She smoothed the strands the best she could without her hairbrush and rebraided the tresses. Her ivory hairbrush—her mother's hairbrush—lay at the bottom of the ravine in one of her trunks.

The broken saplings and crushed underbrush defined the path the wagon had taken, carrying all their belongings with it. Despite the few items they'd found, her heart longed for those precious things that belonged to her mother. A hairbrush, a lace collar, an embroidered handkerchief, and a cameo brooch. Such a pitiful collection of keepsakes to connect her with a woman she couldn't even remember.

She ambled back to the fire and sat near Florrie, who listened as Mr. Danfield answered her questions about yesterday's skirmish with the bandits.

"I noticed that one of them carried a revolver and the other had a flintlock pistol. When we started fighting, once the pistol discharged, I knew it was useless. He didn't have time to reload it. The one who climbed into the wagon worried me the most. He had one of those new Colt revolvers. A few of the officers I knew carried them. When they are fully loaded, they can fire five times without reloading."

In the frantic tension of the struggle, Abby hadn't noticed the details. She knew two things: both men had guns, and they planned to steal the few mementos she had of her mother's. Mr. Danfield's description sounded like a chess match.

"I was amazed he didn't see my rifle under the wagon seat." He cast a rueful glance in the direction of the ravine. "Of course, it went down the hill with the wagon." A scowl creased his brow, and Abby couldn't tell if he was planning to recover his gun or if he was in pain.

"Do you need more willow bark tea?"

He blinked. Mild surprise revealed itself on his face. "Uh, no, thank you." He lifted his hand and touched his bandage. "Perhaps later, though. It did seem to help." His eyes lingered on her for an extra moment, and she ducked her head as telltale warmth stole into her cheeks. A quick change of topic seemed to be in order. She turned to the Cherokee woman sitting beside her.

"Wren, you were going to show me how you make your poultices."

The woman's piercing black eyes twinkled. "First I go check the snare.

Maybe we have rabbit for dinner." She stood and motioned toward Abby. "You want to learn to skin rabbit?"

A stifled, grunting sound reached Abby. She jerked her head to see Mr. Danfield press both lips tightly together and pin his gaze on the ground beside him. A flare of indignation propelled her to stand and join Wren.

"Sounds fascinating. And I'd love to learn more about the leaves and roots you use to make medicines." She raised her chin a notch and followed Wren up the slope.

Keeping Mr. Danfield down for two days was a three-woman job. Abby considered his impatience a good sign, for no healthy man wished to stay put doing nothing.

Mr. Danfield examined the braided rope Abby had created—with Wren's guidance—from the vines that climbed the trees and spread throughout the underbrush. "It's good and strong. It should work fine." His appreciation warmed Abby's face.

Florrie pointed to the contraption Wren and Mr. Danfield had been working on. "What do you call that thing again?"

"Travois," Wren told her. "It is small. You have no horse to pull it."

Mr. Danfield held Abby's vine rope over his arm. "I don't know how much I'll be able to salvage, but without horses we won't be able to carry a lot."

Anxiety tightened Abby's stomach. What she wanted most was in her smaller trunk. Mr. Danfield said he'd try his best, and she'd already done more than her share of complaining on this trip. She opted to keep her mouth closed, a decision she was sure would please Mr. Danfield.

He tied one end of the rope around his waist. With all three women gripping the braided vine and easing it around the smooth bark of the beech tree, Mr. Danfield gingerly picked his way down the steep slope. Within minutes, Abby lost sight of him through the trees and underbrush, but the tension on the rope testified to his continued slow descent.

"I found some of the bedding," he yelled. "I'm going to tie the rope around the bundle."

For the better part of three hours, they worked together to haul up as many items as Mr. Danfield could find. At last, he came climbing hand over hand on the rope to where the women waited. Abby's worst fears were realized. He had no trunks with him. Mr. Danfield had no way of knowing her cherished keepsakes were in one of her trunks, and she didn't intend to tell him. She couldn't bear it if he scoffed at their importance.

They had two quilts, a few foodstuffs, some cooking implements, and Mr. Danfield's canvas valise.

"My trunks. Where are my trunks?" Abby wrung her hands.

Mr. Danfield shook his head. "I'm sorry, but they fell too far. I couldn't reach them."

She curled both hands into fists. The distress that sliced her heart evidenced itself in her voice. "But I *must* have my trunks."

Mr. Danfield gave her an incredulous look. "You'll have to do without your fancy trinkets. I suggest you be grateful to be alive." The sharp gruffness in his voice sliced as deeply as an army saber. She winced under his implication.

After fighting outlaws, nearly being shot, almost losing Mr. Danfield, being left stranded in the middle of nowhere, and struggling with nature to survive, she had now lost her last connection with her mother. Her fortitude crumbled. Tears burned her eyes, and she couldn't hold them back another minute. She picked up her skirt and stalked down the trail to find some solitude where she might have a private cry.

Chapter 5

Shafts of remorse arrowed through Nathaniel. He never could stand to see a woman weep. By the time he'd climbed back up the ravine, his head throbbed and weariness saturated his muscles. Her pouting over the lost trunks seemed petty in comparison to what they'd been through, but he hadn't intended to make her cry. Nathaniel kicked at the layers of matted leaves that lined the trail.

The gratification he'd felt at salvaging a few more things diminished with the memory of Miss Locke's tears. She remained quiet all the next day as they hiked, sometimes single file in spots where the trail narrowed barely wide enough for him to drag the small travois. Once he caught a glimpse of her face and read great sorrow written there. Women sure could get peevish about their personal things.

"How far do you think we've come?" Mrs. Cobb walked side by side with him.

He cast a look at the sky to gauge the location of the sun. Figuring the rocky trail, the ascent, and stopping for short rests, they'd gone perhaps two miles every hour. "Maybe six miles since this morning." He cut his eyes to the widow. She hadn't complained, but weariness etched its mark in the slump of her shoulders. "Why don't we rest here awhile. We might be able to make another couple of miles or so before dark."

Ahead of him, Wren paused and waited. He set the poles of the travois aside, glad to be relieved of his load. Wren turned back to join the other women while Nathaniel retrieved the canteen from the cargo and handed it to Mrs. Cobb. After all three women had quenched their thirst Nathaniel made his way down a gully to a small stream and refilled the canteen.

The gurgling water invited him to dip his hands and cup the refreshing coolness to his face. He returned to the ladies and stretched out on the ground. An ever-changing patchwork of light and shadow skittered with the wind, and the cushion of fallen leaves and pine needles offered comfort. A rest would do all of them some good.

Closing his eyes, he allowed his mind to drift. As it had several times in the past few days, his memory recalled snippets of the encounter with the outlaws. Nathaniel couldn't shake the feeling of familiarity of one of the men. Both had their faces covered and hats pulled low, but something

. . .*something* about one of them nagged at him. His subconscious groped for something firm to grasp.

Let it go, Danfield. The more you chase it the farther away it slips.

He tucked his hands behind his head and turned his gaze to the tree branches overhead dancing in the breeze. Puffy clouds scuttled across the cornflower-blue sky. The tension in his shoulders relaxed, and his eyes lazed closed again.

After several minutes he shook himself. It wouldn't do to get too comfortable. They still needed to cover more ground before they—

"Bivouac." Nathaniel jerked to a sitting position.

"Nathaniel?" Mrs. Cobb leaned forward. The wrinkles lining her forehead defined her concern.

"One of the outlaws—the one wearing the vest—used the word *bivouac*. Only a military man would use a word like that." Nathaniel got to his feet.

Mrs. Cobb shrugged. "What's bivouac?"

"I know what that means." Miss Locke met Nathaniel's gaze. "It means to make camp, right?"

He nodded. "That's right. Did either of you ladies recognize him? Might you remember seeing him at the fort?"

The two women exchanged glances and shook their heads. Miss Locke stood. "Do you remember him?"

Nathaniel squeezed his eyes shut. "I don't know. I think so, but my brain is still muddled." He rubbed one hand over his forehead. "His voice . . .I've heard that voice before."

Miss Locke touched his arm. "Don't worry." Her soft voice stroked his frustration. "It will come back to you."

Her touch sent a tingling sensation of delight all the way to his shoulder, and when she removed her hand, he felt a sense of loss. Her brief word of gentle encouragement revitalized him better than a two-hour nap.

His eyes fastened to hers for a long moment, and something unspoken exchanged between them. He couldn't allow hope to bud. Not after the way Felicia betrayed him.

ฌ

Impatience niggled at Nathaniel as the travelers prepared to move ahead on the morning of their third day of walking. He itched to push on to the town of which Wren had told them, but in consideration for the ladies, especially Mrs. Cobb, he disciplined his restlessness.

Despite Miss Locke's soothing words, Nathaniel pressed his mind to remember, but no further revelations clarified the identification of either outlaw. As he pulled the travois up the trail, he asked God to impart wisdom and remove the veil from the shadowed images in his mind. Nathaniel blew out a stiff breath. If God willed it, it would happen.

Thick gray clouds gathered on the western horizon behind them. Nathaniel glanced back at them from time to time, calculating their nearness. Thus far, they'd been fortunate to enjoy decent weather since they'd been left without the wagon. He wanted the women safely sheltered before bad weather endangered them.

"Wren?"

The Indian woman paused and allowed Nathaniel to come abreast with her.

"Looks like there is some rain coming. How much farther is this town?"

Wren sent a cursory glance at the clouded sky. "Not far. We reach there before sun is high."

Despite the sun being hidden, Nathaniel understood Wren's meaning. Perhaps another hour or two. He gave Wren a nod, and they continued up the trail.

Quiet conversation between the ladies had fallen silent for most of the morning. Fatigue wore on all of them. Nathaniel could have sworn the travois was heavier. His muscles complained after three days of pulling the conveyance up the trail. He looked forward to finding a place of rest where he could be done with hauling the burden. Guilt smote him, however, for having to leave the women's trunks at the bottom of the ravine, and once again the memory of Miss Locke's tears made him wince for having spoken so sharply to her.

Ridiculous. Being tough was the only way to survive. Here he was, letting a woman's tears make him soft. He stiff-armed the mental picture he had of the moisture in her eyes and the despair in her voice. He'd not allow such silliness to affect him.

"Who am I trying to convince?" he muttered. He shook his head and gripped the travois poles a little tighter. Resolve stiffened his jaw. He'd do whatever was necessary to prevent tears from filling her eyes again.

At that moment, Wren stopped and turned to face him. She pointed farther up the trail. "There. You see many pines close together. Town hides in trees."

Miss Locke stepped up to Wren. "Aren't you going with us?"

Something akin to alarm skittered through Wren's eyes. "No. Not safe." She sent Nathaniel a pointed look.

He gave her a nod. "How can we thank you for all you've done, Wren?" She shook her head. "We thank *you*."

With that, she slipped past him and returned down the trail the way they'd come. The inclination to go after her and ask what she meant by her response almost moved his feet in that direction. But the gray skies coaxed him to escort the ladies forward and find the town that Wren indicated was beyond the thick stand of pines.

Sure enough, about a quarter mile farther, they came to a crude sign secured to a tall stump. TUCKER'S GAP. FOUNDED 1827.

He turned to the women. "Welcome to Tucker's Gap, ladies."

Minutes later, Nathaniel's joy over having finally arrived at the town dwindled. The entire community could be seen in one sweeping circle. Nowhere within the range of his sight was there a tavern, an inn, or boardinghouse. The general store, a whitewashed, clapboard building, sat in the center of the tiny village and bore a hand-painted sign: TUCKER'S GENERAL STORE AND TRADING POST. Groves of hardwoods and pines hugged a few other buildings. A feed and seed and a harness maker's shop, both constructed of unpainted boards, flanked the general store. A rhythmic *clackety-clack* sounded from a large building that sat farther back at the edge of the woods next to the swiftly running creek. The sign posted on the front of the building declared it to be WISE'S SAWMILL, SAM WISE, PROPRIETOR.

Beyond a shady grove of trees in the middle of town, Nathaniel spotted a man working at the livery. As good a place as any to inquire.

"You ladies rest here. I'll go and speak with the blacksmith and see if he knows of any place I can secure lodging for you." He left the travois and strode toward the livery. The mountain of a man working at the forge wore a leather apron and faded chambray shirt, rolled up at the sleeves to expose glistening, muscular arms. He swung a ten-pound hammer like it was a child's toy.

"Good day, sir. Might I trouble you for some information?"

The blacksmith looked him over, and Nathaniel watched as the man's eyes took in his military blouse devoid of stripes and epaulets. Nathaniel sucked in a quiet breath, ready for the sneer of disdain that was sure to come.

Abby watched Nathaniel approach the livery. His earlier anxiousness had dissolved when they saw the size of the town. There was a fenced area beside the livery. Behind the structure, a narrow path led to a small house nearly hidden among the trees.

She scanned the rest of the town. A small church sat tucked away in a grove of maples and sweet gums. She imagined the beautiful picture it would make in the fall with the tiny chapel surrounded with gold and scarlet. Just across the road, Tucker's General Store waited to be explored.

Florrie stood and brushed off her skirt. "I'm going into the store and ask about mail delivery."

"All right. I'll wait here." Abby leaned against a tree trunk and watched Florrie climb the steps to the store.

The sound of children's laughter caused her to turn. A little girl, perhaps six or seven years old, with honey-brown pigtails chased a younger boy in and out of the trees in a crazy game of follow-the-leader. Beyond them, a woman with a market basket over one arm struggled to catch up with the two. As they drew closer, Abby watched the boy climb a tree as nimbly as a squirrel.

"Mama, look at me!"

Abby grinned at his childish antics. He pulled himself up to a higher limb to avoid the outstretched hands of the little girl, who attempted to follow him up the same tree.

The mother, obviously in the family way, fanned her face with the hem of her apron. "Beau, get down before you fall. Dulcie, come back here."

Then, to Abby's horror, the woman dropped her basket and crumpled to the ground. In a wink, Abby snatched up her skirt and raced across the way and knelt beside the prone woman whose face was pasty white.

"Ma'am?" Abby patted the woman's cheeks. "Can you hear me?"

"Mama!" One of the children wailed behind Abby. She turned to find both youngsters staring wide-eyed at their mother lying on the ground. The boy began to cry.

A faint moan escaped from the woman's lips, and her eyelids fluttered. Abby reached for the little girl's hand. "Honey, can you go get a cup or a dipper of water? Your mama just fainted. She'll be all right, but she could use a sip of water right now."

The little girl didn't hesitate but bolted back in the direction Abby had seen them come. The little boy knelt beside Abby and reached for his mother's hand.

"I'm sorry, Mama. Wake up." His straw-colored hair flopped in his eyes, and he wiped his nose on his sleeve as he blubbered.

Abby glanced at the distraught child from the corner of her eye as she used the woman's apron to blot moisture from her face. "She'll be all right, little man. She just needed to take a quick nap." She reached to brush the boy's hair from his face.

He turned his chocolate eyes on Abby. His bottom lip stuck out and trembled. "Is Mama gonna be mad 'cause I climbeded the tree?"

Abby wanted to hug the little fellow and assure him all would be well, but at that moment, the woman opened her eyes. "Dulcie? Beau?"

"I'm right here, Mama." Beau patted his mother's arm. "Dulcie went to bringed you a drink of water."

A feeble smile wobbled the mother's lips. She turned her gaze on Abby. "What happened? Who are you?"

Abby supported the woman's arms and helped her to a sitting position. "I expect you fainted. My name is Abby Locke. We just arrived in Tucker's Gap." She fanned the woman with her apron. The little girl trotted back up the footpath with a tin cup only half full of water, most of it sloshing down the child's arm and dripping off her elbow.

The mother took several sips and gave her children a reassuring smile. "Thank you, Abby Locke. I'm Beth Rutledge and this is Dulcie and Beau." She handed the cup to Dulcie and caressed the chin of each child.

Abby ruffled Beau's already-unruly hair and patted Dulcie's shoulder. "It's a pleasure to meet all of you." She returned her gaze to Beth. "Are you feeling better?"

Beth sighed. "Yes, some better. I've been having such a hard time with . . .this baby." A rosy blush chased away the pale pallor. "Keeping up with these two doesn't allow much time to rest."

The two impish children on either side of her each bore a stamp of their mother. Beth's startlingly blue eyes were duplicated in her daughter, and Beau had inherited his mother's gold hair along with a dusting of freckles across his nose.

Abby sat back on her heels and took in Beth's swollen stomach and slight build. Her pronounced cheekbones and thin arms gave indication that perhaps she wasn't eating properly. The babe within her certainly must be a taxing load to carry.

"Do you have anyone who can help out while you're—" Abby took a turn at blushing. "In the family way."

Beth shrugged. "My husband works all day and sometimes goes out to help some of the farmers. I had hoped my younger sister could come and stay with me until the baby comes, but my family lives too far away." The wistfulness in Beth's voice tugged at Abby and a wave of compassion nudged her. Hesitation hampered her tongue for only a moment.

"Will I do?"

"Pardon?"

Abby lifted her shoulders. "I'm not your sister, but I need a place to stay for a short time, and you need someone to help out. I can clean and cook and look after Beau and Dulcie so you can rest." She stopped short and covered her cheeks with both hands. "Oh, I'm sorry. My aunt always tells me being presumptuous isn't ladylike. Besides, you don't know a thing about me."

Beth leaned forward. "No, it's a wonderful idea." She grasped Abby's hands. "Do you really mean it? Would you help me at home in exchange for a place to stay?"

Abby glanced in the direction of the livery where Mr. Danfield still stood talking with the blacksmith. What would he say if she made such arrangements on her own? She didn't want to go to Raleigh, and her father didn't want her at the fort. Why couldn't she stay in this little community and help Beth Rutledge? She lifted her chin and squared her shoulders.

"Yes." Abby nodded. "Yes, I will. And I'll stay for as long as you need me."

Tears filled Beth's eyes. "I don't know how to thank you, Abby. You have no idea what a blessing this is. It's true, God sometimes sends angels among us."

Angel probably wasn't the word Mr. Danfield would use. A week and a half ago she wouldn't have cared. Now, she could only pray he wouldn't force her to break her promise to Beth. Giving her word wasn't something Abby took lightly, and she was beginning to think Mr. Danfield didn't either, no matter what the army said.

Chapter 6

With Beth comfortably seated on the grass under the sprawling oaks, Abby turned her attention to the youngsters.

"Do either of you know how to play hopscotch?"

Both children shook their heads. Abby smiled. "I can show you."

Dulcie gave her a gap-toothed grin. "I like to play games."

Beau's bottom lip pooched out. "I don't. Dulcie always beats me 'cause she's bigger."

Abby sent a wink to Beth. She took Beau's chin in her hand. "Well, this is a game everyone can play. You might even beat me."

Beau's freckles seemed to dance as his eyes widened. "You're gonna play, too?"

"I sure am." Abby plunked her hands on her hips. "Do you think I'm going to let you have all the fun?" She ruffled his hair. "Help me find a stick so we can draw in the dirt. Dulcie, see if you can find a small flat stone."

Beau searched the ground in close proximity to the oaks and quickly produced a twig. Abby set to work drawing a grid of lines in the smoothed-out dirt of the road next to the grass. Dulcie returned a minute later and held out a smooth flat rock in her grimy palm.

"That's a perfect stone. Now watch." She tossed the stone, and it landed in the seventh square. With a grin to the children, she picked up her skirt and hopped, first on one foot and then on both feet, until she reach the rock. With a deft movement, she bent and scooped the stone in her hand, turned, and hopped back.

She placed the piece of granite in Dulcie's hand. "Now see if you can do it." Within minutes, the children were absorbed in the activity of tossing the stone and hopping after it. Their giggles rang across the shady common.

Abby clapped her hands and cheered encouragement to them, remembering the happy times she'd spent with her school chums. Her aunt had considered the games vulgar and unladylike. But as Abby watched Dulcie with her pigtails flopping and listened to the music of Beau's giggles, their cheeks flushed rosy from effort and delight, Aunt Charlotte's reprimands faded from her memory.

She cast a glance over her shoulder toward the livery where

Mr. Danfield remained engaged in conversation with the blacksmith. His back was to her, and she allowed herself a moment to take in the outline of his sturdy form. He stabbed the air with his thumb over his shoulder. Doubtless the men were discussing her and Florrie.

With a gasp, Abby clapped a hand to her forehead. *Florrie.* Having a roof over her own head in exchange for helping Beth with the housework and the children so excited her, she'd forgotten about the widow.

At that moment, Florrie called her name. Abby turned to see the older woman, a broad smile on her face, hurrying over to where Abby supervised the children in their game.

"Abby!"

Abby's heart lifted. Judging by her friend's animated tone, she bore good news. She must have discovered the tiny town had mail service.

"Abby, I have just met the two nicest people." Florrie cocked her head toward the store. "Leon and Mercy Tucker run the trading post here in Tucker's Gap. For the time being, Mercy is trying to run the place by herself." A frown worked its way into the space between Florrie's brows and worry inflected her tone. "Mr. Leon Tucker had an accident last week and broke his leg." She tsked. "Poor man. Anyway, Mercy has her hands full trying to take care of him and run the store alone, so—" Florrie hesitated, a tentative smile on her lips.

"What, Florrie?"

The widow lifted her shoulders. "I told Mercy that Dewey and I ran the sutler's store at the fort. She asked if I would be interested in helping out until Mr. Tucker gets back on his feet. She said they have an empty room since their daughter married and moved away."

"And you said. . ."

"Why, Abby," Florrie shook her finger, "you know I'd never make such a commitment without first discussing it with you and Nathaniel."

Heat flooded Abby's face and chagrin trampled her toes. She glanced at Beth who sat watching the children. "Florrie, you see the woman sitting over there?"

Florrie's gaze followed Abby's pointer finger. "Looks like she's expecting."

Abby grinned. "She is, and those two children playing hopscotch are hers. She's having a difficult time with. . .you know, being in the family way." Abby shrugged. "So I offered to help her with the children and housework. In exchange for a place to stay. Until the baby comes."

She expected Florrie to admonish her for agreeing to work for Beth without Mr. Danfield's knowledge. But instead, Florrie just grinned.

"Well then, since that is the case, I'll go and tell Mercy I'll take the job, at least until her husband's leg heals." She started to turn but halted. "Should we wait and talk to Nathaniel first?"

Abby clamped her lips down on the giggle that bubbled up inside her. "Mr. Danfield will find out soon enough he has *two* headstrong women on his hands." She took Florrie's hand. "Come and meet Beth."

Abby made the introductions and helped Beth to her feet. "Looks like Florrie is going to be helping out the Tuckers for a while. Beth, why don't you go with Florrie to the store, and I'll watch the children so you can take your time shopping?"

A relieved sigh passed Beth's lips. "That would be wonderful." She called to Dulcie and Beau who were still laughing and tumbling over each other as they hopped back and forth. "Children, you stay here with Miss Abby."

Florrie picked up Beth's basket and looped her arm through Beth's. "Let's go tell Mercy Tucker she has a new employee."

Abby couldn't keep the smile from her face. Would the smile remain, however, when she and Florrie informed Mr. Danfield of their arrangements?

"Miss Abby, can we play ring-around-the-rosy?"

Abby pushed aside her concern over Mr. Danfield's reaction. "Certainly. Let's play over here in the grass."

Beau latched on to her hand and sent her an endearing grin. She was already falling in love with this family. A measure of assurance came over her. This was where she was supposed to be—for now.

❧

Feeling like a failure was getting to be an annoying habit. Quinn Rutledge, the blacksmith and livery owner, told Nathaniel he could sleep in the livery loft in exchange for keeping the place cleaned out and caring for the stock. But he was no closer to finding accommodations for the ladies. Rutledge suggested he ask at Tucker's General Store.

Distant thunder rumbled under the leaden sky. He cast his gaze toward the thickening clouds. "Lord, I need to find a place for the women. I can't expect them to stay in a stable." A check in his spirit slowed his steps. "Lord, do You ever get tired of me telling You what to do? It's just that I had hoped for something a little…nicer smelling for the ladies." He could almost see the Lord's smile.

He found Miss Locke holding two young children by the hands, her face wreathed in a radiant smile. They skipped in a circle and their singsong voices carried to his ears.

"Ashes, ashes, we all fall down."

The corners of Nathaniel's mouth twitched as Miss Locke dropped to the ground and the youngsters fell on her, their giggles rivaling the singing of the birds.

"Let's do it again, Miss Abby." The little boy couldn't have been more than five, and he seemed entirely taken with the colonel's daughter. *Miss Abby.* The name fit her.

"Oh my, I think I need to catch my breath." She shook her skirt, brushing off the bits of grass and twigs. When she straightened, her gaze collided with Nathaniel's. A pink glow filled her cheeks in sharp contrast to the gloomy countenance she'd worn for the past few days. Nathaniel stared at the sparkle in her dark-brown eyes, hypnotized by their vibrant depth. She broke the spell when she dropped her gaze.

"Mr. Danfield." Her voice, breathless and airy, captured his senses. "I apologize for my unladylike behavior."

His tongue stuck to his teeth, and he groped to form an intelligent answer. His brain refused to function. "I, uh. . .no, that's quite. . .you don't, uh. . ." He clamped his mouth shut before any more insipid noises fell out and glanced at the ground, half expecting to find his wits lying at his feet. Heat raced up his neck and burned his ears. He cleared his throat and prayed for composure.

He jerked his thumb toward the livery. "Mr. Rutledge, the livery owner, suggested we check with Mrs. Tucker in the general store—"

"Mr. Danfield." She broke in before he could finish. "I met the mother of these children. Her name is Beth Rutledge, so I assume she is wife to the blacksmith. She's—" Her eyes widened, and her cheeks turned bright red. "She's. . .well. . ."

Miss Locke coughed and gulped simultaneously. She took a slow deep breath. "Mrs. Rutledge is going to need some help for the next few months, keeping house and caring for the children. She and I have arranged for me to stay with her family in exchange for providing—"

"You did what?" Nathaniel sucked in a breath. A scowl pulled his mouth downward. What did she think she was doing? Her well-being was *his* responsibility.

The little boy looked up and tugged on Miss Locke's arm. "He looks mean." The whimper in the child's voice smote Nathaniel as effectively as Quinn Rutledge's hammer at the forge.

46

She bent and slipped her arm around the little fellow. "It's all right, Beau. Mr. Danfield isn't mean." She tipped her head and shot an incriminating glare at Nathaniel and then returned a soft smile to the boy. "He's just had a hard day."

Nathaniel pressed his lips together and rolled his head from side to side to work the kinks out of his neck. He didn't wish to confront her in the presence of these children.

"I think we need to discuss this." He lowered his voice and spoke through clenched teeth. "Your safety is my responsibility. I can't let you—"

"Let me?" She folded her arms across her chest. "I beg your pardon?"

He held his hands up. "Sorry." He had no idea why he was apologizing for doing his job, but for some reason he couldn't explain, it mattered to him that she understood his caution. "I simply want to be certain you are in a safe situation. Of course, I won't be far away. Quinn Rutledge is letting me sleep in the loft at the livery. So I can keep an eye—no, that's not what I mean either."

He scrubbed one hand over his face, the stubble on his chin raking his palm like sandpaper. The tapping of her foot on the packed dirt beat out a rhythm that matched the pulsing of his heart.

"Exactly what do you mean, Mr. Danfield?"

He pulled his head up and looked her square in the eye. "I mean I have been entrusted with your safety. If at any time I feel the arrangement is unsatisfactory. . ."

Her stormy stare rivaled the roiling clouds overhead. Then she cocked her head to one side and unfolded her arms. "I do understand your position, regardless of what you may think."

"Oh, Nathaniel, there you are." Mrs. Cobb's cheerful voice broke through his gathering ire. He turned to see her coming from the general store with a loaded basket on her arm and accompanying a woman who was obviously with child. "I can hardly wait to tell you my news."

News? He'd had about all the news he could handle for one day, but he forced a smile. "Mrs. Cobb." He tipped his hat to the woman beside her. "Ma'am."

Miss Locke stepped over to take the basket from the widow. "Mr. Danfield, this is Mrs. Rutledge." She turned to smile at the woman. "I was just telling Mr. Danfield about our arrangement."

Mrs. Cobb clasped her hands in front of her waist. "Did you tell him about mine?"

Hers? Nathaniel jerked his head to face the older woman. "You

47

have an arrangement, too?"

As Mrs. Cobb explained Mercy Tucker's need for help in the store while her husband convalesced, Nathaniel started to raise his index finger but quickly folded it back within his fist. He couldn't shake his finger at a woman old enough to be his mother. He shifted his glance to Miss Locke who appeared to be failing miserably at suppressing a chuckle.

"So you see, Nathaniel, Abby and I both have places to stay. I must tell you, though, that Mr. Tucker is going to need several weeks to heal, and I promised Mercy that I'd stay until he was back on his feet." Mrs. Cobb sidestepped over to stand next to Miss Locke. "See? God has worked everything for good. Such a blessing."

Blessing wasn't the first word that popped into his head.

"What about your niece, Mrs. Cobb? And your aunt, Miss Locke? You both have family members awaiting your arrivals."

Mrs. Cobb waved her hand. "Mercy tells me that mail goes out about once every two weeks or so. Some of the miners who pass through here bring the mail they pick up in Gainesville, and they take the outgoing mail and drop it off at one of the forts. We can get word to our loved ones."

Nathaniel looked from Mrs. Cobb to Miss Locke. He had a suspicion that Mrs. Cobb was every bit as stubborn as Miss Locke. She just had a different way of winning an argument.

"If you could get my satchel off the travois, please, Mr. Danfield." Miss Locke caught the little boy's hand. "Mrs. Rutledge needs to get home to rest." She peered at the sky. "I don't think this rain is going to hold off much longer."

"Of course." Nathaniel blew out a sigh of resignation. "Which house is yours, Mrs. Rutledge? I'll bring Miss Locke's things." He assured Mrs. Cobb he'd do the same for her.

Mrs. Rutledge gave Nathaniel a warm smile and pointed toward a small place nearly hidden by the trees behind the livery. Miss Locke gathered the children and hesitated before following the livery owner's wife.

"Thank you, Mr. Danfield." The defiant edge of her tone had been replaced with a softer inflection. "I suppose I'll see you later, then."

Those eyes. Fathomless depths of dark-brown enchantment. How could he be angry at the owner of those eyes?

He watched Miss Locke and the children follow Mrs. Rutledge toward the little house. A dark-haired man wearing a faded plaid shirt raised his hand and called out something Nathaniel couldn't quite hear. Mrs. Rutledge stopped as the man approached. They spoke, and the fellow tipped his hat in an exaggerated fashion to Miss Locke. Nathaniel strained to hear, but a rumble of thunder drowned out their words. When the women and children moved on toward the house, the dark-haired man stood and watched them.

Every nerve in Nathaniel's body snapped to attention and bristled with distrust. Rain began to fall, but the man in the plaid shirt remained in place.

Needles pricked Nathaniel's gut. He had no real reason to be alarmed—he didn't know anything about the man. He simply didn't like the way the man watched Miss Locke.

Chapter 7

Raindrops splatted on the hard ground, and the thunder growled its warning to take shelter before the deluge let loose. Abby and the children followed Beth to the house. The man she'd just met—she didn't quite catch his name—had a peculiar look in his eye when he'd swept his hat off. The way he'd studied her sent an uncomfortable shudder through her.

"Beth, who was that man?"

Beth cast a quick glance over her shoulder. "His name is Teague Jackson. He's a harness maker, but he also works at the sawmill. His shop is right over there." She indicated the small building of unpainted boards adjacent to the path that led to the Rutledge home. "He's lives in the back of the place."

Abby glanced behind her and found Teague Jackson still standing there in the rain watching them hasten down the path. Her line of vision carried her gaze past Jackson to the grassy area of trees in front of the general store. Mr. Danfield stood beside the travois, a scowl darkening his features. She jerked her focus forward, but the images of both men remained in her mind. Anxious to put a closed door behind her, she ushered the children inside. Mr. Danfield's frown gave her pause. If he was angry about the bargain she'd struck with Beth, no doubt she'd hear about it when he brought her valise.

She sent a sweeping glance around the cabin. Despite its small size and rough construction, it bore a few distinctly feminine touches. The table in the center of the main room bore a blue and white tablecloth that appeared as though it had seen almost as many washes as meals. The corners were frayed and a few stains interrupted the pattern of faded-blue checks. A small crock occupied the middle of the table with a variety of partially wilted wildflowers. Four stools sat at cockeyed angles on either side of the table.

Across the room, the coals glowed in the stone fireplace, and the kitchen area needed straightening. Tucked between the fireplace and a corner cupboard, a well-used rocking chair with a sagging woven-rush seat offered a silent welcome. A bed with a rumpled quilt crowded into the far left corner, and a crude ladder provided access to the overhead loft.

Beth sent her an apologetic look. "I haven't had the energy to keep up with the housework."

Abby set the basket on the worktable. "I'll fix lunch while you get off your feet. Dulcie, can you show me where you and your brother wash up?"

The little girl led Abby to the washstand sitting just outside the back door. Abby cringed at the soiled towel that hung from a peg. The water in the bucket looked as though it had been used a number of times. A worn piece of lye soap stuck to the corner of the stand. A broom leaned against the log wall of the cabin.

Abby bent down and smiled at Dulcie. "Where do you get your fresh water?"

The little girl pointed several yards away to an odd-looking structure of stone with rough-hewn boards forming a cover. "There's a spring under there."

Abby tossed out the used water and scurried through the rain with the empty bucket. A second bucket with a rope tied to the handle sat ready to be lowered into the depths of the spring. She directed the children to wash up, hoping she might discover a supply of clean towels.

Abby tossed some chips she found in a basket onto the glowing coals to coax them to life, and soon a cheery blaze chased away the gloom of the rainy day. Beth pointed out where to find various items, and Abby set salt pork to fry over the fire while she gathered the makings for corn cakes. While she dropped spoonfuls of batter into the hot skillet, she glanced at Beth who sat with her head leaning against the back of the rocker and one hand on her abdomen.

"Are you feeling well?"

A tiny smile lifted the corners of Beth's lips. "Just tired. It seems strange to sit and let someone else do the work."

Abby slid a thin wooden spatula under the corn cakes and flipped them over. "Perhaps you can take a nap after you eat something." She ladled water into the kettle and hung the vessel on the crane over the fire.

The door opened just as Abby was scooping the crispy salt pork and corn cakes onto tin plates. The man who filled the doorframe must be Mr. Rutledge. His broad shoulders barely fit through the opening, and he had to duck his head to enter.

"Papa!" Dulcie and Beau both ran to him.

Beth rose from the rocker with one hand pressed to her lower back and introduced her husband to Abby. Quinn Rutledge looked from Beth to Abby and back again as his wife explained the plan for Abby to help with the housework and care for the children in exchange for a roof over her head.

"Please, Quinn." Beth's pleading eyes sought her husband's approval. "Dulcie and Beau already love her, and having her here would be such a help. She can sleep in the loft with the children."

The blacksmith's thick eyebrows knitted together and were almost lost under the thatch of brown hair that overhung his forehead. "It means two more mouths to feed, Beth. Her, and the man stayin' in the barn." He cut his eyes to Abby. "Ain't meanin' no offense, Miss."

Beau tugged on his father's pant leg. "Papa, Mama fell down today."

Quinn stooped to eye level with his son. "She what?"

The child's lower lip trembled. "She falled down. Miss Abby said she... she..."

"She fainted." Abby stepped over and laid her hand on Beau's head, smoothing the hair from the lad's face. "I'm glad I was there when it happened. The children were frightened."

Quinn rose and in one long stride was at Beth's side. He took her arm, concern in his eyes. "You all right now?"

Beth nodded and massaged her belly. "This one is giving me a hard time, like the last two."

Abby cocked her head. "You had difficulties with Dulcie and Beau, too?"

Beth's eyes glistened with unshed tears, and she shook her head.

"No." Quinn ran his huge hand up and down Beth's arm. "She means the two that's buried over by the church."

Abby swallowed back the gasp that rose in her throat. "Oh, Beth, I'm sorry." How grievous was it to lose a child? Abby had no way of knowing except by the anguished look on Beth's face. The pain Abby read there sliced her heart.

Quinn cupped his wife's elbow and led her to one of the stools at the table. He brushed his thick fingers across Beth's cheek. "She can stay as long as she's a help to you. I reckon we'll manage somehow."

Beth responded with a weak smile.

If Abby needed to prove her worth to Quinn Rutledge, she'd determine to give him no reason for complaint. She put lunch on the table and set some aside for Mr. Danfield, unsure if he would come to the house or if she should carry it to the livery. The water in the kettle boiled. Abby measured out tea leaves into the chipped china pot and added the steaming water for a relaxing cup of tea for the expectant mother.

"Abby?" Beth turned in her seat. "You come and eat, too."

She shook her head. "I'll eat something later. I want to get the bed straightened so you can rest after lunch."

Abby bustled over to the bed in the corner, tugged the muslin sheet taut, and folded the quilt neatly at the foot of the bed. When she looked up, she found Quinn's stony gaze on her, as though measuring the value of her work against what it would cost to feed her.

❧

Surely Nathaniel misunderstood the order. Open fire? Gunshots scattered the Cherokee who'd tried to plead for more time to gather their belongings. The screams of women and children raked his ears. When he twisted in his saddle to confront the captain and protest the order, the officer's sickening sneer assaulted his senses with the comprehension that the order was no mistake.

This isn't right! It's murder!

He vaulted off his horse and ran toward three Cherokee women who were trying to hide their children. Snatching up two crying toddlers, he instructed the women to follow him into the woods. Gunfire exploded around them. He pushed the children behind some scrub pines and motioned for the women to stay low. Only then did he discover one of the women had fallen.

Scrambling back toward the village, he looked up to find a gun barrel shoved in his face.

Lieutenant Danfield, you're under arrest.

Sweat dripped off Nathaniel's face as he jolted awake. The nausea that always accompanied the dream twisted his gut, and he willed himself to breathe evenly. The smell and crackle of fresh hay reminded him he was in the loft in Quinn Rutledge's livery.

A nearby rooster crowed. Pink and gold stained the sky through the eastern-facing window. Nathaniel sat up and pulled his boots on, scrambled to his feet, and climbed down the ladder. Horses whickered a greeting, impatiently stamping for their breakfast. He grabbed two buckets and headed out through the misty dawn and tramped toward the spring behind the Rutledge's house.

Soft lantern light spilled from the open window of the house. Someone was up and stirring. He rounded the corner of the house and saw a figure pulling the cover away from the spring. As he approached, he heard her quiet humming.

"Miss Locke, let me do that for you."

"Oh!" She jumped and dropped the heavy wooden lid. "I didn't hear you come up, Mr. Danfield."

He set his buckets down and dragged the cover to one side. "Sorry if I frightened you." The bucket on the rope splashed into the spring. Nathaniel hauled it up and poured the clear, cold water into her bucket. "Can I carry this for you?"

"No, thank you, I can manage." She started to lift the bucket but hesitated. "I've been expecting you to tell me how wrong it was of me to agree to this arrangement without your knowledge."

Nathaniel dropped the roped bucket back down into the spring. "It's a bit late to argue the point of right or wrong. It's done." He drew the full bucket to the surface and poured it into one of his empty containers. He paused before lowering the vessel down again. "Are they treating you all right?"

She glanced toward the cabin. "I don't think I've won Mr. Rutledge's approval yet, but it's only been a few days." She shrugged.

Nathaniel gave a soft snort and let the spring bucket fall back down into the water. He understood what she meant about Quinn Rutledge. He'd felt the man's eyes boring into him as he worked.

He filled his second bucket and hoisted one in each hand. "I hope you won't think me presumptuous, but I believe under the circumstances it wouldn't be improper for you to call me Nathaniel."

The wispy glow of daybreak fell across her face revealing a hint of a smile. "I suppose then you should call me Abby."

"Abby." The name felt so right on his lips.

"Breakfast will be ready in about a half hour. . .Nathaniel."

She turned and headed back to the cabin. Nathaniel sucked in a breath. His accelerated pulse had nothing to do with the effort required to transport the water buckets. However tiny her smile, he'd carry it with him throughout the day.

❧

Nathaniel maneuvered the load of soiled hay to the pile that sat down a slope downwind of the house. On his way back to the livery he caught a glimpse of Abby and the children at the edge of the woods. The little girl with honey-colored pigtails, Dulcie he thought was her name, held a small bouquet of white flowers. Abby pointed to a spot next to a stump and the child trotted over and added more flowers to the ones in her hand. Little Beau held up what appeared to be a variety of rocks for Abby's approval. It wasn't hard to see the Rutledge children adored Abby, and apparently the feeling was mutual. The arrogance that defined the colonel's daughter at the beginning of their journey had evaporated.

Their journey. The thought erased his smile, and a frown took its place. Had he still been in the army, his mission would be deemed a failure. He'd fallen short of the goal, and the women were stranded, working for their keep in a tiny community far from their destination. He glanced toward the forge where Quinn's hammer rang against hot iron. Perhaps the blacksmith could be talked into helping Nathaniel retrieve the broken wagon to see if it could be repaired. Nathaniel shook his head. Even if repairs were possible, he had no horses. How long might he have to work for Quinn to barter for a team?

The sound of hoofbeats drew his attention across the way where a squad of soldiers rode up to Tucker's General Store. Nathaniel stood and watched as the officer, a lieutenant, dismounted and handed the reins to a sergeant mounted beside him. He noted by their uniforms they were Georgia Guard, not federal troops. The lieutenant climbed the steps to the front porch where Leon Tucker sat with his broken leg propped up on a crate. The two men conversed for several minutes, and Tucker pointed in the direction from which Nathaniel and the women had first arrived in Tucker's Gap almost a week ago.

The lieutenant gave the order to dismount. The remaining Guard soldiers led their horses to the shaded grassy area in front of the store. A bitter taste in Nathaniel's mouth made him grimace. The Georgia Guard had a reputation for brutality. Their presence in Tucker's Gap filled him with unease.

He leaned against the doorframe, watching the men. The sight of their uniforms and the sound of a squad leader barking orders stirred the broken pieces in his mind. Despite the fact that these weren't federal troops, something jogged in his memory—something he'd struggled to remember for nearly two weeks. The bandit who seemed familiar to Nathaniel, whose voice he knew he'd heard before. . .Nathaniel ran his hand over the healing wound on his temple where the bullet had nearly taken his life. *Think!*

He closed his eyes and strained to pull the memory into focus. The harsh, raspy voice, the sneering eyes. . . The connection refused to materialize.

Some of the soldiers sprawled on the grass, others stood, talking and spitting tobacco. The distance didn't allow him to see any of their faces clearly. The wind in the trees, Quinn's hammering, and the repetitive clacking from the sawmill prevented him from hearing their voices. The lieutenant finished his conversation with Leon Tucker and ordered his men to mount. As they did so, one of the soldiers, a sergeant, turned and seemed to notice Nathaniel in the doorway. The two stared at each other for a long moment before the order was given to move out.

Chapter 8

A bby and the children climbed the steps to Tucker's General Store. The whitewashed door stood propped open, and a curious combination of smells greeted Abby. The tangy aroma of spices clashed with pungent lamp oil; the scent of leather and tobacco blended with coffee beans and pickles.

Ceiling-to-floor shelves contained an assortment of foodstuffs, ammunition, and household items. A flour barrel stood to one side of the counter while a coffee grinder anchored the other end. Makeshift tables contained everything from blankets and canvas to pottery. The opposite corner housed a nook, which bore a sign that read TUCKER'S GAP POST OFFICE.

"Mornin', Abby." Florrie came around to the front of the counter with her arms held wide. The women embraced.

"Hello, Abby." Mercy Tucker looked up from the ledger. "It was so nice meeting you at the singing on Sunday."

Abby gave the woman a warm smile. "The singing was such fun, and I enjoyed meeting some of my new neighbors."

Mercy tugged on one of Dulcie's pigtails. "I see you've brought your two helpers along with you today."

Dulcie beamed up at Abby. "I like helping."

"I help, too." Beau shoved Abby's basket onto the counter. "I carried the basket."

His sister rolled her eyes. "That's not helping if the basket is empty."

"Is, too."

"Is not."

Abby stepped between the siblings. "That's enough. If you start squabbling, you won't have any cinnamon bread for lunch."

The two fell silent.

Florrie's eyes twinkled and Abby winked. "Mercy, how is Mr. Tucker getting along?"

"Oh, about the same." She lowered her voice and glanced at the curtain-covered opening that led to their living quarters. "That busted leg is going to take a while to heal. Meanwhile, he's ornery as a billy goat." She shook her head. "He's been able to hobble out and sit on the porch a couple of times, but getting him out there and then back in again is like trying to waltz with a mule."

Abby bit her lip trying not to laugh. The poor man must be going stir-crazy. She wasn't sure if she felt sorrier for him or Mercy.

Florrie's shoulders shook with silent mirth. "Abby, what can we get for you today?"

Abby tapped her chin with her finger. "Let me see. We need salt, a couple of pounds of dried beans, and a tin of saleratus. Do you have dried apples?"

Mercy pulled a crock from the shelf behind her and scooped out two handfuls of dried apples. "Will there be anything else?"

"That's all for today."

Florrie measured out the beans. "I wrote a letter to my niece, and the mail was picked up yesterday." She nailed Abby with a pointed look. "I noticed there wasn't a letter going out to your father. Abby, you have to write to him and let him know where you are."

"But, Florrie." Abby tossed a glance over her shoulder to make sure the children were out of earshot. "If I write to Father, he'll send an entire regiment after me and whisk me off to Raleigh. If that happens, what will Beth do? I promised I'd stay as long as she needs me—at least until the baby comes. All that matters to Father is that people jump when he gives an order." She released a sigh.

"That doesn't change the fact that your aunt is going to fear the worst when you don't arrive as scheduled."

Abby pressed her lips together in annoyance. "I know. I'll write a letter to Aunt Charlotte." She stiffened her jaw. "But I'm going to tell her that I won't be arriving as expected and she's not to send anyone after me."

Florrie dropped the sack of beans into Abby's basket. "And your father?"

Did she dare tell her father not to send anyone after her? A scowl wrinkled her brow. "I really don't look for ways to defy my father. I wish I shared a close bond with him. It's what I've always wanted, but I fear it will never be."

"How can you say that?" Florrie wiped her hands on her apron. "Of course your father loves you."

Abby picked up the basket. "Then why did he continually send me away? He considered me an embarrassment. I've never been able to please him. No doubt he will find fault with my decision to stay in Tucker's Gap and help Beth."

Florrie came around the side of the counter and slipped her arm around Abby's shoulders. "But, honey, if he doesn't know where you are and thinks some ill fate has befallen you, he'll blame Nathaniel."

Abby couldn't dismiss Florrie's reasoning. Postponing her letter writing was simply delaying the inevitable, and it hung over her head like a threatening rain cloud. Imagining what her father might do when he learned of her situation had kept her tossing and turning half the night. Florrie was right, of course. He would hold Nathaniel responsible unless she could convince him otherwise. In order to do that she'd have to write the letter. She pushed the nagging thought away.

After assigning Dulcie and Beau the chore of straightening the sleeping loft, Abby wrung water from a pair of long johns and hung them on the drying line. Dough for salt-rising bread sat on a sunny windowsill covered with a towel, and she'd set a pot of beans to soak. If there was time, Abby wanted to search the edge of the woods for lemon balm. Wren had shown her how to make a tea from the fragrant leaves, and she hoped the infusion would settle Beth's stomach.

Across the path, Quinn and Nathaniel worked together replacing some of the fence posts in the corral. Abby brushed back a few stray strands of hair that had escaped her braid and stood hidden by the laundry flapping in the breeze. Although not as big or tall as Quinn, there was nothing lacking in Nathaniel's effort. His rolled-up sleeves revealed rippling muscles in his forearms as he maneuvered a new post into the ground, and his sweat-dampened shirt clung to his broad shoulders and back. What would Aunt Charlotte say had she known her niece dawdled to admire a man's shoulders? Abby slipped a hand up to her mouth as a snicker danced across her lips.

She picked up the laundry basket and propped it on one hip just as Nathaniel looked up from his task. Their eyes met and her step hesitated. A slow smile spread across his face, and he pulled his hand across his forehead and sent her a short nod. Her fingers tightened and dug in to the woven basket. A moment later he broke the gaze between them when he bent to pick up another post. But his smile sent bewildering tingles through her stomach like nothing she'd ever felt before. She pursed her lips and hiked the basket higher on her hip. Such nonsense. Or was it?

Nathaniel scraped his plate and shoveled the last morsel into his mouth. Taking his meals out in the barn, horses were his dining companions. Mrs. Rutledge had told him he could join the family for meals, but he'd told her he didn't want to intrude. Supper should be a special family time. Some of his best memories growing up were around the supper table. The Rutledges didn't need a stranger in their midst.

The barn door creaked. He turned, expecting Quinn to walk in. Abby stood in the doorway. "May I come in?"

"Of course." He stood and wiped his hand on the back of his pants. The lantern light played off her hair, streaking her dark tresses with gold. He sucked in a breath, noting as he did so his pulse quickened when she stepped inside the barn. "Supper was mighty good. Thank you."

She lifted her shoulders slightly. "It was just beans and biscuits. I thought you might like some shortbread cookies." She held out a napkin-wrapped bundle.

"Th–thank you. That's nice of you." He accepted the offering and flipped back the napkin, extracting a golden brown cookie and sniffing the sweet aroma. "Mm. I haven't had a treat like this in a long time."

"Well. . ." Her hands did a little nervous flip. "I'll just take your supper plate back to the house." She picked up the empty plate and turned to go. "Good night."

"Wait."

She stopped and looked back at him, brows raised in inquiry.

"Can you. . .stay awhile? Share the cookies with me?"

She shrugged. "I suppose. The children are already in bed."

He fell into step with her and guided her out the door to the corral fence. Fireflies winked from the edge of the woods, and the scent of honeysuckle hung in the air. An almost full moon rose above the treetops.

"I saw you with the children today." He reined in the grin that wanted to emerge. "Looked like you were playing in the dirt."

"*Tsk*, I don't play in the dirt, Mr. Danfield."

He detected just enough of a playful lilt in her voice to know she wasn't offended.

"We were using sticks to write the ABCs. Dulcie knows all her letters, but she's never learned to read. Beau is just beginning to master the alphabet." She chuckled. "If I could only get him to draw the loops of the B on the right side of the straight line." Her obvious affection for the children was evident in the way she spoke.

He bit into a cookie and offered Abby one. "Mm, tastes just like the ones Mrs. Danfield used to make."

Abby cocked her head. "You called your mother Mrs. Danfield?"

He took another bite and wiped the crumbs from his mouth. "She wasn't my mother. The Danfields took me in when I was about seven or eight. I never knew my birthday so they weren't sure how old I was. I was a street urchin—in Boston. My mother died when I was quite young. I never knew my father. Reverend Danfield found me living on the streets and took me home. He and his wife raised me, and they were good to me, but I never could think of them as mother and father. They were fine people, though."

Abby's eyes softened, and she smiled. "Isn't it curious how we've been through so much together, but I never knew you were an orphan."

"No reason for you to know." Nathaniel propped one foot on the bottom rail of the fence. "Come to think of it, you're the first person I've ever told."

She lowered her eyes, and the corner of her mouth curved like she was enjoying a private thought. "May I ask you something?"

"Sure."

"How do you know Wren?"

"Wren? What makes you think I knew her?"

Abby clasped her hands, loosely interlocking her fingers. "Several times on the trail I saw her staring at you, like she knew you. And you looked at her the same way a couple of times, like you'd met her before."

Nathaniel shrugged. "I knew many Cherokees. Most of them are just regular folks." He stared hard at the treetops against the darkening sky. "I never did agree with the federal mandate to remove the Cherokees from their land. Seemed to me they had more right to it than we did since they were here first."

Abby crossed her forearms on the top rail. "My father never knew it, but one of my best friends at the Salem Female Academy was Jane Ross."

"Ross? Do you mean—"

She nodded. "She is the daughter of John Ross, the chief of the Cherokees. I wonder what is to become of her now."

Nathaniel didn't have an answer. "I wonder what will become of the whole Cherokee nation." He shook his head. "I hated what we had to do, but a good soldier is expected to obey orders."

Abby raised her palm to her chin and leaned on her elbow. "Father said you defied orders and showed contempt for the government. Is that why you were court-martialed?"

The bluntness of her question didn't surprise him. She'd proven on the trail she wasn't afraid to speak her mind. But he wasn't certain he was ready to let all the details of the court-martial come to light. Especially the secrets he kept hidden in his heart.

He let a long, silent minute go by. "Nothing was ever proven." *But Felicia believed it.*

"How could you be convicted without proof?"

Nathaniel worked his jaw back and forth. Funny how he'd felt comfortable sharing the details of his childhood with her, but one simple question closed him up like a shuttered window before a storm.

"Nathaniel, I'm sorry. Perhaps it's none of my business, but the stigma of dishonor will follow you for the rest of your life."

He stared at the silver moon rising higher in the inky sky. "I want to clear my name." If she only knew how much. "But it looks like that might never happen."

He took the last cookie from the napkin and broke it in half, offering one piece to her. "So, have you written to your father yet?"

Abby jerked her head around. "I started a letter, but I haven't finished it. Who knows when the mail will go out again? There's plenty of time." She bit into her half of the cookie.

He eyed her with a smirk. She wasn't fooling him for a minute. He turned around with his back to the fence and leaned his elbows on the rail. The way the moonlight gleamed off her long single braid reminded him of a silvery waterfall, creating such a distraction he almost forgot his own name. Every bit of discipline he learned in the army was required to stay his hand from reaching out and touching her hair.

Abby took the now-empty napkin and folded it. "It's getting late. I should go in so I don't disturb Beth and Quinn when I climb up the loft ladder."

Disappointment needled him. He wouldn't have minded passing the moonlit hours with this fascinating young woman, but he nodded. "I suppose I'll see you tomorrow then."

She took a couple of steps backward. "Good night." She turned and walked toward the cabin.

"Thanks for the cookies." *And for the company.*

She smiled over her shoulder. "You're welcome."

He headed into the barn and blew out the lantern. Up in the hayloft he stretched out and tucked his hands under his head. The open loft window afforded him a view of the stars thrown against the expansive black canvas. The vast number of twinkling lights reminded him of the people of whom he and Abby had spoken. She'd expressed concern, wondering what would happen to her friend, but there were so many more.

"What will happen to them, Lord? To all of them—Wren and the others who are hiding in the hills, and all those already confined to the relocation forts? They're Your children, too. God, I pray safety for them."

Abby's image tiptoed into his prayer. Her demure smile and the way the moonlight gilded her hair caused his pulse to quicken. So many things about this woman drew him, not the least of which was her genuine concern for the people to whom this land belonged generations before white men arrived and claimed it. Her nearness affected him so differently from when their journey started. His earliest impressions of her as a spoiled, opinionated, uncaring woman had crumbled into dust over the past couple of weeks. Other than her petulant grieving at the loss of her trunks, she'd met the challenges along the trail with determination and grace. A smile accompanied Nathaniel's musings as his eyes drifted closed.

Chapter 9

Despite the absence of a regular preacher, the folks of Tucker's Gap assembled in the small chapel on Sunday morning and raised their voices in praise. Nathaniel allowed the joyous time of hymn singing to minister to his soul. After the reading of scripture and exchanging of prayer requests, Sam Wise, the owner of the sawmill, stood to make a few announcements. "Let's remember next Sunday is a regular preachin' Sunday. Pastor Winslow'll be in Tucker's Gap on his circuit stop." He gestured toward the front row. "This here young lady's been stayin' with the Rutledges, helpin' out with the young'uns and such, and she has somethin' she'd like to say."

A keen awareness widened Nathaniel's eyes as Abby stood with a shy blush on her cheeks. Her hair was different this morning. Instead of her normal single braid, she'd pinned it up like a crown. He blew out the breath he was holding.

She turned to face the assembled group, but when her gaze made contact with his, she paused for a moment. Did her blush deepen?

"As Mr. Wise has said, I'm helping Beth with the children for a while. Dulcie, Beau, and I have been working on our letters and numbers." Abby smiled down at the youngsters. "If any other children would like to join us for lessons, they are more than welcome."

Nathaniel's heart swelled. Her graciousness in offering to teach the children was one more attribute that made him realize how wrong he'd been about her.

Sam Wise announced the closing hymn, and everyone stood and joined their voices in song: "O God, our help in ages past, our hope for years to come."

Nathaniel closed his eyes and absorbed the words.

"Sufficient is Thine arm alone, and our defense is sure."

God's peace poured over him. *Your defense is all I need, Lord.*

At the end of the hymn, families gathered to fellowship. He sent surreptitious glances in Abby's direction, hoping to catch a moment to speak to her. Two mothers nudged their children toward the front bench where Beth Rutledge introduced Abby to more community youngsters.

Florrie Cobb joined Nathaniel and gave him a beaming smile. "Such nice folks here. Mercy stayed home with Mr. Tucker this morning. It's so difficult for him to get around. Just helping him out to the front porch is an ordeal."

"Doesn't he have crutches?"

Florrie pursed her lips. "I don't think so."

Nathaniel rubbed his chin. "Crutches shouldn't be too hard to make. I'll see what I can do."

Florrie hugged his arm. "Nathaniel, you have such a good heart."

Nathaniel smirked. "I know a few folks that might disagree with you about that."

૨ટ

Nathaniel stepped inside Tucker's General Store and tipped his hat at a woman who was exiting.

Florrie called out from behind the counter. "Hello, Nathaniel."

"Morning, Florrie. Is Mrs. Tucker around?"

Mercy stepped out from the back of the store, wiping her hands on her apron. "Did somebody need me?"

"Good morning, Mrs. Tucker." Nathaniel gave her a polite nod. "How is your husband doing today?"

She cast a glance behind her toward the doorway from which she'd just entered. "It's so hard for him to move around. He's getting ornerier by the day, and I'm ready to snatch him bald-headed."

Nathaniel grinned. "Well, that's why I'm here. Florrie and I were talking at church the other day, and I think I can make him a pair of crutches. But I need to know how tall he is. I've seen him sitting out on the porch a time or two but couldn't get a good fix in my mind of his height."

A smile deepened the creases across Mercy's face. "He'd love some company. Won't you come back and meet him?"

Nathaniel nodded. "It would be my pleasure." He followed the woman past the curtained opening and across the kitchen to an open door.

"Leon, there's somebody here to see you." Mrs. Tucker stood aside and motioned for Nathaniel to enter.

Leon Tucker lay on the bed, his leg encased between two splints and secured with wound strips of cloth. His thinning hair bore tufts of silver. A twinge of commiseration poked Nathaniel's gut. Lying there day after day would certainly drive a man to distraction.

"Good morning, sir." He extended his hand. "I'm Nathaniel Danfield. I'm a—"

"You're a friend of Florrie's." Mr. Tucker reached up and shook his hand. "We've been mighty pleased to have her with us." He pointed to the chair beside the bed. "Have a seat."

Nathaniel sat and laid his hat over one knee. "It's nice to meet you, sir."

Mr. Tucker waved his hand. "I'm Leon. Florrie tells me ya'll were travelin' from Fort New Echota to Raleigh and got waylaid." He shook his head. "Bad business that. Ne'er-do-wells that rob honest folks and threaten their lives. . ." A scowl dipped the man's brow.

Heat scorched Nathaniel's face at the memory, wishing he'd done more to stop the bandits. If he'd obtained better directions, they wouldn't have been on that trail in the first place. The millstone of responsibility hung around his neck.

As if reading Nathaniel's thoughts, Leon spoke again. "The good Lord works out our circumstances in ways we don't always understand, but they're His ways, nevertheless. We aren't to question. Why, if things hadn't happened the way they did, Florrie wouldn't be here helpin' us out. I hear the other young lady who traveled with you is helpin' out at the Rutledges. And now here you sit, keepin' me company." A smile pulled at the corners of Leon's mouth. "Who can say God's hand didn't bring the three of you here to Tucker's Gap?"

The reference to Abby stirred feelings he still wasn't certain how to define. Dare he indulge in such speculation? No, not while his name was still sullied. Besides, being burned once by a woman's affections was enough.

Mercy still stood in the doorway. "Leon, Nathaniel said he's going to make you some crutches so you can get around a little easier."

"You don't say. Well, that's mighty neighborly of you, son."

Nathaniel glanced over his shoulder. "Mrs. Tucker, if you'll bring some string, we'll measure Leon's length so I'll know how tall to make the crutches."

Mercy bustled out of the room and returned a minute later with a length of string. They held the string from Leon's armpit to his heel and snipped it off. Nathaniel stuffed the string in his pocket. "I should have those crutches done in a few days."

The two men shook hands, and Nathaniel left Leon to rest. On his way out, he stopped to speak to Florrie.

She folded lengths of toweling as they chatted. "Wasn't it nice of Abby to offer to teach the children?"

Warmth rippled through Nathaniel's chest. "Very nice. You know, I can't get over the change in her. At the beginning of the journey, I thought she was self-centered and arrogant."

Florrie cut her gaze in his direction. "She was angry with her father for making her leave the fort. She doesn't care for living in Raleigh."

Nathaniel stroked his chin. "Really? I figured by the way she carried on over the loss of her trunks that she set much store by her fancy city clothes and female frills."

"Oh, goodness no." Florrie chuckled. "Not Abby. She'd far rather have stayed at the fort." She sighed.

"Is that right?" Puzzlement made him pause. "Why was she so touchy about her trunks?"

Florrie folded another towel and added it to the stack. "I suppose you'd have no way of knowing. The few keepsakes she has of her mother's are in one of her trunks. She told me about them. A brooch, a handkerchief, a lace collar, and her mother's hairbrush. Those things are more precious to Abby than anything else she lost when the wagon went over the ravine."

Nathaniel grimaced. To think he'd accused her of being shallow and peevish when her heart was breaking at the loss of the last connection she had with her mother. He had to find a way to retrieve those trunks.

He bid Florrie good day, and as he exited he caught sight of a small boy crouching behind a barrel on the porch. Whatever was the lad doing back there? He paused and took a step backward to get a better look. The boy clutched something in his fist and shoved his hand behind his back.

Nathaniel moved sideways to stand directly in front of the barrel, cutting off the youngster's escape.

"All right, come on out of there."

A young boy about seven years old with tousled blond hair and a sprinkling of freckles slowly rose to stand. "I didn't do nothin', mister."

"Really?" Nathaniel bent so he was eyeball to eyeball with the child. "What are you hiding behind your back?"

The boy's bottom lip began to tremble. "N–nothin'."

Nathaniel arched one eyebrow. "The truth?"

A fat tear made its way down the child's cheek. Nathaniel reached in and took the boy's hand in his. "Let's sit and have a talk."

Nathaniel steered the boy to the far end of the porch and sat on the edge with his legs dangling over the side. He patted the space beside him and the boy complied, eyeing Nathaniel warily.

"My name's Nathaniel."

The boy rubbed a grubby fist under his nose. "I'm Davy Pruitt."

"What are you hiding, Davy?"

Davy opened his fingers to reveal broken pieces of hard candy sticks stuck to his sweaty palm.

Exactly what Nathaniel thought. "Did you pay Mrs. Tucker for that candy?"

Davy didn't answer.

Nathaniel narrowed his eyes at the boy. "I suspect the answer is no. Otherwise you wouldn't have been hiding behind the barrel. Right?"

Davy sniffed and nodded. "Are you gonna put me in jail?"

Nathaniel tried to hide his smile. "Well now, taking something that doesn't belong to you is stealing, even if it's just candy."

Davy's blue eyes widened, and his chin began to quiver. "I don't wanna go to jail."

Nathaniel bit his lip as he slipped his arm around Davy's shoulders. "I don't want you to go to jail either. That's why we're talking about this." He shifted his weight and turned sideways, pulling one knee up onto the porch. "Davy, when I was your age, I didn't always do right. The preacher who raised me told me something that I never forgot. He said a real man, one who loves God, will do right even when no one is looking. Do you know why?"

The solemn expression on Davy's face told Nathaniel the boy was listening. " 'Cause iffen he don't, he won't go to heaven?"

"Going to heaven is another matter." Nathaniel clasped his hands. "A man who loves God *wants* to do right because God has changed his heart. So pleasing God is very important. If other people watch the way the man lives, they will know that man belongs to God just by the way he acts." He paused to give Davy time to digest the words.

"I want to belong to God."

This time Nathaniel didn't try to stop the smile from filling his face. "He wants to be your God, and He wants you to be His child."

"But I already have a pa. My pa works at the sawmill." Davy lowered his lashes. "I don't got a ma, though."

"Davy, you'll always be your pa's boy. But God wants to be your heavenly Father. He loves you, but He's disappointed when you do wrong things, just like your pa."

The tears welled in Davy's eyes again. "Are you gonna tell my pa I took the candy?"

"No." Nathaniel laid his hand on Davy's shoulder. "That's something I think you should do. But there is someone else you need to tell first."

Davy's bottom lip pooched out. "Who?"

Nathaniel cupped Davy's chin and waited until the boy looked him in the eye. "An honorable man admits when he's made a mistake. Whom did you steal the candy from?"

"Mrs. Tucker." Davy looked toward the door of the general store.

"What do you reckon she'll do?"

"I don't know, but I think she'd appreciate if you'd go in there and tell her the truth. It takes a real man to do something like that."

"But I ain't a man yet. I'm only seven."

Nathaniel smiled and bent his head closer to Davy. "Doing the right thing is how you get to be a man—the kind of man who lives to please God."

Davy pursed his lips and cast an uneasy glance toward the door. "Will you go with me?"

Nathaniel got to his feet and helped Davy up. "No." He patted Davy's shoulder. "I think you're man enough to handle this on your own." He ruffled Davy's hair. "But I will pray with you before you go in." He lowered himself to one knee and draped his arm around Davy, bowing his head.

&

Abby stood hidden by the thick bushes near Tucker's General Store. She'd watched Nathaniel sit down at the edge of the porch with a little boy she remembered from church, but she was unprepared for Nathaniel's wise words to the child. The godly character evidenced in Nathaniel belied her father's harsh opinion of him. Only a man of honor could teach a child how to be honorable.

As Nathaniel finished praying with the boy and nudged him toward the door, Abby swallowed back the lump that had formed in her throat. She waited until Nathaniel departed toward the livery before she stepped out from behind the bush and followed the boy into the store.

She found Mercy Tucker bent at the waist, listening to the lad stammer out his confession. He hung his head and shuffled his bare feet on the floor. Abby remained to one side. Would Mercy's reaction reflect her name?

"Well, Davy, I'm very glad you came in and told me what you did. That took a lot of courage." She lifted his chin. "I hope you won't ever steal anything ever again."

Davy shook his head. "I won't. I promise. And I'm really, really sorry."

Mercy straightened. "I believe you, Davy, and I forgive you."

Abby's throat tightened. Playing out before her was a portrayal of

God's love and grace. How many times had He wanted to pour out that same grace on her, if only she'd come to Him like this little child?

Mercy brushed Davy's hair back. "Being sorry and being forgiven doesn't mean you don't have to pay for the candy."

Davy looked up at her. "But I ain't got no money."

Mercy arched her eyebrows. "I see. Well, how about you do some chores in exchange for the candy?"

"What kind of chores?"

One corner of Mercy's mouth tipped up. "I think sweeping is a good way to pay for the candy." She pointed behind the counter. "Take that broom over there and sweep out the store."

Davy gave her a gap-toothed grin. "Yes'm." He scampered over to get the broom.

"Abby, is there something I can get for you?"

She blinked back the threatening tears and held out the envelope in her hand. "I need to mail this."

Mercy took the letter and glanced at the address. "Fort New Echota. Your father?"

Chapter 10

"M iss Abby, can we go out and play games?"

Abby sat back on her heels and brushed her forearm across her brow. "After I finish scrubbing the floor, Beau. Have you finished filling the woodbox?"

He peered into the box beside the fireplace. "It's almost fulled up."

"It needs to be all the way full. Now scoot and get it done. Then we can play."

The child waved to his mother who was propped up in bed in the corner and trotted out the door.

Beth rubbed her hand over her swollen belly. "You do have a way with that boy. I usually have to threaten him with a switch to get him to mind me."

Abby chuckled. "He reminds me of me at that age." She paused to study Beth's pale complexion and the dark circles under her eyes. "How are you feeling this morning?"

"Oh, I'm fine." The weariness in her tone belied her words. "I didn't sleep much last night. This little one kept kicking me awake."

Warmth rose up into Abby's face. "It must be a wondrous thing to carry a new life inside you." The heat intensified, and she ducked her head. "Maybe I shouldn't speak such things."

"Oh, I don't mind." Beth's quick response caused Abby to raise her eyes to her friend.

A tiny chagrined smile tweaked her lips. "I always wanted to be a big sister, but my mother died when I was quite young. Father never remarried, and he sent me to stay with my spinster aunt a great deal of the time." Abby tipped her head to one side. "The Bible says we are fearfully and wonderfully made. I used to imagine what it might be like to have my mother share such miraculous things with me."

A rosy blush stole into Beth's cheeks, accenting her dimple when she smiled. "'Tis a miracle, for sure."

Beau returned with an armload of sticks, ending their conversation. Abby directed him to walk where she hadn't yet scrubbed the floor.

"After you dump that firewood in the box, you and Dulcie each find a good writing stick and practice your letters until I come outside." The boy scampered out the door.

"Speaking of letters—" Beth raised her eyebrows. "Have you written your father and aunt?"

Abby scoured another floorboard. "Yes, I wrote both of them, but I think I might go over to Tucker's and get the letter to my father before the mail is picked up."

"Why?"

A dirty spot by the worktable drew Abby's scrub brush. "I've been having second thoughts about what I wrote to him. I spent most of last night thinking I shouldn't have told him where I am, just that I've been delayed."

She finished the last of the floor and rose from her knees. "My father isn't like most fathers. He finds fault with everything I do." She tossed the dirty water out the door. "Even when I was a child he said he didn't know what to do with me. The morning we left the fort he told me I was petulant and incorrigible."

Dropping the scrub brush inside the empty bucket, Abby turned to face Beth. "When he finds out where I am, I'm afraid he'll send a detachment to fetch me and take me to Raleigh."

"Oh my." Obvious distress rang in Beth's voice. "The baby isn't due for a couple more months. Do you think he'd make you leave before then?"

Abby crossed the newly scrubbed floor to the bed and took Beth's hand. "That's why I want to go and get my letter. I made you a promise and I intend to keep it."

A weak smile wobbled across Beth's face. "You've been such a godsend. I don't know what I would have done—"

Abby hushed her. "You get some rest. After I pick up my letter, the children and I will be outside working on their letters and numbers. I'll peek in to see if you need anything."

❧

"A couple of miners came through here yesterday, Abby. They picked up the mail on their way to Auraria."

Florrie's words twisted Abby's stomach. "My letter to Father is already gone?"

"I'm afraid so." Florrie measured out coffee beans. "Why did you want it back?"

Abby blew out a sharp breath. "Because in the letter I mentioned Tucker's Gap. Last night I realized I shouldn't have told him where I was." She gripped the edge of the counter with both hands and leaned closer, not wishing the children to overhear. "I am not leaving here until Beth has her baby and can manage on her own."

Florrie weighed a scoop of cornmeal. "Did you explain your promise to Beth in your letter?"

"Yes, but I doubt Father will care." She heaved a sigh. "How could I have been so foolish as to tell him I was in Tucker's Gap?" She scuffed her shoe on the wide floorboards. "What am I going to do if he sends a regiment here?"

"It's doubtful he'll send a regiment." Florrie patted her hand. "Abby, it's done. The letter is sent. Fretting over it won't bring the letter back." She came around the side of the counter. "My suggestion is to take the entire matter to the Lord. Certainly you must have prayed over the decision to remain here and help Beth, didn't you?"

"I—I—" Abby brought her clasped hands up to her forehead.

"Didn't you? Abby?"

Abby dropped her hands to her sides and hung her head. "No." Shame rippled through her, and memories of Father's condemnation pointed accusing fingers. If she couldn't please her earthly father, how did she expect to please her heavenly Father? Her voice dropped to a whisper. "I didn't pray. Beth needed help, and before I knew what was happening, I offered." She raised her eyes. "Florrie, why can't I learn to pray before I act? God must be so disappointed in me."

Florrie brushed a few stray hairs from Abby's face. "Oh, my dear, God is most loving and forgiving. And He doesn't hold grudges. It's never too late to pray."

"Wise counsel, madam."

Florrie and Abby turned in unison toward the door where a gentleman in travel-worn garb stood. His white beard and thick eyebrows gave him a grandfatherly appearance, and his cloudy gray eyes spoke of compassion. He pulled off his battered black hat.

"I'm Reverend Winslow. I don't believe you ladies were here when I was last in Tucker's Gap." He slapped his hat against his pant leg, sending dust motes flying in every direction.

Abby tried to swallow the knot in her throat, wondering how much of her confession the itinerant preacher heard. Florrie welcomed the man like she'd known him all her life.

"Pastor Winslow." She stepped toward him and held out her hand. "I've heard a great deal about you. I'm Mrs. Florrie Cobb, and this is Miss Abigail Locke."

Abby remembered her manners and followed Florrie's example. "Pastor."

"Miss Locke. Mrs. Cobb. I'm pleased to meet you." The crow's-feet at the corners of his eyes crinkled when he smiled, but the slump of his shoulders bespoke his weariness. "I met a young fellow at the livery who told me ya'll were new in town." A tiny frown edged its way into his brow. "I understand Leon Tucker has met with an accident."

"Pastor Winslow, is that you?" Mercy pushed aside the curtain and stepped into the store. "I thought I recognized your voice. Leon's been itchy for three days waiting for you to arrive. He said something about beating you at checkers."

The preacher tipped his head back and laughed. "That sly fox isn't going to beat me this time. I've been practicing."

Abby decided she liked the elderly preacher. She gathered her purchases into the basket. "I need to get back and check on Beth. It was nice meeting you, Pastor."

As she turned to call the children, she collided with a man who'd just entered the store. "Oh! I'm so sorry." She looked up into the face of Teague Jackson.

His lips pulled back away from his yellowed teeth into a leering grin. "Miss Locke." He tugged on the brim of his hat.

Heat scorched her ears. "How clumsy of me. I apologize."

Piercing black eyes explored her face and drifted downward. "No harm done."

"Mr. Jackson." Pastor Winslow offered his hand. "Might I convince you to attend services tomorrow?"

Teague pulled his gaze away from Abby and turned to face the preacher. One corner of his mouth lifted in a half smirk. "Don't usually have time for church, but," he cast his glance sideways at Abby, "I might be there."

Abby's stomach clenched, and she beckoned to the children. "We have to be going. Florrie, Mercy, I'll see you tomorrow. Pastor, pleasure meeting you." She herded Beau and Dulcie out the door.

They were crossing the road, hurrying toward the Rutledge home, when a voice hailed her. Her feet slowed, and she paused to turn. Teague Jackson strode across the road, closing the distance between them. "Thought you might need some help carryin' that heavy basket."

Uncertainty about the man lingered within her. "The basket isn't heavy, thank you, Mr. Jackson. Come along, children."

He lengthened his stride and positioned himself in front of her. "Now that ain't very friendly. I ain't a bad fella. Just tryin' to be mannerly."

Knowing the children were watching and listening, Abby tempered her tone and forced a smile. "Thank you for your offer, Mr. Jackson, but we can manage just fine. Good day."

"Reckon I'll see ya'll in church tamorra," he called after her as she hastened toward the house. She released a pent-up breath when he didn't follow.

As they passed the corral, Nathaniel lifted his hand, gesturing for her to wait. She handed the basket to Dulcie and admonished the children to be quiet in case their mother was sleeping.

Nathaniel ducked under the fence and met her on the footpath. He waited until the children entered the house before he spoke. A frown darkened his eyes.

"I noticed that Jackson fellow followed you from the store. Did he bother you?"

Abby sent a quick glance in Teague's direction, but he had already moved on. "No. He just offered to carry my basket."

Nathaniel turned his eyes in the direction of Jackson's harness shop, a couple of hundred yards from where they stood. "You'll let me know if does, won't you?" A hint of caution edged his voice.

She gave a tiny shrug. "I think he's harmless." She looked up into Nathaniel's hazel eyes, and her heart fluttered. Whether his reason for asking was protectiveness or jealousy, his inquiry sent a tingle through her stomach. The way he worked his jaw indicated he didn't agree with her assessment, but he changed the subject.

"The circuit preacher stopped by here to stable his horse."

Abby nodded. "I met him at the store. I'm looking forward to hearing him preach tomorrow."

Nathaniel stuffed his hands in his pockets and looked at the ground. "Would you allow me to escort you to church in the morning, Abby?"

The tingle in her stomach grew into a tremble. She sucked in a soft breath as warmth flooded her middle and climbed into her face. Uncharacteristic shyness tangled her tongue. She coughed to clear her throat of the lump that suddenly took up residence there. "I'd like that, Nathaniel."

The scowl that had pinched his features minutes ago faded, and a smile took its place. His lips parted and he nodded. "I need to get back to work."

"Me, too. I'll see you later."

He tipped his hat, but before he turned away from her, she caught a glimpse of the silliest grin she'd ever seen on his face.

Dew created sparkles on the grass as the morning sun sent shafts of light through the trees. Nathaniel's memory of Abby's hand on his arm as they entered the church last Sunday still pulled his face into a smile. The only thing that tainted the image was remembering Teague Jackson's glower when he caught sight of them. Pastor Winslow had seemed especially pleased to see Jackson there, even though Sam Wise mentioned Teague never attended church before Abby came to town. Nathaniel knew he shouldn't resent the man coming to church, but the thought still needled him.

He finished mucking out the stalls and pitched fresh hay to the horses. Quinn's hammer rang in the air as the blacksmith fashioned a new blade for somebody's plow. Nathaniel entered the forge and Quinn halted his labor.

"The barn is clean, and the stock is fed and watered." Nathaniel wiped his hands on the seat of his pants. "What else do you need me to do?"

Quinn studied him a moment, as if taking inventory of his character. He pointed with his hammer. "Those saw blades over there are finished. They need to go to the mill. And that harrow belongs to Hiram Sizemore. Load them up in the buckboard and deliver them." He concluded his instructions with a brief nod of his head.

Nathaniel's heart lifted. If Quinn trusted him with the buckboard and team, perhaps now was the time to speak to him about borrowing a horse and some equipment.

"Quinn, as you know, Abby's and Florrie's trunks were lost when the wagon wrecked. Could I borrow a horse and a block and tackle? I'd like to go down the trail and see if I could salvage the ladies' trunks."

Quinn stopped hammering and a scowl dipped his thick brows. The man stared a hole straight through him. "Don't know that I can spare a horse."

The blacksmith's refusal stung, but Nathaniel had begun to realize trust took time. He turned and strode to the barn to hitch the team. The sound of childlike singing drew his attention. Morning sun glistened off Abby's hair as she and the children headed toward the woods. She carried a basket over one arm.

"Abby." He jogged over to catch up with them.

"Good morning, Nathaniel." Abby gave him the same shy smile she did last Saturday when he asked to escort her to church.

"Where are you headed?"

She nodded toward the woods. "Wren told me how to make a tea from the root of yellow lilies. She said it will settle the stomach. She also showed me the berries of the squaw vine. They're good for ladies—" Abby dipped her head, and her cheeks turned bright red.

Nathaniel cast his gaze through the trees, recalling the Georgia Guard patrol that came through less than two weeks earlier. The Guard's reputation for questionable practices filled him with unease. "I don't think it's safe for you to go into the woods alone. I have a couple of errands to run for Quinn, then I'd be glad to go with you."

Lines appeared between Abby's brows. "But I wanted to make that tea for Beth as soon as possible."

"This shouldn't take too long. I want to go into the woods myself and cut some of those twisted trunks and limbs. I have an idea how I can use them." He glanced at the children and then back at Abby. Her eyes reflected curiosity over his statement, but he wanted to make certain she understood his warning.

"It really isn't safe for you to venture into the woods unescorted."

Chapter 11

A bby admonished Dulcie and Beau to be good and mind their mother. She'd left Beth comfortably seated in the rocker while the children showed her how much they had learned over the past weeks. Dulcie proudly read entire sentences while Beau grinned as he told his mother the sound each letter made.

With a basket over her arm, Abby snuck a surreptitious glance toward the livery. Not seeing Nathaniel anywhere about, she slipped into the woods. The teas she'd made from lemon balm and yellow lily root had worked wonders to settle Beth's stomach, and Abby was anxious to hunt for other leaves and roots Wren had showed her. The cool shade whispered across her bare arms and beckoned her deeper into the woods.

She plucked several squaw vines clean of their partridgeberries and snipped shiny pipsissewa leaves, remembering how Wren had used them on Nathaniel's wound. Between Beau getting a new cut or scrape every other day and sparks from the forge leaving burns on Quinn's arms, the leaves might come in handy. With her knife she peeled strips of willow bark to add to her basket.

Squirrels chattered overhead, and a chorus of birds accompanied them. A breeze rustled the leaves. The summer music so engrossed her, she almost missed the movement from the corner of her eye off to the right. She halted. Was it an animal? She held her breath and didn't move.

After several minutes, she scoffed at her own apprehension. Nathaniel's warning had her as jumpy as Beau's hoptoad. Moving slowly she scanned the forest floor, hoping to locate some purple trillium.

"I watch you from trees."

Abby dropped her basket as her hand shot up to clutch her throat, muting her scream. Her heart lurched in her chest as she whirled to find a familiar face.

"Wren! You scared me to death." She clapped a hand over her pounding heart.

A twinkle lit the Cherokee woman's eyes, and a tiny smile wiggled the corners of her mouth. "You move through trees like black bear in spring."

Abby's quivering knees buckled, and she sank to the ground. "You move in absolute silence."

Wren knelt beside her and began picking up the forage that fell out of the basket. "Partridgeberries?"

Abby shifted to her knees and retrieved the willow bark peelings. "I tried to remember all that you taught me during those few days we were together. There is a woman in Tucker's Gap who is expecting a baby. She's having... difficulty. You said partridgeberries are good for women in childbirth."

Wren nodded. "Partridgeberries are good. You need vervain to make tea. Not find here." She gestured to the surrounding woods. "Too dry. Vervain need wet. Come, I show you." Wren picked up her own oddly shaped basket and slung it on her back.

Abby scrambled to her feet and followed Wren down a slope where the solid ground gave way to softer, swampy earth. Abby hung on every word as the Cherokee woman described how to use the vervain leaves to brew a tea for Beth.

"Vervain make your friend strong when her time comes."

They followed the low-lying marshy ground out of the woods to a sunnier area. Wren showed her which cattails to pick and described how to use the fuzz for Beth's baby to prevent a rash. As Abby's basket became fuller, they turned back toward Tucker's Gap. Wren pointed out red clover for making a relaxing tea. Entering the deep woods once more, they found the purple trillium Abby sought.

As they hiked, Abby looked at Wren. "After you left us that day on the trail, I wondered if I would ever see you again."

"I see you play with young ones."

Abby stopped in her tracks. "You've been close enough to the town to see us?"

"Mm. I watch."

The very idea of Wren coming so near the town spiked Abby's curiosity. Would the woman answer the question that had niggled at Abby for weeks? "Wren, you knew Nathaniel before the day the outlaws shot him, didn't you?"

Wren let her basket slide off her back. A flicker of wariness piqued her expression, and the woman's narrowed eyes studied Abby for a long moment. "He is a good man. I know this."

"But how do you know it?" Abby's suspicion strengthened.

Wren's chin lifted, her unwavering gaze defined her determination. "Soldiers come to our village. Say my people must leave our homes and go to fort. They take land, home, animals, all things. We can no longer stay in the place where we are born."

The Cherokee woman absently fingered the stems of red clover from the basket. A faraway look fell across her face, as if she no longer spoke to Abby, but to God. "The day soldiers come we say please for more time, so we can gather things. They say no, we must leave now.

"One soldier with long sword tell other soldiers to shoot. I try to hide with my sister and my friend. Children cry. Their fear is great. One soldier—" Wren turned her eyes back to Abby. "Your Danfield, say stop. Do not shoot."

A rush of warmth filled Abby's face to hear Wren refer to Nathaniel as *hers*, but she set the feeling aside. The story Wren related both drew her and repelled her. How could the army commit such atrocities? Abby wanted to cover her ears, to forbid the picture Wren painted from forming in her mind—except for one thing: What was Nathaniel's role in this abomination?

Wren's expression grew hard. "Danfield say to soldier with long sword, 'Do not shoot. This is murder.'" She swallowed once, twice, and her chest heaved with each breath as she continued relaying the incident. "Danfield see me and my sister and friend with children. He push us to the trees. He tell women to hide children in forest. Soldiers still shoot. My sister fall. Danfield run to her but she is dead."

A single tear made its way down Wren's cheek. It was only then Abby realized her own face was wet with sickening sorrow for Wren's story. But the Cherokee woman wasn't finished. "The soldier with long sword take Danfield. Danfield do good thing, try to stop wrong. They treat him with hate and shame." She shook her head. "Soldier with long sword. . .*evil.*" Wren spat the word. An icy shudder trembled through Abby despite the warm summer day. She set the basket down and slipped both arms around Wren. There were no words to convey the tumbled emotions within her. The loathsome memory Wren recounted and Nathaniel's heroic effort to protect Wren and the others swirled in her mind. Nausea rose in her throat when she realized Nathaniel had been branded with dishonor when his deeds portrayed him a most honorable man.

When Abby released her friend, their eyes locked. Appreciation shone in Wren's gaze as she gripped Abby's shoulder for a long moment.

"You're right." Abby's voice came out in a hoarse whisper. "Nathaniel Danfield *is* a good man."

Abby bent to pick up her overflowing basket. She fell into step with Wren as the two made their way back toward Tucker's Gap.

"My father said Nathaniel was court-martialed at Fort Reed. That's nearly two weeks' journey from where you found us on the trail. How did you come to be in this area?"

"My people live in small village one day's journey from New Echota," Wren explained. "After soldiers come and kill my sister, many run and hide in hills. Soldiers hunt. We move east and north. Always move. Do not stay long in one place."

An ache wormed through Abby's heart. "Do you have shelter? Enough to eat? Clothing?"

Wren shrugged. "We have little. Our needs are not great." The corners of her lips curved up to accompany a look of contentment. "The God who cares for the sparrow cares for Cherokee."

They continued walking in silence. When they drew close enough to Tucker's Gap to hear the sawmill, Wren stopped. She removed the V-shaped basket from her back and took Abby's basket, emptying it into hers. Then she handed her full basket to Abby.

"You take this basket. Make easy work when you hunt leaves and roots."

Abby shook her head. "I can't take your basket, Wren. What will you use?"

Wren lifted one shoulder. "I make new one." She grinned. "More big. This one too small."

Abby laughed. "Thank you." She grasped Wren's hand. "I'm so glad you're my friend."

The two parted. As Abby closed the distance to town, she called to mind what Wren told her about Nathaniel. *He saved Wren's life and the lives of those children, and was court-martialed for doing so.* In her frequent arguments with her father, she remembered him stating adamantly the meticulous orders from General Winfield Scott that the Cherokee were to be treated with kindness. What Wren described represented a gross violation of General Scott's orders. But who would take Wren's word over that of a military tribunal?

As the livery came into view, Abby quickened her steps, anxious to speak with Nathaniel about what she'd learned. She set Wren's basket down by a tree and hurried toward the barn. She heard voices as she stepped through the open doorway. Quinn and Nathaniel must be discussing work. She hesitated, not wishing to interrupt. Then she realized she heard only one voice, not two. Nathaniel's voice. "Father, my life, my name, my reputation are in Your hands. Even if it meant spending the rest of my life under the condemnation of the army, I'd still not change a thing. I'd rather be in Your will first, Lord, than have the approval of men. But is it wrong for me to want to clear my name? If I'm labeled dishonorable, my testimony is tainted. Nevertheless, Lord, I trust You and desire to be used by You in whatever way You see fit."

Hot tears burned Abby's throat. She'd never known a man who embodied the term "honorable" like Nathaniel.

ॐ

Nathaniel rose to his feet and brushed hay off his pant legs. He'd made his request to God, but regardless of the outcome, he'd trust God's design for his life. He drew in a breath, filling his heart with the assurance of God's control.

He picked up the two large water buckets and headed toward the spring. He looked past the trees to the footpath leading to the Rutledge home. Abby walked toward the house, carrying a basket. As he hurried to catch up with her, he noticed the basket was full of various greenery, blossoms, and pieces of roots. She'd been in the woods.

"Abby, wait."

Hadn't he made it clear he didn't want her venturing into the woods unescorted? He couldn't remember ever meeting such a stubborn female.

She turned to face him as he approached.

He pointed to the basket. "What's all this?"

She plucked out a couple of leaves and stems. "Red clover, vervain, pipsissewa—"

"I didn't mean *what* is it, I meant—"

"I know very well what you meant." Abby cocked her head. "I went gathering these herbals because each one has a specific use and benefit. Beth needs these things."

Nathaniel narrowed his eyes. Some days she was so gentle and beautiful, and other days she was the most exasperating person he'd ever encountered. "I thought I told you not to go into the woods alone."

She gave him a short nod. "I seem to recall you saying something to that effect, but I wasn't alone."

He cast a sweeping survey of the surrounding area. "Oh? Who was with you?" *If she says it was Teague Jackson. . .*

She glanced from side to side and lowered her voice. "I met Wren. Nathaniel, she and I talked and—"

"It's not safe—" The volume of his words increased with his irritation, but he quickly quieted his tone. "It's not safe for either you or Wren to be out there alone. I know you're fascinated with Wren's knowledge of herbal medicine, but Abby, I can't stand by and watch you put yourself in danger."

"We weren't in any danger." She leaned forward, her expression animated. "Wren told me—"

Nathaniel held up his hand. "Miss Locke! Just because we have been waylaid on our journey to Raleigh does not negate my responsibility for your safety. I don't want you going into the woods alone."

She shifted the full basket to one hand and plunked her other fist on her hip. "Nathaniel Danfield, you are not my keeper, so stop being so bossy. I am quite capable of taking care of myself."

"Are you now?" He spread his feet and crossed his arms over his chest. "Are you *quite capable* of fighting off a panther or a bear? How about a pack of wolves?"

Abby's chin jutted out and hardheaded defiance outlined her profile. "The most dangerous animal we encountered was a squirrel."

"That's not the point and you know it." He put both hands on his hips. "I gave your father my word that I would ensure your safety. My word might not mean much to him, but it does to me."

Abby flipped her palm up. "That's what I've been trying to tell you. Wren and I talked and—"

Nathaniel tossed both hands up. "Haven't you heard a word I've said? Panthers and bears aren't the only animals that pose a danger. In fact, I'd say the two-legged variety is far more threatening. Some would like nothing better than to find you alone in the woods, completely defenseless."

She sputtered, and fire glinted from her eyes. "Is that what you think I am? Defenseless?"

Nathaniel fastened his eyes on her face. The curve of her cheek, the scowl across her brow, and the upturned tip of her nose all captured his senses. Against his better judgment, he allowed his gaze to drift to her pursed lips, and he nearly forgot why he was angry. He jerked his focus back to the subject at hand.

This wasn't the first time he'd witnessed her bravado. Her tenacious will waved like a banner the day they'd battled the outlaws. He took a step toward her. She stood her ground. Defenseless? Not by any stretch of the imagination.

His arm snaked out and encircled her waist, tugging her into his embrace. She dropped her basket. Her eyes widened, and he heard her soft gasp as he lowered his head to hers and planted a kiss squarely on her mouth.

When he released her, she wobbled back on her heels. He caught her by the elbow and steadied her. Her dark-brown eyes blinked in astonishment, and her lips formed a perfect O.

Nathaniel let go of her elbow. What had he done? Whatever possessed him to do such a thing? Never before had he given in to impulsiveness. The shock on her face mirrored that which he realized in his own heart.

"I'm. . .I'm. . .s–s–sorry." He took a step backward, then another. He half expected her to lunge and take a swing at him the way she had against the bandits.

But she didn't. She stood there swaying unsteadily like a stiff breeze might blow her over, her mouth opening and closing like a fish out of water.

His hands moved as though detached from his body, in sporadic jerky gestures with no apparent purpose. He bent and picked up her basket, shoving in foliage that spilled out when she dropped it. He straightened and held the basket out to her, wondering if she might dump the contents over his head.

Her stunned, dazed look changed to wide-eyed mortification. Red climbed up her neck into her face. She sucked in a noisy breath as she looked around frantically, presumably to see if anyone had been watching. Pressing her lips into a thin line, she snatched the basket from his hands, spun on her heel, and stalked to the house.

Chapter 12

He kissed me.

Abby stood at the kitchen worktable, kneading bread dough with one hand. The fingers of her other hand touched her lips, checking for the hundredth time if the tingle she felt was real or just a memory.

For the space of three sunrises and sunsets, she'd kept her hands occupied with various tasks and drove herself to exhaustion each evening. Still, she'd lain awake for hours, remembering the taste of Nathaniel's lips.

Had she dreamed it? Wren's basket sitting by the table represented tangible proof that she'd made her trek into the woods that day. It was no dream. Their heated words echoed in her mind, and she could still see his narrowed eyes. He certainly had a unique way of winning an argument.

Abby glanced at Beth seated in the rocker working on her knitting and listening to Dulcie read. Neither she nor Quinn had mentioned a word about seeing Nathaniel's impromptu kiss. Not even Florrie had mentioned hearing about it. Had she known nobody was looking, she might have enjoyed the kiss instead of reacting like he'd insulted her.

In the tension of the moment, she feared every person in Tucker's Gap witnessed the embrace. Despite her initial shock, however, three days of rumination had mellowed her indignation. Each time the memory returned, the edges of her annoyance fell away until she could no longer think of a good reason to be perturbed. A twinge of sorrow stung when she remembered he'd backed away, stammering an apology. Was he really sorry he'd kissed her? She couldn't deny his kiss underscored the growing awareness within her. She was falling in love with him.

Abby rolled Wren's revelation over in her mind, more convinced than ever of Nathaniel's character. Under the circumstances, the court-martial didn't make sense. The officer who gave the command to open fire in violation of General Scott's orders should have been the one court-martialed. While Wren's story answered Abby's nagging question, it raised a dozen new ones.

Abby pushed her fists into the bread dough, focusing her energy into pummeling the dough into a satiny smooth lump. She divided the dough into loaves and left them to rise.

"Beau." She motioned the little fellow over to her. "Please go out to the barn and get Mr. Nathaniel's plate and bring it to me."

"Yes'm." He ran out the door. Abby cast a quick glance at Beth who eyed her with puzzlement.

"Something wrong between you and Nathaniel?" Beth cocked her head.

The question sent waves of heat rising into Abby's face, and she gulped. "Wrong? Why would you ask that?" She stared wide-eyed at her friend.

The corners of Beth's mouth twitched. "Because you've avoided going out to the barn three days in a row."

Abby shrugged and scraped thin peels of lye soap into a pan of hot water. "I've been busy." She immersed dirty dishes into the soapy water. "How did that red clover tea work for you? Did you rest better?"

"I rested fine, thank you. Why are you changing the subject?"

"I wasn't aware the barn was a subject." Abby scrubbed the skillet. Perspiration formed on her forehead and dribbled down her temple.

Beau came bursting in the door with the plate in his hand. "Mr. Nathaniel says thank you for breakfast." He thrust the plate at Abby and roared back out the door.

"Hmm." Beth's musing reached Abby's ears. "Now Nathaniel is using Beau as his messenger. If I didn't know better, I'd say you two had a spat."

Abby dropped Nathaniel's plate, and the tin rang against the floorboards. A hiccup lodged in her throat, and she was seized with a fit of coughing. Snatching up the plate, she scoured it and dipped it in the rinse water. When she felt she could do so without giving away her inner feelings, she turned to look at Beth.

"He was just annoyed because I went into the woods alone."

Beth's eyes twinkled. "Is that why he kissed you?"

"Of course not!" Abby sputtered and grabbed a towel. "He. . ." Obviously Beth had seen more than she'd let on. How was Abby to answer that question?

Why *had* he kissed her?

❧

Abby wrote the word *butterfly* in the dirt with a stick. Using the stick as a pointer, she indicated each letter, and Beau told her the sound the letter made.

"B–u–tt–eerr–fff–l—" Beau's face drew up into a frown. "I can't remember how the Y sounds."

"That's all right, you did just fine." Abby ruffled his already-unruly hair. "Sometimes the Y can sound like E, and sometimes it sounds like I. Which one of those sounds do you think the Y makes in this word?"

The little fellow scrunched his eyes into a squint as he let each letter's sound roll off his lips. Abby stifled a giggle at the boy's intense concentration. As if suddenly enlightened with the answer, Beau's eyebrows leaped up and hid under the hair that flopped over his forehead. "I?"

"So what is the word?"

"Bb–uu–tt–er–f–l–y." A wide, triumphant grin spread across the boy's face. "Butterfly!" He jumped up and ran around in circles flapping his arms.

Dulcie rolled on her back in the grass and cackled. "You look like a duck."

Beau fell into Abby's lap, laughing and breathless. "I ain't no duck."

"I am not a duck," Abby corrected.

He popped his head up and giggled. "You and me ain't ducks."

Abby tugged both children into a hug. "Have either of you ever looked at a butterfly up close?"

Dulcie shook her head, but Beau piped up, "I chased one once, but I couldn't catched it, 'cause it flied up high, and Mama said if I climbed up on the fence one more time she was gonna cut a switch."

A snort drew Abby's attention. She looked up to see Nathaniel pushing the wheelbarrow down the narrow path. A small grin poked a dimple into his cheek.

Abby sucked in a soft breath and tried to return her attention to the children, but an unseen force fastened her gaze to the man. The breeze blew his hair across his eyes, much like Beau's, and sweat glistened off his forearms. His step hesitated for a moment as their eyes met. He gave her the slightest of nods, dipped his head, and shoved the wheelbarrow on its way.

Abby felt her face flush, and she forced her gaze at the children's expectant faces. "When I went to the store yesterday, Miss Florrie gave me some scraps of cheesecloth, and you know what we're going to do with it?"

While the children tried to guess, Abby snuck another glance in the direction Nathaniel had taken. She found him at the end of the footpath. His wheelbarrow was upturned and empty, and he stood leaning on the raised handles, watching her.

A tremor rippled through her, and she hiccuped a sharp intake of breath. A rush of nervous energy ignited in her stomach. Her heart rattled against her rib cage.

"Miss Abby?" Beau pulled on her sleeve. "What're we gonna make?"

She yanked her gaze away from Nathaniel and gave the children a shaky smile. "We're going to make special nets so we can catch butterflies.

First we need a branch shaped like this." She picked up the stick and drew an exaggerated Y in the dirt and pointed to the stem. "This will be the handle, and it has to be a bit long so we can reach those butterflies that fly up high." She tweaked Beau's ear. "Then we will sew the cheesecloth here." She traced the forked area. "But you're going to have to find just the right branch."

Dulcie clapped and Beau jumped up and down. Abby pulled her feet under her, taking care not to snag her hem, when a hand reached down and captured hers.

"Allow me, Miss Abby."

She tilted her head back and looked up. Nathaniel held her hand securely in his. The dimple in his cheek deepened as his mouth pulled into a sheepish half grin. He assisted her to her feet, holding her hand an extra moment. Pressure squeezed her chest, and she couldn't seem to catch her breath.

"Th–thank you."

He released her hand but didn't take his eyes off her. "My pleasure."

Abby shook out Beau's wet overalls and hung them on the clothesline. Her lower back ached from bending over the washtub. She twisted first to the right, then to the left, trying to stretch out her tight muscles.

Quinn had left before first light to go help a farmer cut hay, and Abby glanced toward the livery where Nathaniel worked alone today. She bit her lip. Never before had she been rendered speechless around a man.

As she bent to pick the next wet garment from the basket, she noticed two scruffy, unshaven men, climbing down the steps from Tucker's store. Mercy stood in the doorway and waved to the men. They returned her wave as they mounted their mules and pulled the lead rope of a pack donkey.

Miners. The arrival of miners in Tucker's Gap usually meant mail. Abby's stomach tightened, whether with anticipation or apprehension, she couldn't tell. Just over a month had passed with no word from either her father or her aunt. She shrugged and hung Quinn's shirt on the line.

Buried deep in her heart's secret place she longed to know her father cared. Sorting the reasons from her emotions was too complicated. Her willful attitude and penchant for disagreeing with her father had already carved a chasm too wide to bridge. He'd told her as much the morning she left the fort. Still, hidden beneath layers of defiance and rebellion was a little girl who simply wanted her father's love. Was it too much to wish?

She hurried to get the remaining laundry hung, silently chiding herself for allowing her hopes to rise.

Abby left the empty laundry basket on the peg near the door and peeked to check on Beth. Her friend was seated in the rocker with mending in her lap.

"A couple of miners just left the store. I thought I'd see if there was any mail."

Beth looked up from the sock she was darning. "I hope you hear from your father, but I suppose I'm being selfish in hoping he doesn't make you leave Tucker's Gap."

Abby lifted her chin. "I'll not leave you until you're back on your feet, letter or no letter." A twinge of conscience pricked her. Not five minutes ago she wished for her father's affection, yet she defied him at every turn, even when he wasn't present to witness it.

The children tagged along after Abby, and Florrie met them at the door as they climbed the steps to the store. She held up a letter as she gave Abby a quick hug.

Abby's breath caught for a split second, but the handwriting was too neat and precise to be Father's. Apparently Florrie thought so as well.

"From your aunt, perhaps?"

Abby turned her attention to the missive. Yes, it was unmistakably Aunt Charlotte's flowing script. The thickness of the letter hinted at her aunt's verbosity. She broke the wax seal and unfolded the fine linen stationery— all four pages. Her eyes scanned the first page, noting the date. It was written three weeks ago. Aunt Charlotte must have sat down to write her response the very day she received Abby's letter. As expected, her aunt was horrified, going on and on about the damage to Abby's reputation, her responsibility to take her place in society, and challenging her to consider that a respectable man wouldn't have a young woman who'd spent weeks fetching and carrying for a blacksmith's wife.

"For heaven's sake." Abby looked up at Florrie's amused expression. "You'd think she was trying to marry me off to royalty." She folded the letter and stuffed it into her skirt pocket. "I'll finish reading this later. I'd rather go play with the children. We have butterflies to catch."

❧

Nathaniel smiled at the sound of young Beau's laughter. He leaned to one side and angled his head to see what had the youngster so tickled. From the shadows just inside the barn doors, he watched as Abby pointed to a yellow butterfly, and the children swung their makeshift nets at the elusive insect. The creature's flight path hiccupped to and fro, dipping and twisting as if intentionally leading Beau on a dizzying chase.

"Miss Abby, help me. My net's caught." Dulcie's plaintive call drew Abby over to the child. The little girl's net was entangled in a low-hanging branch.

"Don't pull on it. We don't want to tear the cheesecloth." Abby grasped the branch and directed Dulcie to hold it steady while she meticulously removed twigs from the net. Nathaniel watched, mesmerized. Her every movement—from her reassuring smile to the way she concentrated on her task—captured him, and he was a helpless prisoner of her charm. The memory of the softness of her lips caught his breath.

"Come back here!"

Beau ran toward the corral fence after his prey. Quick as a squirrel, he climbed over the fence and followed the butterfly into the corral.

"No, don't—"

Nathaniel's warning came too late. Beau's exuberance in waving his net startled Shadrach, Quinn's best horse. The animal reared and shied, lunging to one side, tossing its thick black mane and throwing its rear hooves up in a vicious kick. Beau stood paralyzed with his long-handled net in the air, pointing straight at the horse.

Nathaniel sprinted across the path and vaulted over the rail fence, snatching Beau around the middle. He yanked him out of the way a split second before the horse crashed into the fence inches from where Beau had been standing. With one motion, Nathaniel swung the boy over the fence.

"Beau!" Abby screamed and came running, wrapping her arms around the boy as he started to whimper. "Are you all right?" She held him away from her, her eyes searching his frame. Apparently satisfied the lad was in one piece, she hugged him tightly.

Nathaniel caught Shadrach by the halter and spoke quiet, soothing words to him, patting his silky black neck. As the animal calmed, Nathaniel found a gash on the horse's right shoulder. Blood trickled from the gaping wound. Nathaniel led Quinn's prize horse into the barn and cross-tied him in the stall. As he grabbed a bucket to fetch clean water, he met Abby at the door of the barn.

"Thank you, Nathaniel." She touched his arm. "You saved Beau's life." Her eyes glistened with unshed tears, and her hand trembled.

Nathaniel shrugged. "Don't know about that. I'm just glad I was there at the right time. Is he all right? I slung him over the fence a bit hard."

Abby nodded. "He's fine, just frightened."

Nathaniel looked over his shoulder back into the barn. "Quinn's favorite horse. He's got a cut on his shoulder. I need to see what I can do for him before Quinn gets back."

Abby cocked her head and looked past him toward the horse. "Is there anything I can do? Yarrow will help stop bleeding, and you can use pipsissewa to clean the wound."

Nathaniel stared at her for a moment. Abigail Locke amazed him. Some women he knew would be hysterical from such an experience. Despite her scare, Abby still managed to give of herself.

A tiny smile tweaked the corner of his mouth. "I'd appreciate your help."

Chapter 13

Nathaniel sorted through several pieces of twisted limbs and cuttings of small sapling tree trunks, looking for four that would complement each other. The very nature of the spiraling grooves and bulging curves carved into the bark by climbing vines lent a unique flavor to each piece. No two were alike. Nathaniel held one of the twining and gnarled limbs up to the lantern light. His finger sought the path the vine had engraved. If he could recall all the woodworking skills Reverend Danfield had taught him as a youth, surely he could take these God-made works of art and construct them into a piece of furniture.

Jingling harness and clopping hooves announced Quinn's arrival. The sun had long since set, and Nathaniel knew the blacksmith was tired and hungry. But he needed to tell Quinn about Shadrach's injury.

Nathaniel took the lantern and met the wagon. Quinn grunted as he descended over the wheel. Nathaniel grasped the near horse's bridle.

"I'll see to the team." Nathaniel patted the horse's neck.

Quinn mumbled his thanks and turned toward the house.

"Quinn, wait. Something happened today that you should know about."

"Oh?" The big man turned, his thick eyebrows furrowing together like a fat caterpillar in the flickering lantern light.

Nathaniel told him about Shadrach crashing into the corral fence. "I put cold compresses on it, and Abby made a poultice out of some kind of wildflower."

Quinn snatched the lantern from Nathaniel and stomped into the barn. At the big black horse's stall, he held up the light.

Nathaniel followed on his heels. "Let me hold the light so you can examine the wound. It's his right shoulder." He took the lantern and held it so Quinn could get a good look.

Quinn peeled back the poultice to reveal the three-inch gash. Cleaned and no longer bleeding, thanks to Abby's quick work, the wound already looked somewhat better than it had earlier. Quinn ran his hand over Shadrach's shoulder and down the leg, his probing fingers no doubt searching for other hidden damage.

"Why did he crash into the fence? Something spook him?"

Nathaniel hated to implicate young Beau. The boy hadn't acted maliciously, and Nathaniel understood better than anyone how it felt to be wrongly accused. "The children were playing, trying to catch butterflies."

"What's this stuff?" Quinn picked up a small earthenware bowl from the ledge and sniffed it.

Nathaniel hung the lantern on a peg and took a rag that hung over the stall divider. "It's some kind of concoction Abby brewed up from leaves she gathered. She said it will help clean the wound and keep it from festering." He dipped the rag into the bowl and blotted the laceration. "Between this and the cold compresses, the swelling should go down in a couple of days."

"Hmm." Quinn's grunt echoed within the walls of the barn. He bent and ran his fingers over the animal's shoulder once more. With another noncommittal huff, he stood and gave Nathaniel a short nod. "You done a good job. Couldn'ta done better myself." He turned and headed toward the house.

Nathaniel reapplied Abby's poultice to the horse and freshened the cold compress. Shadrach snorted and dipped his head, bumping Nathaniel's arm.

"You're welcome, big boy." He patted the white blaze down the horse's nose. Stretching his arms over his head, he cast a glance toward the loft ladder. How he'd love to collapse on a mound of hay and fall into blissful sleep.

Instead, he held up the lantern to light his way to the back of the barn and rooted around in the bins until he found what he was after. He pulled out an old canvas—frayed along the edges and torn from too much use—which Quinn had rolled up and tossed into the bin. Taking his knife, Nathaniel cut three long strips of the heavy canvas.

"Perfect." He dragged the strips back to the stall and improvised a sling to hold the compress in place against Shadrach's wound. He stepped back and surveyed his handiwork. It wasn't pretty, but it would do the job.

He strode out to Quinn's wagon and unhitched the team, brushing down each horse, then feeding and hauling fresh water. After he'd cared for the team, he returned to pour more cold water on Shadrach's compress.

With a weary groan, he lowered himself to the hay-covered floor in the corner and leaned against the side of the stall, his hands tucked behind his head. Closing his eyes, he listened to the nighttime serenade outside. The crickets and tree frogs provided the background music for the whip-poor-wills.

Despite the fatigue, a smile found its way to his face. The boy was unhurt, Shadrach was going to be all right, and Quinn seemed pleased with how Nathaniel had handled things. But the way Abby's eyes had shone when she'd spoken to him made his heart smile. Working side by side with her as they tended the horse generated a rush of emotion within him that was hard to define. His chest grew tight when she'd looked at him. His breath caught when their hands touched. When their task was done and she left the barn, an ache made his stomach roll over with loneliness.

The whip-poor-wills sounded farther away now. He rose and added more cold water to Shadrach's compress. The animal displayed no signs of discomfort for which Nathaniel was grateful.

He fluffed up the hay and settled down in the corner again where he could keep watch over Shadrach and tend him during the night. As he stretched his legs out, his thoughts drifted back to Abby. She'd mentioned feeling badly that the two children had to share a small stool at mealtime because the family only had four places to sit. Nathaniel hoped the bench he was making—large enough to seat two—would be happily received, not only by the children but by Abby, too. Sam Wise told him he could come and pick up scrap pieces of wood at the sawmill. The twisted limbs he'd selected would become the legs, and uniquely shaped branches would form the stretchers. Bent willow pieces, curved and intertwined, would create the back. He pictured the piece coming together and hoped it would turn out as well as he imagined.

Throughout the night, Nathaniel kept Shadrach's compress cold with fresh spring water. By the time dawn's first light appeared in the eastern sky, he removed the cold pack and ran his hand over the horse's shoulder. The swelling was down considerably. He blotted the wound with more of Abby's brew.

Footsteps sounded behind him and Nathaniel turned. Quinn stood, scratching his head.

"I seen the light out here durin' the night. You been settin' up with the horse the whole time?"

Nathaniel shrugged and sidestepped the question. "Look here." He patted Shadrach's side. "He's better this morning."

Quinn leaned forward and examined the animal, running his meaty hand over the injured shoulder. Giving Shadrach a pat, he straightened. He stood with his arms akimbo, studying Nathaniel.

"Miss Abby and my wife told me what you done." Quinn's jaw muscles twitched. "My boy coulda been hurt bad or even killed if you hadn't acted when you did. There ain't no way to thank a man for doin' somethin' like that."

Nathaniel gave a quiet nod of thanks for Quinn's acknowledgement. "Glad I was there."

Quinn shuffled his feet and brushed his hand over his stubbly beard. "That ain't all. I guess you know I been pretty suspicious of you ever since you showed up here in Tucker's Gap. Them army duds with the stripes torn off—it ain't hard to figure out you were dishonorably discharged."

Nathaniel pulled in a breath and straightened his spine. He'd waited weeks for Quinn to speak what Nathaniel knew was on his mind.

The blacksmith stared at the floor and pushed hay around with his foot.

"I didn't have no respect for you, and I didn't trust you 'cause I figured you didn't deserve respect or trust." He raised his eyes to look straight at Nathaniel. "I was wrong. In this case, I'm glad to be proved wrong." He extended his hand.

They shook, and Quinn slapped Nathaniel's shoulder.

"Thanks. That means a lot."

A small smile twitched Quinn's beard. "If you're still wantin' to borrow a horse and a block and tackle, you're welcome to do that."

Joy rose in Nathaniel's chest, and he couldn't keep a smile from stretching across his face. He gripped Quinn's hand again. "I'd be much obliged. But if you don't mind, don't say anything to Abby about it. I don't want to get her hopes up in case it doesn't work. No need for her to be more disappointed than she already is."

❧

Abby enjoyed the energetic singing that filled the small church but kept casting worried glances at Beth. Nearly every day, the expectant mother spent less time out of bed. By the time the singing and prayer time drew to a close, Abby was grateful Quinn had insisted on bringing Beth in the wagon so she didn't have to walk the short distance to the church.

Once back at the house, Abby fussed over her friend. "You're going to bed. I'll make some lunch for you and Quinn, and then I'm taking the children on a picnic so you can rest."

Dulcie and Beau jumped up and down.

"I love picnics!"

"Me, too!"

"Can I bring my butterfly net?"

"Me, too?"

Abby hushed them and made them scoot up to the sleeping loft to change into their playclothes. Her hands flew through the task of making sandwiches—thinly sliced boiled tongue for the adults and jelly for the children. She added some hard-cooked eggs and peaches to round out the meal.

The children clambered down the loft ladder and ran to fetch their nets. Abby instructed Beth to stay put and get some sleep after she ate and then picked up the collecting basket Wren had given her on her way out the door.

"Beau, you carry both nets. Dulcie, you carry the blanket, and I'll carry our lunch." The children followed her like ducklings. "We're going to stop at the store first. Miss Florrie is coming with us." More happy cries from the siblings accompanied the news.

They clomped up the steps of Tucker's General Store, and Florrie met them coming out the door. "Looks like somebody is going on a picnic."

"We are, and you're going, too." Beau confided the information to her like he was divulging a great secret. The lad cocked his head. "Are you bringin' licorice to the picnic, Miss Florrie?"

She patted his head and leaned down so she was eye to eye with him. "Don't I always have licorice in my pocket for you young'uns?"

Abby shook her head. "You're going to spoil them." She looped her arm through Florrie's. "I thought we'd go just to the edge of the woods. There are plenty of shady spots under those trees."

The children led the way. Florrie gave a curious look at the V-shaped basket hanging on Abby's back. "That's an odd-looking basket. Where did you get it?"

"Wren gave it to me. It makes hunting for leaves and roots easier because I can have both hands free and toss what I find over my shoulder into the basket." She grinned. "Wren said she needed a bigger one."

Abby spread the quilt in the shade of the massive oaks. While the children looked for butterflies, the women set out their picnic.

"Beth looked a bit pale in church this morning."

Abby nodded. "I know. At least Quinn drove her in the wagon so she didn't have to walk. You should have heard her fussing about riding such a short distance. I left lunch on the table for her and Quinn. I hope she's resting."

"How much longer does she have?"

Abby cocked her head. Having no experience with such things, she could only take Beth's word for it. "She thinks about one more month. Mercy told me that Mrs. Sizemore generally attends the births. Her husband works at the sawmill."

"Ah, yes, I've met Eva Sizemore. They have six children. All of them are grown."

Abby called the children to come and eat. After their prayer, the youngsters gobbled their jelly sandwiches and hard-cooked eggs. Abby admonished them to slow down or they'd have bellyaches.

"It was good to see Mr. Tucker at church. Those crutches Nathaniel made sure put a smile on his face."

Florrie nodded. "He was so pleased, and Mercy nearly cried. He can get around without putting weight on the leg."

"Nathaniel is working on a cane for him. He said he should have it finished by next week."

The children begged to run and play, and Abby instructed them to stay close by.

Florrie began cleaning up the leftovers. "You still haven't heard from your father."

It wasn't a question. Florrie knew as well as Abby that no letter had arrived from Fort New Echota. "No." Abby shrugged, hoping the nonchalant gesture hid the turmoil in her stomach. "But remember, I didn't mail Father's letter at the same time I mailed Aunt Charlotte's."

"I received a letter from my niece, Virginia. She and her husband are distressed over what happened with the outlaws and the wagon, but they are glad we're safe, and they understand that I'll be helping Leon and Mercy for a few more weeks." She tucked the napkins into the picnic basket. "Virginia said her husband will come for me around the middle of next month."

"Will Mr. Tucker be up and around by then?"

"Should be. Mercy is having a hard time keeping him down now."

They leaned back on the blanket and watched the children play. Abby slid her gaze sideways to her friend. "Florrie, would you think I was touched in the head if I told you I truly like Tucker's Gap?"

The older woman's laughter blended with the singing of the birds overhead. "Of course not. I like Tucker's Gap, too. We've met some fine people here and—" Florrie turned to face Abby. "Just how much do you like Tucker's Gap?"

Abby sat up and took Florrie's hand. "I don't want to go to Raleigh. I never did. But I didn't have a choice. Florrie, I really like it here. I want to find a way to stay here permanently." She leaned back on her elbows and heaved a sigh of resignation. "That is if Father will allow it."

The sound of horses' hooves halted further conversation. Abby leaned forward and craned her neck. A squad of soldiers rode in, appearing to be headed toward the store.

Abby's breath caught, but taking a harder look, she recognized the uniforms. They weren't federal troops, like her father. They were Georgia Guard soldiers.

Florrie snorted. "On a Sunday? I hope they don't expect Mercy to open up and wait on them."

But the patrol didn't stop at the store. They reined up and appeared to be discussing something. Four of them dismounted, and one of the men took the reins and led all four mounts to water. Two others remained mounted and trotted in opposite directions, one toward the mill and the other directly toward where Abby and Florrie sat watching the children play.

"You there." The soldier, a lieutenant, reined his horse directly in front of the women. "We're patrolling this area looking for strays."

Abby didn't have to ask what he meant by the term. She was well aware of the unorthodox, sometimes brutal, tactics used by the Georgia Guard rounding up the Cherokee.

"You know where they're hiding?"

The children came running back to the blanket, looking up at the soldier with wide, fearful eyes. Dulcie's hand trembled as the little girl clung to Abby's arm.

"I have no idea what you're talking about."

"Yes, you do." The lieutenant pointed to Wren's basket lying on the blanket beside them. "That's an Injun basket. Where'd you get that?"

Chapter 14

Wariness piqued Nathaniel's senses as he strode up to the Georgia Guard soldier who confronted the women. "Is there trouble here?" Nathaniel controlled his tone, but his gut twisted. He flexed his fingers to keep them loose.

The lieutenant pulled his big sorrel around to a forty-five-degree angle and squinted at Nathaniel. "No trouble if I can get this woman to answer my question."

Nathaniel ground his teeth at the way the officer said *this woman* and moved to stand between him and the ladies. "And what question is that?"

The lieutenant pulled his face into a sneer as he looked Nathaniel up and down. Nathaniel felt the man's gaze land on the darkened places on his shoulders where stripes once resided. Of all days to wear his old army blouse instead of one of his chambray shirts.

The officer's tone rang with self-importance. "It's none of your business, mister, unless of course, you're hiding renegade Cherokees."

Nathaniel chose to ignore the belligerent challenge in the man's voice. "It's the Lord's day, sir. These ladies are enjoying a relaxing time after worship. I suggest you do the same and not disturb the quiet Sabbath afternoon in this community."

"I've asked this woman a question about that Injun basket, and I'm waiting for an answer." The lieutenant's voice rose in intensity. "If she's helping to hide Cherokees, I have the authority to arrest her."

Nathaniel heard Abby's soft gasp behind him, but he didn't let his gaze waver. From the corner of his eye, he saw a handful of townsfolk gather. Beyond the lieutenant, three of his soldiers moved in behind their leader. He heard one of the children whimper and Abby's responding *shhh*, but he didn't flinch. He'd not allow this arrogant cad to detect the slightest inkling of the way his heart squeezed at the sound of Abby's distress.

The officer cast a quick glance over his shoulder and made a hand gesture. Nathaniel recognized the signal directing the soldiers to flank him. Now with reinforcements at his side, the lieutenant lifted his chin at a cocky angle and smirked.

Another soldier, a sergeant with long, scraggly hair and an unkempt beard, tugged on the brim of his hat. Nathaniel had the distinct impression showing respect to the ladies was not the man's intent. Between the shadows cast by the trees and the man's hat brim pulled low, Nathaniel couldn't get a good look at his face, but something about the man was hauntingly familiar.

Some of the men from the town moved closer. Sam Wise and his oldest son, Hiram Sizemore, and Eli Pruitt all walked toward the soldiers. Leon Tucker stood on his porch, propped up by his crutches, with Mercy at his side. Teague Jackson strode across the grassy area in front of the store and stood several yards to one side with his hands on his hips.

Nathaniel gave a slight nod to the gathered citizens. He crossed his arms and addressed the officer once more. "Lieutenant, I suggest you and your men leave these good people alone."

The sergeant guffawed. "That's high-toned talk comin' from a coward."

The lieutenant raised his hand and jerked his fingers toward the sergeant. "It's clear you're a *former* military man." He gestured to Nathaniel's blouse devoid of military insignias. He rose up in his stirrups and looked around at all assembled. He raised his voice as though making an official proclamation. "You all can draw your own conclusions as to why this man is no longer in the army. If you want to side with him, that's your business, but if I were you, I'd think twice. Me and my men are of a special brigade, formed for the purpose of pursuing those renegade Cherokees who refuse to comply with the law. If anyone here knows the whereabouts of such Cherokees and does not divulge that information here and now, you are guilty of aiding and abetting."

The men from Tucker's Gap stood, silent and watchful, and the only two sounds Nathaniel heard were a fear-filled, muffled cry behind him and a derisive snort coming from the sergeant. Nathaniel turned to the ladies and spoke quietly.

"Abby, Miss Florrie, take the children home. You can come back later for your things."

Thankfully, Abby didn't argue. She scrambled to her feet and helped Mrs. Cobb stand. Then she took each child by the hand. Nathaniel slid his gaze from the sergeant to the first Tucker's Gap man standing the closest—Teague Jackson.

A muscle in Nathaniel's jaw twitched, and he clenched his teeth for an instant. "Teague, will you please see the women and children home?"

Teague stepped forward to usher the ladies. Was that smirk on Teague's face aimed at Nathaniel or the soldiers? Nathaniel couldn't take the time to contemplate the issue for longer than a heartbeat.

The sergeant spit tobacco juice to one side, landing it dangerously close to the hem of Abby's dress as she passed. Nathaniel stiffened but refused to allow his temper the freedom it sought.

"Lieutenant, I'm only going to say this once." Nathaniel kept his tone even but spoke clearly so his determination would be evident to every person present. "I'm a peaceful man, but don't make the mistake of thinking I would hesitate for a moment to defend anyone in this town if you continue to harass them, because you would be very wrong."

"He ain't even carryin' a gun," the sergeant blustered.

Nathaniel disciplined his every breath. The rising and falling of his chest gave away none of the turmoil taking place in his gut. He sent a quick glance beyond the soldiers. Halfway to the house, Abby turned and looked over her shoulder at him, and his heart turned over. He'd do whatever it took to make sure these men didn't bother her again.

"It's time for you boys to leave."

&

Abby spooned batter onto the hot skillet and listened to the frying apple fritters sizzle in the grease. The sound reminded her of the clip-clopping horses' hooves as the soldiers rode out of Tucker's Gap last Sunday afternoon. She'd never forget pausing in the doorway and watching as Nathaniel stood his ground, eventually ending the confrontation when the arrogant lieutenant and his band of cutthroats left.

Dulcie and Beau climbed down the ladder, and Abby watched their reaction. The bench Nathaniel had constructed sat beside the table, waiting for its occupants. Laughter danced in her middle when the children stopped short and stared at the wide seat.

Beau's eyes grew round. "Did Santa Claus bring that?"

Dulcie elbowed him. "Of course not, silly. Santa comes in the winter." She stepped over to the bench and touched the woven willow branches across the back.

"Look at the legs, Dulcie. They look like peppermint sticks, 'cept they ain't red." He scooted around and plunked his bottom down on the seat and pointed beside him. "Look, there's lots more room."

Abby covered her smile with her fingers. A chuckle bubbled up within her. "What do you think?"

Both siblings looked up at her, grinning.

"It's nice."

"Do we really get to sit on it?"

"Can we sit on it for breakfast? Dulcie keeps pushing me off the stool."

"I do not. Papa, did you make this for us?"

Their father shook his head. "Mr. Nathaniel made it. Miss Abby told him you two were havin' to share one stool."

"Can we go out to the barn and tell him thank you?"

Beth took her place at the table. "You can thank him right here at breakfast, because he's going to come and eat with us. He'll be here in just a minute."

As if on cue, a knock sounded at the door. Beau ran to open it.

"Thank you, Mr. Nathaniel." The child threw his arms around Nathaniel's legs before he could step over the threshold. Dulcie echoed her brother's enthusiasm.

Nathaniel's lopsided grin ignited awareness deep in Abby's heart. Emotions she'd tried to deny clamored for expression just like they had last week when she'd helped Nathaniel with the horse. A smile played across her lips as their gazes met. She hoped her gratitude for the bench showed on her face, but just to be sure, she planned to speak to him after breakfast.

The children led Nathaniel to the stool they once shared. Abby placed the heaping platter of apple fritters on the table and set a small jug beside it.

"What's this?" Quinn hefted the jug.

Abby winked at Beau. "It's sorghum syrup to pour over your fritters. I bartered with Mr. Jackson for it yesterday."

From the corner of her eye, she saw Nathaniel jerk his head toward her. "Bartered?"

She purposely kept her eyes fastened on serving the fritters. "I agreed to do some mending for him and darn some of his socks. Sorghum is a nice treat."

While the children exclaimed over getting two surprises, one to eat and one to sit on, Abby's senses were piqued toward Nathaniel. She couldn't tell from his reaction if he was impressed with her bartering skills or angry.

Or jealous.

Abby mentally shook her head and handed the syrup to Beth. Why would Nathaniel be jealous of her darning a few socks and mending a couple of shirts?

Quinn helped himself to another fritter and nudged the platter toward Nathaniel. "Have another. Mighty good, Miss Abby."

Abby slipped a sideways glance at Nathaniel and caught him looking at her. He yanked his gaze away and speared another fritter, but Abby noticed he didn't use any of Teague's syrup. She drew her lips inward and bit down, suppressing a giggle. He *was* jealous.

As soon as breakfast was over, the men scraped their stools away from the table and thanked Abby for the fine meal. Abby's gaze followed Nathaniel to the door where he paused for a second and gave her a fleeting look she could not interpret. His eyes appeared to ask a question that his lips did not voice. Abby's breath caught. Were it not for the morning tasks requiring her attention, she'd give in to the desire to go after him and ask what was on his mind.

Abby made Beth comfortable in the rocker near the open window and then plunged into cleaning the cabin, her thoughts swirling. Teague sometimes made her feel self-conscious in the way he looked at her, but he'd never behaved inappropriately or shown disrespect. It was entirely possible Nathaniel felt no jealousy at all. His expression could simply be a reflection of what he regarded as his duty to protect her. Disappointment rippled through her at the thought.

Her hands slowed, and a scowl tugged at her brow. She mustn't allow flightiness to send her imagination out of control.

"Why don't you let that wait and go talk to Nathaniel?"

Beth's question startled her, and the tin cup in her hands splashed into the dishwater. She pulled her composure back into place. "Why in heaven's name would you say that?"

"Abby, I know you want to talk to him." Beth sent her a sympathetic smile. "Just look at you. You remind me of myself back when I was a girl in Virginia and I hoped a certain handsome blacksmith felt the same about me as I felt about him."

Abby considered denying Beth's observation, but it would be a lie. Truth be told, Beth had read her correctly.

"Beth, when we left Fort New Echota, Nathaniel vowed he would be responsible for my safety." She hung her damp towel on the side of the worktable and turned to face Beth, arms akimbo. "That's why he was so upset when I went into the woods alone. He's just being watchful. There's nothing more to it, and for me to imagine more would be foolish."

A soft smile bloomed on Beth's face. "Who said love was sensible?"

Love? Only in her most private musings had she allowed the word to tease her senses. The very idea set her heart and her face afire. Dare she speak it?

Abby poured hot water into the teapot to brew Beth's red clover tea. The steam rose and brushed her already warm cheeks. "And how would you have me address the topic? I can't very well march out to the barn and ask Nathaniel how he feels about me." She covered the teapot and went to fetch a clean cup. "The fact is Nathaniel has had plenty of opportunities, but he's never brought the subject up."

A twinkle lit Beth's blue eyes. "I think he's brought it up several times, just not with spoken words. I can see it in his eyes."

Abby shook her head. "I think being with child has turned you into a hopeless romantic." She pulled a stool over to sit next to her friend. "Beth, I don't want to go to Raleigh. Nathaniel has vowed to get me there, but I don't want to leave Tucker's Gap. I love it here. How can I convince Nathaniel—and my father and my aunt—to let me stay?"

ð

"Nathaniel, may I ask you something?"

Abby found the quiver in her voice most annoying and hoped it didn't betray her pounding heart.

Nathaniel's hands paused in their work on the cane he was carving for Leon Tucker. His hazel eyes captured her breath. "Of course."

Are you jealous of Teague? Why did you look at me the way you did at breakfast? Do you have any feelings for me?

"Would you have time—" Her voice cracked. She swallowed hard and commanded her tongue to work properly. "Would you have time to make a baby bed for Beth?"

Surprise flickered across his face, and he brought the cane up and blew tiny corkscrew wood shavings away from the handgrip he was fashioning. "She doesn't already have one? I figured since she has two children. . ."

Abby turned to lean on the corral fence. "She told me they lived in Norfolk when Dulcie was born, and her mother gave her the family cradle. Before they left Norfolk to move to Georgia, her sister had need of the cradle, so when Beau came along all she had for him was a basket. He outgrew the basket so Leon Tucker gave Beth a wooden crate, and they turned it into a little bed for Beau."

Nathaniel rubbed his chin. "Let me talk to Sam Wise and see if he'll let me have some scraps of wood for the bottom. I can use the twisted limbs for the sides." He applied his knife to the handle of the cane once again, as though his blade cutting through the wood also cut a path for his thoughts. "Yes, I believe I can do that."

Giddy excitement tickled her stomach, and she clasped her hands under her chin. "Thank you, Nathaniel. That will make Beth so happy."

His knife paused again, and he raised his eyes to hers. "Now may I ask *you* something?"

Abby's heart kicked against her ribs like an army mule, and she braced herself for an interrogation about talking to Teague Jackson.

Nathaniel slid his knife into its sheath on his belt. His normally hazel eyes darkened into green pools, but the depth of them didn't indicate either anger or jealousy. In fact, if Abby had to find a word to define the lines of his face at this moment, it would be. . .*tender.*

"I'm glad to do something that will make Beth happy, but what will make *you* happy, Abby?"

Chapter 15

Nathaniel took one last swipe with the rake and completed his least favorite task—mucking out the stalls. He hung the rake on a peg and grabbed the two water buckets. Taking up woodworking had given him a new reason to hurry through his daily tasks. There was something about the feel of wood in his hands that awakened a long-sleeping spark of creativity within him. His fingers itched to return to crafting the baby bed Abby had asked him to make.

He rounded the corner of the house with the buckets and hoisted the lid off the spring. Plunging his arms up to his elbows into the first bucketful he pulled up, he washed the disagreeable odor from his hands, and then splashed cooling refreshment over his face and neck.

"Ahh. . ." He shook droplets from his hair like a shaggy dog, spraying them in every direction, then ran his wet hand through his hair to smooth it back.

He filled the buckets and headed back toward the barn. On the way, he saw Abby with a small bundle in her hands, walking down the footpath. He watched as she stepped through the trees and a narrow stretch of underbrush. She paused to smooth her skirt before continuing on to Teague's door.

Nathaniel bit his lip as Abby knocked. Teague appeared and ducked his head to step out, much too close to Abby for Nathaniel's liking. She backed up a half step and held out the bundle of what must have been the mending she'd agreed to do.

Nathaniel's stomach tightened, and he strode toward the barn, sloshing water on his pant legs as he went. She could have sent the children over with the mending. He pushed past the corral gate and slung the contents of each bucket into the trough in the corner of the corral. The sound of Abby's and Teague's voices filtered through the trees, but they were too far away to understand their words. Nathaniel grumbled under his breath, with no one except the horses and the Lord to hear his complaints.

Teague smiled at her and Abby shook her head. The man held up one of the socks Abby had mended. The silly grin on his face sent arrows of displeasure shafting through Nathaniel.

When Abby shook her head a second time, Nathaniel ground his teeth. Whatever Jackson's question, couldn't he take no for an answer?

Abby took another step backward and bumped up against a small stump. She teetered and thrust her arms out like a child crossing a stream on a fallen log. Before Nathaniel could move, Jackson dropped the bundle of mending and reached out both hands to catch her, holding on to her for much longer than necessary.

A growl pushed past Nathaniel's lips, and he vaulted over the corral fence, sprinted through the trees, and grabbed Jackson's arm, yanking it away from Abby.

"Hey! What—"

"Nathaniel, what are you doing?"

He nailed Jackson with a glare. "You'd best remember your manners and keep your hands to yourself. Miss Locke is a lady, and I won't stand by and see her manhandled."

"Now, see here—" Jackson clenched his fists.

"Stop it! Both of you!" Abby planted herself between Nathaniel and Teague, forcing both men to retreat. "You're acting like a couple of schoolboys." She sent Nathaniel a reproving look. "I have work to do, and I'm quite certain you both do as well."

She clutched her skirt, lifting her hem an inch, and marched back toward the Rutledge house. Nathaniel watched after her until she stepped beyond the trees and then turned back to Teague who stood scowling at him.

"Me and Miss Abby was just havin' a conversation. Weren't no need for you to be a hero." Teague's piercing black eyes fired buckshot.

"A conversation does not require that you put your hands on her."

A half smirk tilted one corner of Teague's mouth and stretched his stubbly cheek, but there was no humor in his expression. " 'Lessen she's spoke for, I got the right to ask her if I can come callin'. She ain't attached to you, or any other man from what I can see, so that makes her fair game."

Teague's words skewered through Nathaniel's belly. The man was right. Nathaniel had no claim on Abigail Locke. Chagrin wilted his grit at the thought. If circumstances were different, he'd prove Teague wrong.

Nathaniel grunted and strode away through the trees. Reproach filled him. Until he could clear his name, he could only admire Abby from afar.

❧

Nathaniel carved a paper-thin peeling of wood away from the hole he'd bored into the corner of the small bed frame. He scraped the opening clean and blew away the fine debris. The knob he'd formed with his knife on the end of the twisted-limb leg of the bed needed a few taps of the mallet to force it into the hole where it fit securely. The other three legs hadn't given him much trouble, but the fourth one took some extra work to ensure the bed stood solidly without wobbling.

He turned the little crib right side up, stood it on the workbench, and wiggled it. Satisfaction drew a smile on his face.

"That's a right fine job you done on that little bed."

Nathaniel turned to find Quinn watching him. "It's not quite finished yet." He grinned. "It'll be ready before the baby arrives."

A shadow of a smile flickered across Quinn's face. "Beth had a hard time with the last two—the two we had to bury. Almost lost her, too. When she told me she was in the family way again, well. . .it scared me." He sniffed and ran his thick hand over his face. "Don't know what she woulda done without Miss Abby."

Nathaniel's heart warmed. He didn't know himself how things might have worked out had Abby not taken it upon herself to work for the Rutledges. Despite his initial annoyance over her impulsive decision, he had to agree it was the right one. He dipped a rag in linseed oil and went to work polishing the vine-sculpted legs of the bed.

"If you can spare me and a horse, I was thinking about leaving at first light to go down the trail. I'd like to take three lengths of rope and a block and tackle along."

Quinn grunted and nodded. Nathaniel prayed he could make Abby's wish come true. His heart turned over when he remembered her soft smile the evening he asked her what would make her happy. To think all she wanted was her keepsakes from her trunk. When she spoke of her mother's things the sadness in her voice pierced his heart. With God's help, he intended to do his utmost to put those treasures in her hand again.

"When I took the cane I made for Leon over to the store, Mercy let me take a few supplies, some jerky and hardtack, dried apples and such. I should only be gone a couple of days."

Quinn nodded again. "Take as long as you need." The blacksmith bent his head to examine the crib more closely. "This is fine work. So's that bench you made for the young'uns." He scratched his head. "You ever think about buildin' and sellin' pieces like this? You could make a livin' as a furniture maker."

Nathaniel's hand paused mid-motion. "I never thought about it." He resumed rubbing. "Don't know how much I'll be able to salvage when I go down the trail. Maybe I can make enough furniture to barter for a wagon and team." He gave a bitter laugh. "Suppose it would take me an awful long time to make that many pieces."

Quinn scratched his head and frowned. "You still thinkin' to take the women on to Raleigh?"

Nathaniel nodded. "When we set out, I gave my word I'd deliver the ladies to their destination."

Quinn sat on an upturned bucket. "I guess you ain't heard." He brushed his hand over his forehead. "Miz Cobb says her niece's husband is comin' to get her, and Miss Abby says she's stayin'."

"What?" Nathaniel dropped his rag.

"I just figured the both of you was stayin'." Quinn lifted his broad shoulders. "It'll be nice havin' new citizens of Tucker's Gap. Y'all've already been a real welcome addition to our community, and I know folks'd be right pleased."

Nathaniel held both palms upright. "Wait a minute. What are you talking about? What do you mean she's staying?" He stared, bug-eyed, at Quinn.

An amused chuckle shook Quinn's belly. "She told my wife she don't want to go to Raleigh. She wants to stay right here in Tucker's Gap." He slapped both his knees and laughed again. "You mean she ain't told you?"

A scowl wiggled through Nathaniel's face. "I suppose we'll talk about it." How was he supposed to keep his word if she refused to go? One way or another, he had to make sure she arrived in Raleigh. He bent to pick up his rag when another thought slammed into him. If Florrie's family members came to get her, that would leave Abby and him without a traveling chaperone. He couldn't escort her anywhere, just the two of them on the trail. He'd have no choice but to speak with Florrie about taking Abby with her.

He heaved a sigh. "Remember, don't say anything to Abby about my plans to try and retrieve her trunks. I'd rather she didn't know about it."

"She's gonna wonder where you've gone."

Nathaniel pursed his lips and shook his head. "No, she won't. She might notice I'm missing for mealtimes, but it's unlikely she'll spend much time worrying over my whereabouts."

Quinn rose from the bucket and slapped Nathaniel on the back. "That's where you're wrong. Believe me, brother, she'll notice you're gone, and not just at suppertime."

❧

The eastern sky bore wispy streaks of dawn, as if God's fingertip brushed the muted colors across the heavens as a token of His blessing on Nathaniel's mission. There was barely room enough for him in the saddle between the coils of rope, block and tackle, and sack of rations.

And a gun. Quinn had insisted Nathaniel take his flintlock rifle along in case he couldn't find the one that went over the edge with the wagon.

He picked his way down the still-dark trail, humming one of the hymns they'd sung last Sunday. "Guide me, O Thou great Jehovah, pilgrim in this barren land." A smile tipped his lips at the prophetic words.

Two months ago, the uphill walk pulling the travois had taken them nearly three days. He anticipated a shorter trek this time now that he was mounted. Once he found the place, much of his success would depend on how far the trunks had fallen and if he'd brought enough rope.

"Lord, there is nothing that happens in this world that escapes Your knowledge or You don't allow. All things are in Your hand. You know how much I want to do this for Abby. Please let me find those trunks and haul them to the top of the ridge."

As the sky lightened, Nathaniel nudged the horse into a ground-eating trot. Abby's image tiptoed into Nathaniel's mind. Her declaration to Beth about not wanting to go to Raleigh really didn't surprise him, but he wondered if Quinn had understood her correctly about staying in Tucker's Gap. Nathaniel didn't think it likely Abby's father would allow her to stay in the tiny mountain community, but he puzzled over the absence of a letter from the domineering man. Could it be Abby's fears were correct, and her father had severed ties with her? He hoped not.

He'd lain awake a long time last night thinking about Quinn's suggestion. After he'd rolled it over and examined the possibility, it didn't seem so far-fetched. What if he could make a living building furniture? Was Tucker's Gap the place for him to start over?

Birdsong filtered through the trees, and the air temperature warmed. Pure blue sky peeked through the canopy of lofty treetops. When his stomach growled, he pulled a piece of jerky from the pouch and dismounted to rest the horse.

"It can't be much farther." He chewed a bite of jerky and studied the landscape. The trail had narrowed, barely wide enough for a horse and rider. He remembered navigating this stretch two months ago and having a bit of difficulty pulling the travois over the exposed tree roots. "We're getting close, Lord. Please help me find those trunks."

He swung back into the saddle and nudged the horse down the trail. Fifteen minutes later, the trail widened. He reined in. Yes, this was the place. He remembered the massive twin oaks beside the ravine, and there were broken saplings where the wagon had rolled over the edge. He dismounted and tethered the horse. Walking carefully, he found the earth along the rim wasn't as soft as it was the day the wagon toppled. They'd not had rain for almost two weeks, so the ground was solid.

He removed the coils of rope and knotted the ends together. After securing one end to an oak, he started down the side, lowering himself hand over hand. The underbrush had grown thicker in the two months since they camped here. Beads of sweat popped out from his exertion and the jute rope bit into his hands. Blackberry canes scratched his arms and snagged his britches. Cicadas buzzed their annoyance at being disturbed. More broken branches and crushed underbrush indicated the path the wagon had taken. A wheel with missing spokes lay askew in the thorny vines.

Crows cawed overhead, their noisy admonishment echoing within the ravine walls. His legs became entangled in the torn wagon canvas caught in the brush. He might be able to use it to hold the cargo on the travois. As he pulled at it, his own satchel came into view from underneath the canvas.

He paused to look around and assess how far he'd descended. A glimpse of yellow peeked out from the umbrella of sumac fronds. One of the ladies' dresses. That meant at least one of the trunks had broken open. He pulled it out of its hiding place and tossed it next to the satchel. Several more articles of clothing littered the area. He stacked everything on top of the canvas. He could tie it all in a bundle and drag it up.

A bit farther down the embankment, his foot found something unyielding—part of the shattered wagon bed and another smashed wheel. To his left was the splintered double-tree. He sighed. The wagon was definitely beyond repair, and if he didn't come across the trunks soon, he'd run out of rope.

"Please, Lord, lead me to Abby's trunk."

The steep terrain gentled a little, allowing him to let go of the rope without losing his balance. He stomped down the bushes and kicked at the thick vines. His toe made contact with something solid. He bent to grasp the object. It was a trunk. Nathaniel's heart soared. He pulled hard and freed it from its thorny prison. Initials were carved into the lid. FRC.

"Mrs. Cobb's trunk." He scanned the area, his eyes piercing into the shadows cast by rocks and underbrush. "Abby's trunk has to be here. It has to—"

Late afternoon sun glinted momentarily off something shiny as

Nathaniel moved down the slope. The reflection sparkled and then disappeared, as though teasing him with an ill-timed game of hide-and-seek. He stamped back long, thick blackberry canes and made his way toward the spot that had caught the sunlight. There, partially covered by weeds and vines, battered and nicked by its journey down the mountainside, was a trunk with brass hardware. Heavy leather straps secured the lid. On the front near the latch, engraved initials proclaimed the trunk belonged to AEL.

Chapter 16

"B ut where did he go?" Abby tried to curb her agitation at the secretive expression on Quinn's face. She felt like grabbing his arm and shaking him.

Quinn shifted a glance toward his wife before answering Abby's plea for information. "You'll have to take that up with him, Miss Abby." He ducked his head and lumbered out the door.

Abby spun to face Beth who sat at the table with a cup in her hands. "I didn't think too much of it when Nathaniel was absent yesterday at mealtime. Quinn sometimes sends him on errands." Abby clasped her hands at her waist. "When he wasn't here for breakfast this morning I became concerned. Now the noon meal has passed and he's still gone. Beth, where is Nathaniel? Why won't anybody tell me?"

Beth shook her head. "I don't know where he is, either. It's not like Quinn to keep things from me, but I do suspect he knows more than he's telling." She struggled to get to her feet, and Abby hastened to help Beth get her balance. Her friend gave a soft groan and placed one hand on her lower back as she waddled to the bed.

Abby plumped the pillows and helped Beth lie down before sitting on the edge of the bed. "I'm afraid, Beth. Has he left for good? What if he isn't coming back? Why didn't he tell me where he was going?" She covered her soft gasp with her fingertips. "Do you suppose he told Florrie?"

Beth squeezed her hand. "I don't know the answer to any of those questions, my friend, but I know who does."

Abby nodded, remembering the shame she felt when Florrie asked her if she'd prayed about staying and working for the Rutledges. She'd not stopped to pray then, and guilt stung her afterward when she realized she'd left God out of the decision. Her inclination toward impulsiveness was one of the reasons she'd locked horns with her father so often. But disappointing her earthly father didn't fill her with as much grief as disappointing God.

"I've been praying all morning." She didn't add that she'd also been worrying all morning, but she couldn't fool Beth.

"Praying is good. Have you been trusting as well?"

Regret slumped her shoulders. How many times would God remain faithful when she continued to try His long-suffering? "It's hard to trust when you don't understand what's happening nor can you see around the bend in the road."

Beth laughed. "That's why it's called trusting instead of knowing."

She knew Beth wouldn't be intentionally hurtful, but the admonition still smarted. Before she could pull her hand away from Beth's grasp, her friend caught her fingers and hung on.

"Abby, my husband is a blacksmith. He can shoe a horse blindfolded because he's done it so many times. Prayer is like that, too. When you constantly take burdens and questions to the Lord, you learn to trust because you're walking a familiar path. As you take more and more things to God in prayer, you find it becomes easier to trust Him because He has proven Himself worthy of your trust."

Beth leaned forward and slipped both arms around Abby's neck, hugging her as closely as her swollen belly would allow. "Let's pray right now."

❧

"Did Nathaniel tell you he was leaving?"

Florrie shook her head. "I didn't know he was gone. He didn't say a word to me. Abby, he wouldn't go off and leave us without telling us his plans."

"But that's exactly what he's done." Abby tried to control her misgiving without success.

"Surely Quinn must know where he is." Florrie's frown reflected her confusion.

"If he does, he's not saying." Abby's memory of her earlier irritation with the man rankled her once more. Something about Nathaniel's absence and Quinn's refusal to talk about it struck a strange chord. Did the two of them have a disagreement?

Florrie plunked her hands on her hips. "None of this makes sense. Maybe he's helping out one of the farmers who lives away from town. I know Quinn sometimes does that."

"That's different." Abby crossed her arms and hugged herself. "Beth told me Quinn helps a couple of the farmers bring in their hay crop in exchange for a portion of the hay. If Nathaniel was doing something like that, why wouldn't Quinn say so?" She paced to the window and stared out across from the store where Dulcie and Beau chased each other. Beyond the shady canopy and the open space between the trees and livery was the spot where Nathaniel had kissed her. Even now, three weeks later, her lips tingled with the memory. She ran her fingers over her mouth and tried to push away the nagging questions that plagued her.

"Well then, I suppose we'll just have to wait and see." Florrie's voice pulled her out of her reverie. "In the meantime, Mercy wanted me to give you this." She handed Abby a small crock. "It's her crabapple jelly. She said Beth and the children love it."

Abby took the crock. "Thank her for me."

She started toward the door but paused. Did she dare hope, or was that a futile exercise? "Is there any mail?"

The older woman shook her head. "I'm sorry. Maybe your father didn't get your letter."

Abby shrugged. "Maybe." Or maybe she'd defied him one too many times and he'd had enough. Either way, disappointment stung like a sharp rebuke.

She tried to straighten her shoulders, but a heavy weight pulled them into a slump. Perhaps changing the subject... "How's Leon getting along?"

A smile deepened the lines around Florrie's eyes. "Much better. He says he's coming to church this Sunday. Pastor Winslow will be here, and Leon wants to show him the cane Nathaniel made for him."

The mention of Nathaniel's name swelled the ache that already reigned deep within. She wanted to be angry with him for leaving, but she couldn't. Instead of acrimony and resentment settling into the secret place where she hid her most private emotions, a painful bruise pointed an accusing finger. Why did the people she cared about most in this world desert her? Despite the bright sunshine outside, a dismal gray mood cast gloom over her soul. She rubbed one palm over her middle, but the ache didn't go away. A sigh escaped, and she turned away from the window.

"I'll look forward to hearing Pastor Winslow again." She smoothed her skirt. "I think I'll take Wren's basket and see if I can find some more partridgeberries and purple trillium."

"Do you think that's wise?" Florrie supported her right elbow on her left palm and tapped her fingers on her chin. "Nathaniel doesn't want you going into the woods with the Georgia Guard soldiers roaming about, especially after they confronted you about Wren's basket."

"I'll have the children with me, so I won't go far. Besides, Beth thinks the baby could come in the next two or three weeks, and I want to have the partridgeberries and trillium on hand. Wren says they will make Beth's time easier."

"But Nathaniel said—"

"I never told you what Wren told me that day I met her in the woods."

Florrie cocked her head. "You mean about the flowers and leaves and things?"

Abby turned to face the window again. "No, about Nathaniel."

As she related the chilling story of the officer-in-charge's order to open fire and Nathaniel's heroic attempt to save Wren's sister and the others, tears burned her eyes. "He was wrongly convicted, Florrie."

"You don't suppose he went back to Fort New Echota, do you? He might be trying to clear his name."

Abby pondered the possibility for a moment. "According to my father, Nathaniel's court-martial took place at Fort Reed. Father happened to be at Fort Reed at the time on another matter. That's how he knew who Nathaniel was." She nibbled on her lip. "Do you remember the way Nathaniel looked at Wren on the trail? It was as if she looked familiar to him, but he couldn't place her. But Wren knew who *he* was all along."

She spun to face Florrie. "He doesn't know that Wren told me the truth about that day. I want to tell him that I admire what he did, that I believe he is a man of honor, but now I may never get the chance."

Florrie slipped her arm around Abby's shoulders. "You're in love with him, aren't you?"

Her composure crumpled, and silent tears slipped down her cheeks.

Florrie lifted the corner of her apron and blotted the moisture from Abby's face. "There, there. Don't you fret. You just told me you believe Nathaniel is a man of honor." She took hold of Abby's shoulders and gave her a little shake. "He'll be back."

28.

Nathaniel paused in his upward climb to wipe sweat from his eyes and catch his breath. The midday sun beat down with tenacity in the belly of the ravine. The quicker he could transport Abby's trunk to the top of the ridge, the sooner he could enjoy the shade and cooling breeze. He lifted his gaze and squinted at the treetops waving to and fro above him. The saplings and brush down the side of the ravine weren't moving an inch. No wind currents stirred below the ridge.

Many of the saplings up and down the ravine bore the unique twisted trunks carved by twining vines. Once he'd raised all the salvaged items safely to the top, he planned to make one more descent for as many cuttings as he could carry. The more he thought about Quinn's suggestion, the better it sounded. If he could homestead a small parcel and make furniture as well, he could build a future in Tucker's Gap.

His fingers tightened around the rope, and he pulled slowly and steadily, raising the trunk a few more feet. The block and tackle he'd borrowed from Quinn hadn't worked well for the trunks, so he simply slipped the rope around a smooth-barked beech tree and used pure muscle. As a result, each of the three loads he'd already raised had taken longer than expected. The anticipation of fulfilling Abby's wish was worth every drop of sweat, every aching muscle, and every gouge inflicted by the thorny blackberry vines.

The pile of belongings at the top of the ledge grew with each load he raised, beginning with the torn wagon canvas, pieces of clothing and other personal items he'd found strewn about yesterday afternoon. He located the remains of the one trunk that had burst open in the fall and brought as many pieces as he could find to the top. Perhaps he could rebuild it.

A troubling thought badgered him. He'd picked up many articles that had obviously spilled out of the broken trunk, but how many more things still lay scattered in the underbrush that he didn't find? What if Abby's keepsakes were among them? On the other hand, they could be in the smaller trunk that didn't break apart, but he didn't feel right opening the trunk to check.

He dug the toes of his boots into the dirt and braced himself as he pulled the trunk higher. Just a few more yards and he'd push the load over the edge. His chest heaved with the effort and the muscles in his shoulders begged for rest. Sweat dribbled down his face and neck. The image he held in his mind's eye of Abby's face when she saw her trunk kept him going.

Late afternoon shadows were lengthening when he gave the trunk a final shove that put it on almost-level ground. He gripped the rope and pulled himself up the last few feet and flopped down beside the trunk. The shade of the tall oaks and sweet gums caressed his sunburned skin. He lay there a few minutes and then reached for his canteen to quench his thirst.

He glanced at the sun to gauge how much daylight he had left. He didn't want to be caught down the side of the ravine once the sun set. Best he used what light he had to construct a travois big enough to hold everything he'd salvaged and make another trip down in the morning to collect the wood cuttings he wanted to take home.

Home. The ease with which the thought slid through his mind gave him pause. "Lord, are You trying to tell me Tucker's Gap is home?"

And where would Abby's home be? Despite what Quinn had told him, he'd promised her father he'd see to it she reached Raleigh. Once he returned to town, he must speak with Florrie. Surely she would see the wisdom in taking Abby along when her niece's husband came to fetch her. He would not risk Abby's reputation by escorting her alone.

He rummaged through his sack of provisions and pulled out a piece of jerky. While he bit off a hunk and chewed, he took his knife and cut long bands of the wagon canvas, some wide, others narrower. The canvas strips, along with the poles he'd already cut and stripped of leaves, would form a sturdy travois.

He led the horse up the trail a short distance to a tiny trickling waterfall. He refilled his canteen and watered the horse. On his way back, he picked up more firewood. He'd need plenty of light by which to work tonight.

Shadows had deepened by the time he returned to the campsite. He started his fire and ate another piece of jerky and some hardtack. Leaning back against a tree, he enjoyed a few pieces of dried apple. The meager meal filled his belly, but he looked forward to Abby's cooking when he returned to Tucker's Gap. With his appetite somewhat satisfied, he set to work bundling the loose items, readying them for the travois.

By the light of the campfire, he lashed strips of canvas around the poles to form the frame. The wider lengths of canvas were snugly woven in and out of crisscrossed limbs, forming a sturdy platform to support the trunks.

Firelight danced off the pile of salvaged items he hoped would bring a smile to Abby's face. "Just wait until she sees these things." The corners of his mouth tweaked upward. He relished the anticipation of seeing her delight. "Lord, I sure hope the keepsakes of her mother's are in that trunk. I want her eyes to light up when she holds them in her hands again." When he made his last trek down the ravine tomorrow morning, he intended to be extra diligent to look through the thicker underbrush for signs of anything left behind.

He tied off one corner of the travois where the poles intersected and inspected the construction for a moment, nodding in satisfaction. As he began weaving another strip of canvas, a thought occurred to him. His hands halted. "Did Quinn say *when* Mrs. Cobb's nephew was coming to get her?" He tried to think back on the conversation but couldn't recall Quinn mentioning when the man was expected.

What if he came before Beth's baby was born? Abby had adamantly stated she intended to stay with Beth for as long as necessary. He knew he'd have an argument on his hands just convincing her to accompany Florrie, but how would he persuade her to go if Beth still needed her?

Chapter 17

Nathaniel wiped sweat from his brow. The sun hadn't been up more than two hours, and the day promised to be a hot one. As soon as there was enough light to see, he'd climbed back down the ravine, cutting sapling trunks and limbs he selected for their most unusual spiral patterns. Wild grapevine came in handy for lashing the pieces together in a bundle.

Impatience nibbled at him to finish loading the travois and head back to Tucker's Gap. He'd already been gone a day longer than planned. Despite Quinn's generosity, telling him to take as long as he needed, Nathaniel didn't want to presume on the blacksmith's benevolence. Besides, he couldn't wait to see Abby's reaction when she saw her trunk. Nathaniel whispered another prayer that those precious things Abby most wanted back were in the trunk that bore her initials.

As he wound the vines around his wood bundle, he recalled Quinn's amusement the night before he left. What if the man was right and Abby missed him? He couldn't allow his feelings for Abby to become evident, regardless of anything Quinn imagined seeing from her. He reined in his emotions. It wouldn't do to let Quinn, or anybody else, perceive his delight in pleasing Abby. He wasn't in the position to court her. Not as long as he had a blemish on his name.

He knotted the rope around the bundle of cut wood and pulled hand over hand on the rope that circled the beech tree at the top of the ledge. Coiling the slack as he went, he climbed up the steep incline. Much of the underbrush was flattened by his treks up and down, making the raising of the wood bundle a bit easier than hauling the trunks up.

About twenty yards from the top, he halted. The hair on the back of his neck stood up. He sensed he wasn't alone. He strained his ears but heard nothing but birdsong and the breeze stirring the tree branches. Taking a slow turn, he scanned the area on both sides of him as well as the opposite side of the ravine. Panthers sometimes roamed these mountains. Or bears. He remained stock-still, listening and watching, but nothing revealed itself.

Not wanting to carry a cumbersome weapon with him while he cut and bundled the wood, Quinn's flintlock, as well as his own rifle he found under the remains of the wagon, sat up on the ledge by the travois. *Foolish!*

Why didn't he bring one of the guns with him?

A thought occurred. If Wren hid in these wooded highlands, other Cherokee likely did as well. Perhaps they watched him work. He doubted they meant him any harm and were simply wary of his presence. He was as anxious to be on his way as they were to see him go, so he resumed hauling the wood bundle to the top. Just as he reached the ledge and grasped the base of the beech tree, he heard it.

The unmistakable sound of a rifle being cocked.

Nathaniel froze.

"C'mon up here." The voice was vaguely familiar.

Hands reached down and grasped his arms, dragging him the last couple of feet. When he looked up he found the barrel of a flintlock musket pointed directly at his head. Men in Georgia Guard uniforms surrounded him.

"You again!" The voice belonged to the same lieutenant with whom he'd exchanged words nearly three weeks earlier. "What are you doing out here?"

Nathaniel stood and worked to keep the contempt from showing on his face. "I'm trying to salvage what I can from my wrecked wagon."

One of the soldiers hooted. "He brought a wagon up here? How'd he think he was gonna drive a wagon and team through these woods?" The rest of the men joined in the chorus of guffaws.

The lieutenant raised his hand and put an end to the laughter. He motioned toward the loaded travois. "So you're claiming all those things are yours?"

"No." Nathaniel didn't blink. "Only one satchel and a rifle are mine. The other gun belongs to my friend, and all the rest of those things belong to the two ladies I was escorting."

"Are you referring to the women I was attempting to interrogate back at Tucker's Gap the day you interfered?"

The flame of Nathaniel's ire grew in his belly. "I stepped in to stop the harassment of a lady who happens to be the daughter of an army colonel." He kept his steady gaze on the lieutenant but noticed from the corner of his eye the same foul-mouthed sergeant he remembered from that Sunday afternoon in Tucker's Gap. Another inkling of familiarity pervaded Nathaniel's senses. Something about that man set Nathaniel's teeth on edge.

"Surely you don't expect me to believe that. If she's aiding Cherokees, her papa is no army colonel." The lieutenant's sarcasm brought another round of howling laughter from the soldiers. "I want to know who that woman is and where she got that basket."

Nathaniel lifted his chin a fraction of an inch and pressed his lips together. Did this imbecile really think he was going to divulge Abby's name?

"Are you refusing to cooperate?"

The scruffy sergeant stepped forward. "She's Colonel Ephraim Locke's daughter from Fort New Echota."

The blood froze in Nathaniel's veins, and he shot an icy stare at the sergeant. How did this man know Abby?

"And I can tell you who this sorry coward is, too, Lieutenant." The sneer on the sergeant's lips pulled his beard askew. He turned to address all six soldiers as well as their leader. "This here's none other than Lieutenant Nathaniel Danfield—or should I say ex-lieutenant. He was caught givin' aid to the Cherokees and helpin' 'em escape when they was bein' rounded up. Y'all are lookin' at a bona fide, dishonorably discharged traitor."

It wasn't the humiliation of the announcement that widened Nathaniel's eyes. It was the dawning of realization. Finally, he remembered. . .

"And I know who you are, Sergeant Browning. And *what* you are. You're a liar who will testify to anything under oath if you're paid well enough." Nathaniel took a couple of steps in Browning's direction, but he directed his words to the lieutenant. "This man used to be aide-de-camp to Captain Bane at Fort Reed. I wonder why Sergeant Browning is no longer in the federal army. I believe an investigation will uncover evidence of a bribe Captain Bane paid him to lie at my court-martial."

A solid fist coldcocked Nathaniel from the side. He staggered and fell but immediately sprang to his feet again. Browning came at him with fire in his eyes. Nathaniel sidestepped his charge, and the maneuver struck a chord in his memory. The foggy veil lifted from the bits and pieces he remembered from the day he fought with the outlaws on this very piece of ground.

"You're also one of the thieves who accosted me and the two ladies three months ago and stole our horses."

Browning took another swing at him. Nathaniel dodged the man's fist.

"I didn't recognize you with the long hair and beard. That's why you kept your hat pulled low that day in Tucker's Gap."

The sergeant emitted a throaty growl and lunged, seizing Nathaniel around the waist and throwing him to the ground. Nathaniel grappled with Browning, trying to block the man's punches. Browning landed a fist on Nathaniel's mouth and then got his hands around Nathaniel's throat. Pulling to one side and then the other, Nathaniel managed to wedge his arms in and heave the sergeant off him.

"Sergeant! Stand down!"

Browning ignored the lieutenant's command and came at Nathaniel again, this time connecting his fist into Nathaniel's gut.

Air left Nathaniel's lungs in an *oomph*. He sucked in a gulp of air and returned the favor to Browning with a belly punch followed by a mighty uppercut to the man's chin. Browning fell backward, sprawled in the dirt.

Nathaniel bent at the waist and swayed a moment, shaking his head to clear the cobwebs. He pulled in a couple of breaths, as deeply as he could manage, and wiped the back of his fist across his bloody mouth. He straightened and turned, blinking to focus on the lieutenant.

"You have any more questions?"

The lieutenant narrowed his eyes at Nathaniel. "Could be your word against his."

"I can prove what I say is true. Why else would the sergeant attack like he did if not to silence me? All I ask is—"

"Sergeant!"

Something solid connected with the back of Nathaniel's head. A blinding white light and stabbing pain accompanied the blow, followed by a narrowing of the field of his vision, and then blackness.

❧

Four days.

Lord, what if he doesn't come back? Why didn't I tell him I knew the truth about him? Please tell me what I'm to do.

Nearly the entire population of Tucker's Gap and the surrounding farms turned out for Pastor Winslow's preaching service. Even Teague Jackson.

Abby forced a polite smile and a "thank you" at Teague when he stepped aside to allow her and the children to enter the church ahead of him. Taking Dulcie and Beau each by the hand, she found a place for the three of them beside Florrie. Teague took a seat directly behind her.

Florrie turned to greet her and tsked. "Abby, you don't look well at all. You aren't ill, are you?" The lines around Florrie's eyes defined her concern.

Abby lifted her shoulders. "I haven't slept in a couple of nights. Nathaniel still isn't back." Her throat tightened. "I'm so worried. It's been four days."

Florrie slipped an arm around Abby's shoulders. "We have to have faith, Abby. It's out of your hands. All we can do is pray, and prayer is the most important thing we can do."

Tears burned Abby's eyes and her voice broke. "I just wish I knew where he was and why he left."

Pastor Winslow stepped into the pulpit and made a few announcements before the opening hymn. While the congregation lifted their voices, singing "A Mighty Fortress Is Our God," Abby closed her eyes and whispered a prayer. "Where is he, God? Is he safe? Not knowing is so hard. I feel so helpless. If only I'd let him know my heart—maybe he wouldn't have left." A tear slipped down her cheek, and she whisked it away. By the time Pastor Winslow began his sermon, Abby's heart was ragged and frayed.

The preacher cleared his throat. "Friends, I know every one of us in this room have faced times of hardship. We find ourselves at a point in our lives when we know not what to do, and we have more questions than answers."

A startled tremble quaked through Abby's middle and rose into her throat. The preacher had read her very thoughts. She sent a wide-eyed glance to the pulpit, but Pastor Winslow wasn't looking at her.

"Let me direct your attention to the book of Proverbs—the book of wisdom." The sound of pages turning rustled across the room. "This is where I always begin when I'm facing a dilemma. Look at chapter four, beginning in verse twenty-three."

Abby ran her finger under the lines as the preacher read them: *Keep thy heart with all diligence; for out of it are the issues of life.* The issues of life—an all-encompassing phrase. Did God include the maelstrom occurring in her heart at this moment as one of those issues?

The preacher continued. "God's Word tells us to keep our hearts, to protect our steps, and carefully nurture our relationship with Him, so when we face these issues, our faith can carry us over the rough spots."

Pastor Winslow's words reminded Abby of the analogy Beth had used about Quinn shoeing horses blindfolded. Those things of which the pastor spoke were accomplished over time and repetitive practice. *Keep thy heart*—it sounded so simple, but Abby realized she'd only caught a glimpse of the impact the words carried.

Flipping back a page in his Bible, the pastor went on: "God's instructions are clear. Chapter three, verse five says to 'trust in the Lord with all thine heart; and lean not unto thine own understanding. In all thy ways acknowledge him, and he shall direct thy paths.'"

The words smote Abby's heart. It was just as Beth and Florrie had said. Trusting was more than simply praying. She'd prayed. But had she ever waited to hear God's answer? Over and over she'd wrestled for control—with her father, with her circumstances, and with God. Ignoring God's sovereignty time and again, she'd barged ahead. Had she ever truly trusted God to direct her as Lord of her life?

She closed her eyes and spent time communicating with her heavenly Father. When she opened them again, Pastor Winslow was saying something about being a servant and placing oneself under God's direction. But her cup was already overflowing with the richness of God's treasure. Fully trusting God was going to take practice, beginning with acknowledging His presence and power moment by moment.

Fighting to control the details of her life left her exhausted. A breath of relief and freedom blew across her soul. Nathaniel was in God's hands. Whether or not she ever saw him again or had the chance to share her heart with him wasn't up to her.

As they stood to sing the final hymn, peace greater than anything she'd ever known flooded her spirit. Her heart smiled.

Pastor Winslow offered the final prayer and benediction, after which neighbors greeted neighbors and spent a few minutes fellowshipping. Abby gathered the children before they could escape to play with their friends.

"Florrie, could you watch the children for a moment? Beth asked me to speak with Mrs. Sizemore this morning and see if she could drop by in the next few days."

"Her time is getting close, isn't it?"

Abby nodded. "She thinks it will be in the next couple of weeks."

And after that? The unspoken question hung in the air. Putting Nathaniel in God's hands wasn't the only issue of her heart she needed to entrust to God. Her desire to stay in Tucker's Gap must also be offered up.

Chapter 18

Abby opened her eyes as a rooster crowed from the yard below the loft window. The peace God gave her yesterday had lulled her into sweet sleep all night. She knew consciously trusting God with every circumstance wouldn't be learned in one day, but He promised to hold her in His embrace if she'd simply cling to Him. Last night before she closed her eyes, she pictured God taking her hand and she asked Him for peaceful sleep.

The restful night she'd spent was God's kiss.

Abby dressed quietly and slipped down the ladder. She coaxed the glowing coals in the fireplace back to life with some kindling. Tiptoeing to the door, she took the water bucket and slipped out to the spring. Dawn stretched pale-gold fingers into the retreating dark sky. Lace-edged clouds traced the mountain horizon.

"Lord, I pray Nathaniel comes home today, but wherever he is, I know You'll keep him within Your care. Thank You for Your faithful presence."

She filled her bucket and returned to the house. Quinn was up and adding wood to the fire.

"I'll have the coffee boiling soon," Abby whispered.

Quinn nodded. "I'm going out to feed and water the stock."

Nathaniel's job. She mentally reached out for God and treasured the assurance of His promise.

Her hands went through her morning tasks with practiced precision, and by the time Quinn came in from the barn, she had fried mush and cooked apples ready. The aroma of fresh coffee permeated the cabin.

Abby helped Beth sit up and swing her feet over the side of the bed.

"I feel like a turtle on its back. It's all I can do to roll over." Beth gave Abby a wry smile. "I think this baby better come soon before you hurt yourself helping me up."

"Come on. You need a cup of tea." Abby grasped Beth's arms and pulled the mother to her feet.

The children clambered down the ladder and came to the breakfast table. It wasn't until the blessing was asked and Abby began serving up the mush and apples that she realized she'd brought six plates to the table.

"Is Mr. Nathaniel back?" Dulcie asked between bites. "He's gonna make a bed for my dolly."

Abby hesitated. "No, honey. He's not."

Beau spoke around a bite of mush. "But when is he comin' back? He said he's gonna show me how to carve a wooden soldier."

Abby's throat tightened, and she lowered her eyes. Beth hushed the children and told them to finish their breakfast.

Forcing a tiny smile, Abby rose from the table. Trying to swallow anything would be useless. She hung the water kettle on the crane over the fire. *I trust You, Lord. Help me trust You more.*

She brewed Beth's tea and found unnecessary chores to fill her hands. As soon as the children scampered out the door and Quinn headed for the forge, she began clearing the breakfast dishes.

Beth rose with her teacup, obviously uncomfortable. Abby watched her settle into the rocker.

"Mrs. Sizemore said she would stop by this morning to check on you."

"I'd best keep walking then. Eva Sizemore always tells expectant mothers to move about as much as possible." Beth heaved herself up from the rocker. "You've spoiled me so much, I'm afraid I've become quite lazy."

Abby smiled. "You needed the rest, and you aren't lazy."

"Are you all right?"

Abby glanced up. There was no point in pretending her feelings for Nathaniel didn't exist. Beth knew better. "I took your advice, and I'm determined to trust God. Only He knows if Nathaniel is coming back, and—" Abby gasped and widened her eyes. "Oh, Beth!"

"What?"

"He *is* coming back." Intuition stirred in her chest. She scurried over and grabbed Beth's hands. "He said he would make crutches and a cane for Leon Tucker, and he did. He said he'd make a bench for the children and he did. He said he'd make a crib for the baby, and he did."

Beth nodded slowly. "Yes. . ."

"Don't you see? He told Dulcie he'd make a bed for her dolly, and he told Beau he'd carve him a wooden soldier. He wouldn't make idle promises to the children. Wherever he went, he intends to come back." Tears sprang into her eyes.

Beth embraced her for a moment and then framed Abby's face in her hands. "You need to go talk to Quinn."

Abby nodded vehemently. She dashed to the door and then skidded to a stop. "Will you be all right if—"

Beth laughed. "Just go!"

Abby picked up her skirt and ran across the footpath to the forge. "Quinn!"

The blacksmith looked up, alarm widening his eyes. "What is it? Is Beth—"

"She's fine." Abby paused to catch her breath. "Quinn, you know where Nathaniel went, don't you?"

Quinn nodded. "He didn't want to disappoint you, so he told me not to tell you. But I'm gettin' worried about him, too. I expected him back two days ago."

"Disappoint me?" Abby shook her head. "What are you talking about?"

Quinn grimaced. "He borrowed a horse and went on down the trail to try and fetch your belongin's that was lost with the wagon."

Abby brushed a hand over her forehead. "I don't understand. Why wouldn't he want me to know about that?"

"Reckon he didn't want to get your hopes up, in case he couldn't find anything."

Pacing back and forth with her hands on her hips, Abby halted and spun to face Quinn. "He's been gone since Thursday. Today is Monday." Panic rose in her throat, and she raised her eyes heavenward. "What if—"

The blacksmith held up a hand. "I know." He pulled off his leather apron. "Soon as I can get a horse saddled, I'll head out. Can you get me a canteen and—"

The sound of hoofbeats drew their attention. A squad of soldiers rode up to Tucker's store. Presuming the band to be Georgia Guard again, Abby gave them little more than a cursory glance. As she turned back to Quinn, however, recognition jarred her. She spun back to give the group a hard look. They were bluecoats.

She took a few steps closer to the open door and stared. The officer in charge dismounted and handed the reins to an aide. His hat sported a sweeping cock's feather on one side. He strode to the steps in front of the store and paused, casting a wide scan of the town.

Abby sucked in a sharp breath. Was it possible?

Father?

After waiting for a reply from him for weeks, she feared he'd washed his hands of her. But here he stood in the little town she'd grown to love. What if he came to force her to go to Raleigh?

She opened her mouth, but all that came out was a strained whisper. "Father." Joy battled apprehension. *He came.* Tears pricked her eyes. But *why* had he come?

She moved forward, first walking and then running toward the store. Her father, hat in hand, climbed up the steps. As his boot landed on the porch, Abby reached the edge of the road and halted.

"Father!"

He jerked around. The moment his eyes fixed on her, angst lined his face like chiseled granite.

"Abigail." Instead of his customary booming voice, strident tones threaded the single word.

Muscles along his jaw tightened, much like she'd witnessed numerous times during their confrontations. But this time a sheen brightened his eyes, and he moved with uncharacteristic awkwardness.

He climbed down the steps, his long strides closing the distance between them. As he approached, his chin quivered and the space between his brows crumpled. He wrapped her in his arms, pulling her tightly to his chest. A tremble rippled through her, smothered in her father's embrace for the first time she could ever remember.

"Abigail." His relieved whisper blew the loose hairs beside her ear.

The trepidation that twisted her stomach when she first realized her father's presence melted away as the morning dew, and she simply relished the strength of his arms enfolding her.

As though suddenly realizing his men watched the emotional reunion, her father abruptly set her away from him, cleared his throat, and gathered his military bearing. But when he spoke, his voice was low and husky. "Are you all right? Have you suffered any ill from your ordeal?"

"I'm fine, Father." She stopped short of saying she was glad to see him until she learned his intentions.

A familiar scowl dipped his eyebrows as his gaze took in the surrounding area. "Where is Danfield?"

Abby bit her lip. "I don't know. He left last week, and he's two days overdue. We're worried—"

"Sergeant." Her father commanded. "Take the men and spread out. Comb every inch in and around the town. When you find Danfield, take him—"

Abby caught his sleeve. "Father, listen to me. Nathaniel isn't here. He's—"

"Miss Abby!"

She and her father both turned. Quinn stood by the livery, pointing toward the narrow trail that led into town from the west.

"Look there."

Emerging from the cluster of trees, Nathaniel rode one of Quinn's horses pulling a loaded travois. Teague Jackson followed him mounted on a mule.

Abby gave a tiny cry and covered her mouth with her fingers. When she'd loosened her grip on the situation and left it with God, He proved Himself faithful. Grateful tears burned her eyes.

Her father strode in the direction of the two riders, barking orders. "Sergeant! Corporal! Take this man into custody."

Abby ran after him. "Father! Stop!"

The last person Nathaniel expected to see upon returning to town was Colonel Locke, but here he came stomping across the road wearing the expression of a bulldog about to attack.

The corporal snatched the horse's reins, and the sergeant reached up and seized Nathaniel, pulling him off the horse.

Colonel Locke stood with his hands curled into fists, his narrowed eyes filled with venom. "Danfield, you're under arrest."

Abby tugged at the colonel's arm. "Father, listen—"

He shrugged off his daughter's hand. "This man was entrusted with delivering you safely to your aunt. Instead, he endangered your life and your reputation, and left you stranded here with no means of support or protection."

When Nathaniel pulled his hat off, Abby's eyes widened and her lips parted, presumably when she saw the bandage around his head. He wasn't trying to garner sympathy. Removing his hat was simply a respectful gesture.

"Colonel Locke, you are correct in that I failed to complete my mission. However, I did everything in my power to ensure your daughter's safety."

Quinn approached and took the horse's bridle from the corporal. Florrie came scurrying across the road faster than Nathaniel thought a woman of her age could move.

"Ephraim Locke! I could hear you bellowing all the way in the store." Florrie planted her hands on her hips. "Furthermore, Nathaniel did not endanger Abby's life. He treated her with the utmost respect and fought to protect her." She leaned slightly forward. "Your charges against him simply are not true, and even if they were, what crime has been committed? You can't arrest a man if he's committed no crime."

If the tension in the air hadn't been so thick, Nathaniel would have grinned at the spunky widow.

Abby cast a quick glance at him. The moment their eyes met, something precious, yet unspoken, was communicated. She turned to the colonel.

"You're mistaken, Father." Her tone was soft and entreating. "Nathaniel has been a true gentleman and guardian from the very first day. He saved my life. The day the two highwaymen accosted us, Nathaniel threw himself in front of me when one of the outlaws fired his weapon. He was nearly killed protecting me."

Nathaniel couldn't take his eyes off Abby. The moody, irascible young woman he first thought her to be had been transformed into a compassionate, thoughtful person. Her praise caused a warm rush to fill his belly and rise up his chest to his neck.

I love you, Abigail Locke.

She pointed to the travois. "He's been gone these last four days, and it was only this morning I learned that he went back to try and retrieve those belongings that were lost when the wagon crashed. Does that sound like a dishonorable man?"

"She's tellin' the truth, Colonel." Quinn stood by, still holding the horse's bridle. "Nathaniel asked more'n a month ago if he could borrow a horse so he could try and get the ladies' things back." He gestured to the travois. "There's your proof."

Colonel Locke took three long strides to the travois and quickly scanned the load. He ran his hand over Abby's initials on her trunk.

Teague dismounted his mule. "He musta worked plenty hard fetchin' all this stuff up that steep ravine."

All eyes turned toward Jackson, and Quinn cocked his head. "How is it that you came ridin' in with him, Teague?"

With a slight shrug, Teague rubbed his chin. "I heard Miss Abby tellin' Miz Cobb on Sunday how she was frettin' about Danfield bein' gone. Wished I could do somethin' to ease her mind. The preacher said we's supposed to be servants and let God use us." He scratched his head and knocked his hat askew. "Well, I seen Danfield leave before sunup last Thursday, so I knew what direction he took. Found him knocked in the head and bleedin', and I brought him home." He straightened his hat. "Done it for Miss Abby so maybe she'd think better of me."

Abby clasped her hands at her waist. "Thank you, Mr. Jackson." She gifted him with a smile, but it didn't send arrows of jealousy through Nathaniel like it had before. He, too, was grateful for Teague's help.

Abby stepped over to the travois and loosened the straps on her trunk. She opened the lid and pushed aside several items of clothing. A smile sweeter than anything Nathaniel had ever seen lit her face. She lifted out a small bundle. Unfolding the flaps, she revealed an ivory-handled hairbrush, a lace collar, and a dainty handkerchief with fancy stitching on it. Lastly, she extracted a cameo brooch. A tear slipped down her face, but her smile didn't fade.

"Thank you, Nathaniel."

He'd do it all again, even getting hit over the head, to see that smile.

Chapter 19

A bby held her mother's handkerchief to her cheek. She'd given up hope of ever seeing it or her other treasures again. As she ran her finger around the gold-filigree edge of her mother's brooch, a flood of praise rushed over her. An overwhelming urge to shout with joy-filled laughter sent tingles dancing through her chest. How could Nathaniel know how God had used him to bless her? When she raised her eyes she found him watching her. His tender smile and brief nod set her heart to pounding.

What an amazing and faithful God she had!

Father stepped to her side and examined the items in her hands. He touched the brooch, and a tight smile lifted the corners of his mouth. He cleared his throat, but his voice was still husky: "Your mother's."

She looked up into his face. He seemed much older than Abby remembered. Silver hairs outnumbered the dark ones, and the lines around his eyes mapped out the strain of his burdens and responsibilities. But a softness she'd never seen before gentled his gray eyes.

"Aunt Charlotte told me you gave Mother this brooch on your wedding day."

He nodded and sniffed. "She was beautiful. And you look so much like her."

Mercy Tucker walked over to the group. "Abby, why don't you and your father and Nathaniel come and sit on the porch where you can talk. I'll bring coffee."

"Thank you, Mercy. That would be very nice."

Father took her arm and led her toward the store, but she hesitated and glanced over her shoulder at Nathaniel. *Thank you* rolled through her heart for his safe homecoming. Oh, how she'd missed him.

They reached the broad porch, and Nathaniel stepped aside and waited for her and her father to ascend the steps. He held Abby's chair, and Father maneuvered to sit between them. Abby stifled a grin.

Mercy reappeared with a pot of coffee and cups while Florrie fussed over Nathaniel's bandaged head.

Abby wished she were the one caring for Nathaniel, but she clasped her hands tightly in her lap and winced inwardly as she watched Florrie unwrap the strips of cloth that swathed his wound. She had just the thing back at the house to make a poultice to speed the healing, and she suspected a cup of willow bark tea would ease his discomfort. Distracted as she was, she almost missed Nathaniel telling her father he still intended to accomplish his task.

"Sir, a family member of Mrs. Cobb's is coming in a couple of weeks to transport her on to Raleigh."

Abby yanked her attention back to the conversation. What was Nathaniel saying?

"Even if I could barter for another wagon and team, it would be unseemly for me to escort Miss Locke without a chaperone. So," he glanced over his shoulder at Florrie, "I planned to speak with Mrs. Cobb and arrange for your daughter to travel with her and her niece's husband."

Abby's heart plummeted. Weren't the events of the past two and a half months evidence of God's hand orchestrating her circumstances so she wouldn't have to go to Raleigh? She'd hoped Nathaniel felt the same and didn't want her to go either. Her joy wilted as a protest wrestled within her for expression.

I trust You, God. You know the desire of my heart, but whatever Your will is for me, I'll follow wherever You take me.

Florrie paused in her ministrations and gave Nathaniel a motherly look. "I would love to have Abby for a traveling companion, but my opinion isn't the one that is important. You'd best hear what she has to say on the matter."

Abby silently blessed Florrie and lifted a prayer heavenward. She drew in a deep breath, locked eyes with Nathaniel for a moment, and then turned to her father. "I'm *not* going to Raleigh."

Father's eyebrows arched. "Now see here, young lady—"

"Father, please. I'm not trying to be contrary, but I'm not a child anymore." She sat up a little straighter and sent her father an imploring look. "Did you receive my letter?"

He tapped his fingers on the arm of the chair. "I did, but judging by the date, it followed me around awhile."

"Followed you around?" Abby frowned. She'd sent it to Fort New Echota. "I don't understand."

"A few days after you left, I was called to Fort Cass and then to Fort Butler." He took a sip of coffee and continued. "A supply detail came in carrying mail, and there was a note from your aunt."

"How did Aunt Charlotte know you were at Fort Butler?"

"She didn't. The note was addressed to New Echota. When the

mail was sorted, the corporal noticed an envelope addressed to me and delivered it."

He sent a stern look to both Abby and Nathaniel. "My sister was obviously distraught when she mailed the note because all it said was that you had not arrived as expected due to an accident." His tone tightened, and he cleared his throat. "I left the following day for Raleigh."

"But I told Aunt Charlotte in my letter that I was fine."

Father nodded. "When I arrived in Raleigh, she let me read your letter." He shifted in his seat. "But I don't see what this has to do with your refusal to go now."

Abby slid her gaze to Nathaniel. If anyone would understand what she was about to say, it was him. She turned to face her father. "You've always said a man is only as good as his word. Doesn't that also apply to a woman?"

He pursed his lips and gave a short nod.

She shifted her attention between both men. "I promised Beth I'd stay for as long as she needed me. I intend to keep that promise." She lowered her eyes for a moment. *God, please help Father understand.* "Father, we've argued for years about where was best for me to live: with you at your post or with Aunt Charlotte in Raleigh. When I was younger, I didn't have a choice." She reached over and touched her father's hand. "But I'm not a little girl anymore. I believe this is where God wants me."

A frown worked its way into her father's brow, but he didn't reply.

"Father, there are some things you need to know—things I didn't write in the letter." She risked a glance at Nathaniel, and it was nearly her undoing. The look in his eyes took her breath away. He'd proven he had a heart of honor. It was time the erroneous stigma was removed.

"Nathaniel was wrongly convicted at his court-martial." She hurried to explain the story Wren had told her and the miscarriage of justice that had occurred. Her father had the power to clear Nathaniel's name if he would listen to the truth.

"Who is this Wren woman, and why should I regard her word as valid? As I understand you, this woman is a Cherokee."

❧

Nathaniel sat dumbstruck for several moments. He had no idea Abby knew about the circumstances surrounding his court-martial. The growing assurance of his love for her nearly tied his heart in a knot. But he leaned forward in his chair and found his tongue. "Sir, may I speak freely?"

Colonel Locke eyed him with suspicion but nodded. Nathaniel straightened his shoulders.

"What your daughter has told you is true. When Alpha Company set out from Fort Reed that day, our orders were to locate and advise those Cherokee who had yet to vacate their homes. When Captain Bane gave the order to open fire, I couldn't believe it. I tried to stop him, but the other troopers were already shooting." The recurring nightmare flashed across his mind once more. His stomach rolled. "The Cherokees we encountered weren't hostile. They protested and asked for more time to gather their belongings, but they showed no aggression. Captain Bane's actions were in direct violation of General Scott's orders. I considered it my moral duty to protect unarmed women and children, and given the same circumstances, I'd do it again."

"And one of those women was the one named Wren?"

"Yes, sir. After I was arrested, I never knew what became of her or the others. She must have evaded capture that day. I can't say I'm sorry."

The Colonel stood and paced the length of the porch. "Why weren't Captain Bane's actions brought into testimony? If what you say is true, you could have been exonerated, unless you didn't have anyone who could confirm your story." Speculation etched lines on Colonel's Locke's face.

How could he give an honest answer without hurting Abby? He looked at her and hesitated. He'd hoped his trek down the ravine would demonstrate what he'd not felt the freedom to speak. After a quick prayer for God to protect her heart, he turned to the colonel who sat waiting for an answer.

"I was. . .courting Felicia Bane, Captain Bane's daughter. When this incident occurred, I knew Felicia and her mother would be devastated— their family shamed, so I declined to implicate Captain Bane."

Colonel Locke's eyebrows furrowed. "You withheld evidence?"

Nathaniel shook his head. "No, sir, not exactly. Even though I did not accuse him, I had supposed some of the other men in Alpha Company would. I now suspect, although cannot prove, some bribery took place.

"Bane's aide-de-camp, Sergeant Browning, testified falsely that the shooting was in response to the Cherokees' aggression." Nathaniel glanced at Abby and found her hanging on his every word. If she was displeased at learning he was once sweet on Felicia Bane, it didn't show. "Browning is now riding with the Georgia Guard. He was one of the outlaws we met on the trail. I didn't recognize him at first."

The colonel stood with his hands clasped behind him, his face a study in deliberation. For months Nathaniel prayed for God to clear his name. Now, instead of Colonel Locke's conclusions, all he could focus on was

Abby's reaction to his admission about his former courtship.

During the past four days he'd held the image of her face in his mind. He imagined the joy of her countenance when she saw her keepsakes and dreamed of the softness of her lips. Now that she sat across from him, his heart throbbed in his chest, and he longed to take her hands in his and share every secret of his heart—how thoughts of her accompanied his waking and lingered in his dreams. The ache in his chest swelled as his eyes traced the plane of her cheekbones and the tip of her nose.

Colonel Locke halted his pacing and cleared his throat. Nathaniel tore his gaze away from Abby. He stood and faced her father. The colonel pressed his fingertips together and eyed Nathaniel.

"It appears I owe you my gratitude for the way you've protected my daughter." Locke removed his hat and fingered the cock's feather before tossing the hat on the chair. "As for the brand of dishonor, what you have told me today bears investigation. If what you say is true, your actions were a reflection of your officer's oath." He clasped his hands behind him. "It is an injustice, when a man knows his own rectitude of conduct, to have his loyalty debased and held in contempt."

The colonel folded his arms across his chest. "Now I'd like to know more about this Cherokee woman."

Nathaniel sent a quick glance toward Abby. "I can honestly tell you that I don't know where she is. We met her on the trail after the encounter with the outlaws. She doctored me and gave aid to the ladies, and led us to the closest town." He gestured to the community around them. "Then she disappeared into these mountains."

Abby spoke up. "Father, she's been generous and kind, and I wouldn't betray her even if I did know where to find her."

Her father raised one eyebrow. "*Hmph.* I suppose one Cherokee woman living in the mountain wilderness isn't much of a threat." He looked at Abby then rested his steely eyes on Nathaniel. "As soon as I return to Fort Butler, I will initiate an investigation into the incident regarding Captain Bane. If there was any bribery that took place, it will be uncovered. You stand a very good chance of having your conviction reversed and your commission restored."

Nathaniel looked down at Abby who remained in her chair. He wished he knew how she felt about the disclosure regarding Felicia, but her eyes gave nothing away. Her expression offered only a suggestion of peace. Even now, her face brightened with pleasure at her father's statement. Perhaps his courtship with Felicia didn't matter to her. There was only one way to find out.

He turned back to the colonel. "I will appreciate anything you can do to clear my name, sir. However, in the past few months I've come to love these mountains and wish to settle down here. That is. . ." He reached for Abby's hand and drew her to her feet. "If I may have permission to court your daughter."

Colonel Locke lifted his chin and cocked one eyebrow. "Judging by the glow on my daughter's face, isn't that what you've been doing already?"

"N—not formally, sir. I didn't have the right as long as my name was sullied."

Locke gave him a long, unblinking look. Then he leaned over and took Abby's face in his hands and kissed her forehead. "You may court my daughter."

Epilogue

A bby glanced shyly up at Nathaniel. He took her hand and tucked it into the crook of his arm as they walked to the edge of the woods. She relished the touch of his hand.

"Why didn't you tell me about Miss Bane?"

He shrugged. "There wasn't much to tell. I had debated whether or not to ask for her hand, but I kept remembering Reverend and Mrs. Danfield and the love I could see between them. It wasn't there with Felicia, and God never gave me a peace about it. When I was released from the stockade, she wanted nothing to do with me."

Disbelief widened her eyes. "After you took the blame so her family wouldn't be shamed? Why, she doesn't deserve a fine man like—"

Heat flooded her face, but Nathaniel's smile sent ripples of excitement up her spine. After fretting over his whereabouts for four days, she squeezed his fingers to be sure her hand was safely enclosed within his.

They stood beneath the shade of the oaks, and Nathaniel bent to pluck a buttercup. He spun the flower between his thumb and forefinger and held it out to her.

"I'm grateful your father is going to see to it my name is cleared. It means I'm finally free to ask if you could consider spending your life with a man like me."

A twinge of regret pinched her as she accepted the bright-yellow blossom. She wished she'd shared her heart with him sooner. Her voice became a whisper. "A man like you? I've known your heart since the day you kissed me out by the corral."

A mischievous grin poked a dimple into his cheek. With a quick glance over his shoulder, he leaned down and cupped her face in both hands, placing a soft kiss on her lips. "I never want you to wonder what my heart feels."

Her heart danced against her ribs and her breath caught. "Will you tell me every day?"

He ran the back of his fingers along her cheek. "I promise."

The barking orders of the sergeant carried on the wind, and Abby angled her head to look toward Tucker's.

"It looks like my father is getting ready to ride out."

Nathaniel took her hand, and they walked back to the store. Her father stood next to his mount, adjusting his cinch and stirrups. When he turned to address them, his gruff military demeanor had returned, but Abby smiled and stood on tiptoe to kiss his cheek.

He harrumphed and straightened his frock coat, but a pleased smile tweaked his mustache. He extended his hand to Nathaniel. "Take care of my daughter, Lieutenant."

"I will, sir."

A sheen lit her father's eyes. He snapped a crisp salute, which Nathaniel returned.

Nathaniel enclosed Abby's hand within his as they watched the soldiers disappear around the bend in the road.

"Trust in the Lord with all thine heart." The words graced Abby's mind so gently, she was barely aware she'd spoken them aloud. She looked up into Nathaniel's eyes. "God is still teaching me that He'll direct my path if I simply place my circumstances in His hands."

Nathaniel cradled her fingers and lifted them to his lips. "That's something we'll learn together."

Harvest of Hope

To my prayer team:
Ann, Diane, Pam, Chris, Ginger,
Tracy, Angela,
and of course, The Posse—Kim, Eileen,
Margie, Darlene, and Kristian.
Thank you for praying me through
the writing of this book.
We serve an awesome God.

Chapter 1

Covington Plantation
Near Juniper Springs, Georgia
April 1860

Auralie Covington's heart pounded within her rib cage as she clutched the letter and dashed up the grand staircase with unlady-like haste. The pattern of the ornate carpet swam before her, but not from tears of joy. She closed her bedchamber door and stared at her name penned across the front of the letter. The masculine script sent an involuntary chill through her. Perry had never written to her before. In the past, his communications were always sent to Father who told her what he thought she should know. Judging by the rumpled condition of the paper and the water-stained corner, the missive had experienced an arduous journey before reaching the Covington Plantation in the foothills of the north Georgia mountains. Oh, how she prayed the letter didn't say what she dreaded. She took a deep breath and broke the wax seal.

Dear Miss Covington,

"Miss Covington?" Auralie snorted. "We're engaged to be wed and he calls me Miss Covington. What am I to call him? Mr. Bolden?" The irony of her own statement pricked her. Was it not a paradox to feel such trepidation upon receiving a letter from the man she was to marry? Perhaps if the man had been one of her choosing, her emotions wouldn't be in upheaval.

The moisture that had stained the outside of the carefully folded and sealed document blurred the ink in various places within the message, including the date her intended had written it. She glanced over the penned lines that remained unaffected by the water stain.

. . .leaving London sometime in. . . If destiny smiles on the ship, the voyage ought not to take more than. . . I trust your father has impressed upon you the importance of our union. Therefore. . .

141

Auralie held the letter closer to the light streaming in the window and squinted, trying to decipher the smeared handwriting. Since she'd been informed four years ago that an agreement joining her in marriage to the son of one of the most powerful landowners in Georgia had been reached, her father had kept her apprised of Perry Bolden's European travels. As long as Bolden remained an entire ocean away, Auralie's apprehension of the arranged unholy wedlock stayed tucked away like a postponed sentence of death. Upon receipt of his letter, however, anxiety exploded through her. The letter echoed the words of her father, leaving no room for doubt that her marriage to Perry Bolden was her duty.

She scanned down the page at the legible parts of the letter. Perry's expectations of her were spelled out like a list of instructions. Between blotches of smeared ink, he described in detail his demands for their engagement soiree, including the names of certain influential people he considered essential to the guest list. Of course, she was to make herself available upon his return to Georgia, and he went so far as to insist she wear a gown of pink silk upon his arrival.

"Pink! I hate pink."

She tossed the letter on her dressing table and parted the lace curtains at the window. The ancient oaks and sweeping willows outside her window wafting in the spring breeze didn't lend their usual calming effect as she bit her bottom lip and twisted the sapphire ring on her right hand. She could no longer pretend the marriage wasn't going to happen. Her destiny was sealed. She now knew how a trapped animal felt.

Her gaze fastened on to a mockingbird perched in the massive oak tree. After it sang through its repertoire, it took flight, making Auralie long to do the same.

" 'Oh that I had wings like a dove! for then I would fly away, and be at rest.' "

"Mmm-hmm."

Mammy's soft response caused Auralie to jump as she turned and clapped her hand over her heart. "I didn't hear you come in."

The creases in the face of the ageless black woman deepened. "Them be mighty comfortin' words from our Lawd's Book. Psalm fifty-five, verse six."

Auralie instinctively glanced toward the door that stood ajar. Teaching Mammy to read had been a precious secret between them since she was a child.

Mammy glanced over her shoulder as well. "Ain't nobody creepin' up behind." She gestured to the letter on the dressing table. "That be from Mistuh Bolden, ain't it?"

Auralie picked it up and sighed. "I haven't laid eyes on him since we were children. I can't even remember what he looks like. Mammy, what am I going to do?"

The woman who was more of a loving parent to Auralie than a slave drew her into a tight embrace. "Ah don' know, chile. We's gonna pray on it. My God ain't so weak He be caught by surprise." She set Auralie away from her and cupped her chin. "But right now, yo' fathah want to see you in his study."

Auralie's eyes widened and she clasped her hands together, her fingers working the sapphire ring to and fro. "What does he want? Does he know this letter arrived?"

"Don' know that either, chile, but iffen you keep twistin' on that there ring, you gonna wrench yo' finger off." Mammy patted Auralie's shoulder. "You best be goin', now. Massah Covington don' like to be kep' waitin'."

A tremor quivered through Auralie. If Father demanded to see the letter, she'd have no choice but to hand it over.

❧

The morning rays filtered through the trees and sparkled off the dew that still clung to the grass. Auralie gathered her billowing yellow skirt and stepped into the carriage, Mammy close at her heels. After Father had blustered about the illegible, water-stained parts of Perry's letter yesterday, he'd admonished Auralie to ready herself for the man's return to the States. If she had to endure one more lecture about Perry's extensive European education, his family's money, or the honor he'd bestowed on her by consenting to the marriage arrangement, she'd surely be ill. But a smile tweaked her lips when she recalled how she'd nodded in feigned agreement to everything her father had said and then asked permission to visit the dressmaker in Juniper Springs to commission three new gowns. Father had mumbled something about looking her best and waved her away in dismissal.

The carriage pulled away, and Mammy leaned slightly forward, her black eyes twinkling. "Yo' gonna have the dressmaker sew you up a pink silk gown?"

Auralie pressed her lips together and sent Mammy an exasperated look. "You read Perry's letter!"

" 'Course I did. You lef' it on yo' bed table las' night. An' since when you and me kep' secrets from each other?" Deep dimples of amusement sank into Mammy's cheeks.

Auralie could never be annoyed with Mammy. The woman protected her heart like a precious thing hidden away in her pocket. "Never." She shrugged. "And I'm *not* ordering a pink gown. I don't care what that letter says."

They rode in silence for a time. After a few miles, the playful expression returned to Mammy's eyes. "Ah hear'd yo' mama talkin' with yo' brother's intended."

Auralie's older brother, Dale, and his fiancée, Gwendolyn, had announced their wedding date months ago. Gwendolyn and her mother had visited Covington Plantation on a few occasions to discuss wedding plans with Auralie's mother. It was apparent that her soon-to-be sister-in-law was much more eager to become a Covington than Auralie was to become a Bolden.

Mammy broke into her reverie. "I hear her say she havin' six bridesmaids. Mmm, gonna be some fancy doin's. She showed yo' mama swatches o' cloth for the dresses, and ever'one of 'em was pink."

"No!" Auralie stabbed the floor of the carriage with her yellow parasol.

Mammy slapped her knees and threw her head back with a deep-throated chortle. "Yo' gonna wear pink one way or the other."

❧

The knot in Colton Danfield's stomach tightened the way it always did when he prepared to go to town and leave Barnabas working alone. He swept his gaze across the field all the way to the tree line. Even though Barnabas was no longer a slave, Colton wasn't so naive as to believe a slave catcher who thought Barnabas might be worth a bounty wouldn't try to take him, despite the paper he carried in his shirt pocket.

The law stated Colton was expected to see to it that Barnabas left the state upon being freed, but Barnabas rejected the idea. Colton could still hear the man's impassioned plea.

"Please don' make me leave you, Mistah Colton. Dem bounty hunters search fo' ever' colored man who travel no'th, free or not. I's gettin' too old to run from dem dogs. Let me make my mark on a paper sayin' I workin' fo' you. Dat's what I want to do. Please, Mistah Colton. . ."

The memory made Colton smile. He'd written up an indenture agreement, read it to Barnabas, and let him make his mark, just to keep everything legal. But in Colton's heart, the man was an employee and friend. He slept in the lean-to behind the cabin, and Colton paid him a wage. Even after four years, Barnabas's eyes glistened every month when

Colton placed eight silver coins in his work-scarred hand.

Colton slipped his arms into the black wool coat Pastor Winslow had given him. Though slightly too large for Colton, he didn't care. The coat, given to the pastor by a parishioner, was the only garment of fine quality the old preacher ever owned. The elderly saint had precious little to his name when he died, other than the forty acres and small herd of sheep, all of which he'd bequeathed to Colton. Over the past four years, Colton had made a few improvements as he was able and was pleased with the way his corn crop was growing and with the number of spring lambs that frolicked in the pasture. But Colton would give it all back in a moment if it meant sitting with Pastor Winslow one more time and gleaning nuggets of wisdom from the dear old man.

He ran his fingers over the well-tailored sleeve and smiled with remembrance. How he missed his friend and mentor.

Colton glanced at the position of the sun. If he didn't get moving, he'd miss the meeting at Maybelle's Café in town this morning. No doubt much of the debate would center on the upcoming election. While Colton wasn't overly vocal about his opinions, this morning was different. Jack McCaffey, the owner and publisher of the *Juniper Springs Sentinel*, had asked Colton to speak on behalf of the area farmers. Joseph E. Brown, the current governor, had yet to take a stand one way or the other regarding secession, but Colton had serious doubts about the scruples and ethics of Shelby Covington, the man running against Governor Brown.

He saddled his horse, Jasper, and led the animal out to the edge of the cornfield where Barnabas worked. The former slave straightened and sent Colton a grin.

"You must be fixin' to go to town. You's wearin' the preacher's coat."

Colton smiled and nodded. He normally saved the fine garment for going to church, but he hoped wearing Pastor Winslow's black worsted might rub a bit of the preacher's sage insight onto him before he spoke at the meeting.

He pointed to the far side of the cornfield. "What do you think? Should we wait another week before planting the other half?"

Barnabas raised his hand and shaded his eyes. "Yes suh, that be about right. This here first plantin' oughta be over a foot tall by then."

Colton turned and glanced across the footpath from the cornfield where a black-and-white dog sat in the shade of the pin oaks and kept vigil over the three dozen sheep and another dozen lambs. Colton turned to look over his shoulder at Barnabas. "I have to admit you were right about getting a dog to help watch the sheep. He's been worth every penny."

The presence of the dog also eased Colton's mind somewhat when he had to leave Barnabas alone on the place, knowing the animal would bark if he picked up the scent of any strangers nosing around. It always made Colton smile when he remembered the day he brought the pup home and let Barnabas name him. "Freedom," he'd said. And from that day on, they called the dog Freedom, or Free for short.

Colton hoped to one day acquire more land, expand the flock, and plant more acreage, but not until he could afford to pay another man to help work it. It pleased him to pay Barnabas a wage, even if it did mean they ate beans and salt pork most days. The corn crop looked good, and his herd of sheep had doubled in size. The future held promise, but only with God's blessings.

Barnabas dragged his faded sleeve across his forehead. "Mistah Colton, you gots any plans fo' gittin' yo'self hitched?"

"What?" Colton shook his head, certain he'd misunderstood.

Barnabas grinned and his eyes danced. "Iffen you was to marry and have yo'self a passel o' sons, you and me could set on the porch in a couple o' rockin' chairs while the young'uns worked the field."

Colton snorted. "Marriage is a long ways off for me. If God wants me to marry, He's going to have to put the woman right in front of me so I trip over her."

Colton put his foot in the stirrup and swung into the saddle, but tugged the reins to hold Jasper in place. "Barnabas, do you have—"

Barnabas patted his shirt pocket where the paper declaring him a free man lay folded and tucked. "Right here, Mistah Colton, jus' like always."

An uneasy smile stretched Colton's face as he returned Barnabas's wave. He bumped his heels against Jasper's flanks and pulled his thoughts back to the meeting being held at Maybelle's Café. In addition to the speculation over the governor's race, the topic of secession had several folks engaged in hot debate. None of the landowners attending today's meeting used slaves, and most of them, like Colton, had farms under a hundred acres. The wealthy and powerful plantation owners whose holdings were vastly larger than Colton's claimed they couldn't turn a profit without slaves. That philosophy always soured Colton's stomach.

The town of Juniper Springs came into view. He reined in the chestnut gelding and dismounted, taking note of the men headed in the direction of Maybelle's Cafe. Colton knew most of them and didn't see anyone who stood out as suspicious. The last thing they needed was someone carrying information back to the plantation owners.

He stepped aside to let a young woman in a sweeping yellow dress with a matching parasol pass. The older Negro woman with her scowled at Colton, as if she considered him a threat to the lovely young woman in front of her. He tipped his hat and mumbled a good morning, moving on to the door of the café.

A lively discussion was already underway when Colton stepped inside. Maybelle Gooch, proprietor of the café, put a cup of coffee in his hand the moment he entered. He gave the plump, middle-aged woman a smile and a nod of thanks, and made his way to a table already occupied by two other men. As Colton listened to the speakers, most agreed on the immorality of slavery and thought secession was a bad idea. Colton took the floor and presented the position of the farmers with small acreage, the most pressing issue being how to protect their properties in the event the politicians in Atlanta voted to secede and war came to their part of the country.

Several of the attendees called out their agreement as he made his way back to his seat.

"I'm with you, Colton."

Another added, "Colton knows what he's talking about."

Slight movement of yellow near the entrance caught Colton's attention. The same woman he'd passed on the boardwalk stood just inside the door, listening intently. Judging by her attire, she was from a wealthy family, and if the Negro woman with her was an indication, her family owned slaves.

Colton fixed his eyes on the woman in yellow. What was she doing here? Did she plan to take a list of names of the attendees back to her fancy home? At that moment, the woman's eyes met his and his breath caught. Something flickered across her face, as though she recognized him. But Colton had never seen her before in his life. If he had, he'd remember a woman as beautiful as this one.

The door opened and two more men shuffled in, blocking Colton's view. When the men moved, the woman was gone. But what information might she divulge? He rose, hoping to see which way she went.

Chapter 2

Needles of panic spurred Auralie from the café where she'd merely stopped for something cool to drink. How was she to know she'd stumbled upon some kind of political meeting? Distracted over the arrival of Perry Bolden's letter, she was completely taken by surprise when she heard some of the men call him by name.

Confused thoughts raced through her mind. How did he arrive back in the States so soon? Had he traveled on the same ship with his letter? And why was Perry attending such a meeting? When she realized she'd just stared into the face of the man whose return she dreaded, the blood in her veins turned to ice. All she wanted to do was hide behind her parasol and set her feet to flying as fast as she could run. She shoved the questions away and allowed flustered confusion to carry her out the door.

The parasol resisted her effort to thrust it open, and the horrid thing took on a mind of its own. She gave it one more hard yank, and it leaped from her grip like a rock from a slingshot. A man on the boardwalk made his acquaintance with the cantankerous thing when it propelled itself into his stomach.

"Oof!" He doubled over and grabbed his middle, gasping like he'd just run uphill.

To Auralie's further mortification, the poor man fell forward just as she bent to retrieve the parasol, and he tripped over her, sending her sprawling across the boardwalk in a most unladylike fashion.

With a groan that sounded like a strangled cat, the gentleman untangled his arms from hers and scrambled upright. Flames rushed up Auralie's throat and into her face. Her stomach twisted into a knot. From her face-down position on the boardwalk she could hear Mammy sputtering close by. But the hands that reached down to cup her elbows and help her stand weren't Mammy's. They were strong, calloused hands. Masculine hands. White hands.

Once she was steady on her feet, the man released his grip on her arms and proceeded to retrieve his hat and brush dust off his finely-tailored coat.

She sucked in a breath and whisked an errant curl away from her face before raising her eyes to meet his.

It was him.

While he continued to wheeze air in and out as he clutched his hat, mahogany eyes arrested her and she froze in place. She'd tried a hundred times to remember what Perry Bolden looked like as a child. Were his eyes this dark? Was his hair the color of walnuts? She certainly didn't remember him being this devastatingly handsome. But then, he was only fourteen years old, and she eleven, the last time she recalled seeing him. She opened her mouth, but the only sound that emerged was an undignified squeak.

"Now see what you done?" Mammy sent a venomous look at Bolden before fluttering like a mother hen over her. "You all right, honey girl?"

Auralie tried to snatch her composure and stuff it back into place. She cleared her throat and begged God to give her coherent words to speak to this man who stood before her. But he spoke first.

"I'm terribly sorry, miss. Please forgive me. I hope you are unhurt."

Her throat tightened like it was trussed up in a corset. Ever since his letter had arrived yesterday, she'd tried to imagine what she might say when she faced her fiancé for the first time. Nothing she'd learned from Miss Josephine Westbrook at the Rose Hill Female Academy came to mind. She commanded her scrambled thoughts back into some semblance of order.

"Ah, yes. . .I'm unharmed." Finally. A lucid thought.

Mammy fussed for a few more moments, and Auralie used the time to regain her poise. She fixed her feet in place and refused to allow them the freedom to do as they pleased, which was to flee in the opposite direction. But no amount of finishing school training or memories of Miss Westbrook's prim examples could curtail the angst that twisted through her over Perry's arrival. She'd barely had time to digest the implications of his rumpled letter tucked under her handkerchief box in her bureau drawer. Couldn't God have at least given her a couple of weeks to get used to the idea? She shrugged off the plea. She'd had four years to get used to the idea, but the arranged betrothal appealed to her even less today than it had on her sixteenth birthday when her father announced it. She disciplined her lungs to draw a slow, even breath and then discreetly release it.

"I, too, apologize, Mr. Bolden." Had her father orchestrated this encounter, he'd have her strike an aristocratic pose of resplendent grace and reply with demure dignity. No such formalities fell within her grasp at the moment, so she merely lifted her chin. "I had imagined our first meeting would take place under much different circumstances. I only received your letter yesterday, and as you can imagine, we haven't had time to prepare for your arrival. My father will be pleased that you're here of course. I suppose you will be coming by the house to finalize the terms of the agreement."

The man's eyebrows dipped and he shook his head, puzzlement etching lines into his features. "You must have me confused with someone else, miss. My name isn't Bolden. It's Danfield. Colton Danfield." He drew his hat up over his heart in a gentlemanly gesture.

Auralie blinked and her heart paused before resuming its erratic tapping. While embarrassment still heated her face, wilting relief coursed through her—a bewildering duet of emotions. Her knees wobbled as the tension drained from her and reprieve took its place. She started to flap her hand in front of her face, but genteel restraint curled her fingers closed and she returned her hand to hide within the sunny folds of her skirt.

"Oh my. It does seem as though I've made an error." How she wished she had a fan in her possession to obstruct Mr. Danfield's view of her fiery countenance. She didn't dare give her parasol another opportunity to inflict further damage. "In addition to nearly skewering you with my parasol, I've compounded the insult by assuming you were someone else. Dear me, do accept my apology, Mr. Danfield."

A slow, polite smile stretched Mr. Danfield's lips and he gave a slight bow. "Think nothing of it, Miss. . ."

"Covington. Miss Auralie Covington." She extended her hand, which he took and held for the briefest of moments.

❧

Covington? Surely she wasn't. . .

"Of the Covington Plantation?"

Her light brown hair reflected the sun, and the curl she kept pushing back tumbled again when she nodded. "That's right."

Shelby Covington's daughter?

Cautionary flags waved in his brain. He'd noticed her standing by the café door long enough to hear much of what was said, but he mustn't allow his imagination to run rampant. Still, it was entirely possible she'd been sent to spy and report back to her father the names of those in attendance at the meeting. After all, who would suspect a lovely young woman with her mammy in tow?

Shelby Covington would like nothing better than to bully the area farmers into deference to his ambitions. Small farmers may not have the money or power the larger plantation owners did, but each one still had a vote. Covington's ability to gain votes in exchange for political favors might work in wealthier circles, but for those farmers who had to sweat and scratch to eke out a living, money might sway people to cast a ballot for a man with whom they otherwise had no affinity. Colton hoped he was wrong about Miss Covington's reason for being at the meeting, but for the moment, he couldn't think why a refined young woman would patronize Maybelle's Café.

Maybelle's place was clean, but the furnishings were plain, and she served tasty, but simple fare. It wasn't the kind of place Colton expected to see a person of wealth.

He switched his hat from one hand to the other and gave her a polite nod, guarding his words and measuring her reaction. "I see." *Careful.* "The news of your father's run for the governor's seat is all over town."

After the initial humiliating encounter, Miss Covington now appeared to have a tight grip on her dignity, but she didn't resort to batting her eyelashes or employing flirtatious coyness. His level of respect increased a notch.

She looked him straight in the eye. "Father doesn't discuss such matters around me or my mother. Perhaps I'll buy a newspaper after I visit the dressmaker so I can read about my father's political ambitions."

The young woman's statement surprised Colton, and he would have pursued the subject, but at that moment the older black woman who accompanied her continued her solicitous care of Miss Covington.

"Miss Auralie, iffen we don't hurry, you gonna be late fo' yo' appointment with the dressmaker." The old slave woman cast a defensive, sideways look at him.

"But I don't have—" Miss Covington pressed her lips closed for a moment. "It's all right, Mammy. Why don't you go along and tell Mrs. Hyatt I'll be there in a moment."

The woman shifted a distrustful scowl in Colton's direction. She reminded him of a ruffled hen guarding her chicks. He half expected her to flap her arms at him to hold him at bay, and he bit his lip to keep from grinning. She tossed one more treacherous glare at Colton and turned to Miss Covington. "I be waitin' fo' you outside the dressmaker's door. You call out iffen you need me." With that, she huffed her way down the boardwalk.

Miss Covington wiggled the mechanism on her parasol up and down a few times. Colton took a half step backward and eyed the frilly contraption warily as it finally whooshed open. He wondered if Miss Covington consciously clutched the thing like a shield or if perhaps it was only his imagination.

She'd not mentioned some of the uncomplimentary comments made about her father in the meeting, but she must have heard them. How could she be unaware of the questionable tactics and special favors her father employed to gain support of wealthy, influential people?

He pasted a smile in place and steered the conversation in another direction. "The name Bolden—were you referring to the Boldens at Ivywood Plantation?"

A flicker of something akin to alarm blinked across her face. No doubt she regretted mistaking Colton's identity, but he suspected something more. There were rumors afoot that the Bolden clan was backing Shelby Covington for governor. Since she professed to not knowing anything about her father's plans, would she deny knowledge of her father's connection with the Boldens?

She lifted the parasol over her head and shaded her face.

"The Boldens have been friends with my family for as long as I can remember. Before I was born, actually." Her gaze darted about like a wren seeking a safe branch on which to perch. Was that a tremor in her voice?

It seemed to Colton if the Boldens were old family friends, wouldn't she know them on sight? Why would she mistake him for a Bolden? His curiosity piqued, but she took several tiny side steps and twirled her parasol.

"If you'll excuse me, Mr. Danfield. I really must be going. Good day."

He placed his hat on his head and tugged the brim as she stepped gracefully down the boardwalk in the direction of the dressmaker's shop. It wasn't polite to stare, but Colton couldn't tear his eyes away from the retreating figure of Auralie Covington. Her father's political ambitions weren't the only reason for the bad taste in his mouth. Shelby Covington was also the man from whom Colton had bought Barnabas. The cruelty Barnabas had endured at Covington Plantation was evident from the scars carved by the whip on his back and shackles on his legs. Colton gritted his teeth. Only a man devoid of common sense would be attracted to the lovely Miss Covington, given the differences in their backgrounds. But fascination overrode the warnings.

❧

Auralie ran her hand over several samples of material the dressmaker showed her. Despite Frances Hyatt's attempts to convince her pink would bring out the roses in her cheeks, Auralie adamantly refused to consider the color, rejecting anything that remotely resembled Perry Bolden's instructions. Instead, she selected a sapphire blue lawn with ivory trim for a morning dress and a mossy green satin for a new dinner gown.

"What you goin' to pick for when Mistah Bolden come to meet you?" Mammy's eyes twinkled as she fingered a pale pink silk.

Auralie sighed. A sinking sensation weighted her stomach, taunting her with anticipation of the inevitable. Still, she retained enough rebelliousness to shove aside the pink. The array of fabrics spread across the dressmaker's worktable rivaled the colors in the most meticulously tended garden. She reached past the pink and grasped a bolt of royal purple taffeta.

"Wouldn't this be lovely with orchid embroidery along the neckline?"

Mrs. Hyatt beamed. "You do have an eye for quality, Miss Covington. That's an excellent piece of goods." She unrolled a length and draped it across Auralie's shoulder, letting it cascade down in front of her. "Oh my, it's exquisite. You will look like a princess in this gown." The woman's loosely pinned, gray bun flopped from side to side as she cocked her head one way and then another.

"I think so, too." Defiance tickled Auralie's stomach, and she pulled her lips into a smile. "I also like that tiny lavender floral for a morning gown."

The dressmaker opened one fold of the material. "Instead of the blue lawn?"

"No." Auralie picked up the corner of the fabric and held it against her. "In addition to the blue. Would you have any eyelet lace to edge it?"

"Indeed I do." The woman bustled back and forth to her storeroom, bringing out a number of trims for Auralie's approval. "This cloth is so springlike. It will look lovely, my dear. So, that is a total of four dresses." Delight tinkled in Mrs. Hyatt's tone, and the woman scurried to gather her pencil and order book.

Mammy sidled up close to Auralie's shoulder. "Honey girl, yo' fathah agreed to three."

"I know, Mammy." Her gaze locked with Mammy's warm chocolate brown eyes, knowing the dear woman would understand what Auralie couldn't speak. "My choices are slipping away from my grasp. I doubt Father will even notice that I have four new dresses instead of only three."

"He be noticin' when he got to pay the bill." No scolding edged Mammy's tone, but Auralie detected a hint of sympathy.

With a small shake of her head, Auralie curled her fingers around Mammy's. "He might bluster awhile, but I'll remind him that he said I was to look my best." The very idea of primping and preening for Perry Bolden twisted her stomach into a knot. "Who knows how much longer I'll be free to make my own decisions about what dress to wear or which color looks best on me? I realize I'm only feeding my own vanity, but in a few months I may not have a choice."

Her throat tightened, and the lavender print of the material she still held blurred in her hands, but she refused to give in to tears. Her father might have intimidated her mother into submission, he may have stolen his only daughter's privilege of choice, but she'd not let him rob her of her grace. She blinked back the burning in her eyes and forced a smile. For now, she'd grasp whatever freedom was within her reach and relish it.

Chapter 3

The aroma of freshly brewed coffee wafted up the stairs to greet Auralie when Mammy came to awaken her, but Auralie had been up for hours. Every time she closed her eyes, images of Colton Danfield wouldn't let her rest. While relief had skittered down her spine yesterday when she realized it wasn't Perry Bolden to whom she spoke, she never conceived meeting a man like Colton Danfield could linger in the recesses of her mind to such a degree as to interrupt her sleep.

She stepped away from the open window and clutched the edges of her dressing gown, wrapping it around herself against the cool morning air as Mammy plunked the tray containing coffee and cinnamon toast down on the tea table.

Mammy clucked her tongue and waddled across the room. "Honey girl, what you doin' standin' there breathin' in that chilly air. You's goin' to catch the grippe. Now come on away from there." She shut the window and nudged Auralie over to the chair upholstered in rich tapestry roses. "Here now, you drink this coffee and warm yo'self. What you doin' up so early anyway?"

Auralie took a sip of the steaming brew. "I can't get that man out of my mind."

"What man? You frettin' over Mistah Bolden comin'?"

"No. Well, yes, I am, but that's not the man I'm talking about." She nibbled on the cinnamon toast. "That man I met yesterday in town, Mr. Danfield—"

"You mean dat man who knocked you down? I wanted to kick him right in the shinbone. Who do he think he is, bargin' out the door thataway and tramplin' my honey girl?" Mammy snorted her displeasure. "He oughta be put in jail till the sun don't shine no mo', that's what."

Auralie patted Mammy's hand. "It's all right, he apologized. He didn't mean any harm."

"Hmph." Mammy muttered under her breath and began brushing Auralie's hair.

The recurring picture of Mr. Danfield bent over and holding his stomach filled Auralie's face with heat. "I've never been so embarrassed. I nearly ran him through with my parasol. The poor man."

Mammy harrumphed again as she deftly twisted, curled, and pinned each lock of Auralie's hair. "Po' man! I'd like to give that po' man a piece o' my mind. A proper young lady ain't even safe walking down the street with men like him crashin' through doors."

Auralie suppressed a giggle. If she'd let Mammy have her way, Mr. Danfield might be the one in mortal danger. Other than the initial chagrin over the awkward encounter, the one thing that continued to niggle at Auralie was the way Mr. Danfield regarded her with an air of contempt. Something in his tone and demeanor bespoke disapproval, but she didn't think it had anything to do with their collision. She pushed the thought aside as she listened to Mammy's prattle.

"Glad he had the good manners to 'pologize and tip his hat, but I don't mind tellin' you I weren't comf'table leavin' you standin' there with him while I went on ahead to the dressmaker's." She leaned this way and that peering at her handiwork. "Leastways he *not* Mistah Bolden."

"He asked what my connection was with the Bolden family. I hardly knew what to tell him." Auralie finished her toast and took another sip of coffee.

"Why he ask that?" Mammy put the finishing touches on Auralie's hair and turned toward the wardrobe.

She stood and let her dressing gown slip off her arms. "He was speaking in that meeting and some of the other men called out to him. I thought they said *Bolden*, but there were so many people talking and so much noise, I must not have heard them correctly. Now I understand they were calling him by his given name, Colton. But at the time, I panicked. I thought Perry had arrived, and all I wanted to do was run away. When we collided on the sidewalk, I called him Mr. Bolden."

Mammy helped her step into her hooped petticoat, adjusted the stays, and tied the satin strings. "So what you tell him when he ask about the Boldens?"

Auralie pushed out her breath as Mammy laced her corset. "I just told him the Boldens were old friends of the family." She turned and faced the mirror, watching Mammy's animated expression in reaction to her statement.

"You didn't tell him you was engaged to Mistah Perry?"

Auralie shook her head, her face warming. "It hasn't been formally announced yet, so I'm not obligated to tell anyone. I never met Mr. Danfield until yesterday, so it was hardly any of his business."

Mammy's arched eyebrows said more than her silence as she fastened the long row of buttons down the back of Auralie's morning dress.

Curiosity itched her sense of discretion and she longed to scratch it. "Mammy, what do you suppose he was doing at that meeting?"

A low chortle rumbled from Mammy's throat. "Doin' what men do. Talkin' and talkin' and not makin' much sense. 'Sides, didn' you say it was some kind o' political meetin'? Best you ask yo' fathah 'bout that, but ain't likely he'll be tellin' you nuthin'. He always say he want his women to be beautiful, and dat's all."

His women, indeed. Frustration competed with her curiosity. "I can't understand how Mother can sit to one side, doing nothing but being beautiful, like some kind of—*ornament*. Why do men assume women have no ability to think for themselves or contribute something to society? I want to be more than that. I just wish I knew what it is that I truly want."

She released a sigh and wished some of her vexation could leak away with it. "What's so wrong with asking questions? How am I supposed to learn about the events that might steer us toward secession? I know my father holds some strong opinions about it, but he doesn't speak of it in front of me."

"Mmm-hmm." Mammy's tone warned her she was treading too close to the firmly established line that divided the sexes. "You best watch yo' words. Massah Covington not like it iffen he know you sayin' such things, 'specially to me."

"And to whom should I say them?"

Mammy's fingers paused halfway up the back of Auralie's dress. "Honey girl, this here be yo' twentieth spring. You stopped needin' a mammy a long time ago." Her voice grew thick and husky. "You couldn't be mo' dear to me if you was my own chile. The secret place in my heart is glad when you talk to me like a baby girl with her mama. But darlin', yo' gots to remember I ain't nuthin' but a slave, and yo' mama is a refined mistress of the house."

Auralie turned and slipped her arms around Mammy's neck and sighed. "But I can't talk to Mother the way I can talk to you. When I try to draw her into conversation about what's going on in the South, she shushes me and says it's not appropriate for a proper lady to discuss such things."

Mammy cupped both hands on Auralie's cheeks and placed a kiss on her forehead, then turned her around and continued buttoning the dress up to Auralie's slumped shoulders.

"Mother tells me Perry would disapprove if I persist in expressing opinions about things that don't concern me." She blew out an exasperated breath. "I don't care what Perry thinks. Every night I pray God will help me find some way out of this arranged marriage."

She whirled to face Mammy again. "Marrying Perry would be like marrying a complete stranger. I'd rather marry the man who collided with me yesterday."

"Here, now. You keep jumpin' around like dat and I'm likely to get yo' buttons in the wrong buttonholes." Mammy finished the buttons and fastened an ivory lace collar to the peach-colored dress.

Auralie stood still a moment longer. "Mr. Danfield spoke at that meeting, and I heard some of the men there say Father was a man of questionable ethics. At first it made me angry to hear it, but deep in my heart—" She lowered herself to the tapestry chair. "I wonder if they may be right. Does it make me a terrible daughter to question my father's honor?"

Mammy stooped to button Auralie's shoes. "You stop that talk now. You might be headstrong, but terrible is somethin' you never be."

"I stood in the doorway of that café yesterday long enough to hear they were talking about secession and how it would bring hardship on many people. They debated over the upcoming elections and most of the men in attendance believed Father wouldn't make a good governor. I never realized how secession could hurt some of the smaller farmers." She propped her elbow on the arm of the chair and leaned her chin on her hand. "I think Father is for secession because he wants to continue using slaves."

She reached down and grasped Mammy's hands, halting their task. "I never thought much about it before, but here I am, old enough now to take care of myself, but you still have to bring me my breakfast and dress me. You aren't free to do as you please."

"What make you think I ain't pleased to tend to you every day?"

A soft smile tipped Auralie's lips. "I know your heart, and you do everything with love. I just wish you had a choice."

Mammy shook her head. "No sense in wishin' for somethin' that ain't never gonna be. Now prayin' for God to help you find a way out of dis here arranged marriage? Dat be somethin' else. We sure can pray, 'cause I don' want my honey girl to be anything but happy."

"Mammy?"

"Hmm?"

"Do you think God cares about us being happy?"

Mammy jerked upright and plopped her hands on her ample hips. "Well, 'course He do. Why you even ask such a question?"

Auralie lifted her shoulders. "Just look around. You and those like you don't want to be bound in slavery, but you are. If God is my heavenly Father, is He as domineering as my father who sits behind his desk in his study?"

The lines across Mammy's forehead smoothed out and she picked up the Bible that lay on Auralie's bedside table. Her thick fingers wandered through the pages until she found the place she sought. Auralie's gaze followed Mammy's quick glance toward the door. It was shut tight. Mammy began to read.

"I will say of the Lawd, He my refuge and my fo'tress: my God; *in Him* will I trust." She ran her finger further down the page. "Because he hath set his love upon Me, therefo' will I deliver him: I will set him on high, because he know my name. He call on me, and I will answer him: I be with him in trouble." She lowered the book. "Do that sound like a heavenly Father who don't care 'bout His chillun?" She replaced the Bible on the nightstand and took Auralie's hands in hers.

"Honey girl, God's Word say if you love Him, He know your name, and He promise to hear you and be with you, no matter what kind o' trouble you be goin' through. Dat's the kind o' heavenly Father we have."

❧

Colton wrangled a bleating ewe from a patch of blackberry vines into which she'd gotten herself entangled. Without so much as an appreciative *baa*, she ambled back to join the rest of the flock.

Colton pulled off his gloves and dragged his sleeve across his forehead. "We probably ought to chop down these thorny vines so the sheep don't get caught again."

"No suh!" Barnabas shook his head. "Dem vines give some o' the sweetest blackberries in the summer." He smacked his lips. "Make my mouth water jus' thinkin' 'bout it. Blackberries make a mighty fine cobbler."

Colton grinned and relented. "All right, but it'll be your job to keep the sheep out of the vines."

"Sheeps must be th' dumbest animals God evah created." Barnabas declared as he helped Colton and Free herd the woollies toward the small barn. Without the dog's help, the chore might've taken the two men half the morning.

"Put the lambs in that far pen." Colton pointed. "Once we start the shearing, we'll do the young ones last and keep their wool separate."

When they had all the critters corralled, Colton grabbed the horns of one of the young rams and steered the 125-pound animal toward the shearing stall. As the two men worked together, Barnabas plied Colton with questions about the sheep. Having been a field hand most of his life, working with sheep filled the former slave with fascination.

"Mistuh Colton, how come dees sheeps don't have no wool on da faces or underbellies?"

After watching Barnabas emerge from his shell of oppression and submission into a man who glowed joy and wonder, Colton didn't mind answering his friend's endless questions as they clipped the valuable wool and gathered it into burlap sacks.

"These are Gulf Coast sheep, and they are bred especially to thrive in the heat here in the south. Their wool is finer than the sheep raised in the north because the breed was developed with Spanish Merino sheep. The finer wool and not having any wool on their faces, legs, and bellies helps them adapt to hot weather and humidity in this area of the country."

Barnabas clipped the last of the wool from the ram and turned it loose in the pen. The sheep bleated its indignation, and then trotted over to shove its face into the feeding trough.

Barnabas snagged the next candidate and guided it into the shearing stall. "You learn all dat from da preacher?"

"Mm hm." The question stirred Colton's heart. He'd learned that and so much more from the man he considered his mentor. He wished Pastor Winslow could lend him wise counsel regarding the young woman with whom he'd collided a few days ago. His inability to get Auralie Covington out of his mind disconcerted him.

"What you thinkin' on so hard?" Barnabas's voice interrupted his thoughts.

Colton bent over another sheep and began shearing. "I met a young woman in town the other day."

Barnabas's dark face split with a wide grin. "Dat so?"

"It's not what you're thinking." Colton shoved a pile of wool to one side and continued working. "This girl is Shelby Covington's daughter."

At the mention of Covington's name, Barnabas halted mid-task and their gazes connected. After years of living on the Covington Plantation, the former slave no doubt had vivid memories of the cruelty he'd endured at the hands of Shelby Covington and his overseers. Painful memories engraved their marks in Barnabas's eyes, prompting Colton's stomach to tighten. Once again, gratitude spilled over Colton's heart for God allowing him the opportunity to purchase his friend's freedom.

Barnabas squatted and quietly returned to work, stuffing wool into the burlap sacks. "I recall he had a daughter. Long time ago, I 'member her—she couldn't've been more'n eleven or twelve years old—she used to come sneakin' down to Slave Row with a basket. She give cookies and fruit to the chilluns, sometime she even play with the younger ones." He leaned back on his heels and stared at the barn roof like the memory was painted there.

"She used to bring storybooks, and some of the li'l colored chilluns would sit with her and she showed dem words in the books." He looked Colton in the eye and lowered his voice, even though there was nobody to overhear except the sheep. "She taught a lot o' dem chilluns to read. . . ." He lowered his gaze. "Till the day the overseer caught her and take her to her daddy. After dat, I don' 'member seein' her no more. Heard she went off to a school somewheres."

Shelby Covington's daughter taught slave children to read? Colton could only imagine what her father must have thought about that. This new revelation gave him pause. He'd assumed Miss Covington was a pampered, indulged young woman who cared for nobody but herself. Perhaps he'd judged her too quickly. True, she'd been accompanied by her maid, but the slave was obviously owned by Shelby Covington and as such was obliged to do his bidding.

What Colton couldn't figure out was why Miss Covington seemed so relieved to learn his name wasn't Bolden, and why alarm flickered through her eyes when he asked about her connection with the Bolden clan.

Even more bewildering was why the memory of his encounter with Auralie Covington pervaded his senses and refused to leave him alone. He had no answer other than his initial wariness of her taking information to her father. But in the light of what Barnabas told him, that likelihood dimmed. No, for the first time since making Miss Covington's acquaintance, a different picture of the young woman emerged, and it appealed to him.

Chapter 4

C olton heaved a satisfied sigh as he finished loading the bulging burlap sacks into the wagon. He planned to set out for Juniper Springs
right after breakfast. The sale of the fine wool meant he could
replenish their supplies, and he tucked his list into his hip pocket. He
looked forward to drinking real coffee instead of chicory, and although
Barnabas would never ask, Colton planned to bring home some peppermint sticks for his friend's sweet tooth.

Colton climbed aboard and clucked to the team. Barnabas worked at
repairing the corral gate next to the barn and waved as Colton rounded
the curve in the road. Colton always advised Barnabas to stick close to
the barn whenever Colton had to be away. Did it mean he lacked faith, or
was it simply prudent? Colton pursed his lips. Nothing wrong with being
cautious.

The late April morning treated his senses with the fragrance of
spring grass and dogwood. A hint of honeysuckle lingered in the air.
Jingling harnesses and the clopping of hooves blended with the song of a
mockingbird. The serenade put a smile on Colton's face.

Within the hour, Colton pulled the team to a halt in front of the Feed
and Seed. Sloan Talbot stood out front with a record book, counting sacks
of grain.

"Mornin', Sloan."

Talbot shaded his eyes and squinted. "Hey Colton." He peered into
the back of the wagon. "You got somethin' for me?"

"We finished our shearing a day early." Colton set the brake and tied
off the reins. "Sure am glad, too." He climbed down over the wheel.

Sloan glanced over the load. "What have you got there, about sixteen
sacks?"

"Eighteen. The two bags tied with red cording are lambs wool." Colton
nudged his hat farther back with his thumb. "Are the prices you quoted me
last month still holding?"

"Far as I know." Sloan gestured toward the open door. "Bring 'em over
here, and I'll start weighing them."

Colton hauled the sacks to the scale and watched as Sloan balanced
each load with counterweights and tallied them up.

"Say, what do you think about Covington running for governor?"

Colton hoped he'd be able to take care of his business, pick up his supplies, and head home without having to engage in any debates about Shelby Covington. "He's not my first choice."

"You don't say? Why not?" Sloan appeared genuinely surprised that Colton wasn't a supporter of the local candidate.

"I don't feel he has the best interests of the small farmers at heart, and I suspect he'd lead us into secession." Colton dusted off his hat.

Sloan flapped one hand at Colton. "That ain't going to happen, because that Lincoln fellow can't win the presidential election." The man pointed toward the sky, as if testifying to gospel truth. "You mark my words. Either Breckenridge or Douglas is going to win the presidency, and all this talk of secession will fade away. Won't be no need with one of them running things in Washington." Sloan stopped short. "That's right, I forgot. You're one of those fellows who's speaking out against secession. Don't understand why you wouldn't want to preserve Georgia's right to choose the way of life we want to follow."

Colton drew in a slow breath. Sloan Talbot wasn't the first man with whom he'd disagreed over the issue of slavery. "But I do believe in preserving the right to choose. I believe all men should have that freedom." He paused, letting his words settle with the full impact of their meaning. "It's morally wrong for one man to own another."

Sloan smirked. "What are you talkin' about? You got yourself a slave out there at your place. You wouldn't be able to get all your work done without that boy of yours."

The words hung on the tip of Colton's tongue. Barnabas wasn't a slave any longer. He worked for Colton because that's what he chose, not because he was forced. Barnabas gave Colton an honest day's work and took pride in what he did, the way man was made to do. Yes, Barnabas was free, but telling Sloan would be like spitting into the wind.

Sloan smiled like a bird-fed cat and appeared to think he'd won the argument. Changing Sloan's mind was unlikely, but Colton had to try.

"I believe Abraham Lincoln is going to be our next president. Georgia's current governor, Joseph Brown, is indecisive. He's not taken a position one way or the other on these issues. Shelby Covington thinks secession will preserve states' rights, but all it will preserve is big landowners' right to own slaves. If he's elected and alienates those businesses in the north who purchase the goods produced by Southerners, it will break the backs of the small farmers.

"But the ones who will suffer most of all are those people who are bought and sold at the slave markets and live in bondage, forced to work like animals. Some live in worse conditions than the animals. I can't vote for a man who endorses slavery."

Sloan clamped his mouth closed. His lips thinned out and curved downward at the corners. He closed his tally book and tucked it under his arm. "You know, Colton, I just remembered. I got a notice the other day from the mills in New Jersey and Massachusetts that the price of wool dropped. Ain't going to be able to pay you the price I quoted last month." He stuck one thumb in his belt and straightened his shoulders.

Colton stared at Sloan, a man he considered a friend. Or he had at one time. A spark of anger ignited in his belly, but he doused it. Going toe-to-toe with Sloan on the sidewalk wouldn't raise the price of wool, nor would it change Sloan's thinking. "What is the going rate now?"

Sloan quoted a price per pound that equated to approximately half what Colton expected. Before he had a chance to digest the bad news, Sloan tossed the record book down on the boardwalk and spoke again. "Owen Dinsmore at the freight depot tells me shipping rates are going up. He said it costs twice as much to ship freight as it did last month. Must be all those ugly rumors about Lincoln getting elected." Sloan finished his declaration with a sneer.

Colton shook his head. "Would you mind showing me that notice you received from the mills?"

Sloan lifted his shoulders and held out his hand, fingers splayed. "My desk is so messy. It'd probably take me all day to find it."

"That's all right." Colton kept his tone even. "While you search for it, I'll go by the freight office and confirm that shipping price with Owen." He slid his gaze sideways at the stacked burlap sacks. "In the meantime, I'll just take my wool and load it back on the wagon so nobody makes a mistake and accidentally spills coal oil on it, or something like that."

He began hefting the packed wool into the back of the wagon, indignation swelling in his chest.

"There ain't no need for you to do that, Colton." As Colton expected, a thread of desperation rang in Sloan's voice at the prospect of losing his agent's commission.

Colton continued loading. It wasn't hard to figure out Sloan intended to get full price for the wool when he sold it to the Northern mills.

"Where else you going to take your goods? I'm the only agent in town who buys wool."

Colton didn't miss a beat. "You're not the only agent in north Georgia.

The agents in Gainesville have always paid about three cents a pound more than you do. It'll take me a couple of days to get there and back, but the money will make the trip worthwhile. If Harry Jeffers in Gainesville tries to tell me the price of wool has dropped to half of its former price, I'll take it to Athens." He thumped a sack into the wagon and paused to shoot a pointed stare at Sloan. "I'm not giving my wool away."

Colton brushed past Sloan to pick up another sack. He hoped the apprehension over leaving Barnabas alone for a few days didn't show on his face as he continued to reload the wagon. He lifted another sack and slung it to his shoulder. Before he could step off the boardwalk, Sloan caught his arm.

"Look, Colton. There's no need for this." He jerked his thumb toward the doorway leading to his office. "I don't think I can find that notice, and maybe I was mistaken about what it said. You know my memory ain't what it used to be." He took the sack from Colton's arms and tossed it back onto the boardwalk. "We'll just write up the deal for the same price as before and call it square. That all right with you?"

Colton leveled a stony gaze at Sloan. "That's always been all right with me. But know this. I won't continue to do business with a man who treats me unfairly because of a difference of opinion."

Without another word, Sloan picked up the record book and began tallying the weights he'd written down. A few moments later, he showed Colton the totals.

Colton gave a nod and a grunt. "That's a fair price. I'll just finish loading these sacks while you get my money."

Confusion etched deep wavy furrows across Sloan's forehead. "Where're you taking them?"

Colton lifted his eyebrows. "I just want to make sure they arrive at the freight depot safely. I'll be back in a half hour with the shipping invoice."

Sloan's face reddened and he curled his hands into fists at his sides, but he turned on his heel and stomped into the office.

Colton finished loading the sacks and turned the wagon around. Relief washed through him. Leaving Barnabas alone at the farm for days at a time, even with Free there to bark a warning, filled him with trepidation. After dropping off the wool at the freight depot, Colton confirmed his suspicions. Owen Dinsmore quoted him the same shipping rates as always.

Colton's rumbling stomach reminded him it was nearly lunchtime. He pulled up at the hitching rail outside the mercantile and climbed three steps up to the boardwalk.

Clyde Sawyer greeted him as he entered. "Howdy, Colton. How's things out at your place?"

"Just fine, Clyde. How's Betsy?"

A wide smile filled Clyde's face, and his gray whiskers wiggled the way they always did when he spoke about his wife. "You know my Sweet Pea. She knows everything that goes on in Juniper Springs and doesn't mind talking about it. Jack McCaffey at the *Sentinel* told me the other day Betsy's going to put him out of business."

Colton grinned. "You better not let Betsy hear you say that."

"Did I hear my name?" The curtains dividing the storeroom from the front of the mercantile parted and a gray-haired woman with snapping green eyes stepped out. "Clyde, are you telling tales again?"

"Aw, Sweet Pea, you know I'd never do that." Clyde winked at Colton and lowered his voice to a conspiratorial whisper. "After you've been married for as long as me and my Sweet Pea, you learn to just let them have their way."

"I heard that." Betsy narrowed her eyes and batted her hand at her husband. "Now what can we do for you today, Colton?"

Colton pulled his list from his hip pocket and handed it to Betsy. "I have some empty crates in the wagon. Thought I'd go grab a bite to eat over at Maybelle's and pick up the supplies afterwhile."

Betsy sent Colton a warm smile. "That'll be fine. Clyde honey, go and get the crates out of Colton's wagon."

"Yes, Sweet Pea." Clyde's placating tone brought an immediate hissing sigh from his wife, but before she could retort, he pecked her on the cheek.

Colton guffawed. The couple pretended to fight like a pair of alley cats at times, but their affection for each other was always evident. He backed up in mock wariness.

"Think I'll just go on to Maybelle's before the fur starts flying in here." He grinned at Clyde and exited.

He greeted a few folks on the boardwalk as he strode past the cabinetmaker and hotel. A small crowd gathered down the street near the newspaper office. As Colton approached, a man held up the latest edition of the *Sentinel*. Splashed across the front page, the headline read COVINGTON RUNS FOR GOVERNOR.

❧

Auralie stepped out the door of the newspaper office having dropped off the note to the editor as her father had directed. She picked up her flowing lavender skirts to keep from dragging the hem in the dusty red clay as she and Mammy made their way across the street to Frances Hyatt's dressmaker shop for her fitting.

A small crowd congregated on the side of the street nearest the newspaper office. As she and Mammy stepped around them, Auralie heard one man declare, "Joseph Brown is bad enough, but Covington would make a worse governor than Brown, if that's possible."

She slowed her steps and listened to the derogatory remarks being made about her father.

"All Covington is interested in is putting more money in his own pocket."

"Speaking of money, did you read the part of that article about the Boldens? That entire clan is backing Covington."

"Thick as thieves, they are."

"What do you think, Colton?"

Auralie froze in her tracks. The very man whose image invaded her dreams stood among these people who had nothing but negative things to say about her father. She peered through the crowd and caught a glimpse of his profile, and her heart hiccupped.

"I believe we must examine our own conscience to determine whether or not a man like Shelby Covington is the best choice for governor. It's the responsibility of every man who casts a vote to seek God's guidance and not be swayed by unethical granting of political favors."

Auralie couldn't tear her eyes away from Colton. Deep in her heart, she couldn't deny what he said was true. When he finished speaking he turned, and for a fleeting moment their gazes collided. She tried to read his expression when he caught sight of her. His eyes softened into an apologetic grimace, but she doubted he regretted saying what he did. Only that she'd heard him say it. He lifted his hand and started to speak, but she spun around.

Deciding to forego the dress fitting, she snagged Mammy's arm and hurried toward the carriage, barely waiting long enough for their driver to open the door and hand her up to the seat.

"What is it, honey girl? What dem folks say what's got you all upset?"

Auralie sat in silence for a full minute clutching Mammy's hand. When she trusted her voice to speak without breaking, she replied in a voice so hushed, Mammy had to lean close.

"I don't think it's what they said so much as it is that I fear they are right. Father has always preached to me about the Covington name and how respected it is, but how can he force his own daughter into a marriage just so it will benefit him politically? Where is the respect in that?" Tears threatened and she pressed her eyes closed.

"You been prayin' on it like I tol' you?"

Auralie shook her head. "Sometimes I still feel like God is so far off, so big and mighty and powerful. How could He care about someone like me?"

"Mmm-hmm." Mammy wrapped Auralie in her arms and hummed while rocking back and forth. "Oh honey girl, jes' you look at me. I ain't nuthin' but an ol' slave woman, and He care 'bout me."

Auralie straightened. "But how do you know?"

Pure bliss and adoration filled Mammy's face. " 'Cause I done talked to Him jus' dis mornin'."

When the carriage finally turned into the long, winding drive that led to the main house, another carriage approached from the opposite direction heading toward the road. Auralie stared. The fine, ornate gray carriage drawn by a pair of perfectly matched black horses looked vaguely familiar. As the two carriages passed, Auralie's stomach clenched. She'd seen that carriage before. It belonged to Thaddeus Bolden, Perry's father.

She twisted in her seat trying to see the occupants, but the interior of the carriage was too shadowed. A shudder began in the pit of her stomach and traveled up her spine. Had Perry returned? Was he here? With trembling hands, she gripped the seat, wishing she could fly away like the dove in the psalm.

Chapter 5

Colton bent his back and swung the hoe at the weeds growing between the rows of knee-high corn, wishing he could rid himself of worries as easily as he hacked away the unwanted undergrowth. Rumblings about the upcoming elections and rumors of secession continued to spin out of control, and every time Colton went into town—even to church—the topic of discussion was as predictable as the sunrise. He carried on a running conversation with God, bringing the burdens of his heart to the throne, but it seemed no sooner had he laid one worry down another sprang up.

"Kind of like weeds." Colton and the Lord shared a smile.

He straightened and twisted to stretch the kinks in his muscles. Putting a hand to his forehead to shade his eyes, he searched the next field for Barnabas. The man could work circles around Colton. Judging by Barnabas's position, he had already planted more than half of the second cornfield.

Across the footpath, Free patrolled the meadow where the sheep grazed. A soft breeze stirred the trees, and the sun warmed the earth to bring forth a bountiful crop. Colton couldn't ask for a more peaceful scene. But an unsettled feeling of impending danger lurked, taunting him like a schoolyard bully.

"Lord, I don't know why I keep looking over my shoulder, waiting for some unseen catastrophe, but it's like an ache that won't go away, no matter how much I rub it. Pastor Winslow used to be able to tell when a storm was coming, even when the sky was clear. That's the way I feel. There's a storm on the horizon that I can't prevent. All I can do is ask You to be with us and give us shelter from the storm. Forgive me for trying to carry burdens that aren't mine to carry or control. Only You, Lord, can control the winds and the storms, no matter what form they take."

Free's bark interrupted Colton's prayer. He looked beyond the meadow and past the second cornfield into the trees. To the south of the cornfields lay a small apple orchard. Colton's searching gaze swept across the fields and beyond the orchard, but couldn't see any intruders—of the two- or four-legged variety. In the distance, his neighbor's house perched between several tall pines, but Colton could see no one stirring around there either.

When the sun was high overhead, Barnabas came tramping up the slope, carrying his shirt in one hand, his canteen slung over his shoulder. Colton joined him, and they hiked back to the house to see what they could scrape together for lunch.

Colton pumped water into a bucket and raised handfuls to his face to rinse off the sweat and dirt. "You've made great progress on that second field." He shook the water from his hair.

"It be finished by sundown. I's holdin' out some seed fo' one more plantin', jus' 'nough fo' another acre." Barnabas gulped down a dipper of water and then poured a second dipper over his head. "Ahh."

Colton tossed him a towel and went inside the cabin to put their lunch together. Barnabas came to the open door and knocked on the doorframe before stepping inside. Despite Colton's repeated invitations, the former slave couldn't seem to leave behind his old habits of submission. "Come on in. Grab a jar of those peaches from the pantry. There's some coffee left from breakfast. Push the pot over the fire while I make some biscuit and bacon sandwiches."

Barnabas smacked his lips. "Real coffee. Don' wanna waste none o' that."

They settled at the table, and Colton asked the blessing on the food. As they dug in, Barnabas pushed a stray crumb into his mouth. "Seen some men pokin' around in the woods out pas' the orchard this mornin' while I's workin'."

Colton almost choked on the bite of biscuit in his mouth. "Slave catchers? What were they doing? I wondered what Free was barking at."

"Don' think dey's bounty hunters, didn't look like it. Dey seen me workin' but didn' pay much mind. Deys mo' interested in the trees, and they done some pointin' and lookin' 'round. One of 'em had some kind o' spyglass settin' up on three legs. He point it 'cross yo' land and look through it and write sumpin' on a paper."

Colton leaned back in his chair. "Surveyors maybe? But I can't imagine what they were looking at across my fields. Have you ever seen any of them before?"

Barnabas's hesitation in answering piqued Colton's concern.

"Meybe. One of 'em look familiar, like meybe I seen him long time ago." He took another bite of biscuit and rubbed his chin while he chewed, like he was turning something over in his mind. "Don' wanna say fo' sho'. I might be wrong."

Colton let him think on it while they ate in silence for a couple of minutes. After they finished off the peaches, Colton poured the last of the coffee into their tin cups. "Well, do you think you know who the man was that you saw?"

Barnabas blew on his coffee and took a noisy slurp. "Could be. Seem like the one fella put me in mind o' Massah Covington's boy."

"Shelby Covington's son?"

"Mm hm. Massah Dale Covington. I ain't seen him in a mighty long time, but sho' did look like him."

"That's peculiar—if it was him. What would Dale Covington be doing tramping around in the woods next to my land?"

❧

Auralie tapped on the door of her mother's sitting room and cocked her head to listen for Phoebe Covington's soft response. The woman never raised her voice, and most times spoke so softly one had to strain to hear her.

Auralie cracked the door open. "Mother? May I come in?"

"Come in, Auralie."

Mother sat on her ivory satin brocade chaise with flowing skirts primly arranged around her ankles. Her impeccably coiffed ash blond hair crowned her delicate features, and a leather-bound volume with gold filigree edging the corners graced her soft hands. One might think she was posing to have her portrait painted.

"Mother, I need to ask you something."

A hint of disapproval flickered across her mother's porcelain complexion, dipping her eyebrows and accentuating the tiny lines across her forehead—lines she never admitted existed.

"Auralie. You are no longer a child, and therefore should have learned long ago how a refined lady enters a room." She wafted the air with one hand in a graceful gesture. "Proper etiquette dictates we step softly, courteously greet those present, and engage in polite conversation."

Auralie stifled a sigh. She loved her mother but grieved the distance between them, even when they were in the same room. Phoebe Covington embodied the epitome of everything Auralie resented but dared not express. "I apologize, Mother. How are you this morning?"

"I'm quite well, thank you. And you?" Mother gave a slight nod, as if prompting Auralie to respond in kind.

Eager to dispense with the formalities, Auralie answered with the replies she'd been trained to give. For a fleeting moment she envied the daughters who could share trivial things with their mothers, like the new dresses she'd ordered from Frances Hyatt.

"Please sit down." Mother gestured to a nearby chair, also upholstered in ivory brocade. "Shall I ring for tea?"

"No thank you." Auralie took her seat. The request she came to make fidgeted within her for expression. "It's a lovely morning."

Her mother sent her gaze to the window. "Yes it is. Perhaps this afternoon I shall walk in the garden before tea."

"I'm sure the outing will be quite pleasant."

"Auralie, will you please refrain from doing that."

Auralie blinked and dropped her guarded bearing. "Doing what?"

Exasperation edged her mother's carefully controlled tone. "A proper lady does not show nervousness by twisting her ring."

Auralie glanced down at her hands and pulled her fingers away from the sapphire ring, gently interlacing them instead. "Mother, I've received a message this morning from Cousin Belle."

"And what does your cousin have to say?"

Auralie willed her hands to be still. "As you know, her husband, Lloyd, is away in Atlanta on business."

"I was not aware of that."

"Yes, an architectural firm in Atlanta has requested several drawings from him for a project. It seems they admire his work and have retained him for a rather prestigious undertaking." She paused to gauge her mother's reaction, but could not detect any emotion one way or the other on the woman's face. "It will require that he be away from home for several weeks, and Belle hasn't been feeling well. She has asked that I come and stay with her for a while, until Lloyd returns home."

Her mother pressed a lace handkerchief to her lips. "I see. Have you spoken with your father about this?"

"No." Her fingers encircled the ring again. "I was hoping you could ask him for me."

For the first time since Auralie entered the room, her mother allowed her poised demeanor to slip, and Auralie glimpsed apprehension.

"You must send word to your father that you wish to speak with him and request that he inform you what time would be convenient." Her mother's reply wasn't what Auralie wanted to hear. She'd hoped for an advocate in coaxing her father to give his permission, but now she must enter the lion's den alone.

&

Auralie drew in a silent breath and held it, awaiting her father's response to Cousin Belle's request. Stepping inside his study felt akin to approaching a king's throne room, and Auralie fought the urge to run. She sat on the fine leather chair in front of the massive polished desk and locked her crossed ankles under her skirt in an attempt to imitate her mother's perfect posture.

Her father's scowl made her shrink into the chair despite her best efforts to emulate her mother's grace. He tossed the folded note across the desk, and his voice boomed within the walnut walls of the stately room.

"Do I need to remind you we are awaiting Perry Bolden's return, which could be any time." He picked up a brandy snifter and swirled the amber liquid in the glass before taking a sip. Auralie hated the effect the drink had on her father and usually hid herself away in her room whenever he indulged—especially so early in the day.

"Yes sir, I'm aware of that. The new gowns I commissioned are ready, the invitations have been written and are waiting to be sent, and Cook is planning the menu for the—" The word strangled in her throat. She covered her mouth with her fingertips and coughed. "Excuse me. The menu for the. . . engagement party."

"Then you know that your presence is required here." Father stood and paced behind his desk. "Thaddeus Bolden was here last week to finalize some. . .details. He said the last letter he received from his son indicated Perry would set sail from England on April twenty-fifth."

"But that was just a week ago. A trans-Atlantic voyage takes—"

"I'm well aware of how long it takes." He tossed down the remainder of his brandy and poured himself another.

Auralie's pulse pounded in her ears and her throat tightened. Her fingers shook as she twisted the ring and waited for her father to continue the tirade she knew was imminent.

As she expected, his voice gained volume as he repeated his expectations that she make herself available to the Boldens and reminded her how important this union would be to his political aspirations. He slammed the brandy glass down on his desk, sending shards of glass sailing in multiple directions. An involuntary flinch rippled over her. She instinctively yanked up her hands in a defensive posture and drew back.

"When are you going to learn to maintain an attitude of dignity instead of sitting there simpering like an empty-headed fool? Perry Bolden wants a woman of elegance and composure by his side, not one that quavers at the sound of a man's voice."

Auralie's stomach twisted into a knot, and her trembling hands grew clammy. Without warning, the image of Colton Danfield manifested in her mind along with a fleeting thought that she doubted he was the type of man to intimidate a woman. She had no basis for her belief, other than the warmth of his dark eyes and the quiet way he'd recommended the people around him seek God's wisdom in casting their vote. She blinked the image away. Her father towered before her like an overlord awaiting her response.

She raised her chin and adjusted her posture. Her voice must sound perfectly modulated and controlled, ringing with the grace her father demanded. And it was.

"Of course, Father. I'm merely requesting your permission to visit with Cousin Belle for a time. She lives less than an hour away. I could return home immediately should we receive word that Perry has arrived."

Father planted both hands on the desk and leaned forward, leveling a sinister glare at her. "You'd better hope to Saint Peter you'll return home immediately."

A spark of hope ignited in her middle. Did that mean he was letting her go?

Father bellowed for one of the house slaves to bring him another glass then resumed his barking about "her duty." With one final admonition, laced with a threat about her not embarrassing him, he waved his hand in dismissal.

She struggled to control her feet to refrain from taking wing as she exited the study. The moment the door was closed, she fairly flew up the grand, curving staircase to find Mammy. When Auralie burst into her bedroom, Mammy startled, jerking her head away from her task of putting freshly laundered clothes in Auralie's bureau.

"Mercy, chile. Where you goin' in such a hurry?"

A silly grin stretched her lips, and she grasped Mammy's hands. "I'm going to visit Cousin Belle. And you're coming with me."

"Massah Covington say yes? Dat be a s'prise to me."

Giddiness crept up Auralie's throat and emerged as a giggle. "He didn't say no. He just said I have to return immediately if we get word that Perry Bolden has arrived."

A smile played around Mammy's lips. "I send one of the menservants to bring yo' trunk down. When we leavin'?"

"As soon as possible." She sat down at the small secretary and pulled out her stationery box and pot of ink. "It will only take a minute to write this note to Cousin Belle. Can you please call Reuben to take it over to her? Then I'll help you pack."

"Give my heart joy to see you this happy, honey girl. You deserve dis kind o' happiness."

She scribbled the note and blew on the ink to hasten its drying while Mammy went to find the coachman to transport the note to Belle. Auralie sat back and closed her eyes. Imagine having the freedom to come and go as she pleased indefinitely. Realization pinched her stomach. Her happiness was short-lived. Looming in her future like a vulture over a dead animal was her forthcoming marriage to Perry and a lifetime of living just like her mother.

Chapter 6

Auralie sipped the glass of lemonade Belle handed her and leaned back against the porch swing. Regardless of how long or short her visit with her cousin, she intended to enjoy every minute, like a prisoner being handed a commuted sentence.

Squirrels argued in a nearby oak tree, and a pair of wrens flitted back and forth to their nest where three scrawny heads raised up with beaks wide open every time one of the parents landed on the adjacent branch. A lazy white cat stretched out at the opposite end of the porch.

"Aren't you afraid the cat will get to the baby birds?"

Belle laughed, a delightful tinkling sound, and shook her head. "No. Frank is too old and fat to be a danger to anything other than the scraps we feed him. I've never seen a cat sleep as much as he does." She picked up a sugar cookie and nibbled on the golden edge. "Have you decided how long you can stay?"

Auralie sighed. "If it was up to me, I'd stay indefinitely—at least until Lloyd comes back. But Father says I must return home the moment we receive word that Perry Bolden has arrived."

Belle pooched her bottom lip out in a feigned pout. "I still can't believe that you didn't tell me you were engaged. I thought I was your favorite cousin."

Auralie blew out a stiff breath. "You *are* my favorite cousin, but—" She lowered her voice. "This engagement isn't anything I wanted to celebrate."

"What?" Belle's eyes widened and she set her lemonade down. "What do you mean?"

"Belle, I haven't laid eyes on Perry Bolden since you and I were in pigtails. Thaddeus Bolden and Father arranged this marriage four years ago. Father announced it to me and Mother on my sixteenth birthday, as if it were a grand birthday gift, and I'm expected to go along with it."

Her cousin's round blue eyes glistened. "Oh Auralie, how awful. I can't even imagine joining myself in marriage to a man I didn't love. Didn't Aunt Phoebe object?"

Auralie shrugged. "If she did, she certainly didn't tell me. You know Mother. She wouldn't dream of going against anything Father says, or even letting him think she has an opinion." She rose and walked to the railing where Belle's roses were just beginning to bloom. "All during our childhood, we never stopped to consider those people who don't have a choice about their lives. They do as they're told and are completely subservient to their owners."

Belle cocked her head. "Are you talking about the slaves? What do they have to do with you marrying Perry Bolden?"

"Don't you see? We're alike." Auralie returned to sit sideways facing Belle on the swing. "Once I'm married to Perry, I'll be living in just as much bondage as any of the slaves."

Defensiveness threaded Belle's voice. "You say *bondage* like all slaves are treated cruelly."

"You must admit that some are, even if ours are not. Mammy is dearer to me than my own parents." She gestured toward the back end of the porch. Beyond the railing and on the opposite side of the vegetable garden, the summer kitchen sat separated from the main house. Within its walls, Mammy helped Belle's servants. "You grew up with Sam and Maizie in your home, and when you married Lloyd, your father gave them to you. But think about it. Even though they have a good home here and you treat them well, they don't have a choice about their lives, and neither do I."

Belle's expression grew perplexed. "I think I see your point, but surely being married to Perry can't be equated to being a slave. His family is wealthy. You'll have a beautiful home, the finest clothes, servants to do your bidding—you'll never want for anything."

"Except the thing I crave the most—a man who loves me. A man for me to love in return."

"There's nothing you can do?"

Auralie shook her head. "Nothing, short of sneaking out my window in the middle of the night and running away. Where could I go that Father couldn't follow and find me?"

They sat in silence for a while, and Auralie let the gentle rocking of the swing soothe her frazzled nerves. Lloyd and Belle's house was small compared to the sprawling manor house in which she lived. The house she'd been told Perry was having built was even grander. But Belle's house felt much more like a home. Belle didn't have fifteen bedrooms, a lavish ballroom, or an elegant study. There was no immense dining room big enough to seat a dinner party of forty. The gardens surrounding the place were not ostentatious. But there was something the Covington plantation house lacked. Genuine, heartfelt love.

Belle stood and stretched. "I think Maizie is making roast chicken for dinner. I hope that's all right. You're probably used to much fancier meals."

"Roast chicken sounds marvelous." She joined her cousin and they went back into the house. A large bookcase filled almost an entire wall on one end of the spacious front parlor, and Belle's curio cabinet sat in the corner displaying china doll figurines that she'd collected since she was a girl.

"I remember some of these." Auralie picked up one with golden hair swirled up like a crown and wearing a stunning ball gown with flowers around the edge and a daring neckline. "This one was always my favorite. Remember we used to dream about dressing up in beautiful gowns and waltzing all evening with dashing young gentlemen lined up waiting their turn?" She returned the figurine to its shelf. "Isn't it ironic how the things we dreamed of and wished for as young girls are now the very things I dread?" She ran her fingers over several of the dolls.

Belle took her hand. "Is it the marriage you dread?"

Hearing Belle voice the question helped Auralie put it into perspective. "It's more than just the marriage. I'm. . .restless, and frustrated at the role I'm expected to fill. I wish I could have goals and ambitions, but I feel like one of these china dolls—nice to look at, perhaps, but serving no purpose."

"Oh Auralie, you have a purpose. You're a sweet person, kindhearted and sensitive to the feelings of others."

She turned to face her cousin. "But I have nothing to occupy my time and my hands, nothing I can do to make a difference in someone's life. All that is expected of a well-bred, Southern lady is to marry well." She grasped Belle's hand and urgency filled her voice. "I want more than that, but I don't know what." She shook her head. "I know what I *don't* want, but I don't know what I *do* want."

Belle slipped her arms around Auralie and hugged her close. "Then we shall pray for God to show you."

"Belle, are you ever afraid of God?"

"Goodness, no!" Belle jerked her head back and looked Auralie in the eye. "Why would you be afraid of a God who loves you?"

Auralie bit her lip. She didn't want to be afraid of God, but she couldn't comprehend a Father who loved and cared for her like the Bible promised He did. She sighed deep within the recesses of her soul.

❧

Auralie took the cup of weak tea Maizie handed her and smiled her thanks to the gray-haired black woman who clucked her tongue like a fretting hen.

"I stirred some honey in it. Miss Belle like her tea sweet. She need sumpin' on her stomach, and she didn't eat no breakfas'."

Before Auralie could turn to carry the tea upstairs to Belle, Maizie stopped her. "Miss Auralie, meybe she listen to you if you tell her go see the doctor."

Maizie's concern touched Auralie. She sounded just like Mammy. "I think I've convinced her to go. Could you please ask Sam to hitch the carriage?"

Maizie beamed. "Sam sho' be glad to do that. I'll go tell 'im right now."

Auralie climbed the staircase to Belle's room and found her cousin pale and blotting her face with a damp cloth.

"Are you feeling any better?"

"A little. This doesn't last all day. It comes and goes."

Auralie set the teacup down on the bedside table. "Maizie made you some tea. She said you needed to put something in your stomach."

A faint smile lifted Belle's lips. "That's Maizie's answer for every ailment. I probably just need a tonic or something."

"Sam is hitching up the carriage." Auralie covered Belle's hand with hers. "Are you sure you don't want me to go with you?"

"No, I'll be fine." Belle took a few sips of tea, rose from the bed, and patted her hair in place. "Besides, I need to stop by Pastor Shuford's house and speak with him about having someone take the children's Sunday school class—at least until I'm feeling better."

"All right." Auralie hugged her cousin. "I think I'll explore your bookshelves while you're gone."

Belle picked up her parasol and they descended the stairs. "Help yourself. If you'd like to go for a walk, there are some lovely wildflowers in the meadow between our house and our neighbor."

Auralie watched Sam solicitously hand Belle up into the carriage and make sure she was comfortably seated before climbing up to the driver's seat and urging the horses forward. Auralie sighed as she watched them leave and whispered a prayer that whatever ailed her cousin could, indeed, be remedied with a simple tonic.

The last time she recalled having a day all to herself, she was a carefree child with no more concerns than plucking petals from daisies. Perhaps she'd take that walk later and see if she could find some daisies to grace their dinner table.

She found a volume of *Wuthering Heights* on the parlor bookshelf. Smiling, she carried it out to the shady side porch and curled up in a

cushioned rocker. Emily Brontë's story and characters mesmerized her—
the brooding Heathcliff and the beautiful and free-spirited Catherine—
and she was surprised when Mammy poked her head out and asked if she
wanted her lunch brought out.

"My goodness, I must have lost track of time." She tucked a piece of
ribbon between the pages to mark her place and stood to stretch. "Just
something light, Mammy. I'm not terribly hungry."

Mammy returned a few minutes later with a tray. "Maizie and me
make chicken salad from that roast chicken las' night. She say she don'
never throw away food dat's lef', and Miss Belle don' mind at all." She
set the tray on the small wicker table beside the rocker. "Maizie's makin' a
fresh pitcher o' lemonade. I tol' her it one o' yo' fav'rites."

The chicken salad was delicious and Auralie ate every bite. A warm
breeze swayed the treetops and set the wildflowers and grasses to dancing,
inviting Auralie to join in the celebration of spring. She shaded her eyes
and gazed out across the meadow to see if any daisies bloomed. Instead,
she caught sight of two men working in a field beyond the boundary of
Belle's place. One was a black man, bent over his task. The other arrested
her attention. Even at a distance he looked familiar. She studied him for
a minute, the way he moved, the angle at which he held his head.

"Colton Danfield."

Belle said she had neighbors but didn't mention the name. She
observed the two men working side by side for a time. Peculiar. . .she'd
gotten the impression from the way he spoke in town that he was against
slavery, but the Negro man laboring beside him indicated differently.

❧

Colton jerked his glance up when Free started barking. A woman walked
toward them carrying a jug of some sort. Her wheat-colored hair peeked
out from a wide-brimmed green bonnet. Even though the bonnet
prevented him from seeing her face, his pulse picked up when she drew
closer. It couldn't be. . .

"Freedom, hush up."

The dog quieted but remained on alert, watching the stranger approach.

Colton quickly buttoned his shirt and strode to meet the visitor. He
ran his hands over his wind-tossed hair to push it into submission and
brushed at his clothes in a vain attempt to rid himself of some of the dirt
he'd attracted.

"Miss Covington." His voice sounded unnatural and forced. "This is
a surprise."

Her smile rivaled the spring sunshine. "For me as well. I had no idea you were my cousin's neighbor."

"Lloyd Hancock is your cousin?"

"No, his wife, Belle. I'm visiting with her for a while."

"I see." He eyed the pitcher and cups in her hands.

"When I saw the two of you working so hard, I thought you might like something cool to drink." She held out the two cups. "I also felt I owed you an apology."

Colton took the cups and held them while she poured lemonade into them. "An apology? You've done nothing for which to apologize."

"Oh, but I did, Mr. Danfield. You started to speak to me in town the other day and I rudely turned and walked away from you."

Colton handed one of the cups to Barnabas, who lowered his eyes and gave a slight nod.

"Thank you kindly, miss."

Colton watched Barnabas take a long drink. Perhaps he'd been wrong about Auralie Covington. He turned and gave her an appreciative smile. "Thank you. This was very kind of you, but I fear it's I who owe you the apology. You heard me say some rather uncomplimentary things about your father—"

"Things that were true." She finished his sentence.

Colton blinked his surprise at her candor. "I'm still sorry you heard me say it. I'm afraid when one runs for political office he is vulnerable to public criticism from those who disagree with him."

"I'm not blaming you for disagreeing with my father. Truth be told, I disagree with him myself, but nobody asks a woman's opinion."

Yes, he could say with all confidence that he'd been completely wrong about this woman. "Well, thank you again for the lemonade."

She tipped her head to one side. "May I ask you a question?"

"Of course."

She began in a hesitant voice. "When I heard you speak in town, at the meeting in the café and again on the street, I got the impression you were against slavery."

Colton nodded. "Yes ma'am, I am."

Confusion wrinkled her brow, and she glanced over to Barnabas and back to Colton. "But—"

"Barnabas isn't my slave. He's my employee. I pay him a wage. Not a big wage, but certainly more than he ever got as a slave." He cast a quick look over his shoulder and caught Barnabas listening to every word. Colton turned back to Miss Covington. "I realize the law states that once a slave has been freed, it's the responsibility of the owner who freed him to ensure that he leave the state. However, Barnabas is also my friend and as such has chosen to remain and work with me. Just to make sure everything is done decently and in order, he made his mark on an indenture agreement, but it's merely a formality. If Barnabas wanted to leave here tomorrow, I'd make sure he had safe passage to wherever he wished to go."

Her eyes widened, not in shock but with enlightenment. Warmth flooded Colton as he watched her smile.

"Mammy is more than my friend. I can't describe how dear she is to me." Her smile faded. "But she's still a slave because she belongs to my father."

Colton nodded. An affinity grew between them. "God holds the times and seasons in His hand. I believe some changes are on the horizon, hopeful changes, but I fear the circumstances to achieve those changes might be tragic."

Chapter 7

A uralie stepped into the summer kitchen the next morning. Mouth-watering aromas of bacon, biscuits, and fresh coffee greeted her.

Mammy looked up from the fresh strawberries she was cleaning. "What you doin' downstairs so early, honey girl?"

Maizie glanced at her. "Miss Belle sick again, ain't she?" She and Mammy exchanged a meaningful look. "Why don' you go on up an' sit wi' her, and I'll bring up a tray of chamomile tea and dry toast."

Auralie twisted her ring. "I don't know if she'll be able to eat anything yet. She's quite ill." At the moment, food lost its appeal for her as well. "I'm worried about her."

A tiny smile poked a dimple in Mammy's cheek, and she patted Auralie's shoulder. "Don' you fret, honey girl. I 'spect the doctor know what the problem be. You go on up to her now. When she ready, she tell you her news."

News? That seemed a strange way to refer to one being as sick as Belle, but Auralie didn't linger for an explanation. She picked up the hem of her dressing gown and hurried up the stairs.

Belle sat on the small balcony outside the french doors in her bedroom. "The fresh air seems to help. I couldn't abide that awful smell."

Awful smell? Auralie sniffed, thinking perhaps the wind had shifted and was coming from the direction of the stables, but the only thing she could smell was breakfast cooking. "Didn't Doctor Greenway give you any medicine?"

A weak smile wobbled across Belle's face. "No. As far as he knows there's no medicine that can fix me."

Auralie's heart turned over. "Oh Belle, I—"

"Sit down, cousin. I have something to tell you, and it's good news. The best news."

What a brave woman her cousin was, facing an illness the doctor declared incurable with a smile on her face. Auralie sat opposite her and reached to take her hands, determined to be strong for her cousin.

Belle's smile deepened. "Doctor Greenway says I'm expecting."

Expecting? "What are you exp– Oh! You're. . .you're. . ." She clapped both hands over her mouth.

Belle giggled. "I wanted to wait until Lloyd came home so he could be the first person I told, but under the circumstances, I don't think I could keep you in a state of worry any longer." She laughed again. "I think Maizie and Mammy already figured it out."

Auralie threw her arms around her cousin. "I couldn't be happier for you. I just hate it that you're sick."

Belle placed her hand over her stomach and took a couple of slow, deep breaths. "Yes, well, Doctor Greenway said that would pass in a few weeks. I hope he's right."

"Let me bring you a shawl if you're going to sit out here on the balcony." Auralie found a shawl on a hook in Belle's wardrobe cabinet. She hurried back to the balcony and draped the wrap over her cousin's shoulders. "Did the doctor say when the baby might come?"

"Late autumn. Sometime in November." A crease carved a path between Belle's brows and tiny waves of alarm rippled through Auralie.

"Is there something else? Did the doctor say you were all right?"

"I'm fine." Belle patted Auralie's hand and sighed. "I picked up the mail while I was in town. There was a letter from Lloyd. He says he's being retained by the architectural firm in Atlanta."

"That's wonderful!" Auralie clapped her hands then caught the faraway look in Belle's eye. "Isn't it?"

"Yes. It will keep him in Atlanta longer than we planned, but he's worked very hard for this." She turned her head. "All this talk about secession and forming a state militia. . ."

Auralie sensed her cousin's concern. "Are you afraid Lloyd might join the Georgia Militia?"

A single tear made its way down Belle's cheek, heightening Auralie's concern. "The elections will be held in early November. If Mr. Lincoln is elected and Georgia secedes. . ." Her voice broke. "It makes me wonder if Lloyd will even be here for the birth of his child."

❧

Everyone else in the house had gone to bed hours ago, but Auralie sat in the bedroom window seat watching a storm build toward the northwest, not unlike the tempest unfurling in her soul. Mammy and Belle had both encouraged her to pray, but uncertainty jerked her this way and that until she no longer knew how to pray. The realization startled her. What if she prayed wrong? What if this marriage to Perry *was* God's will? If she asked God to stop it, wouldn't He be angry with her? She lit a candle to chase her doubts into hiding.

Flashes illuminated the oak tree nearest the window in a ghoulish glow. Each rumble of thunder built on the last, as if in competition with each other. An unearthly yowl sent shivers up Auralie's spine, and the next flash of lightning revealed Belle's cat, Frank, crouched on a branch of the tree.

Auralie opened the window. "Frank, do you want to come in before this storm hits?"

As if understanding every word she said, Frank meowed, shinnied across the limb as close to the window as he could, and leaped gracefully to the windowsill. He preened for a moment then hopped down into the bedroom.

Auralie laughed. "Belle said you were too old and fat to climb trees. Won't she be surprised?"

Maow. Frank rubbed against her leg then proceeded to make himself at home on the foot of her bed. She rubbed his head and he purred in response, leaning into her touch.

"You can stay here tonight, old fellow, as long as it's storming. It'll be our secret."

Lightning flickered again, followed by a roll of thunder that seemed to rumble endlessly across the nearby mountains and echo in the valley beyond. The call of the storm drew her back to the window seat where she watched nature's wrath in fascination. Rain that had begun as a soft sprinkle now intensified. She closed the window and listened to it tapping on the glass like an evil thing demanding entrance. The similarity to the impending upheaval in her own life was too uncanny. She shuddered.

Forks of lightning sent jagged slashes across the sky. Bewildering emotions roiled within her in rhythm to each clap of thunder. Yesterday's visit to Colton Danfield's place left her feeling even more unsettled than her dread over Perry Bolden's return. Here she was, engaged to one of the richest young men in the state, from a very influential family. Yet she couldn't stop thinking about Colton Danfield—a man with dirt under his fingernails, who made his living by sweat and calluses. What did she have in common with him?

Learning the black man working on Colton's land was no longer a slave intrigued her. Curiosity picked at her to learn how the man's freedom came about. She'd heard accounts of men buying slaves only to set them free and wondered if that's what Colton had done. Speculation of him doing such a thing didn't seem far-fetched at all. In fact, the more she learned about this man, the more she wanted to know.

Thunder boomed and shook the house like a definition of her father's intimidating roar. A tremble rattled through her, imagining his response if he could read her thoughts. The storm raging outside her window was nothing compared with the maelstrom that would hail down around her if she defied Shelby Covington.

The booming thunder awakened Colton, and he rose from his bed. Crossing the cabin to the front door, he peered out through the sheets of rain to the barn, its form outlined by flares of lightning. Everything seemed in order. The sheep were safely tucked into the barn with Free, and his presence kept them calm despite the storm.

He returned to his bed and stared up at the ceiling, the interesting analogy drawing lines of perspective in his mind. Unsettled times, debate over political opinions, and the outcome of elections drew frightening pictures of possible consequences. But if one remembered the Shepherd who never slept—the One who always guarded and sheltered His children from the storms of life the way Free guarded and calmed the sheep—he could rest in the Shepherd's promise. A small smile lifted the corners of Colton's lips.

There was one thought, however, that kept slumber at bay. The image of Auralie Covington stepped into his mind. The memory of her walking through the meadow grass, the wind catching her hair and tugging it from the confines of her bonnet, lingered in Colton's subconscious like a drop of honey on his tongue. The sweetness remained long after the source was gone.

Colton listened to the storm retreating in the distance, grateful for the rain that nourished the earth. Rain to a farmer should be a soothing lullaby, but sleep slipped into some elusive hiding place. He needed his rest to energize him for the day's work ahead. He closed his eyes. Surely if he lay very still, slumber would overtake him.

It didn't.

How was he supposed to sleep when a woman like Auralie graced his thoughts? He rose to sit on the side of his bed, wondering if the storm had awakened Barnabas in the lean-to. Perhaps, but the man likely rolled over and went back to snoring. Colton stood and groped his way in the darkness to the east-facing window. No streaks of dawn painted the sky yet.

He felt his way to the table and lit the oil lamp. The soft glow danced across the room. He nudged the wick a little higher and the light grew. One of his mother's favorite scriptures eased into his memory.

"But if we walk in the light, as he is in the light, we have fellowship one with another, and the blood of Jesus Christ his Son cleanseth us from all sin."

"Lord, keep reminding me if I stay close to Your light, I'll always be able to see where I'm going."

He made his way to the small kitchen and shoved a few pieces of stove wood into the banked coals. While the stove heated, he measured ground coffee beans into the pot and ladled water over them. If sleep refused to be his companion, he could always count on the Lord and a fresh cup of coffee.

He pushed the pot over the hottest part of the stove and crossed the room to stand at the window. Distant lightning flickered within the clouds, like summer fireflies at dusk playing tag in and out of the field grasses. He tried to fix his eyes on the spot where he thought the next glimmer would be, only to have it blink in a different direction. Gratitude filled him as the scripture continued to roll through his mind. He didn't have to chase God's light, wondering where it might next appear. He could put his trust in the Lord's presence, knowing it was always constant.

The bracing aroma of coffee called to him, and he answered the beckoning invitation to fill a cup. He pulled out a chair and settled at the table where he'd left his Bible last night.

He opened the Book to Isaiah seeking encouragement for his heart. He soaked up the words, letting them bathe him in the comforting presence of the One who inspired their writing. He drained one cup of coffee and poured another, eager to return to the precious fellowship he found between the pages of God's Word. By the time he finished his second cup, pale light gilded the sky out the east window.

The latch on the back door rattled, and Barnabas knocked on the doorframe. "Mistah Colton? You got the coffeepot on already?"

"Come in, Barnabas. The Lord and I were having a talk."

Barnabas grinned. "I's finished with the barn chores. Me 'n' Free took the sheeps out to the pasture. Looks like it rained durin' the night."

Colton smirked. "You could say that." He gestured toward the stove. "Help yourself to the coffee."

Barnabas leaned and stared closely at Colton. "You don' look like you slep' at all. Meybe I best make breakfas' so's it be fit to eat."

The offer coaxed a smile from Colton. "Fine with me."

"My mama's co'n cakes." Barnabas smacked his lips. "Wit' sorghum syrup." He pulled a cloth sack from the shelf and held it up. "Mistah Colton, this be co'nmeal?"

Colton turned up the flame flickering in the lamp. "No, that's grits. The other one is cornmeal."

Within minutes, corn cakes sizzled on the cast-iron griddle adding their fragrance to the air.

"There be four or five ewe sheeps that still ain't birthed their young'uns."

Colton grunted in response.

"I think two of 'em is carryin' twins."

"Maybe."

"Mistah Colton, you feelin' all right?"

"Fine. Just tired."

With a deft flip of his wrist, Barnabas turned the corn cakes. "Sump'in mo' than that botherin' you." A knowing twinkle glittered in his eyes.

If there was ever another soul on this earth besides his parents and Pastor Winslow that Colton knew he could trust, it was Barnabas. He stood and walked to the stove, poured himself another cup of coffee, and wandered back to the table. How did a man blurt out—even to a trusted friend—that he couldn't get a woman off his mind?

"Those corn cakes smell good."

Barnabas scooped the crispy cakes onto two plates, placing one in front of Colton. They bowed their heads, and Barnabas began to speak to God.

"Lawd, I thankin' You for this new day and the way You take care o' us. An' Lawd, please bless my frien', Mistah Colton. He be troubled this mornin', but I 'spect You already know 'bout dat. Now I ask You to be blessin' this here food, Lawd. It ain't as good as my mama made, but if You blessin' it, I be mighty thankful. In the name o' Your precious Son, sweet Jesus." When Barnabas raised his head, that same twinkle appeared in his eye, but Colton wasn't in the mood for teasing.

"Pass the syrup."

Barnabas pushed the syrup jug across the table, a twitch jiggling one corner of his mouth. "Womens sho' is puzzlin', ain't they?"

Colton sucked in a deep breath and blew it out. The man's ability to read his thoughts was downright uncanny. "I'm beginning to find that out." He stabbed a bite of corn cake and shoveled it into his mouth. He chewed thoughtfully for a minute and pointed his fork at Barnabas. "You know what bothers me?"

"Mmm-hmm, she be a pretty woman an' you don' know what to say to her."

An exasperated scowl twisted Colton's lips. "Besides that." He poked another forkful of corn cake into his mouth. "You lived on the Covington Plantation for over fifteen years, yet she acted like she didn't know you."

Barnabas shrugged. "No reason fo' her to know me. I was a field slave. All dem times she come down to Slave Row, she jus' be with the chilluns and some o' the mamas. She never did talk much to us workers, 'cause the overseer always around. I know who she be, but she never seen me."

"Hm." Colton mulled over Barnabas's reasoning. "Makes sense, I suppose." Colton polished off his breakfast and gulped the last of his coffee. He started to clear the table, but Barnabas stopped him.

"I take care o' the dishes, Mistah Colton. It be the Lawd's day. You gots to get ready fo' church."

Colton nodded, and for the hundredth time, wished Barnabas could come to church with him.

Chapter 8

Colton hated that Barnabas couldn't accompany him to the church in Juniper Springs. Leaving a man of Barnabas's faith behind to worship alone felt so wrong. There was no doubt in his mind his friend would spend time worshipping the God he loved, whether it took place in the barn, out in the meadow with Free and the sheep, or between the rows of growing corn. Barnabas never let a day go by without thanking God for His blessings. The way Barnabas found joy in the little things most people took for granted taught Colton that none of God's blessings were insignificant.

Colton finished shaving and dressing and pulled Pastor Winslow's black worsted wool coat from its hook. Slipping his arms into the sleeves, his memory echoed with the words of admonishment from the white-haired gentleman.

"Son, don't ever forsake the assembling with other believers on the Lord's Day."

Wearing the old preacher's coat to worship seemed like the man accompanied him. The thought made Colton smile.

Barnabas had Jasper saddled and ready when Colton stepped out the door. He mounted up and noticed his saddle had been freshly soaped and polished. Like he always did, Colton asked if Barnabas had his papers with him, and his friend responded by patting his shirt pocket. The practice had become a ritual.

Puddles dotted the road to town, and Colton carefully guided the horse around them so he wouldn't arrive at church mud-spattered. He drew in a deep breath of rain-washed air and remembered to thank God for providing the precipitation.

"And God, please watch over Barnabas while I'm gone. Keep him safe and let him find joy in his time of worship this morning."

Jasper's rocking chair gait made for an easy ride. Lack of sleep tightened the muscles in Colton's neck, and he reached around to rub the tense places. Maybe he'd find time for a nap this afternoon.

Try as he might, he couldn't convince himself to leave the thoughts of Auralie Covington behind. According to Barnabas, he needed to get himself hitched and have a passel of young'uns. Colton snorted. Even if he had time for a woman in his life, it certainly wouldn't be Shelby Covington's daughter. The ludicrous thought reproached him.

Dogwood trees winked their white blossoms at the spring sky, rhododendrons unfolded their flowers in celebration of the new day, and purple violets dotted the shaded slopes. A wagon carrying a family loomed up ahead, and rather than risk the wheels splashing mud up on his polished boots or clean britches, Colton slowed the gelding to ride at a safe distance behind. The four children in the back of the wagon—two boys and two girls, all dressed in their Sunday best—laughed and teased each other and made up a silly song as they rolled down the road. The children's parents turned around and smiled at the young ones and joined in the laughter. The scene stirred a longing in Colton's chest. Perhaps God had a family in store for him some day, but not now.

The church bell pealed through the trees. Colton hated arriving at church late, but a pang of disappointment pinched him when the father whistled to the team to hurry them along, ending Colton's enjoyment of watching the children. He followed the family into the churchyard and found a shady spot to tether Jasper. A few other folks arrived and exchanged greetings. At least he wouldn't be the only one walking in just as the bell ceased its tolling. He searched for a seat before Pastor Shuford stepped into the pulpit.

Colton smiled at the other members of the congregation around him—hardworking people like himself who observed the Lord's Day by gathering together in the simple church. He turned to glance across the aisle. Auralie Covington sat beside Belle Hancock. Surprise blinked through him. He knew she'd been visiting her cousin, but it didn't occur to him that a woman like her might attend church in this modest little house of worship, even though the Hancocks attended regularly. Before he could discipline his focus, Auralie turned and their gazes collided.

He sent her a polite nod and forced his attention to the front where the pastor announced the first hymn. But halfway through "How Firm a Foundation" he caught himself sliding his gaze sideways while everyone else had their faces buried in their hymnbooks. Everyone else except Auralie. The moment their eyes met for the second time, her face flooded with color and she quickly looked back at her songbook.

Heat filled his face, and he wondered what Pastor Shuford must think. He glanced up to see if the preacher had witnessed the exchange. Judging by the twinkle in the man's eye when he looked straight at Colton, he'd not only noticed, he'd been amused.

After three more hymns, the congregation was seated, and Colton admonished himself to anchor his attention on the sermon. But the knowledge of Auralie's presence crept in, taunting his thoughts.

Lord, why am I doing this? I can't be attracted to a woman like Auralie Covington. I'll only make a fool of myself if I keep looking at her. She's of a completely different class. I'm a farmer and shepherd. She's an aristocrat. Please take these unreasonable feelings for her away from me.

Pastor Shuford instructed the congregation to turn to Joshua, chapter one. As he led the worshippers in reading the scripture, the verses Colton had heard a hundred times spoke to him in a way he'd never before considered. Hearing the preacher proclaim with assurance that God would be with him as He was with Moses, that God would not fail him or forsake him, left Colton breathless. What a precious promise. Was such a promise meant for someone like him? A simple farmer? Could he be a Joshua? Colton attuned his heart to drink up the preaching of God's Word.

Like many of the promises in the Bible, this one came with a command. *"Be strong and of a good courage."* The very words drew a picture of unwavering trust in the One who promised to always be with him. If God loved him enough to never forsake him regardless of the circumstances, then God believed he had a place in this world, a place of significance. Otherwise, why would He waste His time?

The message spilled over Colton in much the same way Pastor Winslow's encouragement did. Be strong and of good courage. The admonition that rang in his ears carried with it a thread of warning as well. Events were unfolding around the bend in the road, beyond the horizon where he could not see, but God's promise meant He was already there, and Colton need not fear the unseen or unknown. Heeding God's command to be strong and courageous meant fortifying his heart and reinforcing his foundation of trust.

&

It never occurred to Auralie that she'd run into Colton at the little church her cousin attended, but she wasn't really surprised to learn he was a churchgoing man. His public statements, urging people to pray and seek God's will before supporting a candidate or casting a ballot fell into line with watching him sit in rapt attention of the preacher's sermon. The way he'd spoken of the land and his sheep the other day— like they were blessings, gifts from the hand of God—left her feeling a bit ashamed for never realizing the value God placed on hard work. Colton regarded the work of his hands as a gift, not drudgery, with peace and contentment rather than resentment. Such a man piqued her curiosity. She'd certainly never seen her father dirty his hands. In fact, more than once she'd heard him speak of working people with disdain. Even though she'd not set eyes on Perry Bolden since they were children, she suspected her fiancé leaned toward her father's notions.

She sneaked several peeks at Colton during the service. His demeanor intrigued her. She'd grown up thinking sitting in a worship service was a stiff, formal affair. Colton's profile was etched with an emotion she'd not seen in a man before. In fact, the only other person she recalled seeing with a similar expression was Mammy. When Mammy read from the Bible and when she talked about the Lord, she did so with pure adoration in her eyes. Auralie glimpsed that same worshipful countenance on Colton. He hung on every word the pastor said, even brushing a tear or two from his eye.

Auralie had known from childhood what it meant to trust Christ for salvation, but watching Colton absorb the preacher's words about God's promises pricked her with envy. Was this what Belle meant when she inquired why Auralie would be afraid of a God who loved her?

The rugged lines of Colton's jaw captured her attention. For almost four years, she'd tried to remember what Perry Bolden looked like. As her gaze traced the shadow of Colton's profile, she realized with a start that she hadn't wondered about Perry's appearance in weeks, and she didn't feel the least bit guilty about it. This man, unlike any other she'd ever met, was work toughened and tender at the same time. He showed gratitude for what God had given him and worked hard to care for it. Above everything else, he humbled himself in a way she'd never seen a man do before. This was the embodiment of a real man—not the kind of man who stepped over people to get what he wanted, or used money and power to manipulate his circumstances, not one who lorded over others or talked down to them.

Colton shifted his position, uncrossing and recrossing his legs. He glanced in her direction, and a tiny smile twitched his lips when he caught her looking at him. A flutter tickled her stomach, and she pulled her gaze back where it belonged, but not before returning his smile.

A gentle nudge poked her ribs. Belle covered her mouth with her fingers and coughed. When Auralie looked up at her cousin, an odd expression filled Belle's eyes. Heat rushed up Auralie's neck and chagrin filled her. The announcement of her engagement to Perry Bolden was scheduled within a few weeks, and here she sat in church, experiencing flutters and exchanging smiles with Colton Danfield. The word *hussy* tiptoed through her mind and fanned the flames in her cheeks.

"Your pastor must think I'm some kind of heathen." Auralie covered her face with her hands as they rode home in the carriage. A fresh wave of discomfort washed over her. "I couldn't even look him in the eye when he shook my hand at the door."

Belle giggled. "If you had, you would have seen that he was smiling." She grasped Auralie's hand. "It could have been worse. You might have fallen asleep and started snoring."

"Belle!" Auralie glanced up at Sam driving the carriage and saw his shoulders shake silently.

A wicked grin worked its way into Belle's face. "One time a man—I think he was a deacon—went to sleep and fell forward and hit his head on the pew in front of him. They had to carry him out." Her cousin stroked her chin. "Then there was the time—"

"Belle, it's not funny. I was mortified. What if this gets back to my father?"

"I doubt there is anyone from our little church who is on casual speaking terms with Uncle Shelby." Belle shrugged. "Except maybe Jack McCaffey."

Auralie spun in her seat, her eyes wide. "The editor of the newspaper? Oh, I think I'm going to be sick."

Belle emitted a tinkling laugh. "I was kidding. He wasn't even there today." She turned sideways and grasped Auralie's shoulders. "Relax. I was just trying to make you see the funny side of this." She rocked back and forth with laughter.

"Oh of course. It's sidesplitting." She lifted her eyes heavenward. "You always did have an odd sense of humor." She took off her gloves and fanned herself with them. "I shall never forgive you for teasing me."

Belle wiped tears from her face. "Don't you remember the time we had a contest to see which of us could climb a tree faster and I got stuck and your brother had to get me down? You teased me about that for months. I'm simply paying you back."

"That was more than ten years ago!" Auralie batted her cousin with her gloves. "How long do you hold a grudge?"

Hoofbeats sounded behind them. Sam steered the horses to move the carriage over so the rider could pass, but instead the chestnut horse pulled up alongside.

"Mrs. Hancock. Miss Covington."

Sam slowed the carriage, and Auralie turned at the sound of the familiar voice. Her breath strangled in her throat and all that came out was a squeak.

Amusement threaded Belle's voice. "Hello, Mr. Danfield. We don't see much of you, even though you are our nearest neighbor."

Auralie wanted to return the favor and elbow her cousin in the ribs. She managed a smile and polite nod, but her face flamed.

Mr. Danfield removed his hat. "I missed paying my respects to you ladies at church. When the service ends, it's often difficult to speak to everyone." His warm eyes locked with Auralie's. "Miss Covington, I wanted to tell you again how much we appreciated the lemonade."

Belle cocked her head and gave Auralie a curious look, her eyebrows arching like a pair of hissing cats.

Auralie found her voice. "It was my pleasure, Mr. Danfield. I'm glad you enjoyed it."

Belle's lips pressed together as if she was trying to keep from bursting into laughter. "Mr. Danfield, I feel I've been remiss. We've been neighbors for almost three years, and I've yet to extend an invitation to dinner. We would be pleased to have you join us this afternoon for Sunday dinner. I heard Maizie say she was preparing a roast."

Auralie tried to swallow and nearly choked. She wanted to shake her cousin. What in heaven's name did she think she was doing? Surely Mr. Danfield would see through Belle's ploy as nothing more than a matchmaking scheme and refuse the invitation.

Surprise flickered over Mr. Danfield's features, and he hesitated. His eyes shifted from Belle to Auralie, and the same tiny smile he sent across the aisle at church tweaked his lips again. Pleasure danced in his eyes.

"Why, that's very gracious of you, Mrs. Hancock. I really must go home first to check on—" He glanced downward for a moment, then smiled. "There are a few things that require my attention, but I would be pleased to accept. What time should I be there?"

A smile sweet enough to melt butter graced Belle's face. "Around one o'clock would be perfect."

He slid his gaze to Auralie. "I shall look forward to it." He replaced his hat and tugged on the brim. "Until later, ladies." He nudged his horse into a canter.

"Belle. . ." Auralie lowered her voice to a growl.

"Don't Belle me." A smirk danced through Belle's eyes. "What is this about lemonade?"

Chapter 9

I must be losing my mind."

Colton muttered to himself all the way home. Whatever possessed him to accept Mrs. Hancock's dinner invitation? True, she was a neighbor, but judging by the mischief that twinkled in her eyes and the way Miss Covington's eyes widened like she was facing the gallows, he'd just stepped into something better left alone.

Images of Auralie Covington kept him awake half the night, and he'd adamantly instructed himself to remain aloof. Seeing her at church took him by surprise, and he berated himself for repeatedly looking her way. Now he could only surmise that his brain had taken a holiday. What was he thinking?

Was it proper to have accepted the invitation to the Hancock home since Lloyd was away? It wasn't as if Mrs. Hancock was there alone, but he had a suspicion the invitation was more of a nudge to get to know Miss Covington rather than a neighborly gesture.

Barnabas met him in the yard by the barn as soon as he rode up. He took Jasper's reins while Colton dismounted.

"Mistah Colton, you look like yo' best frien' just up and died. Don' you know you s'posed to come home from church wi' th' joy o' the Lawd in yo' heart and on yo' face?"

Colton hung his head. "I did something stupid."

A soft snort reached his ears, and he looked up to find Barnabas rubbing his hand over his mouth. "Mistah Colton, yo's a lot o' things, but stupid ain't one of 'em." He started to lead the horse into the barn.

"Don't unsaddle him. Just give him some water and a little bit of hay." Colton took off the preacher's coat and folded it carefully over his arm. "I've been invited to Sunday dinner."

Barnabas bobbed his head. "That be right nice."

"But I *accepted* the invitation."

"I don' understand." Barnabas planted a hand on his hip. "Ain't that what yo's s'posed to do?"

Colton ran his hand over his forehead and pulled his hat off. "Well, yes. Normally it would be a very nice thing to do. But in this case, I'm having dinner with our neighbor, Mrs. Hancock, and her cousin, Miss Auralie Covington."

Barnabas's eyes crinkled into merriment. "Then I didn' make no mistake. That be right nice." He led the horse into the barn and tethered him.

"That depends on your perspective—how you look at it." Colton shook his head. "Having dinner with Miss Covington is like smacking a hornet's nest with a big stick."

Barnabas dipped a bucketful of water for the horse and deposited a small mound of hay in front of him. "I agree wi' you 'bout one thing. Smackin' a hornet's nest sho' be a stupid thing to do. But how can settin' down to dinner wit' a pretty lady be stupid?"

The two men walked side by side from the barn to the house. "She's Shelby Covington's daughter." Stating what Barnabas already knew didn't clear up the muddy water. Colton wasn't sure he could put into words what he didn't want to hear with his own ears, much less speak to another man.

"Barnabas, don't you see? She comes from an important, powerful, wealthy family. Her father is running for governor, and I detest most of the things he stands for. She's been raised in luxury and privilege. I was raised learning the value of hard work. I'm nothing but a farmer and shepherd." He turned to face the man who once toiled as a slave for Auralie's father. "I have forty acres of land that I sweat over with your help. Covington Plantation is nearly a thousand acres that uses over a hundred slaves to work. Sitting at dinner with the likes of Auralie Covington would be akin to tramping into the palace of Queen Victoria with muddy boots."

Barnabas dipped his head and rubbed his stubbly chin. Colton never noticed before how gray Barnabas was getting. He'd never even thought to ask how old the man was or if he'd ever fallen in love or had a family. The realization pinched a nerve in Colton's heart and shamed him.

"Mistah Colton, is you tryin' to tell me you ain't good enough to have dinner wi' Miz Covington? 'Cause that jus' ain't so. You is a man who loves God and always try to live in a way that please Him. You know what right and wrong, and you stand up fo' it. You ain't never hurt no one that I knows about. Yo's honest an' a man can trus' what yo' say." Barnabas's voice cracked. "An' you save my life, Mistah Colton. Them overseers woulda killed me fo' sho' iffen I'd stayed there too much longer. You give me my freedom and dignity, lettin' me work like a man oughta work, takin' pride in what he do, an' earnin' his way in dis here world." He shook his head. "No, Mistah Colton, I cain't let you say you ain't good enough. I'd go to fightin' any man who say you ain't good enough. You the bes' man I evah know."

In all the time Colton had known him, Barnabas had never made a speech before. Colton didn't know what to say. He'd grown up with the encouragement of godly parents, and Pastor Winslow was as dear to him as anyone in this world. The old preacher taught him by example what it meant to have a servant's heart. What Barnabas just said to him was exactly how he felt about Pastor Winslow.

His throat tightened, and he must have gotten something in his eye. Dust, no doubt.

He clapped his hand on Barnabas's shoulder, holding it there for several long moments. The two men spoke without uttering a word.

Colton cleared his throat. "I think I'll go freshen up."

Barnabas took the preacher's coat from Colton. He hung it on the peg and began brushing it meticulously. A smile creased Colton's face.

છે

Colton politely held Mrs. Hancock's chair as his hostess was seated. "Thank you, again, for the invitation. It's been a while since I sat at such a nice table."

Miss Covington seated herself at the opposite side of the table, and Colton gritted his teeth at his inability to move quickly enough to hold her chair as well. Her soft smile made him catch his breath.

She reminded him of a cameo brooch that belonged to his mother. He used to stare at it when he was little boy, thinking the lady whose ivory profile appeared there surely must be the most beautiful woman in the world, next to his mother, of course. Manhood had changed his perspective, and Auralie Covington now rivaled every other woman he envisioned, including the woman on his mother's cameo brooch.

The black woman Mrs. Hancock called Maizie set bowls of savory vegetables and a platter of succulent roast beef on the table. Miss Covington's mammy carried a tureen heaped with mashed potatoes and a pitcher of gravy and set them near the head of the table, while a man called Sam filled the glasses.

"Mr. Danfield, will you please ask the blessing?"

Colton smiled. "It would be my honor." He bowed his head and lifted his voice to the throne room of God, asking special favor on this house and those who lived under its roof and the hands that labored to prepare the meal. Finally, he asked God to bless the food to nourish and strengthen them, thanking God for His provision, mercy, and grace.

When they said amen and raised their heads, Colton caught a glimpse of Miss Covington's wide brown eyes reflecting wonder. Didn't she think he knew how to pray?

As they passed the dishes and platters, Colton turned to his hostess. "What do you hear from Lloyd?"

While Mrs. Hancock recounted Lloyd's last letter, Colton forced himself to pay attention to his hostess's report, but the sweet distraction sitting across from him tested his willpower. "It sounds as if he has made an impression on the senior heads of the firm in Atlanta. You must be very proud of him."

"Oh, I am. But I miss him terribly." Mrs. Hancock took a sip from her glass. "I'm hoping he can come home before—" She cleared her throat. "Before too long."

Colton took a deep breath. Barnabas declared him "good enough" to sit at dinner with Miss Covington. The least he should do is include her in the conversation. "Miss Covington, it's so good of you to keep your cousin company while Lloyd is away."

She'd done little more than push the food around on her plate. Was she uncomfortable with him sitting across from her? Perhaps she didn't agree with Barnabas's view. He gave himself a mental kick. He shouldn't have come. He should have. . .

A smile filled her eyes when she looked up. "I am the one who is the beneficiary. I love it here. If I could, I'd stay indefinitely."

Her statement surprised him. While the Hancocks weren't poor by any means, they didn't possess the wealth reflected on the Covington Plantation. She picked up the basket of biscuits and handed it to Colton.

"I was walking in the meadow the other day, watching the lambs in your pasture." A charming expression lit her eyes. "They're so adorable."

"You must come over and get a closer look at them some time." The invitation fell out of his mouth before he could snatch it back.

"Perhaps."

Change the subject, you fool. "Have you and your cousin always been close?"

Mrs. Hancock managed a mischievous grin, but Miss Covington responded with a look of exasperation. "Yes, but my cousin can be a terrible tease at times."

Mrs. Hancock's eyes twinkled. "Ah, but we laugh a lot."

The very idea of laughing with Auralie Covington filled Colton with a notion of such pleasure he dared not try to define it.

❧

Auralie stood beside Belle at the front door and watched Colton Danfield ride off toward his house. Misgivings disturbed her better judgment when she admitted—albeit only to herself—that she'd enjoyed the time spent with Mr. Danfield.

"See, that wasn't so bad, was it?" Belle closed the door and arched her eyebrows at Auralie.

"Belle. . ." Auralie brushed her hand across her forehead. "What do you think you're doing? I'm *engaged* to be married."

"To a man you don't love and didn't choose." Belle looped her arm through Auralie's as they walked away from the door. "And the engagement hasn't been formally announced yet, so it's perfectly proper to have a simple meal with a neighbor in the presence of a chaperone." She waved her fingers in a swooping motion at herself, indicating her presence ensured the afternoon had been completely appropriate. "All I'm trying to do is make you visualize how it could be if you were to do your own choosing."

A sigh, festered on despair, rose into Auralie's throat. "But that privilege has been taken away from me."

Belle gave a soft snort. "Whatever happened to my feisty cousin who dared to dream about the impossible? Think about it, Auralie. What's the worst that can happen if you refuse to marry Perry Bolden?"

Refuse? The word smacked Auralie in the face. The very idea of refusing her father's demands sent a shudder through her.

Belle stifled a yawn. "While you're thinking about it, I'm going upstairs to take a nap. Care to do likewise?"

"No thanks." Auralie gave her cousin a quick hug. She couldn't very well blame Belle for meddling when all she'd done was invite a neighbor to dinner. "You know, you've always been more like a sister to me than a cousin."

"I know. And you got me in trouble more times than I can count when we were children." A wicked gleam glittered in Belle's eye. "That's why I can get away with playing matchmaker." She giggled and headed for the stairs.

"Belle!"

Auralie shook her head. Belle meant no harm, and truth be told, she loved her cousin for what she was trying to do. But stirring up desires she'd buried long ago was a dangerous thing when her father was involved.

She headed for her favorite rocker on the side porch and curled up. Once comfortable, she realized she'd forgotten to bring the copy of *Wuthering Heights* with her, and she didn't feel like going back into the house after it. She snuggled into the cushions and laid her head back. Without anything to read, her mind lay vulnerable to imaginings.

Belle prodded her to remember the adventurous childhood they'd spent, when Auralie was usually the one to dare Belle into taking chances. Now it seemed things were turned around.

Belle's question rang in her ears. What *was* the worst that could happen? In the fairy tales she'd read as a child, the beautiful princess was locked up in a tower, but locking her up wasn't what her father wanted. His intention was for her to be on display, like Belle's china dolls—an elegant, graceful woman who exuded the lifestyle, kept her mouth shut, and hung on her husband's arm like an ornament.

When one was raised in a culture in which crossing class lines was unconventional, breaking such a tradition shook her foundation. She let her eyes drift closed and the image that came to mind was Colton Danfield sitting in church, intently listening to God's Word preached, wiping away a tear, saturating himself with the presence of God.

Had she ever done that? She believed in God and had trusted Christ as a child. But there was something missing in her faith. Mammy had tried to make her see it, and Belle had hinted Auralie's relationship with God was lacking. But she didn't understand until she watched Colton Danfield sit in awe and pure adoration of the God he loved.

Conviction.

That's the word that described what she saw in Colton, not only in the way he viewed God, but in the way he lived his life.

What convictions could she claim? Did she have that level of belief that God loved her and kept His promises? Despite having just finished eating Sunday dinner, she felt ravaged by hunger, but not a hunger for anything tangible. What she longed for was a filling of unshakable hope that she could cling to God in utter and unspoiled trust. That's what she saw in Colton Danfield. Everything about him bespoke of a deeply rooted conviction that God remain enthroned in the very center of his life.

She'd never witnessed such a faith from her father. The motive for everything her father did was greed and lust for power. When she'd questioned almost two years ago why Perry wrote to her father rather than to her, she was harshly silenced and told to stay in her place. A month ago she'd finally received a letter from Perry, and he hadn't mentioned God one time, but rather communicated the same dictatorial air she'd grown accustomed to seeing in her father.

She opened her eyes and raised them to the puffy, white clouds that drifted lazily across the blue sky. Last night's storm had rattled the walls and roof like a demonic thing seeking to devour her. Today, the cornflower blue skies, wispy clouds, and balmy breeze defined how God could keep her through the storm. Not all storms were comprised of slashing lightning, booming thunder, and wild winds. Some storms raged in the heart. Could God calm a storm within the same way He'd sheltered her during the treacherous lightning and crashing thunder?

Chapter 10

Colton stared at the colorful banner flapping in the breeze, declaring Shelby Covington the best candidate for governor. It stretched the entire width of the main street, from the lamppost next to the courthouse across the street to the saloon. Colton shook his head in disgust. The accolades borne on the banner were a stretch at best and fabrications in reality.

Clyde Sawyer stepped out the mercantile doors and stood next to Colton, hands on hips and a scowl twisting his gray whiskers. He pointed to the pretentious sign. "Is that a joke?"

"No. Covington is running for governor." Colton did his best to disguise his personal dislike of the man. Being asked to speak on behalf of local small farmers at a private gathering was one thing, but he'd not make a spectacle of himself on the street, publicly denouncing a candidate.

Clyde flapped his hand like he was shooing away an annoying gnat. "I mean that other stuff." He splayed his fingers and waved his hand in a grand arc imitating the size of the banner. "Best man for the job? A man you can trust?" Clyde's voice rang with contempt. He angled his head and looked sideways at Colton. "That's the biggest crock of—"

"Clyde?" Betsy's shrill voice carried from inside the mercantile.

The merchant cast a look of mock exasperation heavenward. "I'll be there in a minute, Sweet Pea," he called out before turning back to Colton. "So what brings you to town in the middle of the week?"

Colton pulled a scrap of paper from his shirt pocket and handed it to Clyde. "Just need a few things. I have to pick up some feed and a couple of rolls of fencing from Sloan Talbot. I'm enlarging the chicken coop. Can I pick up those supplies on my way back?"

"Sure thing." Clyde leaned closer. "Say, did you hear the news. Stephen Douglas got the most votes at the Democratic Convention, but he didn't win a clear majority. They say there was quite a rhubarb going on down there in Charleston. Fussin' and fightin' to beat the band."

Colton slapped his hat back on his head. "I was planning on picking up this week's edition of the *Sentinel* today. There ought to be something in there about the goings-on in Charleston."

Clyde dug a nickel out of his pocket and held it out. "Pick up a copy for me, will you?"

"*Clyyyyde!*" Betsy screeched for her husband again. "Where did you get off to? I need your help."

A wide grin stretched Colton's face. "You're going to be in trouble if you don't go see what she wants."

"You're right." Clyde chuckled. "Just between you and me, sometimes I think she enjoys getting all in a flutter." He raised his voice a few notches. "*Coming, Sweet Pea.*" He turned and waved. "Talk to you later, Colton. Oh, Betsy made some strawberry preserves and she wants to give you a jar, so remind me when you—"

"*Clyde Sawyer!* Do I have to come lookin' for you?"

Clyde beat a hasty retreat back inside, and Colton climbed aboard the wagon seat. He whistled to the team and headed off toward Talbot's Feed and Seed. The enterprise's owner—the man with whom Colton had exchanged words the week before—stood on the loading platform, counting stacked burlap sacks.

Sloan gave him a cool nod. "What can I do for you, Colton?" His tone bore a thread of malice, left over from their previous encounter, no doubt.

Colton climbed down from the high seat. "Morning, Sloan. Nice day, isn't it?"

A scowl wormed its way across Sloan's brow. "Haven't had time to notice. You need somethin'?"

If the man didn't want to be civil, there was nothing Colton could do about it. "I need a hundred pounds of oats, a hundred of barley, and two hundred of cracked corn. Do you have any of that crushed sorghum cane?"

Sloan gave a short nod. "How much you want?"

"A hundred pounds of the crushed cane, and a roll of poultry netting." He pulled his wallet out of his pocket.

Sloan's frown deepened. "Don't you want to put this on your account?"

Colton shook his head. "Cash on the barrel. I trust the prices are still the same?"

A rush of red filled Sloan's face and he jerked his head toward a crudely lettered sign hanging against the board and batten siding. "Price chart is right there."

Without giving the list more than a cursory glance, Colton pulled a few bills from his wallet and extended them to Sloan. The man who Colton once called a friend snatched the money, stuffed it in his pocket, and stomped into the warehouse to fetch the purchased sacks of grain.

Colton sighed. He remembered Pastor Winslow telling him once that sometimes all a man has that he can call his own are his principles.

If taking a stand against secession, and more specifically against slavery, caused Sloan to cut friendship ties with him, then so be it.

Sloan dumped the heavy sacks on the platform and let Colton load them himself.

෨

Colton set the brake and tethered the team outside the mercantile, but before going inside to pick up his supplies, he jogged across the street to the *Juniper Springs Sentinel* office and bought two copies of the latest edition. He exchanged greetings with the editor, Jack McCaffey, and wandered out the door reading the headline.

COVINGTON PROMISES RAIL SERVICE IF ELECTED

Reading as he ambled back toward the mercantile, he collided with a man and dropped Clyde's copy of the paper he'd tucked under his arm.

He jerked his head up. "Oh, excuse me. I'm sorry."

The gentleman in the fine gray frock coat and silver brocade vest scowled and brushed imaginary dirt from his sleeve. "Watch where you're going." He straightened his silk maroon paisley cravat and proceeded to his waiting carriage, stepping on Clyde's dropped newspaper in the process.

Familiarity rang in the man's face and voice. Colton had seen him before but couldn't recall when or where. The landau carriage, with its crest-adorned door and polished brass lamps, pulled away. Colton glanced up at the sign over the door the man had just exited. The land office.

"Not very polite, is he?"

Colton turned his attention to the one making the comment. Cyrus Fletcher, Juniper Springs' only lawyer, sent a derisive frown after the carriage and bent to pick up the newspaper, brushing off some of the dirt before handing it back to Colton.

"Thanks." Colton glanced at the soiled paper. It wasn't ruined, but he switched it with the paper he'd been reading, intending to give the clean copy to Clyde Sawyer. "No, I'd say the gentleman definitely lacked manners. Do you know that fellow?"

Cyrus snorted. "I wish I didn't. That's Maxwell Rayburn, Esq."

Colton pondered the name. "Wasn't he that fancy attorney from Athens you went up against a time or two?"

"That's right. That land right-of-way case a few years ago. Shelby Covington sued to prevent local farmers from using a trail they'd used for years because it went through the tract where he was building his brickworks. The farmers weren't damaging anything—they were just passing through on their way to transport their harvested crops downriver. The trail was the easiest and straightest way, but Covington denied them access. Rayburn pulled a dirty trick or two out of his sleeve, the court ruled in Covington's favor, and the farmers suffered." Cyrus looked in the direction the fancy carriage had taken, then at the building Rayburn had exited. "Wonder what he's doing up here."

&

Auralie trembled and paused halfway down the stairs. A man she didn't know stood beside the bottom step with one hand on the ornately swirled rail. The harsh glare of light behind him made his features impossible to distinguish. She hesitated, her feet frozen in place on the stairs. Every instinct told her to dash back up the stairs, run to her room, and bolt the door behind her.

"Come." His voice sounded far away and he held out his hand.

Panic spiraled within her, but her full, sweeping skirts of pink silk hampered her movements. She sent a frantic look over her shoulder. Mammy stood at the top of the stairs, shaking her head and wiping a tear away with the corner of her apron.

"Come." The voice sounded closer and more commanding.

Auralie jerked her head around. No longer at the halfway point on the stairs, she now stood three-fourths of the way down without having moved her feet an inch. Who was this man ordering her about? His chin lifted and he held his head at an arrogant angle. With outstretched fingers, he beckoned. Beyond the mysterious figure, Colton Danfield stood near the door, his hat in one hand. His other hand extended to her as well, but in a gentle, inviting manner, as if offering her a choice.

Her chest constricted, and it was hard to breathe. She realized her corset was laced much too tightly. Heat rushed into her face. When she looked down at herself, the pink silk was gone. In its place was a pearl-studded gown of white satin and Chantilly lace. A veil of matching lace cascaded from her head across her arms. A droplet trickled down her face. Was it perspiration? Or a tear?

The glaring light outside disappeared and inky blackness blanketed them. A ferocious flare of lightning blazed from the windows, illuminating the face of the man waiting for her at the foot of the stairs. His downturned mouth and sinister, narrowed eyes sent a jolt of fear through her. He pointed to her and then slowly drew a path with his finger, directing her to come and stand beside him. She sent a desperate glance beyond him toward the door, where Colton stood, but he'd vanished. Why didn't she grasp his outstretched hand while she had the chance?

"Come!" The imposing tone pronounced the single word as if it were an edict handed down from a king to his subjects.

A deafening crash of thunder made her grab her skirts and turn to scurry up the stairs, but at that moment a viselike grip encircled her arm with such force, she cried out. Clawing at the hand in a vain attempt to escape, she sought the face of the one who held her. Shelby Covington glowered down at her and pulled her by her arm down the stairs toward the man who waited for her.

"Father, please don't make me do this." The plea tore from her throat.

Beside him, her mother stood dressed entirely in black, fluttering a fan, a passive nonexpression on her face.

"Father. . ."

"Wake up, chile."

Auralie's eyes flew open, and she bolted upright with a gasp. She sat amid tangled bedcovers. A single candle flickered on the bedside table. Sweat dripped from her hair, and she sucked in great gulps of air. Mammy leaned over her, drawing Auralie into her arms.

"Yo's havin' a bad dream, honey girl. Jes' a dream, that all it is, jes' a dream. Mmm-hmm." Mammy hummed in that familiar, soothing voice she'd used to comfort Auralie for as long as she could remember. "Shh, now. Yo's gonna rouse the whole house wit' yo' hollerin'."

Auralie sagged into Mammy's embrace, relief quivering through her. She lifted her trembling hands and clung to the sweet Negro woman like she used to do as a child. Mammy continued to hum, a spiritual Auralie had heard her sing a thousand times, as she gently rocked back and forth and stroked Auralie's damp hair.

After several minutes, Mammy took Auralie's shoulders. "Honey girl, you all right now?"

"Yes." Discomfort scraped her raspy throat. "Better now. I'm sorry I awakened you."

"Nonsense, chile." The thin glow of the candle danced across Mammy's face as she retrieved a towel from the washstand. She began patting Auralie's face and neck, brushing back the damp tendrils of hair. "There now. I's jus' goin' to sit right here beside you while you fall back to sleep."

"No, Mammy. You need your sleep, and I think I want to stay awake for a while longer." She swung her feet to the floor and reached for her dressing gown.

Candlelight outlined the concern in Mammy's eyes. "Honey girl? When you was dreamin', you cried out to the Father." She stroked Auralie's hair. "Was you prayin'?"

Mammy's question jolted her. Praying? "No, I wasn't. But I think it's time I started."

❧

Auralie and Belle relaxed on the east-facing side porch where the morning sun peeked through the trees and sent rays of dappled light skittering across the tabletop. Belle's morning nausea had eased up some, and she nibbled on a piece of cinnamon toast.

"Do you think you could eat some strawberries?" Auralie offered the bowl to her cousin. "Try one."

Belle made a face. "I think I'd better stay with the toast and tea."

"That's not much of a breakfast," Auralie admonished. "Maizie and Mammy said you're supposed to be eating for two."

Belle grinned. "I'll make up for it later."

Fragrant honeysuckle scented the air, and a nearby pair of squirrels bickered over the rights to a pinecone. The late spring breeze waved the tree limbs in an impromptu waltz. The idyllic setting soothed the tension from last night's dream from Auralie's shoulders. She took another sip of coffee. This place had become her refuge, far removed from the impending reality that had prompted last night's terror. She drew in a breath and let it out slowly, easing her head back against the wicker chair's cushion and letting her eyes drift closed.

"I have an idea."

Auralie opened her eyes.

Belle's expression sparkled with anticipation. "Let's go into Juniper Springs to the dry goods store and look at material for sewing a layette for the baby. I'm going to need yards and yards of flannel for diapers, and maybe you could help me make some simple little gowns." She clasped her hands together under her chin, fingers interlaced. "Why don't we stop and see if Frances Hyatt could make something special for the baby. A christening gown, perhaps?"

Enthusiasm sparked within Auralie. "Oh, that sounds like such fun. Why don't we look for some cloth to make a little quilt? Since the baby isn't coming until fall, he—or she—will need a warm quilt."

Belle rose and pulled Auralie to her feet. "Let's go get ready. I'll tell Sam to hitch up the carriage, and we'll go right away."

Delight tickled Auralie's stomach, and she scurried inside and up the stairs to freshen up. Mammy came to repin her hair into a snood so it wouldn't tumble in disarray during the carriage ride.

"I hope the dry goods store has a good supply of flannel." Auralie grinned while Mammy dressed her hair. "Making sweet little things for the baby will be so much fun."

A tap at Auralie's bedroom door drew their attention. "Miss Auralie?" Maizie nudged the door open. "This just now come fo' you." She held out a folded missive.

The very sight of the paper in Maizie's hand sucked the breath from Auralie's lungs. Her heart hammered against her ribs, and she twisted her ring while whispering a prayer. "Please, Lord, don't let it be what I think it is." Fighting to draw a deep, steadying breath, she took the note. "Thank you, Maizie." Her name was written on the outside in her mother's unmistakable flowing script. With trembling hands, she broke the seal and unfolded the paper.

Auralie,

Mrs. Gabrielle Bolden is coming from Athens to visit on Tuesday, the twenty-second of May for the purpose of discussing the planning of your engagement ball. Her plans indicate she will stay through Thursday. Your presence is, of course, required. A carriage will be sent Monday morning, the twenty-first of May, immediately after breakfast to bring you home. Your father will see you upon your return.

Mother

Chapter 11

Auralie tiptoed out of Belle's room and quietly closed the door. Just when they thought her morning sickness had abated, another bout of nausea seized her cousin this morning.

Sympathy tugged at Auralie's heart for the poor girl. She'd finally fallen asleep after Auralie bathed her face and opened the window to allow the cool breeze coming off the mountain to enter. She descended the stairs and exited through the back door. The aroma of fresh bread greeted her at the door of the summer kitchen where she found Maizie and Mammy. "Belle is asleep. I'm going to go for a walk."

She followed the stone walkway that led past the vegetable garden where Sam worked. He nodded politely as she passed. She rounded the corner of the house by the east-facing side porch where she liked curling up with a book. But today, not even *Wuthering Heights* held any appeal.

Her mother's note and the anticipation of having to face Mrs. Bolden stole the usual joy with which she entered each day here at Belle's house. What if her future mother-in-law expected her to have detailed plans for the soiree? Other than writing a list of invitees that Perry had demanded, she'd given no thought to the upcoming event other than to dread its arrival.

She bent to pluck a clover blossom and twirl it between her thumb and forefinger. Her time would be better spent sitting at the desk in her upstairs room, making assorted lists to appease her mother and Mrs. Bolden, but drinking in the freedom of the beautiful day felt far more pressing.

The split rail fence of black locust marked the edge of the yard. She wandered past it, searching the meadow in the distance to see if the lambs were cavorting as she'd seen them do on other days.

"Mr. Danfield said I should come over and get a closer look at them." She only hesitated a moment. In a few weeks, the privilege of choice would be stripped away and she'd be in bondage, just like her mother. Today, she intended to do as she pleased.

The meadow grasses swayed in the breeze, ebbing and swelling much like the ocean billows she'd once seen. The motion eased her mind back to her childhood when she twirled and danced to the music she made up in her head. Those carefree days, spent without thought of what she'd have to endure later in life, etched sweet memories on her soul. Did her mother have similar memories? If she did, she'd never shared them. Perhaps those secret recollections were what sustained her mother now.

She neared the fence line of the Danfield farm and searched the shady slopes for the lambs. A handful of mother sheep grazed while their offspring either played or slept. Mr. Danfield was right. They were even cuter close up than when looking at them from a distance.

The same black-and-white dog she'd seen on her previous visit paced back and forth between the sheep grazing at the bottom of the hill and a secluded spot at the crest of the slope. He seemed friendly enough, but Auralie wondered if he'd mind her coming into the pasture. She carefully gathered her skirts and climbed over the fence. The dog perked up his ears and barked a couple of times but made no aggressive moves. She stood still to see if any of the lambs might approach her.

The wind calmed and plaintive bleating sounded. The dog whined and dashed back up to the top of the slope. Curious, Auralie followed.

Just beyond the crest, a plump sheep lay, periodically thrashing its legs and emitting a pitiful *baa*. Auralie crept closer and peered at the ewe that seemed in obvious distress.

Auralie looked around for signs of Mr. Danfield or his helper but could see neither. Kneeling in the deep grass, she reached a tentative hand to stroke the sheep's head. "Poor thing. Are you sick?"

The animal grunted, its doleful bleats raking across Auralie's heart. Alarmed that the sheep might be in trouble, she stood and swept her gaze across the area as far as she could see. Only the nearest portion of the cornfield was visible from where she stood. Perhaps Mr. Danfield was working on the far end of the field. She picked up her skirt and hurried down the slope.

The dog followed her but halted where the other sheep grazed and didn't appear to want to leave them. Auralie's toe caught her hem, and she stumbled and fell face-first in the meadow grass, knocking the air from her lungs. She struggled to her hands and knees, sucking in as much air as she could before getting to her feet. Dirt and grass stains marked her dress, but it mattered little. She hiked up her skirt a few inches higher and resumed her search for Colton Danfield.

She raced along the fence line that separated the pasture from the cornfield but didn't see either of the men. Stopping to catch her breath, she sent a plea heavenward.

"Lord, I know it's just a sheep, but she's in trouble, and I'm afraid she might die. Please show me where Colton is." When she'd begun thinking of him as Colton instead of Mr. Danfield, she couldn't say. She pushed the thought aside and pressed on.

Beyond the acres of corn, a small orchard perched on a hillside. She shaded her eyes and squinted. Colton's helper, the black man, worked among the trees, his back to her.

She ran toward him, too breathless to call out. As she approached, she realized he was shirtless and she hesitated, but urgency won out over propriety. Holding her skirt to avoid another spill, she hastened through the orchard. Just as she opened her mouth to call to the man, her gaze fell on his bare back. Ugly jagged scars crisscrossed his back. A wave of nausea threatened, but she ordered her stomach to be still and forced her eyes upward to the back of his head where white hairs curled tightly with black ones.

"Sir. . .could you please. . .come help. . ."

The black man spun around, his eyes widening when he caught sight of her. He glanced from side to side and took several strides to an adjacent tree. Snatching his shirt from a low-hanging branch, he shoved his arms in the sleeves and pulled the garment around him. He lowered his eyes.

"Miz Covington. I's sho' sorry. Didn' mean no disrespec'."

She shook her head and gulped air. Pointing behind her, she panted. "One of the sheep. I think it's sick. It's lying in the grass, kicking. . . . The poor thing needs help."

"What's going on?"

Auralie turned. Colton Danfield approached from the opposite side of the orchard. Alarm filled his eyes when he met her gaze.

"Miss Covington. Are you all right? Is something wrong at the Hancock place?"

She held up her hand, her respirations still coming in short gasps. "You said I could come and get a closer look at the lambs." She paused to breathe. "I was walking through the pasture and one of the sheep is down. I think it's sick or hurt. It sounds like it's in pain."

He lengthened his stride. "Where?"

She pointed. "Up past the top of that farthest slope. It's lying in the grass, groaning."

He exchanged glances with the black man. "Probably one of the ewes." He returned his gaze to her. "Most of the sheep can—" His face grew scarlet. "They don't normally need help— That is, when it's time for them to—" He sent a pleading look back to his helper who simply pressed his lips together.

"Please, come." She hoped the insistence in her tone compelled him. "I'm afraid the poor thing is dying." Her voice broke and Colton winced.

"All right. Show me."

She clutched her skirts tightly so she'd not embarrass herself by falling on her face again. He took her arm and helped her up the inclines and over the rough terrain. A fleeting thought whisked through her mind that she might enjoy his chivalry had it not been for the urgency of the situation.

As they approached the spot where the sheep lay struggling, the black-and-white dog barked furiously.

"Hush up, Free."

Free? An odd name for a dog.

She stood back a pace or two, twisting her ring, as he knelt by the sheep. He ran his hands over the wooly body and looked up. "It's as I suspected. She's in labor."

"You mean, she's going to—she's having—"

The sheep let out a groan and sharp bleat. Dizziness invaded Auralie's senses, and she feared her knees might buckle.

Colton examined the animal more closely, carefully probing the underbelly. "Well, you were right. She's in trouble. I need your help."

Auralie blanched. Surely he didn't intend for her to— "Do you want me to go back and get—"

"There's no time. Come here and help me." He sent her an imploring look. "Please."

❧

Colton tramped back up the slope with his bandana soaked in water from the tiny rivulet at the bottom of the hill. Auralie sat in the shade of the oak tree, her hem—soiled with grass stains and rumpled from kneeling next to the sheep—primly arranged over her ankles, watching the new mother and her twins get acquainted.

He couldn't stop the grin from spreading across his face and tucked the memory of their shared experience into a secret place in his heart where he kept those treasures he never wanted to forget.

The twin lambs struggled to their feet and bumped against their mother until they found their dinner. Pure exhilaration glowed on Auralie's face as she watched.

She'd paled at first when he directed her to hold the ewe, but fascination soon replaced the panicked look, and awe filled her expression as she helped Colton with the birth.

He walked over and lowered himself to the ground beside her and handed her the wet rag. She cleaned her hands then angled her head to look at Colton. "They're so beautiful. What a miraculous thing to watch. It was so. . .so. . . ."

He grinned at her. "I'm just glad you didn't swoon."

"Oh." She jerked her head to face him. "Me, too. Look what I would have missed."

He tossed his head back and laughed. He remembered wondering what it might feel like to laugh with Auralie Covington. He wasn't disappointed, and knew at that moment he was losing his heart to her.

Auralie plucked a few clover and dandelion blossoms and gathered them into a small bouquet. "Have you lived here long?"

"Just over five years." Colton relaxed against the trunk of the oak. "When Pastor Winslow retired, he bought this homestead. He'd spent forty-five years in the ministry—thirty of those years as a circuit-riding preacher. He performed my parents' wedding ceremony.

"He was up in years, and before long his health began to fail. I came over from Tucker's Gap—that's where my parents live—and stayed with him, helping him around the place." Colton smiled. "He used to say I was the grandson he never had." His smile faded. "When he went home to be with the Lord, he left this place to me."

Auralie shifted her position and tugged her hem discreetly over her ankles. "I don't remember him." She shrugged. "But then, my family doesn't attend church. The only time I ever went to church was when I visited Belle and her family."

How sad, to have to visit relatives in order to attend worship services. But Colton kept his musing to himself. "Do you visit your cousin often? I don't recall seeing you at the Hancock place before."

She shook her head. "I was away at school when Belle married Lloyd and moved here. I begged to come and visit her, but my father never allowed it until now."

Colton found this puzzling. "But you indicated at dinner last Sunday that the two of you had grown up together."

"Well." She cocked her head as if trying to figure out how to explain. "We didn't really grow up *together*. Belle's family lives south of Athens, so we only got to see each other two or three times a year. Belle is three years older than me, but we got along very well, even when we were young. When I was twelve, my father sent me away to boarding school because he said I needed to make appropriate friends."

Colton studied her dark brown eyes. "He didn't consider your cousin appropriate?"

A tiny frown creased her brow, and she appeared to be studying blades of grass. Her voice took on a pensive tone. "Not my cousin. He didn't like me spending time with the slave children. Of course, he especially didn't like it when he found out I was teaching them to read."

So, what Barnabas told him was true. "I see." He reached over and plucked a dandelion and added it to her diminutive bouquet. "Barnabas told me he remembers you."

She raised her eyes to meet his. "Barnabas?"

"The man who works with me."

Her gaze skittered in the direction of the orchard. "How does he know me?"

"He was a field slave on your father's plantation for more than fifteen years. He said he remembers seeing you coming to the slave quarters and playing with the children."

She stared off at the distant apple trees, fixing her focus on something unseen. Colton could almost hear the thoughts turning over in her mind. When she spoke again, her voice was low and strangled.

"He—Barnabas—was one of my father's field slaves?" She turned to look at him, and her eyes held a stricken look, as if some horrible vision had just been revealed to her. She shuddered visibly.

"Yes." Colton kept his tone gentle. "I bought Barnabas from your father."

She slipped her hand up and touched her trembling fingers to her lips. Tears glistened in her eyes, and an invisible fist punched Colton in the gut. He was about to apologize for upsetting her, but he couldn't imagine what he'd said to evoke such a response. Before he could say a word, she spoke first.

"And you gave him his freedom."

Colton nodded. What kind of cad was he, to make this sweet young lady cry?

Auralie dropped her hand to her midsection and her brow furrowed. "Oh mercy." The words came out as a whisper as if speaking them in a prayer. She turned her eyes back to Colton. "When I came looking for you to tell you the sheep needed help, I saw Barnabas working. He'd. . .he'd taken his shirt off, and—"

Understanding dawned. "You saw his scars."

She gave a slight nod and dashed away the tears. "I admire you for what you did, giving Barnabas his freedom."

Colton glanced off to the side, emotion welling up within his chest.

"He carries papers with him, indicating he is indentured to me, but that's just to prevent a bounty hunter from taking him." He returned his gaze to her. "Barnabas is free to go whenever he wants, and I wrote a statement on those papers saying exactly that. He chooses to stay."

She clasped her hands around her knees. "It must be a glorious thing to be able to take those papers out any time he wants to and read for himself that he is free."

Colton wasn't sure why, but Auralie's statement sent shafts of guilt needling through him. It had never occurred to him to ask Barnabas if he wanted to learn to read. He had all he could handle worrying about some unscrupulous bounty hunter coming by the place when Barnabas was alone and taking him, papers or no papers.

When he didn't answer her, she turned to him with a quizzical arch to her eyebrows. "Can Barnabas read?"

Colton pictured a courageous twelve-year-old girl sneaking off to the slave quarters to teach little colored children to read, and shame leached into his heart. "No. He can't."

Her lips parted in disbelief. "Why didn't you ever teach him to read?"

He hunched his shoulders. "I don't know. It never occurred to me." The moment the words fell out of his mouth, he regretted them. A little thing like breaking the law hadn't mattered to her at the age of twelve. With Barnabas a free man, what prevented him from teaching his friend to read?

Chapter 12

Auralie bit her lip and waited for Mr. Danfield to growl at her, pointing out that how he chose to handle his hired help was none of her business. When would she ever learn to think before she spoke? Sure enough, a frown carved a furrow in his brow, but instead of bellowing his indignation at her comment, he nodded slowly.

"You're right. I'll ask Barnabas if he'd like to learn to read." A small sheepish grin tilted his mouth at a lopsided angle. "After all, if you can teach a bunch of children to read when you were just a kid yourself, I can teach one man."

She gulped. "I'm so sorry. I don't know what comes over me sometimes. It was entirely unfitting of me to ask such a question. My father constantly berates me for stepping out of place. Please forgive me, Mr. Danfield."

A smile stretched across his face. He reached out his hand and covered hers, halting the twisting of her ring she hadn't been aware she was doing. "There's nothing to forgive. I'm glad you pointed out the opportunity to teach Barnabas to read." He gave her hand a brief squeeze before releasing it. The pressure of his fingers sent tingles up her arm, and she stifled a soft gasp. He must have felt it, too, because his eyes widened, and he glanced down at their hands the instant they parted.

Warmth stole into her cheeks. She knew she should tell him about her betrothal, but the familiar ache that pinched her stomach every time she thought about the coming marriage swelled, and she swallowed back the words.

He must have mistaken her reaction for embarrassment over her impulsive statement.

"Really, I'm not angry at you. You opened my eyes and made me see I'd neglected something very important. I should thank you."

She'd never heard a man say such a thing. All her life, she'd witnessed men assert themselves and manipulate others, bluster their authority and wield control like a weapon. Over the years, she'd learned to lower her eyes in submission and shrink into the background to make herself as invisible as possible, quietly excusing herself and tiptoeing away the moment the opportunity presented itself. But Mr. Danfield's gentle tone unnerved her. All the elocution lessons and deportment exercises she'd endured with Miss Josephine Westbrook at the Rose Hill Female Academy did not

217

equip her with a ready reply to his unexpected response.

"Mr. Danfield, I. . .I. . ."

His expression turned solicitous. "Have I upset you in some way? Because that was not my intention."

Wonderment filled her. "You didn't upset me. I didn't expect—that is, I'd assumed all men—" She stopped herself before saying something sure to insult him, but he finished her thought.

"You thought all men were like your father?"

Was she that transparent? Oddly, the idea didn't frighten her, at least not with Mr. Danfield. She relaxed her shoulders and nodded. "Yes, I suppose I do."

He sat forward and rested his arms on his upraised knees. "Pastor Winslow taught me a great deal, and he always seemed to use common, everyday things as object lessons." A twinkle lit his eyes. "Around here, that usually involves sheep."

She couldn't help but smile and raised her eyes to watch the newborn lambs again.

After a moment, he continued. "You've probably heard the parable in the Bible about the shepherd who left the ninety-nine sheep to go out and find the one that was lost. Of course, that parable is meant to illustrate how we should seek people who need the Lord, but Pastor Winslow used it to draw a different picture. What kind of man was the shepherd?"

She cocked her head and pondered the question. "I suppose he was diligent about his job."

Mr. Danfield smiled and nodded. "Yes, he was that. But what made him diligent?"

Auralie turned her gaze back to the twin lambs tottering unsteadily next to their mother. Who wouldn't want to diligently protect something so vulnerable and helpless? She lifted her shoulders. "My father would say the sheep were worth money so diligence ensured a better profit. But I presume the shepherd had a different reason."

Mr. Danfield's rich, deep-throated laugh made her heart skip, and she hoped he'd laugh again.

"The shepherd *cared* about the sheep, and he demonstrated his compassion by showing that even the least of them was just as important as the rest. Pastor Winslow used to say every one of his sheep was important, just like every one of God's children is important." He pointed to the new mother and her babies. "When you found this ewe in distress, you could have just left her to fend for herself. After all, even if she had died, there's still a whole flock of sheep down the hill."

Auralie gave a soft gasp. "I couldn't do that. Look at her. Look at those little ones. How could anyone just leave her to die?"

"Exactly my point." When she turned to look at him, he was smiling at her. "Pastor Winslow emphasized that if Jesus died for the sins of all of us, then He views every person the same way the shepherd does his sheep. The pastor's point was that we shouldn't treat some people better or worse than others because we assign them a different level of importance. It was a valuable lesson that I hope I never forget."

"Your Pastor Winslow sounds like an extraordinary man." *And so are you, Colton Danfield.* She pressed her lips together before the words found their way past her tongue. "I must say this has been a very enlightening morning, but I fear it's well past the noon hour. Belle and Mammy will be sending out a search party if I don't get back."

Mr. Danfield pushed away from the tree trunk and stood. He reached down and grasped both her hands and helped her to her feet. For a moment—an eternity—they stood facing each other with joined hands. His warm eyes and devastating smile robbed her of speech.

He released her hands and took a step backward. "May I see you home?"

At the moment, she couldn't think of anything she'd like better. She nodded and took one last look at the lambs she'd helped usher into the world. "Will they be all right?"

"Oh sure." He gave a sharp whistle. "Free will look after them." The dog came bounding up the hill, and Mr. Danfield gave him a pat. "You have two new babies to take care of, fella."

"I don't think I've ever heard of a dog named Free."

"Barnabas named him."

She smiled. No other explanation was needed.

As they approached the boundary line between the two properties, Mr. Danfield cleared his throat. "Would you be offended if I asked you to call me Colton?"

Her breath caught. *You're engaged. Tell him.* Her heart and her common sense waged war. Until it was announced, the engagement wasn't official. At least that's what she kept telling herself.

At some point, she'd already begun thinking of him as Colton, and she couldn't deny how the silent utterance of his name in her private thoughts set an entire flock of hummingbirds loose in her stomach.

"I find nothing offensive in calling you by your given name, but you must call me Auralie."

"Auralie."

She had to remind herself to breathe at the sound of her own name. The way he said it was melodic, as if the wind whispered. Her heart pounded so hard, the impact vibrated throughout her body.

What was it Belle had told her? "*All I'm trying to do is make you visualize how it could be if you were to do your own choosing.*"

❧

The grass was still wet with morning dew as Colton made his way to the pasture to check on the newest lambs. Free met him with tail wagging, as if proudly showing off *his* new babies. Only three days old, the twins stuck close to their mother, but they looked stronger than they had the morning they struggled into the world. For the hundredth time, the memory of Auralie kneeling in the grass, holding the ewe's head and crooning quietly to calm the nervous mother, slid easily into his thoughts. Who would have thought the daughter of Shelby Covington would exhibit such tender compassion? Chagrin pricked him when he remembered how he judged her—assumed she'd be spoiled and arrogant by virtue of her lineage. He was happy to be wrong.

He'd never stopped to think how a woman like Auralie lived under a cloud of intimidation, but that's exactly what she'd implied. Did Covington really bully his own daughter into submission? The idea rankled Colton more than he cared to admit.

What are you doing, Danfield? He shook his head. Time after time he warned himself against allowing feelings for Auralie to take root, and every time the feelings won out. Hadn't he pushed away the budding attraction? Didn't he try to discipline his thoughts?

"Hmph. If I did, I wasn't very successful." He reprimanded himself all the way back to the barn, but blocking Auralie from his thoughts was an exercise he found impossible. He'd exchanged a few glances and smiles with her at church yesterday—each time setting his heart to thumping like a schoolboy's. At the end of the service, Jack McCaffey snagged him to discuss some information regarding Shelby Covington's pledge to bring the railroad into their area. By the time he broke away from Jack, the Hancock carriage was leaving the churchyard.

No good could come of seeking more than friendship with her. With a heavy sigh, he grabbed a hoe from the barn and headed for the cornfield.

The sun slipped behind a cloud, and the air held the scent of rain. He began swinging his hoe at the intruding weeds, hoping to get several rows done before the skies opened up. Hard work. That's what he needed. Nothing like aching muscles and sweat to take a man's mind off. . .

In the distance, a stylish gray carriage pulled up at the Hancocks' front door. Colton straightened and squinted. Mrs. Hancock's servant, Sam, loaded bags behind the driver's seat. Auralie came out onto the porch, tying her bonnet under her chin. Mrs. Hancock followed. They hugged, and then Auralie turned toward Colton's farm and paused. He couldn't tell from the distance whether she saw him. A minute later, she and Mammy stepped into the carriage and drove off, leaving Mrs. Hancock standing and waving from the porch.

Colton leaned on his hoe and watched the carriage disappear beyond the trees. She'd not mentioned her visit was growing short, not that it was any of his business.

"Just as well," he muttered, but his words rang hollow.

❧

Colton dragged his sleeve across his forehead. His back and shoulders ached and sweat dripped from his hair, but taking out his frustrations on the weeds was better than brooding. When he got to the end of the row, he picked up the canteen looped over the fence post and took a drink. As he returned the canteen to the post, he caught sight of three men beyond his property line.

He instantly turned to ascertain Barnabas's whereabouts and found him working on fence posts near the barn. Colton returned his focus to the trio who now studied an unrolled scroll.

His surly mood kicked a notch higher. He intended to find out once and for all who these men were and what they were doing so close to his land. He strode to the edge of the cornfield toward the men. If grumpiness hadn't already taken up residence within him, he might be tempted to laugh. The men, dressed in fine suits, brocade vests with glittering watch chains, and silk cravats, looked as out of place tramping around through the underbrush as a mule in church. Engrossed in whatever the paper in their hands contained, they didn't look up until Colton called to them.

"Good afternoon, gentlemen."

The three jerked their heads up in unison. Colton stopped at the edge of his property, and one of the men walked toward him. His thick reddish brown hair and square jaw gave him an air of nobility, and Colton wondered if this was the same man Barnabas saw.

"May I ask what you're doing out here?"

The man lifted his chin and sent a sweeping glance down Colton's dirty work clothes and muddy boots. "Are you Danfield?"

"That's right." He held out his hand.

The man gave Colton's hand a brief shake. "My name is Covington." The man's haughty demeanor hung in the air like a stench from mucking out the stalls. Covington paused momentarily, as if waiting for Colton to react to the name. When Colton remained stonefaced, Covington continued. "My men and I are conducting a geographical survey, marking boundary lines for a client—an old family friend."

The hackles on the back of Colton's neck rose, and his spine stiffened. Covington's disdain didn't bother him nearly as much as what he didn't say, but Colton didn't intend to let Covington walk away without confronting him with what he knew.

"A friend of mine witnessed you several days ago, taking survey measurements across my land. I'd like to know why."

A sneer pulled one side of Covington's mouth upward. "*Your* land? Can a man who doesn't have the means to purchase land truly be called a landowner?"

Every shred of self-control Colton possessed prevented him from planting a fist on the side of Covington's aristocratic jaw. "If you'll check the record books in the land office and the tax assessor's office, you'll find I am the legal owner of this piece of property."

"Through another man's benevolence." Covington sniffed. He reached into his inside coat pocket and pulled out a small, leather-bound notebook with gold filigree stamped on the front. He flipped a few pages. "The previous owner was an old man by the name of Winslow, and he left it to you when he died."

Colton clamped his teeth and pursed his lips, determined not to allow the man to detect any inkling of agitation at the disrespectful reference to his dear friend and mentor, or his implied insult. "That is true. Does inheritance make me any less the rightful owner of the property?"

"Legally, no. At least for now."

Colton ached to grab this arrogant snob and bloody his nose, but if he landed in jail, what might happen to Barnabas?

"You didn't answer my question."

Covington tucked the notebook back into his coat pocket. "What question was that?"

Colton spread his feet and crossed his arms. "Why were you surveying across my land?"

The same insolent smirk appeared. "We were using the southeast corner of the little shanty there as a benchmark for locating the corner of the property."

No point in inviting more ridicule by informing Covington that little shanty was his home. Besides, Colton was quite certain all the condescending talk was a smoke screen. If Covington thought he could rile Colton to the point where his anger would make him take leave of his common sense, he might miss what was really going on. The first chance he got, he planned to go to town and make some inquiries with Randall Kimber at the land office. If there was anything underhanded brewing, Colton wanted to find out.

Colton uncrossed his arms and planted his hands on his hips. "I have to get back to work."

Covington snorted. "Of course you do." He turned to walk away, but Colton stopped him.

"Mr. Covington."

The man halted and turned, his forehead furrowed in patronizing disdain. "Yes?"

"A thought just occurred to me. Do you suppose your father is going to live forever?"

Covington's brows dipped. "What?"

Amusement tickled Colton's belly, but he held it in. "Unless your father lives forever, you're going to inherit Covington Plantation some day. How nice that you will become a real landowner through another man's benevolence."

Colton turned and strode back to the cornfield.

Chapter 13

Auralie forced her attention back to the discussion of tea cakes, tarts, and petit fours. Gabrielle Bolden held court in the parlor at Covington Plantation, instructing Auralie on the proper arrangement of the buffet table for tea. The woman destined to be Auralie's mother-in-law arrived armed with lists, schedules, menus, and decoration plans, complete with instructions for Auralie and her mother.

"You do understand, of course, each menu item has been selected with utmost thought and consideration for color, shape, and texture, as well as taste."

"Forgive my confusion, Mrs. Bolden." Auralie intertwined her fingers in her lap, twisting her ring. She curled her toes inside her slippers at the disapproving frown from her mother, who sat across the room. "I was under the impression the engagement party would be held in the evening. I don't understand the need for planning an afternoon tea."

Mrs. Bolden raised one eyebrow. "There will be very important people coming from as far as Atlanta and Augusta—senators and their wives, diplomats, and various dignitaries. Some will arrive in the afternoon, and we must be prepared to serve them refreshments befitting their station."

Auralie wilted under the scrutinizing glare of the woman's green eyes. She didn't care a fig about planning this soiree, but her mother did. As she expected, an indignant cough came from across the room.

"Auralie received the guest list from your son and has spent a great deal of time in preparation for the announcement party."

Auralie's eyes widened. How could her mother speak such an exaggeration? "Mother, I—"

The elder Covington woman merely gave a nearly imperceptible shake of her head to Auralie. "We're quite prepared to entertain the most elite of those listed and will take every pain necessary to ensure a most triumphant event, surpassed only by the wedding itself."

Mrs. Bolden pressed her lips together in an artificial and condescending smile. "Of course."

Auralie wasn't fooled. Gabrielle Bolden intended to dictate every detail of the event.

Phoebe Covington refused to be outdone. "I've commissioned ten ivory tablecloths of the finest Irish linen, to be overlaid with Belgian lace.

In addition, I've ordered twelve dozen napkins in a coordinating brocade." She finished with a slight bob of her head, no doubt intended to put an exclamation point on her announcement.

Mrs. Bolden advised that the etched stemware she'd ordered from Boston should arrive any day. Auralie's mother described the finest of silver and crystal candelabras she'd chosen for the serving table. The duet of egos made Auralie dizzy, and she longed to be back in the sheep meadow with Colton, watching the lambs. She stiffened her jaw against the yawn that threatened to expose her boredom.

Auralie's mother tugged at her cuff and sat forward in her chair. "Mrs. Bolden, our cook makes an excellent pecan shortbread that is particularly nice with tea."

Mrs. Bolden fluttered her hand in a dismissive motion and uttered an airy titter. "Oh my dear Mrs. Covington, we will bring in the best chefs and pastry artists from Savannah and Charleston. Surely you didn't think to entrust such an important occasion to your servants." She pressed a lace-gloved hand to her bosom and shook her head. None of her precise curls dared to slip out of place.

Auralie's stomach rolled over. Is this what her life was destined to be?

"So, let us summarize what we have thus far." Mrs. Bolden perched a pair of bejeweled eyeglasses on the bridge of her nose and looked over the sheet of stationery in front of her on which she'd written several lists.

"For the tea, we shall serve Darjeeling, orange pekoe, ginger spice tea, and a delightful oolong tea I sampled the last time I was in Richmond." She jotted down a notation, and then sent an evaluating glance around the room. "This room might do for the tea. If the weather is nice, we'll leave those french doors open to the veranda. That way the space might not seem so cramped."

Auralie gulped. Cramped? If the cavernous room was any larger, it would echo. She slid her gaze to the window and wondered for the twentieth time that day what Colton was doing, and whether he knew she'd left Belle's.

"Miss Auralie, you mustn't daydream." Mrs. Bolden's voice, while veiled with overtones of refinement, grated on Auralie's ears. "My son will expect his wife to be attuned to his needs and be capable of engaging in intelligent conversation. You can hardly do that while staring out the window."

"Yes ma'am." Auralie itched to have this ordeal over. A quick glance showed Mother's displeasure at her daughter's lack of attention. A knot twisted in Auralie's stomach.

Lord, I'm not giving up praying and asking You to please put a stop to this marriage. I love You, Lord. Help me trust You with this.

She tried to relax her stomach muscles that had begun to cramp. Mrs. Bolden went down her list of delicacies for the afternoon tea.

"Finger sandwiches of cucumber, watercress, liver pâté, and veal pâté. As accompaniments to the sandwiches, tomato aspic, cranberry apple press, and ambrosia will be offered." She checked off the items as she announced them. "We must have at least four different kinds of tarts, equally pleasing to the eye as to the palate. With that in mind, I've chosen red current tarts, lemon chess tarts, marmalade tarts, and ginger buttermilk tarts." She glanced up at Auralie and her mother, as if daring them to challenge any of her choices.

"An exquisite variety." Her mother's stiff smile appeared ready to crack. "They will make an interesting arrangement on the platters."

Auralie's back ached from sitting in such a stiff position, but she dared not move and draw attention to herself.

Mrs. Bolden gave a single nod and turned a page. "I've selected the following pastries: Bavarian cream, chocolate liqueur, brandied apricot, and sherried fig. Of course the finest spiced tea cakes and petit fours will be a necessity." She released a sigh, as if she'd spent the entire morning in the kitchen creating the delectable tidbits listed on her paper.

"Mrs. Bolden, I don't mean to be disagreeable, but none of us are certain when Perry will arrive back on American shores." Auralie swallowed back a spoonful of guilt at her fib. Disagreeing was exactly what she wished to do. "Hadn't we ought to wait until he is home before making such lavish plans?"

A tiny frown tilted Gabrielle Bolden's brow into a V. "The last communication we had from Perry indicated he was sailing on the twenty-fifth of April. Allowing approximately six weeks for the trans-Atlantic voyage, and barring adverse weather, he should arrive within the next two weeks."

"I see." Invisible fingers clutched Auralie's throat. "The letter I received was water stained and the date of his departure was blurred." Two weeks. She envisioned a prisoner counting off the days until his execution.

Dear God, please intervene. The time is growing so short. I beg You to free me from this marriage.

Mrs. Bolden cleared her throat, her annoyance clearly visible. "Now let us discuss the menu for the ball."

The woman droned on for the next hour, introducing an extensive list of rich and impressive foods. By the time their meeting was concluded, Auralie didn't care if she ever saw food again. But she still had to endure a luncheon with both her mother and future mother-in-law. She managed to swallow a few bites but longed to be back on Belle's side porch, listening to her cousin tease and laugh and watching the lambs frolic in the distant pasture.

While her mother and Mrs. Bolden retired to the conservatory, Auralie slipped upstairs to her room. Exhaustion overwhelmed her and she collapsed on the bed. Within minutes, Mammy tapped on her door and came bustling over to the bed.

"Let me he'p you get that gown off so's you can take a nap. You look worn to a frazzle."

As Mammy unfastened the garment, the starch Auralie employed to get her through the hours spent with Mrs. Bolden and her mother evaporated, and she melted into tears. "Mammy, it's awful. If I have to spend another day with that woman, I'll lose whatever sanity I have left." She whirled around to face her dear old friend. "What if Perry is just like her? What if he's worse?" She covered her face with her hands. "I can't do this."

Mammy slipped the gown and crinolines off. "There, there, honey girl. Did yo' fo'get we's prayin'? We beggin' God fo' His mercy, and He hear us. Now you come ovah here and rest, while ole Mammy sit right here in dis chair beside you."

Auralie curled into a ball on the bed while Mammy covered her with a light sheet. "There is one good thing. Father was called away on business at the last minute, so I didn't have to face his inquisition."

"I don' know what dat is, but it don' sound good."

Auralie propped her head up with one hand. "Mammy, I want to go back to Belle's house."

A smile twitched around Mammy's lips. "Did you tell yo' mama that Miss Belle be in da family way?"

"No! And don't you say anything. Mother would never allow me to go back if she knew Belle was expecting. She wouldn't think it proper because I'm yet unmarried." She snuffled a giggle.

Mammy angled her head and plopped one fist on her ample hip. "What be ticklin' yo' funny bone?"

Perhaps it was the depth of her exhaustion, but she suddenly couldn't stop laughing. Gales of mirth brought tears to her eyes, and she pressed her hands to her stomach and held her midsection. "Oh my goodness. . ." She wiped her eyes. "When Mother asked about my activities while I was visiting Belle, I had to bite my lip to keep from giggling. Can't you see the expression on Mother's face if she knew I'd carried lemonade to Colton and Barnabas, had Sunday dinner with a farmer, helped in the birthing of two lambs, and sat in the meadow grass under a tree getting to know Colton?" She burst into laughter again. "She'd swoon."

Mammy's shoulders shook silently and a broad smile split her face. "Honey girl, I jus' loves hearin' you laugh."

Auralie sat up and reached for Mammy's hand. "I want to go back. As soon as Mrs. Bolden leaves, I want to go back to Belle's."

❧

Auralie begged to be excused from the discussion of flower arrangements, candelabras, and string quartets, claiming a headache. It wasn't a lie. Her head hadn't stopped throbbing from the moment Gabrielle Bolden stepped through the front door. Thank goodness the woman was leaving in the morning.

A late afternoon breeze wafted through the double doors leading to the small private balcony off Auralie's bedroom. How many times had she stood out there as a girl, attempting to see past the oaks and pines to the slave quarters hidden beyond the rise behind the stables. Where were those children now—the ones she'd taught to read? Were they still working at Covington Plantation? Had they been sold? Were they still alive?

A shudder rippled through her as she recalled the ghastly scars on Barnabas's back. She turned away from the balcony and tried to banish the unspeakable picture from her thoughts. Instead, she welcomed the image of Colton and his sheep. She reclined on the velvet-covered chaise and let her eyes drift closed. Colton's lopsided grin and the newborn lambs eased into her musings. A thrill danced through her stomach when she remembered his hand over hers.

The urgency of the mother sheep's dilemma and the exhilaration of witnessing the births had taken center stage that day. Afterward, as they'd sat beneath the oak and talked, she didn't think to tell Colton she'd been bidden to return home in a few days. She knew it was presumptuous to think he'd care whether she stayed or left, but she wanted to *think* he cared. When the carriage had arrived from Covington Plantation two mornings ago, she remembered pausing to look across the meadow toward Colton's place. She'd seen him in the cornfield, but the distance prevented her from seeing his face. She wished now she'd told him good-bye.

She shook her head and opened her eyes. "I must stop this. God, unless You act in a miraculous way, I'm going to spend the rest of my life with Perry, not Colton."

She swung her feet off the side of the chaise and sat up. Colton's deep-throated laughter lingered in her mind, as did his promise to ask Barnabas if he wanted to learn to read. Her heart smiled imagining the stirring of realization in Barnabas's eyes when he read his first word. Oh, how she'd love to be there to witness it.

An idea dawned. Of course, why hadn't she thought of it before?

She rose and crossed to her bedroom door, cracking it open. She peeked out and listened. Her mother and Mrs. Bolden must still be trying to outdo each other over the plans to decorate the ballroom for the upcoming festivities. She tiptoed into the hall and headed toward the attic staircase and the wonderland of adventure hidden away on the third floor. She'd spent countless days up there as a child, exploring and playing games of imagination.

One of the steps creaked beneath her foot. She froze and held her breath, listening. A snicker wiggled its way up her throat when she recalled the times she and Belle spent childhood days creeping through the attic, hoping to avoid detection by the adults. No one came to investigate, so she climbed up the steep, narrow staircase to the whitewashed, chipped door.

The attic appeared much smaller than she remembered, and much more cluttered. Sunlight fell in through two small windows. Sheet-covered furniture created ghostly forms, stacks of crates sat haphazardly arranged, and several rolled up carpets leaned against one wall. But the item for which she searched was nowhere in sight. As quietly as possible, she moved crates and pushed a chair to one side, stirring dust motes that floated in the light streaming from the window, like tiny fairies dancing on sunbeams.

A small chest with a broken latch sat beneath the window. Inside she found dresses she'd worn when she was a child. A tug of remembrance caused her to pick them up and finger the cloth. They weren't fancy. No ribbons or special stitching, no pearl buttons or satin sashes adorned them. They were the simple dresses she'd worn to play. She sorted through the pile.

And she remembered.

A spark of anger kindled within her. "These are the dresses I took to the slave children. I remember giving these to the little girls when I sneaked down there with a basket of cookies and fruit. How did they get up here in the attic?" There was only one way, and it grieved her to think her father had ordered the little slave girls to give back the dresses she'd outgrown and had given to them. She tucked them back into the chest and closed it, sadness gripping her heart.

The dancing fairies tickled her nose, and she pinched her nostrils shut to ward off a sneeze. A tapestry lay across an unwieldy lump. Auralie moved a birdcage and an old dress form and pulled back the tapestry to find the object of her search—an old leather-bound trunk where her childhood storybooks were packed.

The hinges squeaked when she lifted the lid. She paused and glanced over her shoulder. No footsteps sounded on the stairs—no voice challenged her right to be in the attic. Her hands rummaged through the trunk, extracting volumes to hold up to the light so she could read their titles. Finally her fingers found the one for which she searched.

"McGuffey's Second Eclectic Reader." A smile warmed her all the way to her toes. The same book she'd used to teach the slave children to read would unlock a whole new world for Barnabas as well. She closed the trunk lid and replaced the tapestry and other items. Slipping the book within the folds of her skirt, she sneaked back down the stairs to her room.

Chapter 14

Auralie removed her bonnet. "It's only been a week, but it feels like I've been gone for a year."

Belle's merry laugh was balm to her soul, and she pulled her cousin into a hug.

"Sam is taking your bags up to your room, and I asked him to open the windows in there as well." Belle squeezed Auralie again. "Oh, it's so good to have you home." She giggled. "I meant it's so good to have you back."

"I knew what you meant." Auralie cocked her head. "Being here feels like what *home* is supposed to mean." She looped her arm through Belle's, and they headed for their favorite wicker chairs on the side porch. "Have you heard any more from Lloyd?"

Belle regaled her with all the details of Lloyd's last letter. "He said he might come home by the end of June, but only for a couple of weeks."

"Have you told him yet?" A warm flush filled Auralie's face. "That you're..."

Belle shook her head. "Some things you just can't put in a letter. But I did write that I had a special surprise for him when he returned home." She sighed. "I could barely contain myself when I answered his last letter. I'm just aching to tell him. He's going to be a wonderful father."

Maizie stepped out onto the porch with a tray and set it down on the small table between the two chairs. "I made some fresh lemonade, 'cause I know it yo' fav'rite, Miss Auralie. An' dem cookies be Miss Belle's fav'rite snickerdoodles." She leaned toward Auralie. "It be real good to have you back. You make Miss Belle smile." The black woman grinned and bustled back to the summer kitchen.

"Poor Maizie. I'm afraid I've been rather grumpy." Belle nibbled on a cinnamon-encrusted cookie. "Does Mr. Danfield know you're back?"

Auralie paused with her frosty glass of lemonade halfway to her lips. She could attempt to pull a veil over Belle's eyes, but her cousin knew her well. "I doubt it. He's much too busy with his farm and his sheep to care one way or the other anyway." She took a long sip of lemonade and allowed herself to hope she was wrong.

Belle arched her eyebrows. "It might interest you to know that he stopped by here two days ago."

"He did?" Auralie's heart turned over, and she knew the spark in her voice betrayed her.

Belle munched on another cookie. "I'm so hungry these days. Maizie says I'm eating for two, so I'm supposed to be hungry."

Auralie waited.

Belle patted her lips with a napkin. "Remind me later to show you the little gown I finished for the baby while you were gone. It's so tiny, but Maizie assures me it's plenty large enough for a newborn. I embroidered a delicate design in yellow around the neck, and the stitches—"

"Belle?"

"Hmm?"

"Are you going to tell me why Colton...uh, Mr. Danfield stopped by?"

The twinkle in her cousin's eyes belied her innocent expression. "Oh, I thought you were much too busy to care one way or the other."

"*Belle*...I said *he* was probably much too busy. Now are you going to tell me or am I going to confiscate the rest of those cookies?"

Giggles bubbled from Belle's throat, and she leaned forward as if divulging a great secret. "When I saw him walking across the meadow, I met him on the front porch. He seemed...kind of lost. He mumbled something about lambs, and then he asked if I'd heard from you. I said no, and he just stood there like he didn't know what else to say." She pressed her hand to her chest. "It was so romantic."

Romantic? Auralie couldn't see Belle's reasoning, but perhaps being in the family way made her take strange notions. "Is that all? I mean, did he say anything else?"

Belle took on a sympathetic expression. "He asked me if I would give you a message the next time I saw you." She sighed and tipped her head to one side.

"And?"

"And what?"

Auralie gritted her teeth. "If you don't tell me what he said, Belle, I swear I'm going to—"

Belle dissolved into a burst of laughter, and Auralie sat there trying to scowl at her cousin. Finally wiping her eyes, Belle fanned herself with her napkin. "He said to tell you the lambs were running and playing. And he said something else—something about keeping his promise."

A thrill swelled in her midsection. He was teaching Barnabas to read. She couldn't contain the joy that fluttered through her. A smile spread across her face.

"Well?"

Auralie glanced at Belle. "Well, what?"

Belle crossed her arms over her chest in mock indignation. "Are you going to tell me what this promise is that he's keeping?"

A song took wing in Auralie's heart, but this was not something she could share.

"No."

≈

Belle pretended to sulk, but Auralie knew her cousin wasn't truly miffed, especially when she gave Auralie a hug and told her she was going to take a nap. Auralie opened her bag and found the McGuffey's reader tucked in between a chemise and a nightgown. After checking to make sure Belle was asleep, she took the book and headed to the summer kitchen where she found Mammy and Maizie singing while they worked.

"Maizie, are there any more of those snickerdoodles left?"

"They sho' is. Miss Belle still hungry?"

"No." Auralie bit her lip and wondered if she should divulge her purpose for asking. "Might I get a dozen or so in a small basket?"

She slid her gaze to Mammy who raised one eyebrow and gave her a knowing look. Maizie fetched a basket and lined it with a checkered napkin, filling it with the spicy confections. All the while, Mammy spoke without saying a word, but her eyes warned Auralie to guard her heart.

"Thank you, Maizie." She glanced back at Mammy. "I won't be long."

It was all she could do to keep from skipping down the stone walkway. With the McGuffey's tucked under her arm, she set out across the meadow, her focus fixed on the hillside where the sheep grazed. A number of lambs pranced and scampered to and fro, but Auralie couldn't distinguish which ones were the twins she helped birth. The closer she got, the greater the joy in her heart.

She lifted her face to the spring breeze, relishing the feel of freedom. She never realized before how sweet the meadow grass smelled or how soothing the harmony of the birds. What a privilege to drink it in and let it saturate her spirit.

"What are you doing here?"

Auralie jerked her head toward the voice that bellowed across the meadow from the wooded area that bordered Colton's place. Three men, looking entirely out of place in their tailored frock coats and fancy vests, stood in a cluster at the edge of the woods with measuring equipment. One of them was her brother. She halted as he strode toward her, his expression stormy.

"Dale. What are *you* doing here?"

He planted his hands on his hips. "Suppose you answer my question first, little sister."

Her hands grew clammy and her pulse tapped out a staccato beat. "I'm visiting with Cousin Belle." She turned and pointed. "That's her and Lloyd's house."

Dale glowered at her. "I know where our cousin lives, and Father said something about you visiting her while Lloyd is away. But what are you doing *here*?" He gestured around them. "This isn't Lloyd Hancock's land. It belongs to a man named Danfield."

She never realized before how much Dale's voice sounded like their father's. "I'm aware of whose land it is. Mr. Danfield said I could come and watch the lambs whenever I wanted."

A sarcastic smirk tipped one corner of Dale's mouth. "The lambs. I suppose you're bringing cookies to the lambs as well?" He thumped his fingers against her basket.

"I'm merely being neighborly."

Dale crossed his arms across his chest. "Neighborly. Dirt farmers are not our neighbors, Auralie."

"Oh, stop being such a snob, Dale. There is nothing wrong with extending a kindness."

He narrowed his eyes at her. "Do I have to remind you that you're engaged to Perry Bolden?"

Her engagement was the one thing of which she needed no reminding. "The engagement hasn't been formally announced. Besides, I'm not doing anything wrong."

"Auralie, think about what you're doing." He hissed through clenched teeth at her. "The Boldens are very influential and powerful. You're endangering your reputation—and Perry's. What will Perry think when he arrives home and learns you've been consorting with the likes of Danfield? Not to mention Thaddeus Bolden is Father's biggest supporter. He'd be outraged if he knew you were traipsing around seeing another man behind his son's back."

"Oh, for goodness' sake. You make it sound as if I'm committing some horrible sin." Auralie's ire swelled in her stomach. Her purpose in coming back to Belle's was to escape the rigid parameters under which she was forced to conduct herself at Covington Plantation—at least for a time. "How is taking a basket of cookies to a neighbor outrageous?"

"A family of our standing in the state is always under the magnifying glass." He leaned in closer so he was nearly nose to nose with her. "And don't forget the effect any indiscretions of yours could have on my future with Gwendolyn. Our wedding is less than a month away, and I won't take kindly to you creating a scandal."

Auralie's mouth fell open. "A scandal! Dale, what are you accusing me of?"

Dale's hand snaked out and curled around her arm. "Anything you do to create gossip will not only destroy your union with Perry Bolden, it could also ruin Father's chances for winning the election."

She tried to yank her arm away, but Dale held it fast. "I'm not as naive as you think, Dale. I know why I'm being forced into this marriage. Thaddeus Bolden is paying a great deal of money to smooth Father's way to the governor's seat in exchange for political favors." She pulled against Dale's grip again and when she did so, the McGuffey's reader she had tucked under her arm fell at her feet.

Dale bent and snatched it up. "What do you plan to do with this?"

She froze and her mouth refused to work. When she tried to take it back, Dale pulled it out of her reach.

"Up to your old habits? I seem to recall Father sending you away to school to protect the family name the last time you used this book." He glanced over his shoulder toward Colton's place. "Little sister, teaching a slave to read is against the law."

"Barnabas isn't a slave. He's free." The instant she uttered the words, she wished she could snatch them back, but it was too late.

Dale's eyes widened. "Is that so? If that is the case, Danfield is in violation of the law. Any slave owner who frees a slave is expected to see to it he leaves the state."

Embers of anger sparked to life within her. "Barnabas carries papers showing he is indentured to Colton Danfield, not that it's any of your business."

"You best mind your place and do what's expected of you." He shoved the McGuffey's into his pocket. "Father isn't going to be happy about this." He started to stomp away, but she called after him.

"Dale, I'm not anybody's property. Not Father's and not Perry's."

He turned with his arms akimbo. "That sounds like you're declaring your independence."

She tilted her head and considered his challenge. "Maybe I am."

From the doorway of the barn, Colton watched the animated discussion between Auralie and her brother taking place on the far side of the sheep fence. Mixed emotions tugged him in multiple directions. When he'd caught sight of her coming across the meadow with a basket over her arm, his heart leaped in his chest. He'd thought he'd seen the last of her after she climbed into that fancy carriage almost a week ago. Emptiness dogged his steps for days. How he wanted to tell her about the way Barnabas's eyes lit up when Colton asked him if he'd like to learn to read. Just when he'd gotten accustomed to knowing she was close by, running into her at church, watching her laughing at the lambs' antics, she left without so much as a good-bye.

Seeing she'd returned initiated explosions of pure joy churning through him he didn't want to contain. After weeks of sending his heart explicit instructions to keep Auralie Covington at arm's length, exhilaration broke through like a landslide.

A check in his spirit snagged his attention. In tandem with the thrill, gall burned in his chest watching the confrontation between her and her brother. He couldn't hear their words, but their posture and gestures bespoke anger. The only thing that prevented him from charging to Auralie's defense was the certainty that the argument was about him. Auralie was, after all, headed in the direction of the sheep pasture when her brother intercepted her. No doubt Dale Covington considered him unfit company for his sister.

The siblings parted, and the slump of Auralie's shoulders sent an arrow of grief through Colton. She stood looking toward his place, as if trying to decide whether to proceed. Finally, she turned and headed back to the Hancock home.

Colton's stomach curled into a knot of frustration. Common sense told him he had no business having feelings for a girl like Auralie. His heart disagreed.

He set aside the ax he'd been repairing and headed to the orchard where Barnabas was pruning some of the apple trees the deer had damaged. His friend waved when he saw him coming.

"We goin' to have a good crop o' apples this year, Mistah Colton, if dem deer don't eat 'em all." Barnabas pulled on one of the limbs pointing out the dozens of buds. "Even better than las' year."

Colton looked over the trees Barnabas had finished. He'd done his usual fine job. But examining Barnabas's work wasn't his reason for hiking down to the orchard. "Those men are back again."

Barnabas craned his neck and looked through the trees. "How many times dey gots to measure?"

Colton swept his gaze around the perimeter of the orchard and down past the pasture where the forested land in question bordered his. "That has me concerned as well. It doesn't generally require a team of three men to make repeated visits over a period of two weeks to determine where the property lines lie. I told you I already had words with Covington and he evaded my question about why they felt the need to take calculations across my land. Something doesn't smell right about this." He slapped Barnabas on the shoulder. "Just. . .be careful. Keep your eyes and ears open, especially when you're out here working alone."

"Mistah Colton, you know I always carry my paper wi' me." He patted his shirt pocket. "God be takin' care o' me, so don' you fret none."

"I know. You must think I have no faith at all, the number of times I've asked you about those papers."

Barnabas grinned. "No suh. You a man o' faith, all right. Otherwise, why you be lookin' over 'cross the meadow a hundred times a day? Mm hm, I seen you—yo' eyes hungry, searchin', expectin', waitin'. It take faith to believe she comin' back."

Colton pursed his lips. The man was downright uncanny sometimes in the way he could look straight through Colton and see his whole being laid out like a page in a book. Barnabas might not be able to read words, but there weren't too many men Colton knew who could read hearts.

He rubbed his hand over his chin. "She's back."

Barnabas threw his head back in a deep, rich, joyous laugh. "See there? Who says you ain't got no faith?"

Chapter 15

C olton walked out of the post office and tucked a letter from his parents into his vest pocket, saving it to share with Barnabas over a cup of coffee. He crossed the street to the general store.

"Mornin', Clyde."

"Howdy, Colton. I'll be right with you. Sweet Pea has me rearranging these shelves."

Betsy cackled. "If I can get Clyde to move faster than a snail."

"No hurry. I'll just help myself to the peppermint sticks." Colton grinned and stuck his hand in the glass jar on the counter.

Clyde dusted his hands on his apron. "What brings you to town today, Colton?"

"I had a letter to mail to my mother and father back in Tucker's Gap." He patted the envelope in his pocket. "Mother must have had the same idea."

He didn't mention his other errand—stopping by the land office. He loved Clyde and Betsy dearly, but Betsy didn't always know when to keep information to herself.

Clyde nodded. "What can we get for you today, my friend?"

Colton sucked on the peppermint stick. "Pound of coffee, couple bars of lye soap, tin of sorghum, and a can of neat's-foot oil."

Clyde gathered the items and ciphered the total. "Anything else?"

He pulled the sweet confection from his mouth and pointed it at Clyde. "Half dozen peppermints sticks. And a box of cartridges—twenty-two caliber, rimfire."

Clyde set the box of ammunition on the counter beside the other items. "Fixin' to do some huntin'?" He caught Colton's eye. "Or are you expectin' trouble?"

Colton bit off the end of the peppermint stick. "Just bein' prepared."

Betsy came around the end of the counter, glancing this way and that. Nobody else was in the store. "You know that fancy-pants lawyer that was nosing around?"

Colton counted out the money for his purchases. "Maxwell Rayburn. What about him?"

"He's back." Betsy pressed her lips into a tight line and gave a single nod. "He was in here this morning. Wanted to order some expensive cigars.

238

I don't trust him. His eyes are too close together."

Clyde guffawed. "Sweet Pea doesn't like him because he called our store a second-rate establishment." Clyde leaned forward, propping his elbows on the counter. "I'd like to know why he was orderin' them ceegars here. Does that mean he plans to stick around instead of goin' back to Athens?"

Colton gathered his purchases and pondered Clyde's question. "I'd like to know the answer to that one myself. See y'all Sunday."

He walked across the street where he had left Jasper and tucked his purchases into his saddlebags. With a pat on the horse's neck, Colton mounted and reined the gelding around to the other side of town. The land office sat tucked behind the newspaper office where Colton could tether Jasper without Betsy peeking out the front window of the general store and letting her imagination run rampant.

The front door stood open to catch whatever breeze might be stirring. Colton stepped inside. A slight man with garters around his sleeves sat at the desk, his balding head bent over his work and his spectacles perched lopsided on his nose.

"Mornin'." Colton greeted the man.

The little man's glasses slid to one side when he jerked his head up. He caught them before they hit the desk. "Good morning, good morning." He set his pen aside and rose. "Mr. . . .Danville? No, no, don't tell me." He studied Colton through squinty eyes. "Danford? No, Daniels? No. . ." He tapped his finger on his nose. "Ah! Dalton! I knew I'd think of it. I never forget a name or a face."

"Uh, yes." Colton held in the chuckle that tried to snuffle out. "You're Mr. Kimber, right?"

"Randall Kimber, at your service." He straightened his shoulders. "And what can I do for you today, Mr. Danville?"

Colton's lips twisted into a half smile. "I was hoping you could give me some information." He gestured toward the map on the wall. "May I?"

"Of course, of course." Mr. Kimber stepped aside while Colton moved over to the map and pointed to a section.

"My land is right here." He tapped his finger on the forty-acre section a half mile from the Chestatee River, then slid his finger over to trace the massive area behind his land. "I understand this section of timber is for sale."

Mr. Kimber shook his head. "No, no, not for sale anymore. That thousand-acre tract has been purchased. Sorry if you were interested in buying it yourself, Mr. Darnell. You're a little late."

Colton tried to appear disappointed. "Oh? Someone's already bought it?"

"That's right, that's right." Kimber bobbed his head. "None other than, uh—Theodore Bolden." He appeared pleased with himself for having such an important tidbit of information. "Prime timberland, prime—from what I'm told. I've never actually seen the land myself."

"I see." Despite Mr. Kimber's mistake on the first name, there was no mistaking Thaddeus Bolden was the "old family friend" of whom Auralie's brother spoke. Uneasiness poked Colton's gut. If Bolden's men went in there and began clear-cutting, they'd destroy the watershed. "Did Mr. Bolden happen to say when he plans to start cutting timber?"

"Oh, no, no." Kimber's head wobbled from side to side. "Mr. Bolden wasn't here himself. It was his lawyer—a Mr. . . .uh, Radford, and of course, Mr. Tom Covingdale, Mr. Bolden's representative."

"Dale Covington?"

"Yes, yes, that's what I said."

Colton swallowed the remark he wanted to make, and it had nothing to do with Mr. Kimber's inability to remember names. "Did Mr. Covington or Mr. Rayburn make any mention of building a sawmill on the property?"

Mr. Kimber scratched his head. "No, no. Not that I recall." A smug smile slid across his features. "And I have an excellent memory if I do say so myself."

"Thank you, Mr. Kimber. Good day."

"Good day to you, Mr. Davenport."

Colton exited the office, pausing by the hitching rail to ponder the revelation. If Bolden had no plans to operate an on-site sawmill, how did he intend on transporting the timber? Dale Covington's skillful sidestepping of Colton's earlier question stirred an uncomfortable inkling in his stomach. He gritted his teeth with the realization he was about to clash with the Covington and Bolden clans.

"Hey Colton. Hold up a minute."

Colton pulled his thoughts out of the shadowy recesses of speculation and looked up. Jack McCaffey headed in his direction, striding with purpose.

"Hey Jack."

Jack held out his hand with its ever-present ink stains. They shook hands and Jack lowered his voice. "There's something I've learned that I think you need to know. Normally, I wouldn't divulge this kind of information until it comes out in the *Sentinel*, but I believe it's going to impact you personally. Thought you might want to know before you read about it in the paper."

The wariness that pricked Colton in the land office heightened. "I'm listening."

Jack glanced over his shoulder toward the land office. "Did Kimber tell you about the land deal out by your place?"

"If you mean Bolden buying up the timberland that borders my property, yes. Is there something else?"

"I have a few sources from all over the state, and I've recently been in touch with a couple of them who have contacts within the Georgia Railroad and Banking Company."

Colton shrugged. "Spur only comes as far north as Athens. What's that got to do with us?"

Jack quirked an eyebrow. "You know the Boldens and Covingtons are thick as thieves and twice as crafty. According to my sources, Covington has a contact or two at the Georgia Railroad who owe him a political favor in exchange for some dealings that went on under the table a while back." Jack flapped his hand, apparently dismissing the history to get to the meat of the issue. "Seems Covington is pulling some strings to bring the spur from Athens up into our neck of the woods—literally."

"I remember reading about his campaign promises in the *Sentinel* a couple of weeks ago, but you know how politicians are. They'll spout just about anything to get elected." Colton propped one elbow on his hand and stroked his chin. "Is this spur extension he's talking about related to that tract of timber Bolden just purchased?"

"Bolden needs a way to ship timber to the mills south of here."

Colton rolled the information over and met Jack's pointed look. "You know why Covington and his team of surveyors were taking calculations across my land, don't you?"

Jack turned his palms up and lifted his shoulders. "All I can say is, if it were me, I'd make a trip to the county seat and make sure my land deed was properly recorded."

%

Auralie ran her finger across the leather spines of the dozens of books occupying the shelves in Belle's parlor. Every title she touched brought back the memory of Dale's face when he scooped the McGuffey's off the ground and glowered at her, knowing her intent. Surely one of these volumes was appropriate for teaching Barnabas to read.

"Have you become bored with *Wuthering Heights?*"

Auralie glanced up and found Belle eyeing her from across the room. Her copy of *Wuthering Heights*—with a ribbon marking her place halfway through the book—lay on the chair she'd occupied earlier.

"No. I just thought I'd look and see what else you have."

Belle rose and crossed to the bookcase. "What are you looking for?"

"Something. . .simple."

Belle cocked her head. "Simple? That's odd since you were always the one with her nose stuck in a book when we were in our adolescence."

Auralie shrugged off Belle's observation and fluttered her fingers. "I wondered if you might have something light and easy to read."

Her cousin narrowed her eyes. "Auralie, what are you up to?"

"Who says I'm up to anything?" She didn't want to engage in a debate of the moral rights or wrongs of teaching a black man to read.

"Perhaps because I know you better than anyone." She plunked her hands on her hips. "And perhaps because I remember the trouble you got into when you were a kid teaching the slaves to read." She glanced out the front window that looked out across the meadow. "You aren't thinking what I think you're thinking, are you?"

"Belle, I—"

"Stop and consider what you're doing, Auralie. Most people frown on teaching Negros to read, whether they're free or not." The pleading tone in Belle's voice pinched Auralie's heart.

A heavy sigh escaped and she crossed to take up her copy of *Wuthering Heights* again. Controlling her frustration, she settled into the chair. "I'm quite aware of the public opinion. I happen to disagree."

Belle thrust her hands out to her sides. "There are thousands of white people who can't read."

Auralie nodded. "Yes, but in most cases, they don't care to learn. They weren't denied the privilege."

"You taught Mammy to read, didn't you?"

Auralie sucked in a breath. For years, she and Mammy kept their secret, and it thrilled her every time she saw Mammy pick up the Bible. "Yes. It's a blessing to know she can read God's Word for herself. I don't regret it."

"Does your father know she can read?"

"Of course not." She stood and approached the window where Belle still stood. "You know what would happen if he found out."

"Auralie, you're asking for trouble." Belle returned her gaze to the bookcase. "I don't think I have anything here you can use."

&

Auralie's heart grieved the silence between her and Belle in the carriage all the way to church. The space in the carriage echoed, devoid of their usual chatter and teasing. Even at the dinner table last night their stilted conversation remained limited to the weather and other inane topics. They'd been so close all their lives. How could one disagreement carve such a chasm between them?

Sam halted the carriage in front of the church and hastened to help the ladies disembark. Auralie followed Belle into the church and found their seats just as the service was beginning. She glanced across the aisle where Colton generally sat.

The black wool coat Colton normally wore to church was absent, no doubt due to the warmer temperatures. Instead, he sat in his shirtsleeves and string tie, looking as handsome as ever, except for the scowl on his face. He appeared as troubled as Auralie felt. She longed to press her fingers to his brow and smooth out the worries she saw etched there, but she didn't know what to do with her own burdens. How could she expect to comfort Colton, for whom she cared so much?

He glanced over at her, as if he could feel her gaze upon him. A small smile tipped the corners of his mouth. The now-familiar tingle she felt every time Colton smiled tiptoed through her.

She shifted her gaze to Belle who sat stiffly beside her. She didn't wish to cause her cousin distress. Perhaps it was time for her to go home. The only trouble was Covington Plantation didn't feel like home, and she couldn't look out the window there and see Colton's sheep and cornfield.

After the hymn singing, Pastor Shuford stepped into the pulpit and invited the congregation to open their Bibles to the book of Matthew, chapter twenty-five. Auralie followed along as he read the words of Jesus, describing the ministering to the hungry, thirsty, naked, and lonely.

" 'And the King shall answer and say unto them, Verily I say unto you, Inasmuch as ye have done it unto one of the least of these my brethren, ye have done it unto me.' "

Pastor Shuford went on to explain giving from the heart and expecting nothing in return, seeking injustices and remedying them with no thought to self. The preacher challenged his flock to find someone to whom they could minister—someone who could not reciprocate.

Auralie soaked up the words like a dry sponge. How she'd fretted her lack of purpose, the absence of usefulness, her china doll existence. Her heart cried out to God. *Lord, use me. Let my hands be filled with something worthwhile to minister to those who have no means to repay a kindness— unto the least of these.* Moisture burned her eyes and she blinked, but a tear escaped anyway. She discreetly dashed it away. She closed her eyes during the final prayer and inquired at God's throne if teaching people like Mammy and Barnabas to read was her calling.

When she opened her eyes, she found Belle looking at her with a mixture of confusion and pain in her expression. The congregation began filing out, pausing at the door to shake the preacher's hand. The line moved slowly and just before she arrived at the door, she felt fingers squeeze hers. She glanced down. Belle held fast to her hand.

They greeted Pastor Shuford and thanked him, then made their way to the carriage.

"Allow me."

The voice Auralie heard in her dreams turned her head. Colton stepped over and offered his hand. She placed her hand in his, and his smile sent butterfly wings fluttering through her middle.

He swept his hat off. "It's nice to see you, Auralie."

Her breath caught, and for a moment she forgot where she was. If only she could feel the touch of his hand and hear him utter her name every day for the rest of her life. For the briefest of moments, she wondered if God would mind if she'd add that to her prayer.

"It's nice seeing you as well. . .Colton."

Belle cleared her throat, rattling Auralie's consciousness. Colton still held her hand. A rush of heat skittered up her neck into her face.

Colton handed her up into the carriage and aided Belle up as well. He fidgeted with the brim of his hat. "I'd like to talk to you sometime. If that's all right."

Auralie gave him a soft smile. "I'd like that. Perhaps tomorrow?"

Colton nodded. "I could come by."

Auralie's smile widened, and the heat in her face intensified. "I think I'd like to meet you at the pasture. I love watching the lambs."

"That'd be fine." Colton took a step backward. "Until tomorrow." And the carriage pulled away.

She and Belle rode in silence for a couple of minutes before her cousin spoke. "I saw your tears in church." She reached across the seat and covered Auralie's hand with hers. "I really didn't understand."

"I know." Auralie swallowed hard. "I'm not sure I understood myself. Do you remember when I complained to you about not having a purpose except to be nothing more than a china doll?"

Belle smiled. "I remember."

"And do you remember when you said you wanted me to see how it could be if I did my own choosing?"

Belle's smile deepened. "I remember that, too."

Auralie twisted around in her seat to face Belle. "Well, I've decided to let God do my choosing for me."

Chapter 16

Auralie clutched the storybook close to her heart. "Oh Belle, how can I ever thank you?"

Belle dabbed a tear away from her eye and shrugged. "No thank-you is necessary. As I told you after church yesterday—I understand now." She touched the book with her fingertips. "This was mine when I was little. I was saving it for when I had children, but—" She slipped both arms around Auralie. "There's no reason why you can't use it now."

A thrill ran through Auralie. Her cousin understood—really understood. "Belle, I'll never forget this." She gave her a squeeze. "I can't wait to show Colton."

"Well then, go." Belle laughed and pushed her away. She flapped her hands, shooing Auralie out the door.

Invisible wings carried Auralie across the meadow. In the distance, Colton worked on the rail fence that divided the sheep pasture from the cornfield. This time, her brother wouldn't stop her. Excitement bubbled within her at the prospect of opening Barnabas's eyes to the world of written words.

"Colton!" She waved when he looked up.

He returned her wave and came to meet her. "You're certainly in a joyful disposition this morning."

Breathless from hurrying, she beamed at him. "Yes, I am." She held out the storybook. "I hope Barnabas won't be offended, but the words in this book are easy, and until he learns how the letters sound and—"

Colton held up his hand. "Whoa." He laughed. "There's no need for apology. This is a very kind thing you're doing." He glanced toward the Hancock home. "Are you sure it's all right with your cousin? Some folks don't approve."

Auralie tilted her head and gave him a nod. "At first, she didn't understand my desire to see people like Barnabas learn to read. But after yesterday's sermon, she had a change of heart."

"Ah, 'unto the least of these'." Colton smiled.

Her throat tightened. "This book belonged to Belle when she was little. She was saving it for her own children."

"Then we shall take very good care of it so we can return it to her in good condition." He reached out and grasped her hand. "Come on.

Barnabas is repairing the lean-to."

The warmth and gentle strength of his hand quickened her pulse and set butterflies loose in her middle.

As they neared the cabin, Colton grinned down at her then hollered for Barnabas. A moment later, the former slave stuck his head out of the lean-to.

"Wha'sa matter, Mistah Colton?" He set his tools down and trotted around the corner of the house. He stopped short when he saw Auralie. "Miz Covington." He dipped his head.

Bursting with excitement, Auralie motioned to the bench and rockers on the front porch. "Let's sit down."

Barnabas shifted his feet, obviously uncomfortable being seated in Auralie's presence. She looked up at him and gestured toward the bench. "Please."

He eyed the book in her hands, and she turned it so he could see the front. "Barnabas, I realize this is a child's book and you're a man. But this book is a wonderful starting place for learning to read. If you'd like, I'd love to teach you." Her heart leaped for joy when his eyes widened and a slow, broad smile stretched across his face.

"You hear dat, Mistah Colton?" His deep voice broke. "I's gonna learn to read!"

Auralie's heart swelled with joy until she wasn't sure her body could contain it. She swiped at a tear and opened the book to the first page.

❧

Colton hated leaving the next morning, especially after watching Barnabas's face glow when he read his first word—*dog*. But he decided to take Jack McCaffey's advice and confirm the land deed records at the county seat. He rode into Mount Yonah by midafternoon. The building being used temporarily to house the county records wasn't hard to find. A crude sign nailed above the door declared it the courthouse, even though it in no way resembled such a building. The residents of the county seat proudly anticipated the completion of the official new courthouse—a fine brick building—before the year was out. In the meantime, the ramshackle framed structure before him served as county offices and courtroom, if it didn't fall down first.

Colton stabled Jasper and then strode back to the courthouse. Two dirty windows at either end of the building allowed in muted light. A man sat at a desk in the corner with his back to the door, diligently laboring over paperwork.

Colton removed his hat. "Excuse me."

The man looked over his shoulder and turned the paper he was working on facedown. "Yessir, can I help you?"

"Yes, you may. I need to look up the recording of a forty-acre tract of land down near Juniper Springs."

The clerk rose from his chair, his legs bumping it backwards. His blond hair splayed out in multiple directions. "J–Juniper Springs, you say?"

Colton laid his hat on a long table that sat under one of the grimy windows. "That's right. It would have been recorded in March of 1856. Where might I find that record book?"

The clerk fumbled through two shelves of bound journals, pulling one out and pushing it back in, stacking three on the desk and then replacing them. Colton watched him, nonplussed. He assumed the records were all kept in chronological order. Finally, after shuffling several volumes, the young man pulled out the book that lay on the bottom of the stack—the one that had sat on the corner of the desk when Colton entered.

"Here it is. What would you like me to look up for you?"

The clerk's nervous mannerisms and disorganization raised Colton's suspicion. "If you don't mind, I'd rather look up the entry myself. These records are all public, are they not?"

"Well, yes. . .but, uh, some of the records aren't completed yet, so you might not be able to find them."

"Not completed?" Colton's eyebrows rose along with his misgivings. "The record I'm looking for dates back over four years ago. Seems to me there's been ample time to record the deed."

He stepped forward and reached for the volume in the clerk's hands, but the young man held on to it. Beads of sweat popped out on the fellow's forehead and upper lip. Colton kept his voice even but firm.

"Sir, as a citizen of this county, I have the right to search any of these public records. I really don't want to go get the constable, but I will if I have to."

The clerk reluctantly released the book and pressed his lips into a tight, thin line. Colton carried the journal to the table under the window. He turned pages until he found February 1856. He ran his finger down to the end of the page. The next page bore two listings entered at the end of March, and then the rest of the page contained April records.

Odd. Colton remembered the day like it was yesterday. Pastor Winslow had told Colton he knew his time on this earth was growing short, and he wanted all his affairs in order. Colton still recalled the grief that sliced through him at his dear friend's announcement. The two of them had come to the county seat together, and Colton had watched as the preacher recorded his will, and signed over ownership of his land to Colton.

He turned to get the clerk's attention, only to find him standing a few steps away, watching over Colton's shoulder. "There seems to be a page missing. March 12, 1856."

The young man wiped his hands on his pants. "Uh, that's. . . that was before I worked here." An unmistakable tremor resonated in his voice.

Colton stood and crossed his arms over his chest. "Are you not responsible for all the records in this office, those established before you were employed as well as after?"

Muscles in the clerk's neck twitched and he blanched.

Pieces of the puzzle didn't all quite fit together yet, but Colton was getting a clearer picture of how they were cut. "I don't know what's going on here, but I do know this." He stabbed his finger on the open pages of the book he'd been examining. "All that juggling around of the books you did was meant to cover up the fact that this ledger was already on your desk when I walked in." He slid his finger along the bound edge of the pages where they joined the spine. "It's not hard to see a page has been torn out. Is that what you were working on when I came in? Is that the paper you turned over so I wouldn't see it?"

The clerk's eyes shifted to and fro. When he thrust his hand out, it trembled. "I don't know what you're talking about. I just work here and do as I'm told."

"And who told you to tear out that page? Was it Maxwell Rayburn?"

A droplet of sweat dribbled down the clerk's temple. He appeared about to crumple in a heap on the floor. "I don't know anyone by that name."

Colton stuck his thumbs in his pockets. "Are you going to let me see that page you were working on?"

"No. Th–that's—it's, uh, confidential."

Anger churned in Colton's stomach, but no good would come of him losing his temper. "I don't know how much you were paid to alter these records, but it's not worth going to jail." He closed the ledger and tucked it under his arm, picked up his hat, and started for the door.

"Wait! Where are you taking that book?"

Colton turned. The fellow looked like he was going to be sick.

"To the constable's office. Would you like come along?"

"Look, mister, I was just following orders."

Colton shifted the volume to the other arm. "Whose orders?"

All the fight seeped out of the young clerk, who probably only saw the altering of the records as a chance to make some extra money. He blew out a stiff breath. "By order of Shelby Covington."

❧

Auralie and Belle carried their teacups to the side porch and settled into the comfortable chairs. The latest edition of the *Sentinel* lay on the small table between them. The headline proclaimed Shelby Covington's political ambitions and promises. The words sent conflicting emotions swirling in Auralie's stomach.

"I've come to realize this arranged marriage to Perry is but one piece in a monumental quagmire. Father is using me as a pawn in a political game of chess." She set her teacup on the table. "He wants the governor's mansion, and he'll use whatever means necessary to get there."

Belle settled her cup into its saucer. "I hate to think Uncle Shelby would do such a thing, but I'm afraid you're right. What are you going to do?"

Auralie released a sigh. "I don't know. After months of fretting and weeks of praying, I think I've finally placed the issue in God's hands. Now if I can just leave it there—"

She avoided filling in the blank. The truth was she still struggled with doubts, but if her faith were ever to grow, fully trusting God with every part of her life was the answer.

A muffled sniff sounded from Belle. Auralie turned and found her cousin blotting away a tear with her napkin. Between being in the family way and missing her husband, her cousin's weepiness attacked with regularity. Auralie reached over to pat Belle's hand.

"Missing Lloyd?"

Belle sniffed again. "Yes, but I'm frightened, too." She gestured to the newspaper. "Did you read the article on page two? The one about the state militia?"

Auralie shook her head. "I know there's been talk."

"They're saying they aren't waiting to see who will win the election, and they're beginning to form a state militia now." Belle swallowed, her effort to be brave evident. "They say they want to be ready in case Lincoln is elected and Georgia secedes. Lloyd mentioned in his last letter that a lot of men are signing up already."

"Did he say he plans to sign up?"

"No, but I fear that's what he's implying."

Auralie squeezed Belle's hand. "But he doesn't know about the baby yet. That will make a difference, won't it?"

Belle laid her hand over her abdomen, a gesture Auralie had often seen her do. "I hope so."

As so often happened, Auralie's gaze drifted toward Colton's place. Sheep dotted the pasture like scattered clumps of snow. She wondered silently if he would enlist in the militia if conflict arose. What a difficult decision. Would he fight to defend Georgia? Every time she heard the topic debated, the outcry was always for state's rights, but in truth, one of the rights for which they clamored was the right to own slaves. She couldn't imagine Colton fighting *for* slavery.

Belle flicked a mosquito from her arm. "Do you think the forming of the militia will affect your father's election?"

Auralie lifted her shoulders. "I don't know. Dale has announced he intends to stand up for Georgia and defend her rights. Father was incensed. He kept telling Dale he could send 'a couple of darkies' in his place, but Dale rejected that. He said he would purchase a commission and be an officer."

Belle's mouth dropped open. "But he and Gwendolyn are going to be married next month. Surely he wouldn't go off to join the militia and leave his bride."

"That's what he said." Auralie sipped her now cooled tea. "I don't know what Gwendolyn thinks about it."

The sound of hoofbeats coming up the drive drew their attention, and Auralie's heart turned over in anticipation. Perhaps Colton had returned from the trip he'd told her he was making to the county seat. She stood and smoothed her skirt. Glancing at her reflection in the window, she gave her hair a pat and pinched her cheeks.

Belle winked at her and led the way around the corner of the porch. But it wasn't Colton. Reuben, one of her father's slaves dismounted from a tired, old gray plow horse. The blood in Auralie's veins ran cold, and she stood rooted in place. Reuben tied the horse and approached the porch. He lowered his eyes and gave a polite nod.

"Miss Covington. I has a note fo' you from yo' mothah." He held out an ivory envelope with her mother's distinctive handwriting.

Auralie stared at the folded missive as if it were a snake. Her feet wouldn't move. Her fingers of her left hand found the ring on her right and twisted it in vicious circles.

Belle stepped forward and took the note. "Thank you. If you'd like to go around to the summer kitchen, I'm sure Maizie will give you some refreshment and Sam will water your horse."

Reuben bobbed his head. "Thank ya kindly, ma'am." He disappeared around the corner of the house.

Belle turned with the letter in her hand. "You have to read it."

Auralie shook her head, as if the vehemence of the motion would keep the words of the letter at bay. But as much as she wanted to pretend it didn't exist, she couldn't tear her eyes from the envelope.

"It's happening." Her own voice sounded like it belonged to someone else. Her prayers had found their way to God's throne room, she was sure of it. He heard the cry of her heart. She'd said that very morning she intended to trust Him with every part of her life. The moment of truth had arrived, and she had a choice. She could cling to God in faith, or she could crumble.

Mammy came bustling through the side door. "Reuben jus' came to the back do', and he say he brung a—"

Mammy's groan sounded like glass breaking.

Auralie took the note and slid her finger under the edge to break the seal. With Mammy on one side of her and Belle on the other, she read her mother's words.

Auralie,
   Perry Bolden has telegraphed from New York. His ship has docked, and he plans to take the southbound train scheduled to leave for Charleston on Thursday, May 31st.

May thirty-first. Perry was boarding the train today to come home. Auralie's stomach churned, but she continued to read.

   After attending to some business in Charleston, he will take the train to Augusta where a carriage will meet him and bring him home. He plans to arrive by June the 5th.
   A carriage will be sent for you on Monday, June 4th.
                                                              Mother

Auralie crumpled the note in her hand. As much as it pained her, she owed it to Colton to be honest with him.

Chapter 17

"Engaged?"

Colton almost choked on the word. His delight at seeing Auralie coming through the meadow with the morning sun playing off her hair evaporated. The impact of her statement left him reeling.

"Colton, I'm so sorry I didn't tell you sooner." She leaned against one of the apple trees and twisted her ring. "At first, I didn't think it was appropriate to even mention it. You and I were barely acquainted."

He stared at her, but she wouldn't look him in the eye. Instead, her gaze shifted everywhere except at him.

"After a while, I kept telling myself the engagement wasn't official until it was announced." She tipped her head. "After we became. . .friends, I didn't want to read more into the friendship than was truly there."

Colton hadn't yet attempted to put into words what was truly there, but he knew without a doubt that it went beyond friendship. Pain sliced through his heart and realization overtook him. *I'm in love with her.*

"Every time I intended to tell you, I simply. . .couldn't." Her voice reflected her troubled spirit.

If he reacted in anger, he would only confirm to her what he now knew. He found his tongue. "I hope you didn't think I'd not want you to be with the man you love."

"But I don't." Strained emotion clouded her tone and her eyes misted.

Confusion caught Colton off balance. "I don't understand. You don't want to be with your fiancé?"

She caught her lip in her teeth. Anguish—the kind born of long, silent suffering—veiled her eyes. Her voice fell to a whisper carried away by the wind. "I don't love him."

Her conflicting statements defied understanding. Colton ran his hand through his hair. "Am I to understand you're marrying a man you don't love?" He had no business asking her such a question, but he couldn't help himself.

The flush in her cheeks evidenced the humiliation racing through her at having made such a declaration. A war raged within him. Part of him longed to take her in his arms and comfort her, tell her she need not say any more. But another part of him he hadn't known existed until now wanted to confront her and demand to know why she waited until he'd fallen in love with her before telling him she was promised to another.

The lines in her brow furrowed and her voice bore a brittle tone. "Do you remember the day we met?"

How could he forget? He'd literally tripped over her. He nodded and she went on.

"I heard some men in the café that day call out to you, but there was so much commotion. I thought they'd called you Bolden."

Colton rolled back his memory to that day. He recalled the misunderstanding.

"I haven't seen my fiancé since we were children. I can't even remember what he looks like. My father and his father arranged this union four years ago. He's been studying abroad for the past five years, and now. . ." The tremble in her voice punctuated her unfinished sentence.

Now? Understanding dawned as all the pieces of the puzzle fit together into an unspeakable portrait of Shelby Covington's selfishness and greed. The man was a canker on everything that being a man, a husband, and a father meant.

"Your father has arranged for you to marry Thaddeus Bolden's son?"

Twin tears slipped from Auralie's eyes, and she nodded. "I've received a letter from my mother telling me that Perry is arriving tomorrow and I must return home." She grimaced as if she'd just tasted something bitter. "A carriage is being sent for me later this morning. I've come to tell you good-bye."

Acid gall rose in his throat as an invisible fist punched him in the gut. His hand reached out involuntarily for her, to pull her to him, but she took a step back. She clasped her hands together under her chin, her arms clamped tightly to her chest.

"Auralie, I—"

"Don't." She shook her head, as if afraid to hear what was in his heart. "Please encourage Barnabas to keep learning. And take care of those lambs." She covered her mouth with trembling fingers that muffled her words. "I'll miss you."

She picked up her skirts and ran through the orchard and across the field toward the Hancock home.

"Mistah Colton?"

Colton turned. Barnabas stood a few yards away, his expression one of sorrow as he watched Auralie leaving. "I's sorry, Mistah Colton, but I needs to tell yo' some o' the sheeps is missin'. Free was barkin', and when I went to see about it, there be a place in the fence where that orn'ry ram musta busted through. Free wouldn't leave the rest of the sheeps."

Colton gazed another long moment in Auralie's direction, wondering if his heart would ever be whole again, before he turned to join Barnabas.

❧

The lump in Auralie's throat nearly prevented her from drawing a breath as the carriage pulled away from Belle's. The sobs she'd valiantly tried to hold back won the battle as tears cascaded down her cheeks.

Mammy slipped her arm around Auralie and drew her close. "There, there, baby, don' you cry. You have me cryin', too." She rocked Auralie back and forth in a comforting motion. "Shhhh."

"Mammy, I did what you said. I prayed and asked God to intervene, to provide a way out of this marriage. Every day and night I begged God for help, but He didn't answer."

"Why you think He don't answer? Jus' 'cause He don't answer the way you want Him to, don't mean He ain't list'nin'." Mammy pulled a handkerchief from her sleeve and blotted Auralie's tears. "Maybe His answer is to change you 'stead o' changin' what happenin' around you. Ever' time a prayer leave yo' lips, yo' faith and trust grow. You know God hear you, He care, and He never leave you."

Auralie clung to Mammy. The woman's wisdom fell over Auralie like a gentle rain washing away her doubts. Until now, she'd not tried to define God's promises to her. In that heartbeat, she knew. . .He loved her. Did that mean He'd answer her prayer the way she hoped? She didn't know that yet. She did know a deeper level of trust she never before knew existed now reinforced her, regardless of what lay ahead.

Mammy squeezed her shoulders. "We jus' keep on prayin', honey girl. Sweet Lawd Jesus, please hear us. We need a touch from Yo' hand, a miracle."

A miracle. Would God grant her a miracle if she asked?

"Whoa, there!" Their driver, Reuben, called out to the horses and the carriage lurched to a stop.

Auralie and Mammy exchanged alarmed looks. "What is it, Reuben? What's the problem?"

"Trouble ahead, miss."

Auralie stuck her head out the side of the carriage and craned her neck to see what was going on. On the road just ahead, a man jerked a black man from the wooded area along the road and dragged him toward a tethered horse. Auralie's heart seized. *Barnabas!*

"Reuben, drive on up there so I can speak to that man."

"Could be dangerous, miss."

Auralie pointed. "Go."

"Yes'm." Reuben clucked to the horses.

Mammy leaned to the side. "What goin' on? Who that man be?"

Auralie glanced back at her. "I'm not sure who he is, but he has Barnabas."

The carriage pulled alongside the two men and halted. Auralie called to the man. "You there. What do you think you're doing?"

Barnabas looked up at her with an expression that made the hair stand up on the back of her neck.

The burly man with greasy hair and an unkempt beard pulled a pair of shackles from his saddlebags and clamped them on Barnabas's wrists. "Pickin' up strays, ma'am. Ain't no concern o' your'n."

Indignation straightened her spine. "It most certainly is my concern if I witness you taking a free man captive."

The white man guffawed and called Barnabas a vulgar name. "Why else would a darkie be hidin' in the woods if he ain't runnin'?"

"I weren't runnin', Miz Cov—"

The man backhanded Barnabas. He staggered backward and blood trickled from the corner of his mouth.

"Shut up." The white man yanked a bowie knife from his belt. "Open your mouth again and I'll slit your tongue."

"Stop that. Don't you dare hit him again." Wrath flamed through Auralie, and she climbed from the carriage. "See here. I happen to know this man is not a runaway."

The bounty hunter smirked. "I say he is. The man I work for will pay me a nice bounty for every darkie I bring in." He swept his hat off and held it over his heart, bowing in a sarcastic demonstration of mock respect. "Beggin' pardon, ma'am."

Auralie gritted her teeth. "Who is the man who pays you to capture men like this?"

He plopped his hat back on his head. "My boss, the honorable Shelby Covington. He hired me to recover his property. Escaped slaves make me a tidy profit."

Bile rose in Auralie's throat and her stomach twisted. "I'm telling you this man is not an escaped slave. He works for—"

"I ain't interested in no petticoat pardon." He cinched a rope around the wrist shackles on Barnabas's arms and slid the other end through an iron ring attached to his saddle.

Mammy stood in the carriage and shook her finger at the man. "You watch yo' mouth. This here is a lady, and—"

The man pulled the knife again and brandished it toward Mammy. "Lady, huh? Well, lady, you need to teach your darkie some manners. Or I can do it for you."

Auralie tried to swallow, but fear choked her. She watched in horror as the man mounted his horse and jerked on the rope to pull Barnabas along.

"Where are you taking him?"

The man's sneer revealed tobacco-stained teeth. "Back where the overseer'll teach him not to run no more." He nudged his horse into a trot, forcing Barnabas to run behind the animal.

Auralie whirled toward the carriage. Both Mammy and Reuben wore pained grimaces. "Reuben, turn around and take the north road."

"But missy, massah say to bring you home."

"I'll tell him you were obeying my instructions." She picked up her skirts and clambered into the conveyance. "The north road, Reuben. Hurry!"

Reuben turned the carriage around and sent the horses running full tilt, veering to the left at the fork, onto the north road. The wind pulled at Auralie's hair, but she wouldn't let Reuben slow the horses until Colton's place came into view.

"Stop!"

Reuben pulled back on the reins to bring the heaving horses to a halt. Auralie discarded propriety and jumped down.

"Colton! Colton!" She picked up her skirts and ran toward the house, screaming Colton's name, but he didn't appear. She ran down the slope toward the cornfield.

"Colton!"

"Auralie?"

She halted and searched in the direction of his voice. He came jogging toward her from the sheep pasture. She ran to meet him.

Trepidation edged his voice. "What's wrong?"

"Barnabas. A bounty hunter took him." She gasped for breath. "Come quickly."

He grasped her hand. "Some of the sheep got out. We split up to look for them." Together they hurried back toward the house. He sent a sweeping search in the direction Auralie's carriage had come. "Where?"

Nausea swirled in her stomach. "Covington Plantation."

Colton's jaw dropped, his expression incredulous. "You go ahead. As soon as I throw a saddle on Jasper I'll catch up with you." He turned and ran back toward the barn.

"Hurry, Colton!"

He called back to her over his shoulder. "I will. Go on. Jasper will catch up with the carriage before you get there."

She dashed back to the carriage where Reuben waited to help her aboard. As soon as she was seated, Reuben turned the team around and lit out back down the road. The distance to Covington Plantation normally took an hour at a more sedate pace, but Reuben encouraged the horses to keep moving.

"Oh dear Lord, don't let us be too late. Please don't let them hurt Barnabas."

Mammy gripped Auralie's hand. "Amen."

When they were within a mile of the entrance, the sound of pounding hoofbeats coming up behind them turned Auralie's head. Colton's sweat-flecked chestnut gelding pulled abreast of the carriage, and he adjusted the horse's speed to keep pace.

Reuben steered the horses through the huge iron gate that yawned open. Colton went ahead and skidded his horse to a stop. He vaulted from the saddle and ran to meet the carriage as the lathered horses halted by the front entrance. He seized Auralie around the waist and swung her to the ground. Grabbing her hand, they ran up the front steps to the wide veranda.

Her father stepped through the open french doors from the parlor with a brandy snifter in his hand. "Auralie," he barked. "What is the meaning of this?"

For once, Father's intimidating growl had no effect on her. "Father, a bounty hunter who says he was hired by you has taken this man's friend. Barnabas isn't a runaway. He doesn't even belong to you. Colton bought him and freed him."

Father turned his glower on Colton. "I know who you are. You're Danfield."

"That's right, and what your daughter says is true. Barnabas is no longer your property and carries papers to prove it, but it seems your bounty hunter took him anyway. I demand to know where he is."

"You demand? Who do you think you're talking to? And take your hand off my daughter."

Instead of complying, Colton tightened his grip on Auralie's hand.

Another man, with thick auburn hair and a daunting, chiseled countenance, stepped out the door behind Father. He scowled from Auralie to Colton and back again.

In the next heartbeat, everyone began talking at once.

"Auralie, how dare you, coming racing in here like a hooligan—"

"Father, please—"

"Covington, I demand you release Barnabas immediately."

"Who is this man, and why does he have hold of my fiancée's hand?"

Auralie drew a sharp breath. Fiancée? Didn't Mother's note say he was to arrive tomorrow? The tall man with the brooding eyes and sinister brows leveled a glare at her. Perry Bolden raked a disapproving scowl over her.

"I don't understand this at all. This can't be Auralie." He turned to look at her father. "You assured me that my future wife was delicate and refined and conducted herself with elegance and decorum." He tossed a disdainful look at Auralie. "I'm appalled at this unladylike behavior."

"How dare you insinuate that I misled you? I am highly offended. Why, she—"

"Covington, answer me. I want to know where Barnabas is right now."

Perry frowned at her again. "Where is the pink silk gown you were instructed to wear upon my arrival? And who is this—this farmer with whom you are consorting?" He shook his head and turned back to her father. "This unspeakable conduct will never do."

Her father bellowed. "Auralie, I am outraged that you have shamed me like this."

"Covington." Colton grabbed the man by his lapels. "Where is Barnabas?"

"Now see here. . ." Perry grasped Colton's arm, causing Colton to spin around and land a punch on the side of Perry's jaw, sending him sprawling.

While the men continued to shout at one another, Auralie dashed down the veranda steps and ran toward the back of the house, past the trees, to a clearing that skirted Slave Row. A large group of slaves stood in a wide circle. In the center of the circle was Barnabas, tied to a thick post with his shirt stripped off. One of the overseers approached him, a whip coiled in his hands, announcing to all assembled that the same treatment awaited any of them who tried to run.

"*Stop! Stop this!*" Auralie screamed at the top of her lungs. She raced toward the horrific scene, screaming as she went. "*Colton!*" She broke through the circle and ran toward Barnabas, gasping for breath and seething with fury. "Stop this, immediately."

The overseer jerked his head, no doubt taken aback at Auralie's presence. "Who are you?"

She stepped in front of Barnabas, drew her shoulders back, and lifted her chin. Her chest heaved as she gulped air. "I am Auralie Covington. This man does not belong to my father. He is not a runaway. I demand you release him at once."

Chapter 18

A mid the bellowing and blustering between Covington and Bolden, Colton realized Auralie no longer stood beside him. He twisted his head to the right and left, searching for her, and caught sight of Mammy standing on the front lawn, pointing frantically toward the back of the house.

At that moment, Auralie's piercing scream rent the air. *"Colton!"*

Colton leaped down the steps.

"Where do you think you're going?" Covington roared.

Bolden staggered to his feet. "Sir, you are a boorish clod, and you will hear from my attorney."

Colton ignored them both and sprinted in the direction Mammy pointed. Another scream reached his ears, and the blood in his veins turned to ice. His heart pounded in his throat as he ran past the stable toward a thick copse of trees. He slid down a steep slope past the trees on a path that opened up to a clearing. Rows of ramshackle hovels lined a rutted road, and the stench of sweat and human waste hung in the air. Dozens of slaves gathered in a circle around the edge of the open area, while in the center of the clearing, a loathsome sight greeted him. Barnabas was tied, with his arms wrapped around a post. An overseer coiled a whip in preparation for use.

But standing between Barnabas and the overseer, hands on her hips and a defiant lift to her jaw, stood Auralie. The vision of her triggered a hitch in his chest, and his breath caught. An exquisite ache filled him as he drank in the valiant picture she made. He moved forward to take his place next to her.

Pounding footsteps sounded behind him, and Bolden called out something about Colton insulting him and he demanded satisfaction. Colton ignored him. The slaves who stood on the fringes of the clearing parted and let Colton slip past.

Auralie looked his way, and the relief in her eyes made him want to take her in his arms. Instead, he let his gaze slide to Barnabas, and acid rage swelled in his chest. He strode, fuming, to the overseer. The man spat tobacco juice at Colton's feet.

Colton grabbed the whip from the man's grimy paw. "I ought to wrap this thing around your worthless neck." He flung it as far as he could into the trees. Barnabas's faded muslin shirt lay on the ground, and Colton bent and snatched it up. He jammed his hand in the pocket and pulled out the indenture paper, unfolded it, and shoved it in the overseer's face.

The man shrugged. "Cain't read."

Colton yanked the bowie knife from the man's belt and went over to cut the ropes holding Barnabas hostage. "Are you all right, my friend?"

Barnabas gave him a wobbly smile despite a swollen lip. "I is now."

Colton folded the paper and handed it, along with the ripped shirt, back to Barnabas before turning to Auralie. Her eyes misted, but she blinked back the moisture.

"Oh Colton. I've never been so glad to see anybody in my entire life."

He held her gaze for a long moment. The tremor in her voice didn't match her bravado, and he longed to whisper in her ear that everything was all right now. He glanced over his shoulder to where Bolden stood fuming, a silk handkerchief pressed over his nose and mouth. This wasn't the time.

The overseer waved his arms and shouted for the workers to get back to their tasks. With eyes held low, they all trudged away while the overseer searched through the trees and underbrush for his whip. Colton's heart ached, but the only thing that would change their circumstances was electing men to office who held to the belief that slavery was immoral.

Shelby Covington approached at a jog, huffing and puffing, his belly jiggling with each footfall.

"Danfield! You're trespassing. Auralie, I'll not permit you to embarrass me any further. Get back to the house this instant."

Auralie folded her arms and turned to face her father with the same expression of confident bravery with which she'd faced the overseer. "No, Father. I am a grown woman, not a child."

Bolden took three strides and grasped Auralie's arm. "I am your future husband, and you'll do as I say."

Colton clamped his hand on Bolden's arm and yanked it away from Auralie, nudging her away from the contemptuous snob. Through gritted teeth, he hissed at Bolden. "You lay a finger on her again, and these folks will have to carry you out of here."

A flinch wavered across Bolden's face, chased into hiding by an expression of indignation.

Shelby Covington barged past Bolden and stood toe-to-toe with Colton. "How dare you come in here and disrupt my daughter's life."

Before Colton could reply, Auralie stepped forward.

"Father, if anyone is disrupting my life, it's you."

Covington's face flooded red and the veins in his neck stood out. He sputtered, but no words formed. But Auralie wasn't finished.

"All my life I've watched you wield your power and authority in such a way that it tramples everyone around you into submission, including Mother and me. It's not my intention to show disrespect to you, but respect can't be demanded." She turned her head and glanced at Colton. "I have far more respect for this man who has dirt under his fingernails and calluses on his hands. He pours his heart and soul and sweat into the land and work God has given him to do. Colton doesn't demand respect. He earns it."

Auralie's words caressed Colton's ears like music. His heart soared.

Bolden, still holding the fancy handkerchief over his face as though he was afraid to breathe the same air as the slaves, looked down his aristocratic nose at Auralie. "Do you have the audacity to insinuate this. . .this *farmer* appeals to you?" Disbelief echoed in his tone.

A tiny smile tweaked Auralie's lips, and she lifted her gaze to Colton. "Yes. Everything about this man, from his dirty hands and sweaty brow, to the way he asks God to bless him with a good crop, the way he rejoices over a newborn lamb—" She gestured to Barnabas. "And the way he stands up for what is right." She turned her eyes back to Bolden. "Yes, Colton Danfield appeals to me, Perry. Being forced into an arranged marriage for business and political purposes repulses me."

Bolden's eyes flamed, and then narrowed, first at Auralie, then at Colton. Finally he whirled to confront Covington. "Everything you told me about your daughter is false. She is a most unsuitable match. I will not have a wife who doesn't know her place. You'll be hearing from my attorney regarding the dissolution of our contract." With an incensed snort, he stomped away.

Tears filled Auralie's eyes. She cast a brief glance heavenward, and her lips mouthed the words, *Thank You.*

Colton understood her tears. The sentiment she'd just offered to God flooded his heart as well.

Shelby Covington stood clenching his fist at his sides, his posture domineering. Poison darts of hostility spit from his eyes. "You are to blame for this. I'll see to it my attorney files papers immediately to sue you for every dime you have to your name."

Colton folded his arms across his chest. "I'm glad you have an attorney, Covington, because you're going to need one."

"What?" Covington sent a piercing glare at Colton and cursed. "What are you talking about?"

Colton stroked his chin. "I had a rather interesting conversation with the county clerk at Mount Yonah when I went there several days ago to confirm the deed to my land was properly recorded."

Covington pooched his lips in feigned disinterest and shifted a glance in Auralie's direction. "What does that have to do with me?"

"I can prove that you paid the clerk at the courthouse in Mount Yonah to alter the record ledger."

"That's preposterous!" Covington almost stood on tiptoe as he emitted the bellow. "What kind of pernicious lies are you inventing to besmirch my name?"

Acutely aware of Auralie's eyes upon him, Colton took no pleasure in exposing Covington's misdeeds in her presence, but he suspected she wasn't entirely oblivious to her father's tactics.

The stench of liquor on Shelby Covington's breath nearly turned Colton's stomach, but he faced the man, "Are you denying you paid the county clerk to remove the page in the ledger on which the deed for my land was recorded and to rewrite a new page to replace it?"

Covington sputtered and his face evolved from red to purple. A vein in his temple pulsated visibly. "This is outrageous. You can't accuse me like this, especially when you can't prove a thing."

"Oh, but I can." Colton didn't blink at Covington's bluster. "You see, you forgot something, Covington. Reverend Robert Winslow recorded his will in the same county office, bequeathing his land to me. Pastor Winslow's will and the land deed were recorded at the same time—the deed in one ledger and the will in a different one. A copy of the will is also on file."

"I don't know any Robert Winslow." Moisture beaded on Covington's forehead.

"That's odd, because your son knows about Pastor Winslow. He and I had a conversation one day about three weeks ago when he was out my way doing some surveying. Your son mentioned that I was a landowner only through Pastor Winslow's benevolence."

Covington huffed and stammered. "Y–you. . . Th–this entire c–conversation is ridiculous."

"You won't think it's ridiculous when you receive a summons from the state attorney general's office." Colton tucked his thumbs into his belt. "Seems the county clerk wasn't willing to go to jail, so he signed a sworn statement saying you paid him five hundred dollars to change the ledger pages."

Covington blanched. "He's. . .he's lying. It was Bolden. Thaddeus Bolden wanted. . . He said he'd withdraw his support if. . ."

"Father, how could you?" Auralie's shocked gasp reminded Colton she was listening to the entire exchange.

Covington turned without another word and plodded up the slope past the trees. No doubt he'd be penning letters to Thaddeus Bolden and Maxwell Rayburn within the hour.

Colton watched him until he was beyond the trees.

Colton turned to Auralie and spoke quietly. "I think it's time for Barnabas and me to leave." Their gazes locked. He'd not leave her here if she feared her father's wrath. He tried to sort out the twisted jumble of emotions on her face. "Will you be all right?"

Some of the starch he'd seen when she stood up to the overseer, and then to her father and Perry Bolden, seemed to seep out of her. Her shoulders drooped a bit, but she managed a tight smile. "Yes, for now."

Barnabas pulled his shirt on the best he could—one sleeve dangled, having been ripped from the shoulder. "Mistah Colton, I jus' go wait fo' you up yonder." He bobbed his head toward the rise.

Colton nodded. "Jasper is by the front entrance. He could probably use some water."

"I see to da hoss. And Mistah Colton, Miz Covington." He laid his hand over his heart. "I thanks yo' both. I be. . .mighty grateful, fo' ever'thin'."

Colton extended his hand and Barnabas gripped it. Then he stepped back with a polite nod toward Auralie. "Ma'am." And he hurried away.

Colton placed his hand gently on the small of Auralie's back, and they slowly made their way together up the pathway that led back to the house. He had so many things on his heart that he wanted to say to her, but getting the words to line up in an order that would make sense suddenly seemed a daunting task. He drew in a deep breath and released it.

"Auralie, how can I thank you for what you did?"

She angled her head and peered up at him, her demure smile nearly doing him in. "What did I do?"

"You showed remarkable courage in the way you stopped that overseer." He took her elbow and turned her to him. "I think I understand a little of what it took for you to stand up to your father after being subjected to his intimidation for so many years." He glanced down at his boots. "I'm sorry you had to hear all those things I said to him."

She touched his hand and a tremble skittered up his arm. "Colton, I'm sorry for what my father did, or tried to do. He wasn't always that way—so filled with greed he'd sell his soul to gain more power. He used to care more for my mother and me. I don't know why or how he changed." She sighed.

They continued walking, passing the stable and entering the sprawling side yard with its majestic magnolia trees and lush rhododendrons. Colton spied Mammy watching them from an upstairs window. She gave Colton a smile and a nod, quite the opposite of his first meeting with Auralie. He couldn't help but grin.

Auralie stopped and sat on an ornate, wrought iron bench among the roses. "I don't understand why Father tried to change the land records."

Colton sat beside her. "Jack McCaffey was the one who suggested I go and check the records. His sources told him there was a deal in the works to bring the Georgia Railroad spur up this way from Athens. Thaddeus Bolden bought a thousand acres of timberland that borders my property, and the shortest route to access the spur extension was through my land. He knew I wouldn't sell, and one of Jack's sources got wind of some under-the-table dealing at the county seat. When Jack saw a map of the tentative route for the spur, he told me about it."

Auralie closed her eyes and nodded. "Thaddeus Bolden is Father's biggest financial supporter."

"That's right." Colton cupped his hands over his knees. "Your father could win the election on Bolden's wallet, and once in office, he'd be Bolden's puppet for political favors—like seizing possession of land that didn't have a properly recorded deed."

Auralie covered her face with her hands. "Oh Colton, I'm so sorry. . ."

"There's no need for you to be sorry." He slipped his fingers around her wrists and tugged her hands away from her beautiful face. A chuckle bubbled up within him. The wild carriage ride had pulled pins from her hair and set the sandy tendrils in disarray, and she had a smudge of dirt on her face, but she was still the prettiest thing he'd ever seen. He brushed back a lock of her hair, and she pressed her head against his knuckles.

"Did you really mean what you said about being glad to see me?"

A rosy blush stole into her cheeks, and her eyes twinkled. "Yes."

Colton cleared his throat. "Well, then, there's something I'd like to say to you, but I'm not sure if this is the right time, or even if I'm the right person."

She dropped her gaze to her lap. Colton reached over and took her hand. She blinked and raised her eyes to meet his. "First I must ask your forgiveness for misjudging you. The day I met you, I assumed you were a spoiled, self-centered young woman who only cared about herself. I happily admit I was wrong."

Surprise flickered across her face. "Why did you think that?"

Colton shook his head. "The reasons aren't important. What matters is that God gave me the privilege of truly getting to know you. I think I was smitten the day you brought the lemonade to Barnabas and me." He grinned when she blushed. "I knew I had lost my heart to you the morning we worked together helping birth the twin lambs."

A shy smile graced her lips. "That was special to me, too."

"A little while ago, you said you respected me for having dirty hands and calluses from working." He hesitated and searched her face. "I have to know if you said that simply to offend Bolden."

Her wide, solemn eyes answered him even before she spoke. "No, Colton, I meant every word. The Bible says a man ought to work with his hands and care for those things the Lord has given him. That's what you do. How can I not respect that?"

Colton pulled in a slow, deep breath. His heart thrummed within his chest. "Auralie, I believe with all my heart that when God created a helpmate for me, He had you in mind."

Her eyes misted, and she gifted him with that endearing smile he'd come to adore. "I believe that, too."

He slid off the bench to one knee, capturing both her hands in his. "Auralie, I love you with all my heart. I'm asking you to be my wife."

"Yes, Colton. With all my heart, I want to marry you."

Epilogue

September 1860

Auralie looked at the house as if she'd never seen it before as Colton drove up to the front and reined in the team. The meeting in town with Lloyd and Belle at Cyrus Fletcher's office had been a celebration, topped off with lunch at Maybelle's Café. The only sad part was the good-bye, and even that was sprinkled with giggles as Belle's swollen stomach got in the way of their hugs and promises to write once Belle got settled in their new house in Atlanta.

"Colton, I'm still pinching myself to make sure this isn't a dream." Auralie could barely contain her excitement. "I spent many joy-filled days in this house last spring."

He lifted her down from the wagon and gave her a peck on her nose. "We will make sure a lot more joy abides with us in the coming days, Mrs. Danfield."

Soft laughter bubbled up from her throat and accompanied a warm flush at hearing her new name. Colton took her hand.

"I want to show you something." They rounded the corner of the house to the side porch swathed in afternoon shade from the stately oaks. There sat the wicker chairs with their colorful cushions and the small table where Auralie and Belle had enjoyed midmorning tea or afternoon lemonade while they talked out the issues they faced.

"Belle left them here for you as a belated wedding gift."

Auralie released a soft gasp and clapped both hands over her chest. "But she and Lloyd already gave us that lovely quilt." She climbed the two steps up to the wide wraparound porch and picked up a book from the chair she'd occupied so many pleasant hours. Amusement tickled her stomach. "*Wuthering Heights.* I never did finish it. Look, she even left my bookmark in place."

"I'm afraid the furnishings will be a bit sparse for a while." Colton joined her on the porch. "Lloyd and Belle took most of the furniture with them. You'll be happy to know they left the bookshelves in the parlor."

Auralie ran her hand over the railing, still in awe the house was now theirs. "Oh look, there's Barnabas." She waved at the man working in the meadow, and he reciprocated. "What is he doing?"

Colton slipped his arm around his bride. "With the purchase of the house and land, we're able to expand the sheep pasture to include four more acres, so Barnabas is working on new fencing."

She looked out across the meadow and imagined the sheep grazing there as soon as Barnabas finished the fence. "What did he say when you told him he'd be living in the cabin now instead of the lean-to?"

Colton grinned. "I didn't tell him." He gave her a sly wink. "I showed him. I wrote it out for him to read. His face lit up like a sunrise. I think he was more excited that he could read it for himself than he was about living in the cabin."

Ripples of delight darted through her. She stepped toward the door that opened to the side porch.

"Where do you think you're going, Mrs. Danfield?"

She pointed. "Can't we go inside?"

A wide grin poked a dimple in her husband's cheek. "Not until I carry you over the threshold." He scooped her into his arms.

"Colton! We've been married almost two months, and we've visited Lloyd and Belle here at least a dozen times as husband and wife." But she snuggled against his shoulder and enjoyed the closeness.

"Ah, but now the house is ours, and a proper husband should carry his wife across the threshold." He lowered his lips to hers. "Are you sure you don't mind that we didn't have the big fancy wedding you would have had with Perry Bolden?"

"Oh Colton, it's not the wedding that's important. It's the marriage." She buried her face in his neck. "God has given me a most priceless gift—the best husband I could ever imagine."

He nudged the door with his shoulder, and it swung open with no effort.

A voice, nearly as familiar as her own, greeted them. "Welcome home, honey girl."

"Mammy!"

Colton set her down and she embraced her dear friend. "What are you doing here?" She looked back at her husband, expecting a mischievous grin, but he appeared as surprised as she.

Mammy pulled a paper from her apron pocket and handed it to Auralie. "Never thought I'd see the day that yo' mama would stand up strong to yo' daddy, but tha's jus' what she done. She talk yo' daddy into signin' me ovah to you, as a weddin' present."

Astonishment dropped Auralie's jaw. "Mother did that?"

"Yes she did. Yo' daddy did some hollerin', but yo' mama got her way." Mammy winked. "Sho' s'prise me, too. But I's mighty happy to be here, takin' care o' my honey girl, again." She leaned close to Auralie and whispered. "An' maybe I gets to take care o' yo' babies, too."

A rush of heat filled Auralie's face. "Maybe sooner than you think." She looked up into Colton's widened eyes.

"What?"

"I've been sick to my stomach three mornings in a row."

Mammy clapped her hands and cackled. "Halleluiah!"

Harbinger of Healing

To JoAnne Simmons, my first editor:
Thank you for letting God use you
to make my dreams come true.

Chapter 1

September 1870

Charity Galbraith choked back the retort dancing on her tongue with a garbled cough. Uncle Luther's opinions of her occupation and the station to which he believed all women were born grated on her nerves. Had she known a nonstop dissertation of his narrow-minded views would accompany her south, she'd never have entreated him to be her traveling escort.

She turned toward the train's grimy window and muttered under her breath, "Perhaps I should feign sleep." If she had to endure five more minutes of his diatribe, she'd surely throw the nearest loose object at him. Said object happened to be her thrice-read volume of *Jane Eyre*. No, she'd never treat the intrepid heroine of her favorite novel so shabbily. Perhaps the stale liverwurst sandwich her uncle had magnanimously bestowed on her would serve as a better projectile.

Two days of train travel with her pompous, cigar-puffing uncle frayed the threads of her poise dangerously thin. She returned her attention to her chaperone and sugared her tone. "It may make you feel better to know that my editor shares your opinion of women writers and therefore requires that I use a masculine pen name."

Uncle Luther's thick, black eyebrows bristled together like a fat caterpillar preparing for winter. "He does? Your articles don't bear your name?"

Pricks of irritation made her squirm, and she glanced at the novel in her lap. If female authors of fiction were now acceptable, why not of magazine articles? The upper crust of society made up the majority of the magazine's audience, and they apparently weren't ready to read the expressed viewpoint of current events from the female perspective. "The readership of *Keystone Magazine* thinks my articles are written by Charles Galbraith."

Speaking her father's name sent waves of sorrow through her. Major Charles Hampton Galbraith of the Federal army never returned home after the War of Southern Rebellion, and the ache to know what became of him still haunted her.

A *harrumph* met her ears, and she braced herself for more of Uncle Luther's unsolicited criticism.

"What would your father think of the unseemly usage of his name?"

Her eyes burned and she swallowed hard. "Even though most everyone in Harrisburg knew him as Hampton Galbraith, I use his first name in tribute to him."

He muttered something she couldn't quite hear over the monotonous rumble of the train wheels. She turned to squint out the soot-darkened window as the landscape lurched past. Where were they? Virginia? No, they changed trains in Washington some time ago, so surely they must be in North Carolina by now.

Had the train carried her enough miles from home to safely inform her uncle of her intentions? She twisted in her seat and found him buried behind his newspaper.

"I hope you'll be able to cancel the reservation for my room at the hotel in Atlanta."

The newspaper crumpled as Uncle Luther lowered it and sent her a scowl. "What are you talking about?"

A hint of defiance tiptoed through her, and she lifted her chin. "I don't plan to stay in Atlanta, Uncle. This trip is not only for the purpose of researching the series of articles for the magazine. I promised my friend back in Harrisburg, Essie Carver, that I'd search for her son."

"What? What kind of nonsense is this? Of course, you're staying in Atlanta under my protection. That Carver woman is a servant."

Ire flared in Charity's belly. "She's a businesswoman. She was born a slave and escaped that horrendous life. Now she makes her living as a seamstress."

Uncle Luther sniffed. "That hardly makes her a businesswoman. She's still a—"

"She's my friend." Charity interrupted him before he could use the despicable word. "You know how dangerous it is for a Negro woman to return to the South alone. Even though it's been six years since the war, Negroes aren't looked upon with favor in those states. Besides, she hasn't the money or the connections for such a search. Essie hasn't seen her son, Wylie, since he was sold to a neighboring plantation eleven years ago. He was only thirteen. She doesn't know if he's alive or dead."

"I still don't see why you must take it upon yourself. Why can't this Wylie initiate the search." He shook his head until his jowls flapped. "What about your family's reputation? What will people think of you going off to find this slave—"

"He's no longer a slave." Her fingers curled around the end of the armrest of the lumpy seat. "That's what my father—your brother—fought for. He believed nobody has the right to own another human being. Essie and Wylie are but two of the people for whom my father fought."

Uncle Luther grunted and snapped open his newspaper without another word. Grateful for the silence except for the clackety-clacking of the wheels rolling down the track, Charity allowed her thoughts to wander back to her last conversation with Essie. All the woman could tell her was the name of the plantation to which Wylie had been sold—Covington Plantation, near a town called Juniper Springs.

There was a third aspect to her journey, the purpose of which she'd shared with no one. Her research assignment for the magazine not only offered the opportunity to search for Essie's son, but also to pursue the desire of her heart for the past six years. She prayed for God's help in learning what had become of her father.

Her mother had kept the few letters they'd received from him in the drawer of the china cabinet, and the paper had grown yellowed and worn from the number of times Charity and her mother had taken them out and read them. The last word from the war department indicated Father had been wounded and taken prisoner at a battle in northern Georgia—some place called Pickett's Mill. She and her mother had been left to wait and wonder. Mama had taken her broken heart to her grave, but Charity still longed to know the truth.

Growling snores emerged from behind Uncle Luther's newspaper. Charity set aside her book and rose, stretching her stiff legs. She gingerly stepped past her uncle's sprawled out form and held on to the corners of the seat backs to keep her balance as the train lurched along, carrying her deeper into the Southern countryside. Making her way toward the back of the railcar, she hailed the conductor.

"Sir? Can you tell me how much longer it will be before we arrive in Atlanta?"

The plump, rosy-cheeked man peered at her over the top of his lopsided spectacles. "This here train don't go to Atlanta, miss. It goes on to Savannah. You'll be changin' trains and headin' westbound at Augusta. We're scheduled to arrive in Augusta at nine forty-five tomorrow mornin'."

"I see." She glanced back at her uncle whose snores could be heard all the way back to where she stood conversing with the conductor. "Do you happen to have the westbound schedule?"

He beamed and proudly pulled a small black booklet from his jacket pocket. "Of course. Let's see." He licked his thumb and pushed back a couple of pages. "Here it is. Westbound train leaves Augusta at eleven ten in the mornin', and it stops to take on water at Madison. It'll get you into Atlanta at six fifteen tomorrow evenin'."

"Is there a northbound train from Madison?"

"Uh-huh. Train runs between Madison and Athens every day."

She thanked the man and returned to her seat, a plan formulating in her head.

❧

Charity rummaged around in her satchel for her comb. There wasn't anything she could do with her rumpled, travel-disheveled clothing, but at least she could tidy her hair. Uncle Luther and some other men had moved to the smoking car to discuss business over brandy and cigars, leaving Charity to watch out the window for the sign indicating they were coming into Madison. The westbound train was shorter than the southbound and didn't haul as many freight cars, thus allowing the train to make better time.

The whistle sounded and the brakes squealed, slowing the train around a bend in the tracks.

"Madison. Madison, Georgia, ladies and gentlemen." The conductor made his way through the car calling out the information. "We'll stop here for about fifteen minutes, so don't go far."

"Excuse me, sir." Charity reached out and touched the man's elbow.

"Yes, miss?"

"I'll be disembarking the train at Madison. Could you please see that my trunk is taken off the baggage car?" She handed him her claim stub.

This conductor wasn't as pleasant as the one from the southbound train. He glanced at the stub and sent her a surly scowl. "Yer ticket goes through to Atlanta, don't it?"

"Yes, it does, but my plans have changed. Please remove my trunk."

He grumbled but headed toward the back of the railcar. Charity picked up her satchel and left the note she'd penned explaining her departure to Uncle Luther on the empty seat. Gathering her skirts about her, she quickly stepped toward the door, hoping she'd not encounter her uncle. Judging by the boisterous laughter coming from the smoking car, the men were well into the bottle of brandy.

Charity hurried across the platform to the ticket window. "One-way ticket to Athens, please." She dug in her reticule for her coin purse. "Might

I be able to hire a carriage in Athens to take me to the town of Juniper Springs?"

The clerk assured her carriages were available at a price. A porter thumped her trunk down on the platform. Minutes later, the train hissed and belched steam. The whistle sounded and the behemoth groaned, rolling westward toward Atlanta and leaving Charity standing in a swirling cloud of soot and dust.

❧

Dale Covington rolled his head from side to side to unkink the tightened muscles in his neck, and once more thanked God for the job he had at the sawmill. It had taken him some time to develop the muscular arms and calloused hands required for the manual labor—work he'd never known before the war. It was a good thing his father couldn't see him now.

Dale limped across the bridge that led to the town of Juniper Springs, but he still had work to do before returning to the small house he rented from Simon Pembroke, the Yankee who moved to Georgia after the war and built the sawmill. How many times had Dale come to the end of a long day and thought about the opulent home he'd once occupied with his parents and later with his wife?

The old wound in his leg hampered his progress as his hitched gait carried him toward the general store and his second job. Clyde Sawyer, the man who ran the mercantile, always had odd jobs for Dale to do and deliveries for him to make. The extra job enabled Dale to add a few more dollars a month to his savings. One day he'd be a landowner again. He set aside his weariness and pushed open the back door of the store.

"Clyde?"

A stocky man with wisps of gray hair around his ears stepped through the curtained doorway and wiped perspiration off his balding head with the corner of his denim apron. "Afternoon, Dale. There's a couple of orders on the clipboard to be delivered, and those crates by the door gotta be unpacked. Why don't you take a sit-down first? You look like you could use it."

Dale shook his head. "If it's all right with you, I'll unpack the new stock first and deliver those orders on my way home."

"Fine with me. Oh, my Sweet Pea made some cookies this mornin'. Said to make sure to save you some." Clyde pointed to a cloth-covered basket. "They're under that blue-checked napkin. Help yourself."

"Thanks. And tell Betsy I said thank you to her, too."

Clyde bobbed his head and returned to the front of the store, whistling as he went. Dale envied Clyde. The man had always led a simple, hardworking life. He'd never known wealth and therefore didn't miss it. He had a wife he adored who loved him in return, and by all appearances he seemed completely content with his life. How much easier would it be to face each day without regrets, disappointments, and grief?

Dale heaved a sigh and munched on a cinnamon-crusted cookie while he pried open the heavy crates. Ammunition and gun-cleaning supplies filled one crate, sewing supplies and button hooks in another. Three more contained canning jars and foodstuffs. Bolts of new cloth were stacked atop the last crate.

By the time he got everything unpacked, checked off the bills of lading, and ready for Clyde to stock the following morning, the sun hovered just above Yonah Mountain to the west. Dale stacked the two crates he'd set aside for the Juniper Springs Hotel and carried them two doors down, entering through the side door by way of the alley. Using the servants' entrance galled him at the beginning, but now he shrugged it off and set the crates down. The head housekeeper signed for them, and Dale made his way back to the mercantile to pick up the crate destined for the boardinghouse. As soon as he dropped off this order, he could head to his little cottage and solitary supper.

He limped across the street with the boardinghouse order and went around to the kitchen door. Amiable chatter reached his ears when he knocked on the back door. Hannah Sparrow, the widow who ran the boardinghouse, greeted him.

"Come in, Dale." She held the door open for him.

"Thank you, Mrs. Sparrow."

She plunked her hands on her hips. "When are you going to call me Hannah like everyone else?" Without waiting for a reply, she fluttered her fingers. "Excuse me. I must see to my new boarder." She left Dale to take the grocery items out of the wooden box and lay them on the worktable, and while he did so, he could hear her making introductions in the dining room.

"Everyone, this is Miss Charity Galbraith. She's a reporter with *Keystone Magazine*."

Dale peered through the crack in the door to get a look at the newcomer. An attractive, dark-haired woman in a maroon skirt and white shirtwaist stood beside Mrs. Sparrow. A collection of greetings blended in disharmony as Mrs. Sparrow introduced Miss Galbraith to everyone seated at the table.

"This is Frances Hyatt. She's our dressmaker. Miles Flint there is the sheriff in our county. Polly Ferguson and her daughter, Margaret, run the bakery down the street. Elden Hardy is a wheelwright, and he's from West Virginia. Arch Wheeler works at the land office, and across from him is Tate Ridley. Tate works at the sawmill."

Miss Galbraith greeted each person in turn, and her northern accent rasped across Dale's ears like sandpaper. The reporter was a Yankee—if he didn't miss his guess, she was from Pennsylvania.

Tate Ridley spoke up. "What sort o' articles you plannin' on writin' 'bout our town, Miss Galbraith?" Dale detected the familiar belligerent tone in Tate's voice.

"*Keystone* has assigned a series of articles to me on the Reconstruction. I'm here to research and document the progress of putting our country back together after the war."

Dale gritted his teeth. Reconstruction, indeed. How many times did he have to be reminded of all he'd lost until the pain finally dulled? For the thousandth time he wondered if his decision to stay in Juniper Springs after the war was prudent. There were any number of places he could have started over, but the ugly memories would have dogged his steps no matter where he'd gone.

Why would a woman reporter travel to Georgia alone? He'd seen more northern carpetbaggers than he cared to count, but she certainly didn't look like someone who was here to snatch up cheap land or make money on the misery of others. He didn't wait to hear any more.

Dale let himself out the back door and headed down the now-darkened street toward his small rented house. There was a crisp coolness to the air—an onset of autumn? Or perhaps the chill that permeated his bones was generated by the voice of the Yankee woman at the boardinghouse.

Chapter 2

Dale opened one eye. An irritatingly cheerful bird perched in the maple tree outside his window proclaiming the dawn of the Lord's Day. After tossing and turning most of the night, his mind filled with images from the war and its aftermath, Dale scowled at the morning light streaming into the room. Sunday morning, the only day he didn't have to work. He rolled over, turning his back to the window, and pulled the pillow over his head. But despite squeezing his eyes closed and pressing the pillow to his ear, he couldn't block out the feathered herald's insistence that he arise and dress for church.

Stupid bird.

He swung his feet over the side of the bed and raked his fingers through his hair. Yawning and stretching, he exited the small bed chamber and shuffled across the main room to see if any live coals remained in the stove. No welcoming red pinpoints glowed from within. Grumbling, he assembled a handful of kindling and wood chips, stuffing them into the firebox. He struck a match and dropped it in among the dry tinder, watching it catch and burn.

"I need a cup of coffee." He grabbed the coffeepot and shook it hopefully, but there was no happy gurgling. Lack of sleep fueled his surly disposition as he shoveled several spoonfuls of grounds into the pot and ladled water over it. While he waited for the pot to boil, he sat at the small, shabby table with the Bible Pastor Shuford gave him. No doubt the preacher would ask him if he'd been reading it. He opened the Book where the scrap of paper marked his place and began reading.

"Psalm thirteen. 'How long wilt thou forget me, O Lord? For ever? How long wilt thou hide thy face from me?'" He leaned back and stared at the words. How did the writer of the psalm know exactly how Dale felt? The verse echoed through his hollow being, rattling the bitter crust around his heart. He looked heavenward and pointed to the pages, as though God were unaware of what it said.

"Why God? The psalmist, David, was a godly man and this says You turned Your back on him. He only asked how long, but I'm asking why. Why was my world devastated? Why did You take everything from me?" The well-kept chronicle Dale hid in his heart emerged, and he mentally went down the list of everything he'd lost.

His old war wounds—the one in his side as well as his leg—began to ache in unison along with the canker in his spirit. He rubbed his hand over the scar on his left side under his ribs.

"God, I really do want to live for You, but every time I take a step toward You, my feet slip out from under me and I'm back where I started. I don't want to live in the pit of despair, but I don't know how to climb out."

The quiet whisper of heaven's voice nudged him to keep reading. He returned to the psalm and found an affinity with the writer in the next verses. "Sorrow in my heart...mine enemy be exalted over me..."

But the last two verses of the short psalm weren't what he expected. "But I have trusted in thy mercy; my heart shall rejoice in thy salvation. I will sing unto the Lord, because he hath dealt bountifully with me."

He shook his head. "Bountifully? How is losing everything meaningful to a man considered bountiful?"

Recurring nightmares from the war weren't the only thing that kept slumber at bay last night. That Yankee woman he'd seen at the boardinghouse yesterday lingered in his thoughts. Her winsome smile charmed him until she spoke. The sound of her Northern accent mocked him with the reminder of all that the war had stolen from him.

How ridiculous. It was unfair to blame Miss Galbraith for his losses by virtue of her birthplace. She was not the one who burned his home, nor did she fire the rifle that inflicted his wounds. Still, did she not represent the ones who did?

Hisshhhhh. The coffeepot boiled over. Dale jumped up and limped over to the stove, grabbing a rag to mop up the mess. He muttered his annoyance and gazed through the open door that separated the tiny bedroom from the main living space. The rumpled bedcovers and lumpy mattress tick called to him. Falling under the alluring spell of his pillow seemed more prudent than shaving and dressing for church, but Pastor Shuford would no doubt come knocking on his door later this afternoon if he didn't go. He sighed and went to fetch his razor.

ॐ

The Sunday service was already underway when Dale hop-stepped up the front stairs of the church. The congregation's fine voice filled the early-autumn morning, much like the mockingbird that had awakened him. Their song gilded the air with praise, but Dale's grumpiness had accompanied him to church. He slipped in the door and found a place near the back, scowling at the toes of his boots. Maybe he wouldn't have to fellowship with anyone if he sat in the back.

From his vantage point, he could study the backs of everyone's heads and noted his boss, Simon Pembroke, sat directly in front of him. His gaze moved down the row, and he picked out Doctor Greenway and the Sawyers. Across the aisle, his sister, Auralie, her husband, Colton, and their two children sat sharing a Bible. Dale gritted his teeth and pulled his gaze away. When Colton fought with the Yankees, Dale had told Auralie she was no longer his sister.

He directed his vision straight ahead. Five rows ahead of him, a woman with dark walnut hair pinned up under a ridiculous purple hat sat beside Hannah Sparrow.

Pastor Shuford's voice filled the room as he announced his text for the morning. Dale paid little attention to the reference, but when the preacher began relating the biblical account of Peter inquiring of Jesus how many times he must forgive, Dale jerked his focus to the pulpit. He narrowed his eyes at the pastor, certain the clergyman spoke directly to him. After all, how many others in the congregation struggled with unwillingness to forgive those who had wronged them? If he rose to leave, everyone would notice his halting gait heading for the door, so he sat still and tried not to listen.

His gaze kept returning to the woman in the purple hat, and when she turned her head momentarily, Dale realized it was Miss Galbraith. How ironic, or appropriate, that the woman whose presence had stirred his rancor and interrupted his sleep, who represented those he refused to forgive, sat not fifteen feet in front of him.

❧

Charity tucked her lower lip between her teeth to keep from standing up and demanding the preacher stop trampling on her toes. If there was a topic to which she did not wish to listen, it was God's instruction to forgive. How dare this minister suggest it was her obligation to forgive the people who had taken her father from her?

She turned to the scripture the preacher indicated with the intention of checking to see if he had taken it out of context and twisted its meaning. Matthew chapter eighteen, beginning in verse twenty-one. She read all the way through to verse thirty-five searching for the smallest detail to which she could point and disagree. But the plain truth of Christ's example lay across the pages in black and white. The thought of graciously granting forgiveness to those who didn't deserve it set her teeth on edge.

It stood to reason many Southerners harbored resentment since they lost the war, but hearing such a message preached in a Southern church indeed surprised her. Charity sent a surreptitious glance around the room, looking for people who appeared as offended as she at the minister's audacity. There were some who scowled or looked away from the man in the pulpit, but many nodded their heads or murmured "amen."

The pastor drew the congregation's attention to Luke chapter six. "In verse thirty-seven, Jesus tells us not to judge so we will not be judged, nor condemn others so we will not be condemned. Our Lord adds that if we expect to be forgiven, we must learn to forgive." The man stepped to the side of the pulpit, reaching out an upturned palm, beseeching the listeners. "Don't allow the spirit of unforgiveness to devour you. Your refusal to forgive another doesn't hurt that person nearly as much as it hurts you."

In the two days she'd been in Juniper Springs, the sound of Southern twang had grated on her ears, and this preacher was no different. But it wasn't the sound of his voice as much as the meaning of his words that offended her. How could she do what he advocated? Some days her anger was the only thing that fueled her motivation to go on. Clinging to malice made her strong. Charity drew the shutters of her heart closed and refused entry to the remainder of the sermon.

She'd begged her editor to let her write the series of articles on Reconstruction. The South started the fight, demanding their right to use slaves or their very way of life would be destroyed. Of course there were casualties inflicted in the South, but after all, they were the ones who rebelled and seceded. Soldiers like her father were defending their sovereign nation. Besides, the very idea of slavery nauseated her. The South's insistence that their agriculture industry would suffer without slave labor was preposterous, and she intended to use her pen as a sword to carve indelible words to that effect.

The latest news from the South had made the headlines only a few weeks before she boarded the train to travel to Georgia. According to the *Harrisburg Gazette*, Georgia was finally readmitted to the Union after five years of refusing to comply with Federal orders. It wasn't until last February that the Georgia legislature finally ratified the fourteenth and fifteenth amendments, and the newspaper said it happened only at the point of military bayonets. Even now Federal troops still occupied McPherson Barracks in Atlanta to ensure no more lapses in compliance. Charity sniffed. Didn't that justify her feelings and prove her point?

Charity folded her arms. Nobody—not this preacher or anyone else—would convince her to extend unmerited forgiveness to people who had wronged so many.

She barely realized the rest of the congregation stood until they began to sing, "O, for a closer walk with God, a calm and heavenly frame; a light to shine upon the road, that leads me to the Lamb."

She rose quickly and added her voice to the hymn, hoping no one noticed her lack of attention. When the singing faded away, the minister closed in prayer and bid everyone a blessed Sabbath. Charity picked up her Bible and reticule, and Hannah Sparrow beckoned a few parishioners over to introduce them.

More Southern accents.

She managed to smile and shake hands with each one; then her gaze collided with that of a young man standing near the back talking to the pastor. He stared at her for only a moment, his expression an odd mix of fascination and distrust. After a few seconds he turned back to his discussion with the pastor, but Charity studied his profile from across the room. She'd seen him before. That haunted look in his eyes jogged her memory. Of course—the man she saw through the kitchen door at the boardinghouse yesterday evening. She thought at first he worked there, but she didn't see him again until now. A darkness clung to him, nothing sinister, but somber and brooding, like he'd known great pain.

The preacher clapped him on the shoulder and turned to greet other worshippers. The young man with the moody eyes sent another quick look her way and caught her watching him. She stifled a gasp and turned to speak to Hannah Sparrow.

"Please excuse me, Mrs. Sparrow. I'd like to speak to the preacher."

"Wasn't this morning's message wonderful? I'm sure you'll enjoy meeting him," her landlady bubbled.

Charity didn't bother to explain that her interest in speaking with the man wasn't to discuss today's sermon. As the pastor of the church, he likely knew everyone in town, and Charity hoped he could supply her with some information. When she made her way toward the pastor, the man she'd seen at the boardinghouse had already taken his leave, and Charity's curiosity remained unsatisfied.

Mrs. Sparrow took Charity's hand. "Pastor Shuford, I'd like you to meet my newest boarder, Miss Charity Galbraith. She is a reporter with *Keystone Magazine.*"

The pastor shook her hand and gave her a warm smile. "I hope you'll be with us for a good long visit, Miss Galbraith."

"Thank you, Reverend. I hope to stay for as long as it takes to research the information I need."

Pastor Shuford smiled and nodded. "If I can be of any help, please let me know."

Exactly what Charity hoped he'd say. "As a matter of fact, I'd like to visit Covington Plantation. Perhaps you could direct me."

A saddened expression drooped the man's smile. "I'm afraid there is no more Covington Plantation. It was burned during the war. Scavengers."

"Oh dear." Charity bit her lip. "I hoped to speak with someone from the Covington family. You see, I'm trying to locate a former slave who worked there."

"A former slave?"

"Yes. His name is Wylie, and his mother is my friend. She's not seen or heard from him for eleven years. I'd like to find him for her."

The pastor sent a stealthy glance around them, and then leaned in and lowered his voice. "That sounds like a fine Christian act, and I pray God's safety for you as you search. Not everyone in these parts will appreciate such a mission. Unfortunately, Covington Plantation no longer exists, but you can speak to Dale Covington."

"I'd very much like to do that. Where might I find him?"

The pastor stepped to the open door of the church and pointed. "That's him, the man in the dark brown coat."

Charity looked at the man to whom the pastor pointed. The brooding man with the hollow look in his eyes limped across the street away from the church.

"He was wounded in the war." Pastor Shuford's voice, hushed and pensive, left Charity to wonder about the extent of Mr. Covington's wounds.

A dozen other questions crowded her mind as well. The Covingtons were obviously a wealthy family at one time if they owned a plantation and slaves. Curiosity needled her. Whatever was a man like that doing in the boardinghouse kitchen?

"Miss Galbraith, I feel I must tell you, Dale Covington probably won't be very receptive to your inquiries."

She turned to look at the pastor. "Why? Is he ashamed of having kept slaves?"

Pastor Shuford gave an almost imperceptible shake of his head. "Sometimes a man's wounds go deeper than his flesh."

She pondered the minister's peculiar reply for a moment. "Could you direct me to his place of residence?"

"It wouldn't be proper for you to visit him at his home. He lives alone. I hope you understand." Pastor Shuford gave her a fatherly smile. "But he works at the sawmill across the creek." He pointed toward the left. "Go past the boardinghouse and the post office. The road curves and you'll see a bridge. You can find him there most days. After he finishes at the mill, he works for Clyde Sawyer at the general store. He helps out in the back, makes deliveries, things like that."

So he'd been delivering Mrs. Sparrow's groceries last evening. Imagine that, a rich man like Covington working in a sawmill and delivering groceries. She supposed she should feel sympathy for him, but instead, an element of smug gratification settled in her stomach.

"Across the creek, you say?" She leaned to peer in the direction the pastor had pointed. "Thank you, Pastor. I'll pay Mr. Covington a visit at the sawmill."

Chapter 3

Dale hurried into the bakery on his way to the sawmill. Despite living alone for six years, he'd still not gotten used to making his own breakfast. Polly Ferguson always had some tempting offerings to satisfy him.

Polly's daughter, Margaret, greeted him. "Good morning, Dale. What can I get for you today?"

Dale peered over the counter to the baked goods lined up on racks behind her. "By any chance did you and your mother make those apple things this morning?"

Margaret's pleasant personality and culinary skills might have been enough to lure some men, but Dale wasn't hunting. Besides, the woman was a few years older than he, and plain-looking with her mousy hair pulled back in a tight bun. Her crooked teeth showed when she smiled.

"You mean the cinnamon apple scones? Yes, we made them. How many would you like?"

One fat scone would keep him going this morning. He'd tried buying an extra one once, thinking he could eat it the following morning, thus saving himself a trip to the bakery. But by the second day the scone was so dry, it was like trying to swallow thatch.

"Just one."

Margaret wrapped a scone in paper and handed it to him with a demure smile. "I gave you the biggest one. Anything else?"

Dale had the distinct impression she was flirting. "No, thank you." He handed over a dime and took his wrapped breakfast.

"See you tomorrow, Dale?"

He hesitated on his way out the door. "Uh, maybe." As he exited, he nearly collided with Pastor Shuford.

"Morning, Pastor." He held up the scone. "Join me for breakfast?"

The preacher chuckled. "No, my wife keeps me supplied with all the baked goods I can eat. Actually, I saw you walking this way and thought I might accompany you to the sawmill if you don't mind."

Dale slid the scone into his pocket and glanced sideways at the preacher. "You thinking on buying some lumber, or is there another purpose to your early morning stroll?

The older man smiled. "I confess I just wanted to talk to you. Let's walk so you aren't late for work."

The two set out in the direction of the sawmill. Dale noticed the pastor shortened his stride to accommodate Dale's hitched gait.

Pastor Shuford sucked in a noisy breath. "I love the smell of autumn."

Certainly the man didn't wish to discuss the changing seasons.

"I was talking with your sister and brother-in-law yesterday after church. Auralie and Colton said they haven't seen much of you."

"I've been busy." The ten-minute walk didn't afford much time for chatting. "What's really on your mind, Pastor?"

The pastor smiled. "I wondered if you'd given much thought to yesterday's sermon."

Dale drew in a stiff breath. He could have predicted this conversation. "Not too much. You know it's still hard for me to think about that. Everything you said is probably true, but I don't see why I should forgive people who burned my home, stole my land, and"—he gritted his teeth— "took Gwendolyn and—" Tightness took up residence in his throat.

Pastor Shuford's voice gentled. "Dale, you aren't the only one who lost someone in the war."

Dale halted and jerked around to face the preacher. "Maybe not, but when soldiers go off to fight, the ones left at home know there is a possibility they won't come back. After months of fighting and trying to heal from wounds, I came home expecting to find my loved ones waiting for me." He shook his head and continued toward the mill, his annoying shuffle-step impeding his determination to end this conversation and get to work.

The pastor fell in beside him. "Dale, have you ever noticed how your limp gets worse when you get angry about the war?"

Dale stopped so fast he almost pitched forward. He spun with an indignant retort on his tongue, ready to demand to know why the pastor would say something so cruel. But the preacher's expression was anything but cruel. Kindness and compassion deepened the lines around his eyes, defusing Dale's irritation.

"Dale." Pastor Shuford laid his hand on Dale's shoulder. The preacher's eyes glistened. "I fear the bullet that injured your leg did less damage than the resentment and animosity you nurture. Don't you see, son? Your old wound has been trying to heal for six years, but your bitterness is making you a cripple."

Pastor Shuford's words, spoken with such tenderness, punched Dale in the gut and robbed his breath. He braced himself with his good leg so he wouldn't stagger. No other person on the face of the earth could get away with saying such a thing to him. But even under the onslaught of pain the preacher's words brought, Dale knew the man well enough to realize he'd spoken in love.

He stared at his friend, watching the moisture gather in his eyes. The pastor squeezed Dale's shoulder before stepping back and dropping his hand.

"I better let you get on to work."

Dale nodded mutely, but didn't move.

"Son, you know I'm praying for you."

Dale somehow found the will to make his muscles work again. He nodded. "Yes, sir. I know."

He walked the remainder of the distance to the mill alone, but the preacher's words accompanied his every step. The morning mist still hung in the air as Dale studied his own impaired stride. Did his limp really worsen when he thought about the war?

Smoke curled from the tin chimney in the sawmill office. Simon Pembroke already had the fire in the potbellied stove going. Dale hitched his way up the dozen steps to the door that bore a sign, PEMBROKE SAWMILL—OFFICE. When he stepped inside, his boss looked up from the desk.

"You all right, Dale? You look a little peaked."

Dale gritted his teeth and worked his jaw. Pembroke's Northern accent always set him on edge, but even more so this morning. The man had arrived in Juniper Springs from Massachusetts the year after the war ended, bought up land cheap, and built the sawmill. It had galled Dale at first to work for a Yankee, but Pembroke paid a fair wage.

He sucked in a breath through his clamped teeth. "Yes, sir, just fine." He pulled the clipboard from its peg, but before he left the office to start on the day's first work order, he dug in his pocket and pulled out a few folded bills. He held them out to Pembroke. "October's rent for the house."

Pembroke frowned. "This isn't due till next week."

"I know." Dale laid the money on the desk and stepped out the door.

Charity walked resolutely down the street, past the post office, to the bend in the road. The bridge appeared on the left, just as the pastor said. She lifted her chin and straightened her shoulders, marching over the bridge. The sawmill was tucked into the rocks beside the creek so the swiftest running water turned the huge wheel. The noise from the mill drowned out the thumping of her heart in her ears. She paused at the end of the bridge.

Anticipation of speaking with Mr. Covington had her nerves tumbling, though she couldn't guess why. Arrogant, self-important people had never bothered her in the past. But something about this man intrigued her. He'd once been an influential man of means, but the outcome of the war had stripped him of his wealth. No doubt his circumstances would steer his reactions to her questions.

A set of stairs on one side of the large frame building led to a door with a sign declaring it to be the office. She pulled in a deep breath to strengthen her fortitude and proceeded toward the stairs. As she placed her foot on the first step, she saw him.

Mr. Covington, his back bent to his task and his sleeves rolled to his elbows, stacked lumber in the back of a wagon. She watched him for a moment. Unsure of what she expected to see, an element of surprise raised her eyebrows as she observed the intensity and zeal with which he performed his job. He appeared different today, other than the fact he wore work clothes instead of his Sunday best. He gripped each board and maneuvered it smoothly into a neat stack with ease. That was it. His limp wasn't as noticeable today.

He straightened and reached for a canteen that hung from the side of the wagon. Just as he started to take a drink he caught sight of her and halted midmotion. He lowered the vessel slowly, his steely gaze fixed on her.

"Can I help you find something?"

Charity had an eerie feeling that he considered her an intruder. "Mr. Covington?"

He set the canteen aside. "That's right."

She pasted the most professional expression she could muster on her face and approached him. He stiffened visibly. Charity decided if he'd been a cat, he might have arched his back and hissed. She extended her hand. "I'm Charity Galbraith."

His hooded eyes and the sullen twist to his mouth sent a chill through her, not from fear, but anticipation. What hovered behind those eyes?

He took her hand for a brief moment, but dropped it like it had burned him. "Miss Galbraith." There may as well have been a No Trespassing sign staked in front of him. This wasn't going to be easy.

"I wonder if you might have time to talk."

His dark eyes didn't blink. "I'm working."

"Yes, I can see that, but I promise I won't take up much of your time."

Several long seconds ticked by, and she thought he was going to tell her to leave, but he didn't. Instead, he gestured to a low stone wall on the side of the building beside the creek. He snagged the canteen and carried it with him.

When they were seated, he took the cap off the canteen and gave her an apologetic look. "Sorry, this is all I have to offer in the way of refreshment."

She waved her hand. "No, thank you, but you go ahead."

He took several gulps. "What is this about?"

Charity took a deep breath. "I have a friend in Pennsylvania. Her name is Essie Carver. She hasn't seen or heard from her son in eleven years. She's not even sure if he's alive."

Puzzlement etched its mark across his brow. "What does that have to do with me?"

"Essie's son's name is Wylie." She paused, searching his face for some flicker of recognition, but none appeared. "Wylie was a slave. He was sold to Covington Plantation in 1859 at age thirteen. That's the last she ever saw of him. I hope you can tell me where Wylie is now."

Distress lines between his eyes gave Mr. Covington a prematurely aged appearance. He rose and paced for a moment, as if unconscious of his limp. When he spoke, the painfulness of the topic was evidenced in his tone.

"I'm sorry, Miss Galbraith. Covington Plantation utilized over four hundred slaves. The only ones I knew by name were the house slaves and the ones who worked in the stables taking care of the horses and carriages." He glanced awkwardly at his crippled leg, hobbled slowly back to the stone wall, and sat, the limp more noticeable now than when he had been working.

"Records were kept, of course, but—" The muscles in his neck twitched as he swallowed. Was he trying to compose himself? "There was a fire. The records were destroyed along with. . .everything else." He rubbed his side with a slow, methodical motion. "It may seem inhumane to keep such a large number of slaves without knowing their names. When my father was alive, he and I frequently disagreed on the care of the slaves. I tried to tell him that treating them with brutality was unnecessary, but he insisted on leaving that up to the overseers." He looked across the lumberyard as if he was searching for the manor house in which he'd lived. "One of the things we disagreed on was splitting up family members. My father did not regard the slaves as having families. To him they were chattel."

Charity shook her head. "Are you telling me that a thirteen-year-old child came to work on your plantation and you were not aware of him?"

He rubbed his hand across his forehead. "Not if he was bought as a field slave." He turned to look at her. The moodiness in his eyes wavered. "I don't expect you to understand how it was."

Charity swallowed hard, trying to control her temper. How it was? How did he think it was for a child to be separated from his mother and for his mother to never know what happened to him?

"You're right, I don't understand."

He stood again and turned away from her with his hands clasped behind his back. "I was away much of the time. In the year or so before the war, I worked on some special projects for my father and out of necessity was away from the plantation for short periods. After—"

Though his back was to her, a visible shudder rippled through him, as though he bit off the words and spit them out.

"When the war started, I was commissioned and, of course, was away from home for much longer periods of time. When I returned home after the war, every—" He paused and sighed. "Everything. . .and everyone. . . was gone." He turned back to face her. "I sincerely wish I could help you find this Wylie. And I wish—I wish I'd known his name when he belonged to Covington Plantation."

Charity sat in silence, uncertain if she should feel pity or outrage toward this man. This conversation did not go as she expected. She'd come to the sawmill fully prepared to dislike Dale Covington. Her wavering emotions unsettled her, like a child walking atop a fence with arms held out to her sides for balance. She'd always held indecisive people in disdain. Now she was the object of her own scorn, the very attitude she'd reserved for Dale Covington.

"I really must get back to work." Mr. Covington fastened the top back onto the canteen.

Charity rose from her seat. "Thank you for your time, Mr. Covington. I suppose I'll have to look elsewhere for Wylie."

"You still intend to keep looking?" His question sounded more like a challenge.

"Of course." Did the man not understand what it meant to persevere? "I promised his mother."

❧

Long after Miss Galbraith had taken her leave, Dale listened to their conversation echo in his mind. A cold sweat popped out on his forehead as the memories tore through him. His stomach tightened, and his leg ached. The picture he'd tried a thousand times to erase from his mind emerged again.

His uniform in tatters, a crutch under one arm, and sinking dread in his belly, he hobbled up the road toward home. Fear accosted him when he saw the great, ornate wrought-iron gates of Covington Plantation hanging askew from the posts. Grass grew down the lane that led to the manor house, and the once-beautiful grounds screamed out for someone to care for them once again.

He smelled it before he saw it. Although slight, the distinctive stench of stale smoke lingered in the air as though it didn't know where else to go. His first sighting of the burned-out ruins of the house nearly brought him to his knees, but that's not what ripped his heart from his chest.

Dale shook his head to rid himself of the memory—the scene he knew would invade his dreams again—and another took its place.

The black face bent over him, wrapping a rag around his leg and offering him a drink. The stranger removed his own shirt and used it to bind the wound in Dale's side. While rifle fire and artillery still roared, the black man whose name Dale did not know lifted him in his work-hardened arms and carried him to safety. For two days, the black man—obviously a slave sent to fight in his master's stead—cared for him until they reached a regiment that had a doctor.

"I wish I'd known his name."

Chapter 4

Charity propped her elbow on the small desk in the corner of her room at the boardinghouse and leaned her chin in her cupped palm. She'd composed a short letter to Uncle Luther, letting him know she was fine, staying in a respectable boardinghouse, and he needn't worry about her.

"*Pfft.* More likely he's glad to be rid of me." She addressed the envelope to her uncle, in care of the Kimball Hotel in Atlanta. Uncle Luther had made certain she'd known the Kimball was the finest hotel in the city, boasting of steam heat and elevators. She smirked at her uncle's pomposity.

Her second letter lay half-finished in front of her. She knew her editor at the magazine waited for a tentative list of interviews and useful research she'd gleaned. Convincing Mr. Peabody to give her this assignment wasn't easy. She couldn't disappoint him. She'd been in Juniper Springs for almost a week and most of her time had been spent simply observing and listening. She crumpled the paper into a ball.

"And trying to find Wylie." Frustration taunted her. She'd hoped one visit to Covington Plantation would supply her with all the information she needed to find the young man. How was she to know the place didn't even exist anymore?

Her conversation with Dale Covington raised more questions than it answered. She leaned back in her chair and gazed out the small curtained window. Orange and red leaves mingled with bronze and gold in a gorgeous crazy-quilt mosaic, a gentle reminder that no matter how ugly war's destruction, God had the power to make things beautiful again.

"What if some things can never be put back together? What if I have to go back to Harrisburg and tell Essie I couldn't find Wylie, or worse, what if he's dead?"

The familiar twinge of grief pierced her chest. Her goal of finding her father remained unspoken. No one but God knew of her intention to learn what had befallen him, and she knew the chance of finding him alive was almost zero. But if she could simply know for sure, perhaps the troubled dreams that invaded her sleep would come to an end.

"Lord, I can't bury him in my mind until I know." Her throat tightened, and burning moisture filled her eyes. "If I know he's with You, then I can be at peace."

Her heart turned over as she thought of her friend wondering all these years if her child was alive. Poor Essie tried to cling to the belief that Wylie would one day find his way to her. But with each month and year that passed, Charity saw the hope in Essie's eyes crumble a little.

"God, please help me find Wylie. I pray he's alive, but if he isn't, then help me know how to tell Essie."

If only Dale Covington had been able to give her a solid lead to follow. Again, she recalled their meeting at the sawmill the other day. The man was not at all pleased to meet her. A twinge of shame nibbled at her heart. She'd marched in there all prepared to revile Mr. Covington with her scathing opinion of people who bought and sold other human beings. But a mysterious aura hung around the man like a cloak of grief that drew a haunted shroud over his eyes. She suspected he had his own version of war miseries. But what could be worse than expecting a loved one—a father, a brother, a husband, a sweetheart—to come home and having that wait stretch into months and years without any word? How did one finalize a bond with a person they loved and put their memories to rest?

She'd often thought it cruel and coldhearted to inform family members of their loved one's demise by telegram or letter. Words on paper seemed so heartless. But even a heartless letter would have been better than a state of oblivion.

Over the past several years, she'd seen and known many people who'd suffered a great loss through the war. Countless men came home blinded or missing a limb. Some could no longer work to support their families. Others were so devastated by what they'd witnessed, they turned to whiskey or opium to dull the pain. Others withdrew into themselves and no longer seemed to be the same person they once were.

Her conversation with Dale Covington became more puzzling every time she thought about it. How could he exude such melancholy over the loss of a house? When he spoke of it, his limp even became more pronounced. With the staggering number of casualties and destroyed lives as a result of the war, if all Mr. Covington lost was his house, he should count himself fortunate.

A twinge of regret poked her. Her parents taught her to be compassionate and kindhearted, not cynical and judgmental. Her father always said to hear an entire matter before making up her mind. Otherwise, she was merely jumping to conclusions.

A lump filled her throat. "Papa was always right about such things." Her own whisper echoed in the emptiness of the room.

Mr. Covington did say he wished he could help find Wylie, and for some reason she couldn't explain, she believed him. As she'd left him that day at the sawmill, the expression in his eyes stayed with her. She was a journalist. She made her living with words. But she couldn't put her finger on the words to define what she saw in his eyes.

Her stomach growled, and she glanced at the dainty watch pinned to her bodice. Nearly six o'clock. She pushed away from the small desk and left her room. Perhaps she could give Mrs. Sparrow a hand.

The enticing aroma of roasting chicken greeted her halfway down the stairs. Three of the other boarders sat in the parlor awaiting supper, and Charity tried to remember their names. The county sheriff—she remembered his last name was Flint—reclined with one leg crossed over the other, a book in his hands. Another man—his name escaped her—read the *Juniper Springs Sentinel*. Did he work in the courthouse or land office? He might turn out to be a source of information if he had access to official records.

The third man she remembered. Tate Ridley slumped on the settee, impatience edging his features. Ridley was the most vocal of the boarders when Mrs. Sparrow introduced her as a magazine reporter. The man clearly didn't take to the idea of someone from the North reporting on the Reconstruction process. She almost suggested he write an article based on his own research and submit it, but she suspected the man couldn't read or write. When he looked over and saw her standing at the foot of the stairs, one corner of his mouth lifted, appearing more like a snarl than a smile.

Charity hurried to the kitchen door. "Mrs. Sparrow, what can I do to help?"

The plump woman straightened and brushed an errant lock of hair away from her face. "Well, you can start by calling me Hannah." She blotted perspiration from her forehead with the corner of her apron. "It's right nice of you to offer to help. Can you check the biscuits?"

"Certainly." Charity grabbed a towel and pulled the pan of golden brown biscuits from the oven. "Mmm, they're perfect. The dog usually tries to bury my biscuits."

Hannah chuckled. "It would be a sad thing if I couldn't make a decent biscuit after nearly forty years of practice." She deposited two fat roasted hens onto a large platter. "If you'll fill the water glasses, I'll put these birds on the table and call everyone to supper."

As soon as all the boarders were seated and Hannah asked God's blessing on the meal, conversation flowed as freely around the table as the serving vessels. Charity listened, trying to pick out the persons who might be the most willing to share information. The man whose name she couldn't remember gave her a syrupy smile and wiggled his eyebrows.

"Would ya pass the biscuits, please, Miss Galbraith."

Charity obliged him with a polite nod.

"Thank ya kindly, ma'am."

Tate Ridley snorted. "Looks like Arch got hisself some fancy manners. You tryin' to impress this here Yankee lady, Arch? Oh, that's right, I forgot. You're a Yankee yourself, ain't ya?"

The man Tate Ridley called Arch growled back. "There's nothing wrong with being polite. You could stand to learn some manners yourself, Ridley."

"Boys." Sheriff Flint held up his hand. The lamplight from the wall sconces glinted off his badge. "I'd be obliged if y'all didn't start anything I'd have to finish, 'cause I'd be mighty vexed if y'all interrupted my supper."

Hannah pointed her fork at both Ridley and Arch. "I've told you before. You two can disagree all you want, but not under my roof."

Ridley grunted and shoveled food in his mouth.

Arch shrugged. "Sorry, Miz Hannah."

Everyone ate in silence for a few minutes. Perhaps now was a good time to inquire if any of these local folks could aid her search.

"I wonder if any of you can answer a few questions for me." Several pairs of eyes looked her way. "You see, in addition to the articles I'm writing for the magazine, I'm also trying to locate someone. Perhaps some of you might know where I could find him."

Sheriff Flint took a sip of water. "What is this person's name?"

Charity blotted her lips with her napkin. "All I have is a first name— Wylie. He would be about twenty-four years old. He is a former slave, having been at Covington Plantation since 1859."

Tate Ridley glared at her and set his fork and knife down with a clatter. "You're lookin' for a darkie?"

"I'm looking for my friend's son whom she hasn't seen in eleven years."

Ridley demanded to know why she'd waste her time and called Wylie by a derogatory reference that Charity detested.

"Mr. Ridley, I would appreciate it if you would refrain from using that term." She mentally counted to ten and cut her glance to the others at the table. "Slave records were kept, but there was a fire and the records were destroyed. Might there be any place else I could look? Were records of slave sales kept in any of the county offices?"

Frances Hyatt spoke up in her mousey little voice. "Miss Galbraith, why don't you ask Dale Covington? He might know."

"Yes, ma'am, I already did, but he couldn't recall the young man."

Another derisive snort came from Tate Ridley's side of the table. "*Young man!* Mighty highfalutin way to refer to a—"

"Tate. I believe the lady has already stated her request for you to mind your mouth and your manners."

All heads turned toward the kitchen door. Dale Covington stood in the doorway, his dark eyes narrowed and his jaw twitching.

ॐ

Dale met Tate's glare without a blink. It wasn't the first time he'd locked horns with the crude fellow, but it normally occurred at the sawmill where they both worked. Most times Dale ignored the man's uncouth language, but not this time.

"Miss Galbraith is a lady, as are the rest of these women. Some of her questions may open wounds better left alone, but she's not being intentionally hurtful. You are. Keep your disrespectful opinions to yourself."

The ladies sat wide-eyed, and Miles Flint smirked, while Arch Wheeler and Elden Satterfield just kept eating. Tate Ridley pursed his lips and clenched his jaw. Charity Galbraith, however, turned a bright red and her eyes snapped with displeasure.

He turned to Hannah. "My apologies, Mrs. Sparrow, if I overstepped my bounds." He gestured over his shoulder. "I put your order from the mercantile on the kitchen worktable." He tugged the brim of his hat at the ladies and turned, striding through the kitchen to the back door.

"Wait."

He stopped and turned. Miss Galbraith hurried through the kitchen.

"I suppose I should thank you for coming to my defense, but what did you mean about my questions opening wounds?"

Before he could answer she rattled off her own indignant defense. "You may not approve of me being here, and perhaps my questions strike a nerve, but what I'm doing is in service to a friend."

"Well, isn't that noble of you." Dale folded his arms over his chest. "I may not be familiar with how things are done in Harrisburg, but around here right now, your questions might be considered inappropriate at best and dangerous at worst."

Her dark brown eyes shot sparks. "Dangerous! That's silly. The war is over."

He returned fire. "It's not over for everybody. Many Southerners are still fighting for their very existence, trying to regain some semblance of the way of life they once knew." He bit his tongue and refrained from spewing his own list of losses, lest it sound like self-pity.

Miss Galbraith stood with her hands on her hips. "Maybe they should have considered that before they seceded from the Union and started the war."

Dale's fingers curled into fists, and he stared hard at her. She had no idea how it was in Georgia during the fighting and its aftermath. He contemplated educating her in the ways of the South, but he had a notion the explanation would be a waste of breath, if she was like most hardheaded Yankees.

"There is some room for debate over which side was responsible for starting the war, but I'm talking about right now, today. You're here to write about the Reconstruction as well as find your friend's son. I'm only cautioning you to use discretion when you ask your questions."

She lifted her chin. "I'll ask whatever questions I need to in order to find Wylie. Your advice is interesting. I wonder if my friend would consider my inquiries offensive if they lead to locating her son."

Dale nudged his hat with his knuckle and blew out a stiff breath. "Miss Galbraith, I didn't say your cause is not a good one. It's a fine thing you're trying to do, even if it is a bit misguided and imprudent. I'm just suggesting you be careful who you ask. Not everyone will appreciate your devotion to your mission."

"Why is it imprudent? If your child was missing, wouldn't you welcome any and all help to find him?"

Her words slammed into him, nearly stealing his breath. Heat rose into his face, and his pulse pounded in his ears. A rush of blood fell into his belly.

She took a step forward, genuine concern tugging her brow. "Mr. Covington, are you all right?" Her tone lost its defiant edge and gentle warmth took its place.

All right? Was that a state of mind? He'd not considered for a very long time what it meant to be all right.

Miss Galbraith's dark eyes softened and a tiny crease formed between her brows. His chest squeezed. Had he noticed her enchanting eyes before? The slight blush in her cheeks? Her hair that glowed in the lamplight?

He stiffened his spine. When was the last time he looked at a woman in that way?

"Yes, I'm fine." He stepped backward toward the door. "Please, just be careful."

She cocked her head. Her piercing gaze seemed to penetrate his soul. "I will."

He stepped out the back door into the gathering dusk. The chilled autumn air pulled him back to consciousness. He shoved his hands into his pockets and hurried down the shadowy street. Miss Charity Galbraith was certainly the prettiest Yankee he'd seen in all the years since the onset of the war and afterward.

He slowed his pace. No point in hurrying home to an empty house. He welcomed the cool evening air on his face and took a deep breath. Someone had baked an apple pie. The crisp air laced with the homey scent spiked his loneliness. If only he could find a way to get past his anger. He didn't like the way it made him feel. Even Pastor Shuford suggested his bitterness poisoned him.

Miss Galbraith's image graced his thoughts again. He sincerely hoped she'd heed his advice, but caution threw a red flag in his face. Caring about a woman, especially a beautiful Yankee woman, spelled trouble. After all, old hostilities were hard to shake.

Chapter 5

Have you gone soft in the head, Covington?"

Tate Ridley's caustic tone stirred Dale's ire, and ignoring him didn't appear to work. He turned to look the man in the eye. "I assume this is about your impolite behavior and crude language in the presence of ladies last evening."

"Ain't nothin' wrong with my way o' thinkin', but it 'pears like you done forgot which side you're on." Tate's sneer pulled his lips into a grotesque frown. "How come you was defendin' that Yankee woman? Are you forgettin' what her and her kind did to us?"

"Tate, you don't know what you're talking about." Dale brushed past him to continue inventorying the stack of logs. "Miss Galbraith didn't do anything to you. She is just doing her job, and I suggest you do yours."

"She's writin' for that magazine of hers. What do you think she's gonna write about?" Tate followed at Dale's heels, and a few other men stopped what they were doing to listen. "She's gonna make it sound like the South deserved what they got and how them Yankees is a bunch of heroes."

Dale heaved a sigh. "You've made me lose count again. Look, Tate. Save your foul language for the gutter rats with whom you associate. Miss Galbraith is a lady."

"She's a Yankee, and a Yankee is a Yankee." Ridley nearly spat the word. "They might've won the war, but that don't mean I hafta stand by and do nothin' while she belittles me and mine."

"What?" Dale gave him a sideways glance. "She didn't belittle you. Have you been drinking that moonshine again?"

Tate's face turned red. "She told me in her highfalutin' talk that she don't like the way I think."

"Simmer down, Tate. She's not the enemy." A twinge of guilt twisted in Dale's belly. Hadn't he thought of Miss Galbraith the same way? He turned his back to Tate and went through the motions of counting the logs, but his conscience nipped at him. "It's none of your business what she chooses to do for her friend, and I'm sure she'll write an honest account of the Reconstruction effort."

"Oh, you're sure o' that, are you? What's the matter with you? You turn into a blue belly?" Tate practically hissed over Dale's shoulder. "Don't you remember the fightin'? Don't you remember it was a Yankee minié ball that blew a hole through your leg? Did you forget how everybody sees you as a cripple now, and it's the Yankees' fault?"

Heat rushed through Dale, from his toes all the way to the roots of his hair. The stigma that dogged him every time he limped screamed in his face.

Cripple!

Bitter acid filled his gut. He clutched his pencil so tightly it snapped in half. Coming out of the war a lesser man spawned rage in his heart. The doctors told him his leg had healed as much as it would, and he should be thankful to have survived. They called him lucky.

Tate's questions were preposterous. No, he hadn't forgotten. He remembered every day, with every step he took, with every sympathetic look of pity.

"Ridley." Simon Pembroke's voice broke the grip Tate's words held on Dale. "Did you get that wagon loaded yet?"

"I'm gettin' to it right now."

"See that you do."

Tate leaned close to Dale's ear and growled under his breath, "She's a Yankee. Don't make no never mind that she's a woman. If you're a true son of the South, you'll see her for what she is."

Ridley sauntered off toward the partially loaded wagon, and Dale listened to his heavy-booted footsteps—his even-cadenced strides—fade away. Shards of animosity wedged themselves in his flesh, and the rancor he nurtured festered a little more.

"Dale."

He turned. Simon Pembroke stood a few feet behind him.

"Don't let Tate get to you. I could stand here and tell you he's a troublemaker, but coming from me it wouldn't mean much since I'm a Northerner." He sniffed. "But I'll tell you this. You're twice the man he is, and twice the worker." He pulled a fresh pencil from his pocket and handed it to Dale. "Thought you might need this."

Pembroke turned on his heel and strode back to the office. Dale's boss was a man of few words and didn't approve of wasting time with idle chat. Dale came to work, did his job, and accepted his pay at the end of the week. In the nearly six years since he'd worked at the sawmill, Simon had never said such a thing to him before.

Dale looked at the two pencils in his hand, one broken and useless, the other whole and purposeful. And he did what anyone would do. He tossed the broken one away.

Dale spent the next hour counting and tallying the logs, but repeatedly had to admonish himself to concentrate. Tate's words rang louder than Simon's, and there was an element of truth in what Ridley said. Dale really didn't know for certain that Miss Galbraith's articles would reflect an honest disclosure of the Reconstruction process. Putting a splintered nation back together required the cooperation of all sides. Men bought lumber from Pembroke to reconstruct those buildings that were destroyed in the war. They carefully measured and cut, squared and nailed each board to create a solid structure. Likewise, each participant in the rebuilding of the nation must measure and ensure the trueness of what was built. If one didn't double-check for truth, imbalance would result. It stood to reason Miss Galbraith would write from a Northern perspective, but she had a responsibility to make sure her articles communicated the truth.

Last night he assumed any explanation to be a waste of breath. It might be wise to rethink that assessment. Perhaps he *should* enlighten her about the atrocities the South suffered. Politics aside, the cruelty of war destroyed much more than the Southern countryside. He just wasn't ready to share with her all the parts of his life that had been destroyed.

Charity stepped off the town doctor's porch and tucked her notebook into her pocket. Doctor Jonas Greenway had some interesting comments about the war and the reconnecting of all the states back into one nation, from a medical point of view. He'd seen and treated his share of war casualties from both sides. As he'd said so eloquently, "Soldiers don't bleed blue or gray. As a doctor, their blood was all the same to me." He told her he'd not prayed for the South or the North to win the war. He simply prayed for the war to be over. She'd filled several pages with notes.

Her only disappointment in the interview with the doctor was that he had no knowledge of a former slave named Wylie. Since he'd been away, attached to a regiment as a field surgeon, he'd not returned to Juniper Springs until after the Covington Plantation house burned.

She wished to interview Simon Pembroke as well, since the man hailed from Massachusetts. His take on the subject might prove interesting, but she didn't know how to approach the man without encountering Mr. Covington. She puzzled over the quandary.

After their confrontation in the boardinghouse kitchen ended with such a strange twist, for some reason, his feelings were important to her. After she'd recalled their heated discussion, she still couldn't put her finger on what had affected him to such a degree that he turned momentarily pale and speechless. But whatever the reason, it moved him visibly, and she desired to sit down with him again for another conversation.

Tate Ridley proved disconcerting. She found him rude and openly hostile, but he wasn't alone. Many Southerners still held deep resentment toward Reconstruction. She'd not anticipated encountering such hateful contention, but like it or not, she must include it in her articles.

Clearly, she didn't have a complete understanding of both sides. Until now, she'd only considered the perspective with which she and her mother had lived during the war and in the months to follow as they awaited word from her father. After her conversation with the doctor, chagrin pinched her as she acknowledged the thousands of Southern women who lost loved ones in the bloody conflict.

Pondering the depth of the research and inquires she still needed, she couldn't put off contacting her editor any longer. Mr. Peabody tended to be a stickler for accuracy, so hopefully he'd agree to extend her deadline.

Charity stopped at the telegraph office and wrote out a brief message to the magazine editor indicating she'd need more time. The telegram cost much more than sending a letter, but she justified the expense, anticipating Mr. Peabody to be pleased with her meticulous fact-finding.

She stepped out the door of the telegraph office into the warm Georgia sunshine. Despite being late September, she didn't need a shawl at midday. The mountains just to the west of town shimmered with dappled autumn colors. Charity paused to appreciate the view. The mountains were strong, enduring for millennia, and even a tragedy like the war couldn't destroy them. They stood as a silent testament of God's power and strength. Charity took solace in the thought.

Up the street, the schoolchildren spilled out of the schoolhouse, scrambling for the best place in the yard to eat their lunch. She had an appointment to speak with the town lawyer, Ben Latimer, and she didn't want to be late. She checked the time. Thirty more minutes—time to stroll around the little town.

She backtracked and walked along a treed lane that led to the tumbling creek. Pembroke Sawmill stood on the opposite bank. On the far side of the lumberyard, Dale Covington wrangled a team of mules, hitching them to a massive log and driving them forward to drag the giant tree trunk into position for the saw blade. As she watched him, she imagined the drastic change the war brought to his life, and she admitted her shame to the Lord for her initial critical attitude in depreciating the man's losses. Enduring wounds on the battlefield and his house burning to the ground would be hard for anyone to bear.

Concealed by a holly bush, she watched him work. No doubt he'd once been a wealthy man if he owned a plantation. Now that he had no grand house or land, and no slaves to work for him, he earned his wage by the sweat of his brow. There was nothing careless or lazy in the way he did his job. For that, he earned her admiration.

She found it interesting that he stayed in Juniper Springs and found employment after the war, especially doing physical labor. How difficult had it been for him to remain in the area where he'd once been a prominent landowner? He must have known humiliation at having his social status jerked out from under him. Why did he stay here? Did he ever consider going someplace where nobody knew him? Her curiosity piqued, and she wondered if she'd dare ask him such questions, even in the name of research.

ஓ

Charity scribbled as fast as she could push her pencil. Mr. Latimer, whose speech patterns identified him as a Southerner, gave her some insightful answers to her questions from the legal angle, explaining the process by which the legislature ratified the amendments required for readmission to the Union. In addition, he clarified the different periods of Reconstruction, outlining the nullifying of the state constitution before reorganization would take place.

Latimer leaned back in his desk chair. "Two years ago, the General Assembly expelled twenty-eight Negro members newly elected to the legislature because the state constitution didn't specifically give blacks the right to hold public office. Then they reversed their own decision on the fourteenth amendment, so the Federals returned and occupied the state again." He shook his head. "It's been a wickedly hard time for the people of Georgia."

Charity paused and tapped her pencil on her chin. "But why didn't they simply go along with the stipulations set down by the Federal court in the first place? It seems to me the Georgia Assembly made it harder on the people by continuing their rebellious posturing."

Latimer stroked his trimmed gray beard. "Some would agree with you, but you must remember Southerners are a proud people. They refused to admit defeat, and noncompliance with the demands of Congress was to them an act of pride and independence. Whether it was good for the people wasn't really taken into consideration."

Charity jotted down the lawyer's comments and closed her notebook.

"I wonder if you could answer a couple of unrelated questions."

Latimer pulled out his pocket watch and flipped the cover open. "I have to be at the courthouse shortly, but I have a few minutes."

Charity breathed a quick prayer. "Would you happen to know of a former slave who worked at Covington Plantation before it burned? His name was Wylie."

Latimer frowned. "A slave, you say." His tone shifted. After being more than willing to supply information for her magazine articles, disapproval now peppered his voice. "A young lady like yourself shouldn't be pursuing a darkie. Why would your magazine send you on such an unseemly errand?"

Charity tightened her grip on her notebook, sliding her defensive bearing into place. "It has nothing to do with the magazine." She straightened her shoulders. "Wylie is my friend's son, and she longs to find him. I promised her I'd do everything I could."

The lawyer's brow furrowed into a V, and he shook his head. "It's unbefitting and crosses the line of propriety. I don't know any darkies by name. There's some that live on the other side of the river, but it's no place for a lady to go."

"I see." She stood and smoothed her skirt. The muscles in her neck twitched, a warning sign that her temper was about make an appearance. "Thank you for your time, Mr. Latimer."

He rose and came around the side of his desk and took her hand. His gracious demeanor returned. "If there's anything else I can do to help you, why you just come by and we'll have another chat."

After acting like her Uncle Luther, showing gross disapproval of her mission to find Wylie, Mr. Latimer turned back into the benevolent sage. She walked toward the door before he could see her smirk. He strode past her to open the door in gallant fashion.

She paused, clutching her reticule in one hand and her notebook in the other. Turning to face the lawyer, she voiced one more hesitant question.

"By any chance would you know where the prisoner of war records are kept?"

Latimer rubbed his hand over his whiskered chin. "There was more than one prisoner of war encampment. The largest, of course, was at Andersonville. But I would suppose those are confidential military files. Why? Was this Wylie fellow a prisoner of war?"

A cold chill ran through her at the mention of Andersonville, the notorious prison where so many men died. The very thought of her father being imprisoned there nauseated her.

"I don't know about Wylie. I'm not even sure if he fought in the war. I'm looking for. . .a particular name."

"No." Latimer shook his head. "I'm not familiar with military courts. Perhaps if you contacted the war department in Washington."

She'd already done that five years ago, but they'd been unable to help since the records she sought were from the Confederacy.

"The man for whom I'm searching was a Union officer who was wounded and captured by the Confederate army in a battle here in Georgia."

The man arched his brow. "Oh?"

"His family is hoping for some kind of official statement. . .one way or the other."

"I'm truly sorry, Miss Galbraith." He sounded as if he suspected the person for whom she searched was dear to her. "I wouldn't know where such military records are kept, or if they are open to the public."

A lump grew in Charity's throat, and she forced a tiny smile. "Thank you, Mr. Latimer." An ominous burning in her eyes warned of eminent embarrassment. She hurried down the boardwalk.

How many dead ends must she encounter before she finally gave up?

Chapter 6

Charity sat at the kitchen table across from Hannah Sparrow. The heavenly aroma of sweet potato pies cooling on the windowsill seasoned the air in the room while they sipped their tea.

"So, now that you've been here almost two weeks, how do you like our little town?" Hannah pushed a plate heaped with oatmeal cookies in Charity's direction.

Charity relaxed in the cozy kitchen and in the comfortable presence of the woman. "It's lovely."

Hannah cocked her head. "That sounds as if there is something you'd like to add but don't want to offend anyone." She softened the remark with a smile that deepened the creases around her gray eyes.

"Well, I will admit I've encountered a few people who will probably not be added to my Christmas list." She took a nibble of a thick cookie and savored the cinnamony flavor.

Hannah's hearty laughter filled the kitchen. "At least you're honest." She selected a cookie and munched. "How is your research going?"

"Fairly well. I've spoken with a few people but have several more I'd like to interview, which reminds me"—she pulled her notebook from her pocket—"would you mind answering a few questions?"

"Me? Merciful heavens, child, couldn't you find anyone more interesting to talk to?"

Charity grinned. She would miss this sweet woman when it came time to go home. "I'm talking with people from all walks of life to get different perspectives."

Hannah reached for the teapot and refreshed her cup. "I can't imagine anything I have to say being of interest to anyone outside of Juniper Springs, but I'll help whatever way I can."

Charity opened the notebook and flipped several pages, but when she pulled out her pencil, she paused. "May I ask you about something else first, Hannah?"

"Of course. What is it?"

Charity explained about her mission to search for Essie's son and asked if Hannah knew of Wylie. The woman's eyes misted.

"No, I'm sorry, but I don't know him. I can't imagine how your friend felt being separated from her child. The practices associated with keeping slaves were pretty heartless." She reached across the table and patted Charity's hand. "I'll be praying you find this Wylie so his mama can hold him in her arms again." Her voice held a wistful note. "Dale Covington didn't remember him?"

"No, and after he explained why, I tried to understand. Things are just so different here from the way I grew up."

Hannah nodded. "Yes. Those differences are what tore our country apart."

Charity tapped her pencil on the blank page of her notebook. "Has the war and the Reconstruction affected your business here?"

"No." Hannah shook her head. "Not much. I had a couple of boarders who joined the state militia when the war first broke out. They were both killed. Owen Dinsmore died at Shiloh and Randall Kimber at Chancellorsville. Both of them had lived here at the boardinghouse for a few years.

"Two of the boarders I have now came after the war. Arch Wheeler is from New York and fought with the Union army. He came to take over at the land office after Randall was killed."

"Is that why Tate Ridley dislikes him so much?"

Hannah sighed. "I suppose. Those two haven't gotten along since the first day Arch arrived. Elden Hardy is from West Virginia. He doesn't talk much about the war, but a few suspect he was one who was denied citizenship in West Virginia because he aided the Confederacy."

Charity sipped her tea. "What about the town? You've been here most of your life, right?"

"I've lived in this area for thirty-five years. There were a lot of hardships during the war. With most of the able-bodied men from age sixteen to fifty off fighting, most of the work fell to the women and children. We didn't experience the food shortages to the degree that the cities did because most folks around here raised their own food, but there were things we couldn't get. Coffee was scarce and salt was rationed."

"How has the town changed since the war?"

"It's grown." Hannah reached for another cookie. "I remember when Juniper Springs wasn't much more than a half-dozen buildings. Now there are over thirty businesses. Simon Pembroke and a few others came to the area after the war and bought up land cheap."

Charity watched Hannah's eyes as she talked—"the windows to the soul" her mother used to say. Emotions lingered behind her landlady's eyes. "Are you saying these men came to make money on the rebuilding?

Sounds like they're war profiteers."

Hannah splayed her hands on the table and shrugged. "I didn't mean to sound harsh, but I suppose they did come for the opportunities. Some resented it. Simon bought several hundred acres of timber and built the sawmill. But now he employs fourteen men—some work in the woods felling trees, and others work at the mill. Not only do these men have good jobs, Simon also provides a service we didn't have before the war. Four other new businesses opened in town, and over a dozen new families make this their home."

Charity laid her pencil down and leaned closer to Hannah. "Doesn't Tate Ridley work at the sawmill?"

"That's right."

Charity rolled the information over in her mind. "Tate doesn't like Arch because he's a Northerner who came here and took the job that one of the local men used to have, but Tate works for Simon, who is also a Northerner who came here, some say, to make money from the war." She cocked her head. "Isn't that a contradiction?"

Hannah rose and pumped more water into the kettle. "Tate says if a man is handing out money, he'll take it." She set the kettle on the stove and poked another piece of stove wood into the firebox. "To answer your question, yes, it seemed so to me as well, but Tate's ethics are his own business."

Charity picked up her pencil again. "So then I imagine Simon has made a lot of money supplying lumber for all the rebuilding over the past five years."

Hannah reclaimed her seat. "There wasn't a lot of destruction in this part of the state, but I think the sawmill has supplied building materials for some places south of here."

Charity tipped her head to one side. "Not a lot of destruction? But what about Covington Plantation?"

Dismay creased Hannah's face. "There were skirmishes, and certainly there were troops who passed through. But the worst were the scavengers toward the end of the war. They looted and burned several places, including Covington Plantation." She shook her head. "It was a terrible time. Even here in town we were in fear for our safety, but more from the scavengers than the actual fighting."

Charity jotted down some notes. She paused. How to address the next part of the conversation? She asked God for discretion and proceeded carefully. "Hannah, yesterday at church I noticed a large plaque on the wall with all the names of those men from this area who were killed in the war."

Hannah seemed to age a few years in the time it took to for Charity to speak her observation, as if the woman knew what Charity's next question would be.

"There are two names on the plaque—Matthew Sparrow and Edwin Sparrow. Were they your sons?"

A faraway look eased into Hannah's gray eyes. "Yes. I lost both my sons in the war. Matthew fell at Chickamauga in September of 1863. I traveled there to see his grave two years ago. It gave me a bit of peace to lay wildflowers there and ask God to take care of my boy."

Charity didn't interrupt. What could she say? How did one comfort a mother on the loss of her child? The ache she felt for Essie grew with Hannah's telling of her grief.

"I think Edwin died at Gettysburg." Her voice fell to a whisper. "So many fine young men, their lives snuffed out like a candle."

She *thought*? Charity couldn't force the words past her lips. She sat without moving, barely taking a breath for fear of disturbing Hannah's deep, sad musing.

"I don't know where Edwin is buried." Hannah pressed her lips together and the tiny lines between her eyes deepened. "That plaque was put up just a few months ago." Her grief was underscored by her strained words. "People fussed and argued over it for five years."

How odd. Why would people not want to put up a memorial to their loved ones and friends who died in the war? Her puzzlement must have shown on her face, because Hannah explained.

"Some folks didn't want all the names engraved on the plaque, just those who fought for the Confederacy."

"Didn't everyone from Georgia fight for the Confederacy?"

"No." Extraordinary sadness taxed Hannah's voice. "It may come as a surprise to you, but there were plenty of Georgians who didn't believe in slavery, and therefore didn't support secession. Many of them fought for the Union. It caused some very hard feelings that some folks won't ever forget." Her eyes locked onto Charity's. "You see, my dear, the war didn't just divide the country. It divided communities, and"—the pitch of her voice rose unnaturally—"it even divided families."

Charity cringed inwardly, dreading to ask what she feared. "What do you mean?"

Tears filled Hannah's eyes. "While both my boys died in the war, Matthew fought for the Confederacy, but Edwin fought for the Union."

Charity couldn't breathe. How long had she considered her plight—not knowing what became of her father—the worst effect the war could have on a person? She was wrong.

ॐ

Dale selected the straightest oak boards with the finest grain, meticulously sorting through the inventory. He stacked them carefully beside the maple already tucked onto the wagon bed. He glanced at the order again to confirm the correct number of board feet. Simon had called him aside this morning with instructions for Dale to work on this order alone. Dale didn't ask questions but merely set to work.

Despite trying to dismiss Simon's words last week, they lingered in Dale's memory. The opinion of a Yankee never mattered before. Why now? An element of gratification tickled his belly to know Simon had recognized how hard he worked.

He ran his hand over a length of red oak, the intricate grain creating a mosaic pattern beneath his fingers. He hefted the board and inspected it for trueness before adding it to the rest of the boards on the wagon. Checking the last of the oak off the work order, Dale initialed the paper and limped across the lumberyard toward the office.

Three men stood talking in the shadow of the mill. When Dale passed by, he caught snatches of their conversation.

"...let that Yankee woman know she ain't welcome."

Dale slowed his shuffling steps and listened. He identified the trio by their voices. Tate Ridley, Amos Burke, and Jude Farley exchanged comments in the cover of murky shadows between the mill and the pole barn.

"What about all them questions she's been askin' around, 'bout some darkie she's lookin' for?"

"And what do you suppose she's writin' in those articles of hers? All she wants to do is throw more mud on us Southerners."

"We don't need no Yankee, 'specially a woman, stirrin' up trouble. Bad enough the darkies are all uppity now."

"Someone needs to make an example out o' her."

"Meybe someone will."

Harsh laughter reached Dale's ears.

"Listen now. The brotherhood is meetin' this Saturday night. We'll talk about what needs doin'."

Dale had heard enough. With his hitched gait, he stepped over to the men. "Couldn't help overhearing you fellows. If you have any plans on harming, or even harassing Miss Galbraith, you'd do well to change them."

"What business is it of yours, Covington?"

Dale turned to face Tate Ridley. "It's my business when I hear what can be construed as making threats on a woman."

Ridley stepped up, inches from Dale's face. "I told you before, a Yankee is a Yankee. You're a traitor to your own people if you defend her."

Amos snorted. "Everyone in the county knows his brother-in-law was a bushwhacker durin' the war."

Dale's gut tightened. He and his sister, Auralie, had argued over Colton's involvement with the Union army. Regret pinched Dale. With their parents both gone, he had no other family. Their differences drove a deep wedge of alienation between them. He saw them when they came to town, and they never missed church, yet he'd barely spoken with Auralie and Colton for almost five years. Something he needed to address.

Tate sneered. "If you was a true gray-blooded Southerner, you'd be makin' plans to come to that brotherhood meetin' yourself, Covington." He pulled a pocketknife from his back pocket. "But I'll bet if I was to cut you, you'd bleed blue, wouldn't you?"

Dale pointed his clipboard at Tate and then swung it to include Amos and Jude. "Leave Miss Galbraith alone or I'll have something to say about it."

"Ooh, ain't ya skeered, boys?" Amos guffawed. "This here crippled man's gonna have somethin' to say."

Dale jerked his thumb over his shoulder toward the mill. "There's three more orders in there that need to be filled today. If you boys are finished taking your break, I'd appreciate some help." He turned and gimped toward the stairs that led to the office. Anger impeded his steps as laughter followed him.

Simon Pembroke sat at his desk and looked up when Dale entered. "You're finished with that order already?"

Dale handed his boss the clipboard. "I picked through every piece of oak and maple to find the straightest boards, and there's not a knot in one of them."

Simon bobbed his head. "That's fine. This order is going to Lucas Adair, and you know how persnickety he is."

Had Dale not been so incensed by the three men in the lumberyard, he might have smiled at Simon's accurate portrayal of the cabinetmaker. "It's loaded and ready to go."

Simon pulled himself around in his chair. "Sit down, Dale." He gestured to the place next to the desk. "I want to show you something."

Dale sat and watched as Simon unrolled a map and anchored the corners down. He pointed to a section Dale knew well. "I understand you once helped survey this acreage."

Dale examined the map. "Yes, I did. It was before the war, though. Ten years ago. My father attempted to purchase this"—he ran his finger across the map between two points already marked—"this is the boundary line to my brother-in-law's land, and this tract is prime timber."

"I know. I bought it last week." He rolled up the map and stuck it in a drawer. "It's going to mean I'll be away from here two or three days a week for a while, and I'm going to need a foreman to oversee the mill operation." He leaned back in his chair. "You're my first and only choice."

The unexpected offer raised Dale's eyebrows. "You want me to be your foreman?"

"It shouldn't surprise you. I've watched the way you work, the diligence you put into everything you do. You certainly aren't lazy." Simon reached into one of the desk's cubbyholes and extracted a key. He laid it in front of Dale. "And I believe I can trust you."

"But you're—I'm—"

Simon smiled, something Dale had never seen him do.

"I'm blue and you're gray?" Simon shook his head. "Not anymore." He extended his hand.

Dale hesitated. He'd managed to put aside his animosity working for this man with the New England accent and do his job. Simon had always dealt fairly with him. He picked up the key and shook Simon's hand.

Strange. At one time he would have looked down his nose at someone like Simon Pembroke. Not long ago he'd have considered the man's offer an insult. As he descended the stairs and hitch-stepped across the yard, he took a moment for introspection.

Hard work, perseverance, and dependability had reaped him a reward, and it felt good.

Chapter 7

The general store, while small in size, supplied everything on Charity's list. The balding storekeeper and his wife—did he call her Sweet Pea?—served her with gracious smiles, unlike some of the receptions she'd received from a few other folks.

Since she'd decided to extend her stay and the evenings were growing cooler, she purchased a heavier shawl, a sturdier bonnet, and a pair of warmer stockings. As she browsed the store, she added a package of hairpins, a bar of Castile soap, a new nib for her pen, and a box of envelopes to the collection of goods in her arms.

As she walked toward the counter, trays of stationery caught her eye. The supply she'd brought with her was dwindling. Just as she picked up a box of paper, the door to her left opened and a man entered carrying two crates, one stacked atop the other. The door swung against her arms, sending sheets of stationery fluttering like autumn leaves in their descent to earth. In her effort to snatch her other purchases before they scattered across the floor, Charity bent and reached out at the same instant the man with the crates did. The top crate crashed to the floor, spilling its contents of ribbons and sewing supplies. In the space of a heartbeat, Charity recognized Dale Covington at the very moment their heads collided with a *thunk*.

Bumped off balance, she plunked down on her backside, holding one hand to her head.

Mr. Covington grabbed for the elusive papers as they sailed in the breeze from the open door. His boot landed on Charity's bar of soap and slid out from under him, sprawling his legs in opposite directions. Unable to regain his balance, he joined Charity in an ungainly position on the floor.

The storekeeper came rushing over. "Well, land o' Goshen, boy, what in tarnation's goin' on here?"

Heat rushed into Charity's face, and her head smarted. She risked a glance at Mr. Covington seated a few feet from her. A stricken expression of mortification surfaced across his face. A giggle bubbled up from her stomach. She tried to hold it back, fearing her display of humor might offend him. But the mirth refused containment and came puffing out her pursed lips. Once escaped, the laughter mocked her effort to suppress it by

315

building into uncontrolled gales.

"I'm sorry—" It was no use. The words came out in a sputter, and she surrendered to a torrent of giggles.

Finally, a deep-throated chortle joined her in a hilarious duet. She caught her breath, wiped her eyes, and looked over at Mr. Covington. The moment their gazes connected, the laughter started anew. After watching his dark, brooding expression since she'd arrived in town, she didn't think the man knew how to laugh, but she was wrong. The sound rippled through her like a symphony.

The storekeeper stood with his hands on his hips. "Well, I declare, if you two ain't a sight. I don't reckon either of you is hurt, judging by the cacklin' goin' on." He shook his head. "Well, don't just set there, boy, help the lady to her feet."

Weak from the expression of unbridled humor, Mr. Covington held onto the doorframe to steady himself. He reached down and cupped her elbow, supported her forearm, and lifted her. Remnants of a smile lingered on his face.

"Are you quite all right, Miss Galbraith?"

"I'm fine, Mr. Covington, but under the circumstances"—she gestured to the scattered merchandise—"I don't think it would be improper for you to call me Charity."

"I do apologize. . .Charity."

"Please don't. I haven't laughed so hard in years."

A tiny, lopsided grin tipped one side of his mouth. "Me either." He stooped and began picking up the sheets of paper, stacking them in a neat bundle.

"Mr. Covington, I—"

"Dale." A momentary glitter in his eye made her catch her breath.

Butterflies danced in her stomach. "Dale." She took the collected stationery he handed her. "I fear the last time we talked I may have come across as a bit abrasive. Please know that wasn't my intention."

He scooped up her package of hairpins and bar of soap. "No offense taken."

She blew out a short sigh of relief and snatched up the pair of stockings while he gathered the ribbons and sewing supplies that had fallen from the crate. As he did so, she noticed he barely limped at all.

"Dale, would you have time to talk?"

He straightened and shook his head. "As soon as I get these things put out, I have deliveries to make."

"I see." She watched as he retrieved the remaining articles from the floor. "I've come to realize I've been looking at the war from only one side. Being here has opened my eyes, and there is much more research needed before I can write unbiased articles."

He handed her the box of envelopes. "Glad to hear it."

Hope sprang up in her chest. "Does that mean you're willing to talk with me at another time?"

He hesitated and withdrew a bit into the Dale Covington she encountered on her first day there. Regret tugged at her. The glimpse of Dale she caught when he laughed was much more desirable.

She hugged her purchases to her. "Sunday afternoon?"

He shrugged. "I suppose." He stacked the two crates again and lifted them. "Sunday afternoon, then."

An odd thread of anticipation tiptoed through her. Three more days.

৵

The sound of the congregation singing lifted Charity's heart as she took her place beside Hannah Sunday morning. "All hail the power of Jesus' name, let angels prostrate fall. Bring forth the royal diadem, and crown Him Lord of all." The praise made her spirit soar.

She settled in with her Bible on her lap and flipped the pages to the text Pastor Shuford announced, Luke chapter fifteen. As he began to speak about the parable of the lost son, Charity's heart pinched. She pictured Essie, standing and watching for her son the way the father in the parable did.

Lord, please be with me as I search, and lead me to Wylie.

Her silent prayer brought Dale to her mind. Even if he couldn't remember Wylie, perhaps he could suggest somewhere to look. The expression that had come over him and darkened his eyes the first time she'd inquired still haunted her. What if there was something more ominous behind that look? Dare she bring up the subject again?

She hadn't seen him before the service started. She turned her head as far as she dared without people sending her disapproving frowns. From the corner of her eye, she caught sight of him sitting near the back. She pulled her focus back to the preacher, but Dale's presence a few rows behind her proved quite distracting.

After the closing hymn and prayer, Charity looked up and found Dale standing beside her.

"Good morning, Mrs. Sparrow. Charity."

A warm flush filled Charity's cheeks. Did he notice? She turned to her landlady who had a mischievous twinkle in her eye. "Hannah, would it be all right with you if Dale came to the boardinghouse later this afternoon? I have a few more questions I'd like to ask him."

The corners of Hannah's lips twitched, and she reached for Dale's arm. "Why don't you come for Sunday dinner, Dale? We'd love to have you."

Charity hiccuped. What did Hannah think she was doing? Playing matchmaker?

Dale raised his hand in protest. "Oh no, I don't want to put you out."

"You'd do nothing of the kind. I have a pot roast simmering, and there is plenty to go around." She patted his arm. "You come right on. I made an applesauce cake for dessert."

A rush of warmth pervaded Charity's middle. Her other meetings with Dale had been more businesslike. Well, except the unplanned meeting they had in the general store. But sitting next to him at dinner? Wouldn't that be considered too. . .friendly? Of course, dinner at the boarding-house with eight other people around the table wouldn't exactly be an intimate tête-à-tête. She smiled.

"You can't say no to Hannah's pot roast and applesauce cake."

A boyish grin tipped his mouth. "It's been a long time since I had a Sunday dinner like that. I'd be happy to accept."

Why was her stomach doing flips? Charity reprimanded herself, but her heart still rat-tat-tatted like a dizzy woodpecker.

※

"That was the best meal I've had in years, Hannah." Dale still stumbled over calling the woman by her first name, but she'd insisted. He held up his hand at her offer of another piece of applesauce cake. "I couldn't eat another morsel." He grinned. "But I wish I could."

When Charity began picking up plates and serving bowls, Hannah flapped her hands. "I'll do that. You young folks go on. Why don't you sit out on the back porch? It's nice and sunny out there, and you won't be disturbed." She spoke the last part of her statement rather pointedly.

Dale slid a sideways glance at Margaret Ferguson. The woman had blatantly aimed all her attention at him during dinner, much to Dale's chagrin. A childish pout poked her bottom lip out, and she marched from the dining room with a huff.

"Well then, I suppose we should go out to the porch." The pitch of Charity's voice rose a notch, along with his own level of apprehension. Such nonsense. He'd spoken with her before. They'd even banged heads and laughed about it together while sitting on the floor. Why was this different?

She picked up her notebook and preceded him through the kitchen. He held the back door for her while they stepped out to the porch. He glanced from one end of the porch to the other. No chairs. The only place to sit was a swing just wide enough for two. He could have sworn Mrs. Sparrow kept a couple of wicker chairs out here. Didn't he remember seeing them when he came to deliver her groceries? He tossed a look over his shoulder at the back door that stood ajar. Inside, Hannah hummed as she bustled about the kitchen. The woman was a sweet, loving person, but she was sly!

Dale held the chain of the swing until Charity sat. Uneasiness flooded the space between them, so thick it felt like a tangible thing. She opened her notebook and turned to a blank page.

"Do you mind talking about the war? I'd like to hear your story."

A lightning bolt ripped through him. The only person he'd really talked with about his experiences in the war was Pastor Shuford, and the preacher's words came rushing back to him.

"I fear the bullet that injured your leg did less damage than the resentment and animosity you nurture. Don't you see, son? Your old wound has been trying to heal for six years, but your bitterness is making you a cripple."

He stiffened and looked away. If he'd known this conversation would turn personal, he'd have turned down the invitation. He expected general questions about politics and Georgia's readmission to the Union. He curled his fingers into fists. Talking about his private pain he'd worked so hard to bury wasn't something he was ready to do. Was that true? Had he tried to bury it, or had he done what Pastor Shuford had said? Nurturing the bitterness took more ongoing effort than burying it.

Charity's quick intake of breath defined her regret. "I'm sorry." Her voice was quiet and gentle. "It wasn't my intention to make you uncomfortable. It's just that I've realized in the time I've been here that everyone has their own story—their own individual experience that isn't the same as anyone else's. My own experience is much different from yours, I'm sure."

He'd not thought of her having an experience from the war. Except for Gettysburg, he assumed Pennsylvania had remained relatively untouched by the war.

"When my editor gave me this assignment, I hoped to use part of my time here in Georgia to look for information—" Her voice tightened. "About my father."

He turned to look at her more fully and saw deep pain in her eyes. "Your father? I thought you were looking for a young slave."

"I am." Her eyes glistened. "But I also want to find out what happened to my father. He was a Union officer. The few letters he sent said he'd been engaged in several battles in Virginia, Tennessee, and Georgia. My mother and I received word that he'd been wounded and taken prisoner, but that was the last we heard." A single tear slid down her face, and her voice dropped to a hushed whisper. "He never came home."

A tiny ache kindled within him as he listened to her bare her heart—the pain of not knowing, or even having a grave to visit. The tremor in her voice gripped him. Her determination to seek out the prisoner of war records and learn, once and for all, what happened to father, gave him a glimpse of the passion with which she persevered. Her candidness pried away his hold from the horror of his memories. Pastor Shuford said it was time he talked about it.

He took a fortifying breath. "When I came home, the house was nothing but a burned-out shell. Nearly all the slaves were gone, the land in ruins with no way to plant or harvest a crop. Scavengers had looted the place. They took. . .everything. The graves—" He clamped his jaw so tightly it hurt, and he recognized something for the first time. That sensation of hardness that crawled up his gut and into his throat wasn't sorrow. It was anger. Bitter, acid rancor. He forced his hands to relax and concentrated on breathing evenly. After a minute, he continued.

"Both of my parents died during the war. My mother from apoplexy, and my father from consumption. The gravestones had been knocked over and trampled." But the loss of his home wasn't what carved the deepest scars into his heart. "My—"

A vise strangled him. No, he wasn't ready yet to speak of the vilest atrocity. There were some things a man couldn't express.

Besides, why should it matter to him that a Union officer didn't come home? Between the fighting itself and those who died in the prison camps or from disease, over 680,000 men didn't come home. He tried to harden his heart, but he couldn't get around the truth. He did care. He cared about her pain, he cared about her search, and—God help him—he cared about her. How could he do that?

It wasn't reasonable to blame Charity. She didn't burn his home or rip the most precious thing in his life from him. Likewise, he wasn't responsible for whatever happened to her father.

Her soft voice broke through his thoughts. "Dale, you don't have to say any more."

He turned to look at her, and unshed tears clung to her lashes. His gaze dropped to the notebook in her lap. She hadn't written a single word.

They sat in gentle silence, swaying to and fro on the swing. Shadows lengthened and the air chilled.

"I wondered if you'd thought of anywhere I might look for Wylie."

Reference to the former child-slave didn't sicken him the way it had with her first inquiry. He released a sigh. "No." He shifted on the swing to look at her. "I know I've mentioned this before, but I want to caution you again. Some people won't take kindly to you asking around about a slave, especially since you're—"

"A Yankee?" Her voice held a hint of animation.

"Yes." He stood. "It's getting late. I should go."

She rose, and they walked to the top of the porch steps where he paused before descending. "Charity, may I take you to dinner one night next week?"

Her smile sent the shadows into hiding. "I'd like that."

Chapter 8

C harity poked her head inside the door of the land office. "Mr. Wheeler?"

The man rushed around the side of the desk. "Yes, yes, please come in. And call me Arch." His silly grin stretched across his face. "After all, we sit at the same supper table every night, don't we?" He pulled a chair out from the corner. "Please have a seat."

Arch's demonstrative manner took her by surprise. At the boarding-house he spent most of his time sparring with Tate Ridley. The two of them reminded her of a pair of alley cats, hissing and spitting, yowling their opinions.

He grabbed his desk chair and maneuvered it to face Charity's. He plunked down in the chair and leaned forward. "It's nice that we finally have some time alone to get better acquainted."

Time alone? Charity wasn't sure what Arch had in mind, but the purpose for her visit was purely business. She scooted her chair backward a couple of inches and quickly pulled out her notebook.

"Would you have time to answer a few questions, Mr. Wheeler?"

A crestfallen expression drooped the man's mustache. "Arch."

She allowed a placating smile. "Arch." She pointed to several file cabinets lining the wall. "Are all these land records?"

"Most. Some are financial documents, property taxes, things like that."

"I see. I understand a lot of people lost their land after the war."

Arch nodded. "Mm-hmm. When the slaves were turned loose, a lot of the big landowners didn't have anybody to work their land and didn't have the money to pay for help. No slaves, no crop. No crop, no money. No money, they can't pay their taxes. People came in droves after the war looking for bargains. They paid the taxes; they bought the land. Simple as that."

Simple maybe, for the buyers. "But what about the people who lost their land, their homes. What did they do? What happened to them?"

The words no sooner passed her lips than she realized she was talking about Dale. She squirmed with discomfiture, but apparently Arch didn't notice.

"A lot of the landowners or their heirs died in the war. Many of the ones who survived were destitute." He rose and pulled open one of the file drawers, thumbing through some of the folders. "A few went upriver or out west. Some took up with relatives in the city. Some just left and were never heard from again."

"But not all. Dale Covington didn't leave. Why did he stay? Something must have kept him here."

"I guess you'd have to ask him about that."

"And the land that was sold for taxes, what is it being used for now?"

Arch pulled out a few files and leafed through the paperwork. He ran his finger down several pages and then stepped over to a large map pinned to the wall. He traced a block of land. "This area right here has been planted in fruit trees and pecan trees." He slid his hand westward on the map. "Here's a pretty large tract turned into grazing land for cattle." He consulted the documents in his hand again and pointed to the corresponding area. "Simon Pembroke bought up several hundred acres of timber that goes from here all the way up to here." He gave the remaining papers in his hand a cursory glance before gesturing back toward the map. "Some of this land has been parceled out into tenant farms. A brick foundry was built on a stretch of land east of here on the other side of the river."

She closed her notebook. "So, Mr. Wheeler—Arch, do you know what happened to the slaves who worked on these plantations?"

Arch shrugged and closed the file drawer. "Most just run off, I suppose. A few stayed and indentured themselves. You still looking for that friend of yours?"

"He is my friend's son. I've never met him."

A flicker of disdain crossed Arch's face. "You gonna write about that in your high-toned magazine?" His question irritated her, but she had to admit his insinuation was true. Since the majority of *Keystone's* readers came from the upper echelon of society, they likely wouldn't care about one former slave and his mother. Charity chose to ignore Arch's question.

She rose and tucked her notebook under her arm. "Thank you for your time, Arch. I appreciate the information."

"Come by any time." He followed her to the door. "It's easier to talk here where we aren't disturbed than at the boardinghouse. We can...get to know each other better." He waggled his eyebrows.

Charity bit her lip to refrain from telling him she had nothing to discuss with him that required privacy. Instead, she forced a tight smile. "Good day, Arch."

She swept out the door with her eyes cast heavenward, hoping she hadn't encouraged him in any way.

The courthouse—rather stately for a small town like Juniper Springs—occupied the space between two majestic oak trees next door to the sheriff's office. Autumn foliage glistened bronze, pumpkin, and scarlet in the sunshine, but a brisk wind pressed Charity to gather her shawl tighter. A gust loosened several dozen leaves and showered them down across the front steps of the courthouse. Charity pulled the heavy door open and slipped inside out of the wind.

The modest lobby opened to expose four doors and a staircase. Charity glanced around and found the last door on the right boasted the title RECORDS on the glass. She opened the door tentatively and peeked inside. A clerk stood at a counter helping a man and a woman with some documents.

"I'll be right with you, miss."

Charity smiled and nodded. "No hurry."

The woman, who wore a plain bonnet and gray dress with purple trim, turned to stare over her shoulder at Charity. She leaned close to the man and whispered something Charity couldn't hear.

Suddenly self-conscious, Charity reached up to make sure the wind hadn't dislodged her hairpins or deposited a stray leaf in the brim of her bonnet. Finding nothing amiss, she stood to one side until the couple moved to an adjacent table. The clerk turned to her.

"What can I do for you?"

"Good afternoon. I'm Charity Galbraith, and—"

"See, George." The woman at the table nudged her husband. "I told you it was her—that Yankee woman whose been goin' around town askin' a lot o' questions."

The man looked up from the papers he was reading and squinted at her. Charity squirmed under their scrutinizing stares but continued on with the clerk.

"I hope you can help me. I'm conducting a search for a young man, a former slave. His name is Wylie, and he worked at Covington Plantation. I understand the house burned and their records were destroyed. Were there any records kept on file here?"

The clerk's eyes darkened with suspicion. "Slave records?"

"Yes." Charity lowered her shawl to her elbows and drew her notebook from under her arm. "I'm specifically looking for records of slave auctions or the private buying and selling of slaves. Birth and death records, perhaps?" She slid her gaze sideways and found the couple at the table still staring.

"The plantation owners usually kept all those records."

"Yes, I know." Impatience nipped at her. "But as I said, the house at Covington Plantation burned. Was the buying and selling of slaves recorded here?"

"If a colored was sold, the new owner would have a record of it."

Charity's fingers tightened around her notebook in frustration. "But I don't know if Wylie was sold. That's why I'm here. Do such records exist?"

The clerk lifted his shoulders. "What difference does it make? Lincoln freed all the coloreds, so even if this boy was sold, he's free now."

Charity gritted her teeth and mentally counted to ten. "If Wylie was sold, perhaps whoever bought him can tell me where he went after the war."

She glanced toward the table where the couple continued to regard her with distrust.

"I don't know where records like that might be, 'cept with the buyers." Contempt dripped from the clerk's voice, and his steely eyes didn't blink.

Dale's warning rang in her ears. She pursed her lips and looked down at her unopened notebook. The reception she'd received couldn't get much colder. She might as well dive all the way in.

"I wonder if I might ask another question."

The man responded with a nearly imperceptible lift to his whiskered chin.

"I'm also searching for battlefield maps and records of battles fought in Georgia, specifically with regard to casualties and prisoners."

The clerk made a rude sound, sucking on his teeth. "Military records are sealed. Someone like you wouldn't be given access."

She clamped the notebook tightly, praying she wouldn't throw it at the man. "Well, thank you for your time." She sent a forced smile to the couple at the table. "Have a nice afternoon."

She turned and marched to the door. As she turned the brass knob, the woman at the table spoke. "She sure got a lot o' nerve, don't she?"

If only the woman knew how much nerve Charity required at this moment to keep from speaking what was on her mind.

❧

Dale knocked on the front door of the boardinghouse and brushed imaginary lint from his cuff. Charity opened the door, rendering Dale momentarily speechless. He'd seen her numerous times over the past three weeks, but there was something different about her tonight. Perhaps it was her smile.

"Good evening, Charity."

"Good evening." She held the door open. "Please come in. I just have to get my wrap."

He stepped inside. Would it be too forward to tell her how lovely she looked?

She returned a moment later carrying an ivory shawl. He took it from her and unfolded it, placing it over her shoulders. A hint of lavender teased his senses.

Her eyes widened and her lips parted as she looked up at him. A silent reprimand slinked through him. If the gesture surprised her, he'd not been acting enough like a gentleman. Something he intended to change.

They stepped out onto the porch and Dale offered her his arm. "Shall we go?"

A tiny smile tipped her mouth, and she placed her hand in the crook of his elbow.

They crossed the street and started down the boardwalk. The hotel restaurant sat between the general store and the hotel itself. Dale opened the door and ushered Charity inside. They paused for a moment while Dale scanned the room, seeking a table where they could speak with a certain amount of privacy. He noticed George and Henrietta Ludwig sitting at a small table halfway across the room. Both had stopped eating and sat glaring in Dale and Charity's direction. He felt Charity stiffen.

When he glanced down, her chin rose slightly and a muscle along her jaw twitched. Tracing her line of vision, it appeared the Ludwigs and Charity had made a less than cordial acquaintance with each other.

He leaned his head down and spoke close to her ear. "It seems a little crowded in here. Would you rather go to Maybelle's Café?"

Relief washed over her expression. "Yes, I'd like that."

Back out on the boardwalk, they strolled past several buildings before either of them spoke.

"Is it safe to assume you've met George and Henrietta?"

Charity shrugged. "We weren't formally introduced, but I, um. . .ran into them at the courthouse a couple of days ago."

She didn't need to say any more. The Ludwigs were among those who declared the war would never be over for them, even though they'd lost far less than most. An urge to put the couple in their place needled Dale.

Lord, please keep reminding me that I'm not responsible for anyone's opinions or attitudes but my own.

He placed his hand protectively atop Charity's as they continued toward Maybelle's. Enticing aromas greeted them at the door of the café.

"Smells like the special this evening is chicken." Dale's mouth watered as he steered Charity toward a table in the corner. Maybelle brought them coffee and took their order.

Dale cleared his throat. "Have you been able to find any information about your father?"

A tiny crease between her brows deepened, lines of sorrow marring her countenance. She shook her head, and Dale instantly regretted asking. He changed topics. "I've been thinking about this slave you're searching for." He took a sip of coffee. "My father and I had more than one argument about the slaves, but as long as he was alive, I had little to say about their treatment."

Charity's warm brown eyes studied him, as if she tried to read his thoughts.

He intertwined his fingers. "I was of the opinion the slaves would be more productive if they had better food and housing, but Father disagreed. Loudly. He did everything loudly."

Charity's expression softened into an understanding smile. He had to be truthful. "When you showed up here and started asking your questions, I began to realize my position on the slaves was to get more work out of them if we fed them better." He lowered his eyes and toyed with his fork. "Many of my beliefs and attitudes were based on how I was raised."

Maybelle brought plates of baked chicken and golden biscuits, along with a small dish of butter and a crock of honey.

"Anything else I can get for you folks?" She refilled their coffee cups.

"I don't think so." Dale sniffed. "This smells wonderful."

Maybelle nodded with a pleased grin and bustled away. Dale bowed his head and asked God's blessing on their meal.

They began to eat, and Charity looked across the table at him with a penetrating gaze of comprehension. "What changed your mind?"

He stopped chewing for a moment. How could she tell? He swallowed hard and pushed his chicken around on the plate with his fork.

"The war had already started. I'd been away for months. I'd barely received word that Father was ill when the telegram came saying he'd died. I couldn't get home for the funeral, but I was told they laid him to rest beside my mother." He knew he wasn't answering her question, but she didn't interrupt, as if encouraging him to take his time.

He buttered a biscuit, but then laid it on his plate without taking a bite. He ran his finger around the rim of his coffee cup. "I had been with Major General Cleburne for some time, but when President Davis relieved General Johnston and appointed General Hood to take his place, Hood needed reinforcements. I was sent, along with part of our regiment to attach to Hood's in July of 1864. The Yankees were threatening to overrun Atlanta, and our job was to stop them at Peachtree Creek."

He sat back, the memory flooding over him, as it often did.

"The fighting at Peachtree Creek was fierce, and we were all exhausted. I was hit in the side." He rubbed the place with his fingers. "I tried to crawl to some bushes, but I was hit again, this time in the leg. I couldn't move, and I knew I was going to die."

Charity covered her mouth with her fingers.

"There was a soldier—I'd not known him before I joined Hood. He was a black man, no doubt a slave who'd been sent to fight in the place of his master. He bent over me and told me I was going to be all right. He picked me up in his arms like I was a child and carried me to some thick underbrush until the battle was over. I drifted in and out of consciousness, but every time I opened my eyes, he was there. He made some kind of poultice for my wounds. I remember him talking the whole time, but he wasn't talking to me. He was talking to Jesus, asking Him for strength to carry me and asking Him to let me live. That man carried me for two days until we reached a regiment that had a doctor." He looked across the table at Charity. Tears shimmered in her eyes.

"I never knew his name."

Chapter 9

Charity took Dale's arm and a flutter of butterflies turned loose in her stomach. She clutched her shawl with her free hand. Darkness had fallen and the lantern light that spilled over the boardwalk cast ghostly shadows against the buildings as Charity and Dale strolled past. The evening air held a chill, but walking next to Dale felt warm.

The short route from the café to the boardinghouse didn't allow much time for conversation, but Dale had spoken volumes over dinner, even when he sat silently poking at his food with his fork. In those moments when their gazes locked, his eyes cracked open the door to his innermost secrets, and Charity caught a brief peek at the man he was on the inside. A surprisingly compassionate person hid behind the sullen, brooding expression she'd met the first day she made his acquaintance. As they made their way through the gathering night, the man he was on the outside barely limped at all.

"I've enjoyed the evening, Dale. Thank you." She looked up at him. The lanterns were spaced far enough apart that the light danced across his face and then hid as they moved along.

His brow dipped in consternation. "Charity, I've never told anybody what I told you tonight, about how that black soldier saved my life."

A warm flush twined up her neck and into her face. "Then I feel very honored that you would confide such a remarkable experience to me."

"But are you going to. . .write about it?"

"Not if you don't want me to."

He gave a short nod, seemingly satisfied that he could trust her not to betray his confidence.

"It's not that I don't want to give credit to that soldier. I should." His voice dropped off, almost as if he was speaking more to himself than to her.

Was he embarrassed to admit a black man had saved him?

He halted and turned to face her. "Charity, there is more to that story that I didn't tell you. During those two days that soldier took care of me and carried me to safety, I never once spoke to him." Self-deprecation laced his tone. "He'd offer me a drink, and I grunted and nodded. He knew I was in a lot of pain, so we stopped to rest often, but he rarely spoke directly to me, other than telling me I was going to be all right. He kept up a running conversation with the Lord, though. I listened to him pray for two days, and he talked to Jesus like a best friend."

He dropped his gaze to the boardwalk. "Charity, I never asked his name. I never even thanked him." He turned his head as if looking her in the eye as he admitted his shortcomings was too difficult.

Charity waited. An owl hooted in the distance and a breeze stirred the air.

"I wish I knew his name, and I wish I'd shaken his hand." A sigh that sounded more like a groan escaped his lips, and he shook his head.

She reached out and touched his cuff. "Dale, have you ever read the parable of the two sons?"

He shook his head. "I don't think so."

"Jesus told a story about a man who had two sons. He went to the first son and told him to go work in the father's vineyard, and the son refused. Later, the son repented and went and worked in the vineyard."

She paused to give him time to digest the scenario. "Then the father went to the second son and told him to go work in the vineyard, and the son said he would do it, but he didn't."

A frown dipped Dale's mouth. "What does that have to do with the soldier who took care of me?"

A fleeting prayer winged toward heaven. *Please, don't let me offend him, Lord.*

"Which one of the sons did the father's will?"

Dale shrugged. "The first one, but I still don't understand."

"You might have started out with a hard heart, but your heart has changed."

A scowl interrupted his features.

She prayed he wasn't angry. "God knows we're going to stumble and fall once in a while, but He doesn't leave us where we fall. He picks us up and gives us another chance."

His expression mellowed and softened, and finally he gave a slow nod. "I understand what you're saying. I'll have to do some thinking about it."

The lanterns hanging from the front porch of the boardinghouse came into view, and Dale's steps slowed. "Would you allow me to read your articles when you've finished writing them?"

She arched her eyebrows. "You want to proofread them, or don't you trust me to write impartially?"

He chuckled. "I'm curious. In your short time here you've been quite thorough in your research. From what I can see you've interviewed quite a few people."

She peeked at him from the corner of her eye. "I'd like to interview Simon Pembroke. Would it bother you if I did that?"

"No, it wouldn't bother me, but I don't know when you would catch him at the mill."

She tipped her head up. "Isn't he there every day?"

"He was. He's purchased more timber land, and he's out there supervising the forming of crews. He left me in charge."

Charity halted at the bottom of the porch steps. "Really? He gave you a promotion?"

"Is that so surprising?" He scowled at her, defensiveness in his voice.

"Oh no! I mean, you. . .I'm sure you can. . .it's just—"

Dale laughed out loud. "Did you know you squeak when you get flustered?"

Charity plunked her hands on her hips. "Dale Covington, are you trying to provoke me?"

He caught her hand and placed it back on his arm. "Simon promoted me to foreman because he needs someone to oversee the mill operation while he's out in the field."

Heat scorched her face. "That's wonderful, Dale. Truly. The reason I was surprised is because I know there are some who consider him a carpetbagger, and you're a Southerner. There is no animosity between you?"

They climbed the stairs and leaned against the porch railing. "I suppose there was at first. But over the past few years we've put aside our differences."

"Did he say when he'd be back at the mill?"

"Probably not until next week."

Charity glanced at the boardinghouse window where a few of the boarders sat in the parlor. She didn't see Tate Ridley but couldn't help wondering how the man felt about Dale's promotion. She shivered.

Dale placed his hand on her back. "You better go inside. It's chilly out here."

"Thank you for a very special evening, Dale."

He gave a slow nod. "It was special for me, too." He walked her to the door and held it open. "Good night."

"Good night, Dale."

She climbed the stairs to her room and closed the door behind her, her head swirling with a half-dozen different emotions. She lit the lamp and sat with her elbows on the desk, her chin in her hands. She couldn't deny it. She was attracted to this man. How did that happen?

When she arrived here three and a half weeks ago, the drawl she heard in everyone's voice—Dale's included—sent shards of irritation through her. She'd wanted to blame every person she met for her father not coming home. The day she disembarked the carriage that brought her from Athens to Juniper Springs, she might have walked on the very soil where her father walked, where Wylie may have walked. The thought should have excited her, but that day she'd felt nothing but animosity. She'd thought her anger fueled her perseverance and gave her the motivation to press on. But now her anger and bitterness tumbled and twisted with empathy for Dale, compassion for those who'd lost so much, and even affection for a few of the folks she'd met. On top of everything, the flutters in her stomach every time she welcomed Dale into her thoughts mocked her with the paradox. How would she ever untangle the web?

"God help me. My feelings are so mixed up. I don't know how to balance what Dale told me about the slaves and how his attitudes have changed. I prepared myself to dislike him. Last Sunday and tonight he was such a different person from the day I first met him—gentler, caring. I don't know what to do."

Only God could sort out her bewildering emotions and put them in the right order. She closed her eyes and prayed. When she finished, she left her turmoil in God's hands.

She readied herself for bed, pulling on the heavier woolen socks and her warm flannel gown. She turned down the lamp and snuggled under the thick quilt Hannah had put on her bed.

Despite closing her eyes and curling up into a ball, sleep wouldn't come. She couldn't dismiss from her mind Dale's story of the black soldier who saved his life. Her chest tightened with emotion as she recalled Dale's telling of the way the man cared for his wounds and prayed for him. He was a slave, sent to fight in his master's place. He could have run off in the heat of battle, but he didn't. Instead, he asked for God's help in caring for a white man he didn't even know.

She breathed a prayer of gratitude for the black soldier and asked God to bless him. "I wonder if such a man might have tried to care for Father."

❧

Dale blew out a frustrated breath. He'd begun inventorying this load of logs twice and lost count both times. A certain lady's face kept pulling his attention into a state of preoccupied distraction. The wistfulness in Charity's voice and the longing in her eyes when she spoke of her missing father wouldn't leave him alone. Their conversation on the back porch of the boardinghouse last Sunday afternoon echoed in his mind as well as the pained look on her face last night in response to his inquiry.

His own circumstances had haunted him for over six years, but at least he knew what happened. He steeled himself against the onslaught of horror crashing over him again. There was no wondering, no speculation. He'd repeatedly tried to put himself in her place, receiving word that her father had been wounded and captured, but then—nothing.

He moved back to the opposite side of the wagon and began counting and marking again. Eight at twelve feet. He scrawled the tally. Ten at eight feet, or was that eight at ten feet?

He and Charity had taken some sure steps toward friendship. How easy it was to tell her about the black soldier who saved his life. He'd never told anyone about that before. A niggling dissatisfaction nipped at him, however. Could he—should he justify forming a friendship with Charity Galbraith, that Yankee woman, as some in town called her? Was it wrong to feel comfortable in her presence and confide in her things he couldn't bring himself to voice to anyone else, not even Pastor Shuford?

Guilt skewered him. Wondering whether or not he should pursue a friendship with Charity wasn't what kept distracting him, and he knew it. As an officer in the Confederate army, he'd been privy to many confidential military files. He knew where the prisoner of war records were kept. Why didn't he share that information with her? Would she desire friendship with him if she knew?

Tate Ridley's words rolled through his mind again. *"A Yankee is a Yankee."* Dale ground his teeth, old hostilities slicing across his heart. His entire focus for over four years had been to destroy the enemy. In the aftermath of the war, the acid desire for reciprocation fueled the bitterness of his soul. Why should he care about Charity's pain? The Federals had inflicted plenty of pain on him. His life had been ravaged. His wounds left him crippled, his home and land stripped away. But his heart screamed when he thought about the one whose very soul mattered more than his own breath; if only he'd been given the chance to lay down his life in place of that one.

He sucked in a ragged breath and limped across the pole barn to sit on an overturned barrel. He wanted to roar out his pain. His heart pounded in his ears, and the familiar burning ache that started deep in his gut rose up to strangle him again. Pastor Shuford said it was bitterness that crippled him, not his wounds. For the first time, Dale realized what the preacher meant. A physical limp didn't make him a cripple, not in God's eyes. The debilitating impairment he dragged around with him was inside, bound by unseen shackles to which he'd clung for so long he wasn't sure how to peel his emotional fingers away.

With elbows on his knees, Dale dropped his head into his hands. "Oh, God, the war ended on this land over six years ago, but it still rages within me. I'm so tired of fighting. I hate the way this anger holds me captive."

"Let go, son. Let it go. Your hunger for revenge will devour you."

Dale raked his hands over his face. "But God, what they did—how do I let it go?"

"Give it to Me."

Letting go of his animosity toward those who took everything from him meant giving God control. Was he ready to do that? Could he take that step?

On the other side of the lumberyard, Tate Ridley and Jude Farley carried sawn boards from the mill and loaded them onto a wagon. The two made no pretense of their sentiments, openly spouting their hatred for everything connected with the North. In many ways they were more honest than Dale.

The way he'd looked forward to his evening with Charity last night proved it. The day she arrived and he'd first heard her speak, her Northern twang bayoneted him, and he hated her without even having been introduced. But the conversations he'd had with her over the past couple of weeks chipped away at the brittle rust around his heart. As he walked to the boardinghouse last night, his limp had all but disappeared in his anticipation of their time together. By the time they'd said good night, he could no longer deny he felt something for her. Was he a traitor, as Tate said? A few conversations didn't change who she was. He'd long equated the word *Yankee* with *enemy*. The two were synonymous.

But the Yankees he faced on the battlefield and his image of Charity weren't compatible. She wasn't a warrior. She was a daughter hoping to reconcile in her mind whatever destiny befell her father, and she was a friend seeking to ease the heartache of a mother.

A thought startled him. What if the black soldier who saved his life was this Wylie for whom Charity was searching? Unlikely, but possible, and a sudden urge to know the answer to that question burned within him.

He rose and walked back to the rack of logs. With the desire to help Charity find Wylie came another realization—another reason he'd refrained from telling her he had knowledge of the prisoner of war records. But this reason had been buried under an avalanche of resentment. Shoveling away the dross, he cleared the way to see his other purpose for keeping that information from her.

Whether he admitted it or not, the feelings he had for her went beyond empathy. If his suspicions were correct, learning the truth about what happened to her father would only deepen her pain, not relieve it. A stirring of protectiveness in his heart awakened a sense within him he thought was dead. Did that mean he was ready to break out of the bonds of bitterness?

In wrestling with the decision of whether friendship with Charity was right or wrong, a thread of dissatisfaction wormed through him. Friendship wasn't what he wanted.

Chapter 10

Dale braced himself for an argument. Tate crossed his arms and sneered in response to the instructions Dale just issued to the crew. A couple of the men resented Dale's new position as foreman, but no one more so than Tate Ridley.

Tate glanced to his left where Jude leaned against the side of the pole barn, whittling. "Seems to me you been dumpin' the heaviest work on me and the boys here while you been slackin' off ever since the boss's been away. He might've made you foreman since the both of you are Yankee-lovers, but it 'pears mighty lopsided, iffen you ask me."

Dale stared, unblinking, at Tate. "I didn't ask you. Nor do I intend to stand here wasting time explaining the number of orders on this clipboard or the time frame in which this crew of six men must complete these orders. I gave you and Jude and Amos your orders for the day. Since today is Saturday, you need to be finished by noon, or you'll stay until you are finished."

Amos hooted while Tate and Jude looked at each other. Tate took a step forward. "Maybe we'll just wait for Pembroke and see what he has to say."

"If you decide to do that, it'll be on your own time." Dale pulled the pencil from behind his ear. "I'm telling you for the last time, Tate. Get busy or go home."

Dale picked up the clipboard and propped one foot on the spoke of a wagon wheel. He made some notes on the side of one of the work orders while he waited to see what Tate and his cronies would do. When the trio stayed in place, Dale called out to one of the other men who worked closest to the office.

"Ned, go upstairs and see if you can find that Now Hiring sign on top of the file cabinet."

After some grumbling under their breaths, Tate and his buddies stomped off in the direction of the log rack. It wasn't the end of the matter, and Dale knew it.

Saturday being a short workday, Dale double-checked the work orders to make certain the most urgent ones would be completed and delivered on time. He went to help Zack and Ned with a load of siding boards. They finished the cutting and stacking in record time.

Dale dragged his sleeve across his forehead. "You fellows go ahead and start on that order of fence posts while I check on the other men." He skirted around the side of the building and came to the back of the pole barn. An ongoing exchange greeted him before he stepped into view of the three men.

". . .oughta be an example to everyone in the county. It's a clear message."

Dale didn't feel like wasting time asking Tate what he meant. He rounded the corner. "How are you men coming? Need any help?"

Tate scoffed. "From you?" The other two men snickered.

Dale consulted the work order and checked their progress. "You only have another hour before the noon whistle sounds. You better get busy if you plan on leaving on time."

He turned on his heel and hitch-stepped back to help Zack and Ned with the fence posts.

The sawdust flew for the next hour, and by the time the shrill whistle blasted signifying quitting time, all the work was completed, checked off, and stacked. Dale handed out the pay envelopes, locked the office door, and made his way toward the general store where Clyde Sawyer was certain to have a number of orders to be delivered. When Dale told Clyde about his promotion, the merchant had rubbed his chin in consternation. But Dale didn't plan on quitting his second job at the store, much to Clyde's expressed relief. The more money he could sock away in the bank, the sooner he could become a landowner again.

He crossed the street in front of the post office. The town always bustled on Saturdays. Farm folk came to do their shopping and trading, along with socializing and gossiping. As Dale drew closer to the mercantile, animated conversations buzzed every few feet along the boardwalk. He couldn't catch enough to make sense of anything, but wide-eyed uneasiness on the faces around him and the foreboding tone in many voices set Dale's senses on alert. He didn't have the time or inclination to stop and chat, however, and he hastened to the back door of the mercantile.

Brisk business kept both Clyde and Betsy Sawyer busy waiting on customers out front. Since there were always extra deliveries on Saturday, Dale used Clyde's buckboard to speed up the process. Dale found the orders to be delivered hanging from a nail where Clyde always stuck them, and began loading the items into crates.

He went to the door that separated the storeroom from the front.

"Clyde, I'm taking six of these orders out. I should be back in an hour."

Clyde waved, and Dale hoisted the last loaded crate. As he shoved it onto the back of the buckboard, he couldn't help overhearing three men on the boardwalk.

"Lynched, I tell you. Right there by the side of the road where everyone can see."

"You don't say."

"I hear tell they stuck a cross in the ground right beside the tree they hung him from, and don't ya know, they set fire to that there cross."

Another man shook his head. "Ain't been any lynchin's around these parts since back in '64."

"Ain't the same. This one was a darkie."

The blood coursing through Dale's veins froze. He limped over to the men.

"What's this about a lynching?"

One of the men thumbed his suspender. "Yup, hanged him there from a big oak tree for everybody to see. Burned a cross beside him, too."

Was this what Tate and the others were talking about? "Where was this?"

"Over by the Athens road." The old timer scratched his head. "Not far from the river."

Dread oozed through Dale's being. His sister and her husband lived out that way. Pastor Shuford urged him numerous times to bury the hatchet, reminding him that Auralie was all the family he had left. If there was anything of which he needed no reminding, it was that his family was gone.

Auralie and Colton had a black man, Barnabas, who worked for them. Dale had never told them so, but he was secretly glad Barnabas stayed on the place protecting his sister and her baby while her husband was off fighting. When the war ended, the conflict between him and Auralie seemed too wide to bridge. The reasons seemed ridiculously petty now.

❧

Every direction Dale turned Sunday morning, talk of the lynching raged like wildfire. It hardly seemed appropriate conversation between worshippers entering the house of God, but the event had sent a shock wave through the town, and everyone had an opinion. Speculation and accusations galloped faster than a runaway horse heading for the barn. Every snippet of conversation that reached Dale's ear sent a blade of regret slicing deeper into his conscience.

All afternoon the day before, Dale made his deliveries for Clyde Sawyer and repeatedly ran into people adding more gruesome details to an already horrendous story. The lynching remained on the lips of every person in town this morning. Dale carried enough grisly memories of the war with him. He didn't need or want to paint a picture in his head of the unholy activities that took place out on the Athens road two nights ago.

Dale hung back from the groups of people gathering in the churchyard. He saw Charity walking toward the church with Hannah and the Ferguson ladies, but the unsettled state of his emotions this morning left him in no mood to talk to anyone. If Charity asked him what he thought about it, he had no answer. He couldn't put into words the turmoil that churned through him, and he had no desire to participate in any of the conversations circulating through the crowd. Instead, he stepped back into the shadows and kept watching down the road as wagons and carriages arrived for the Sunday morning services. When the church bell rang, everyone made their way inside. Everyone except Dale.

The opening hymn drifted through the closed doors, but Dale lingered outside, hoping to greet Auralie and Colton when they arrived. He'd tossed and turned the entire night. If only he'd put his animosity aside when Pastor Shuford encouraged him to do so. He kicked a clod of dirt, watching it burst apart and scatter. He'd wasted so much time fostering his rancor and at the same time feeding his self-pity, privately envying those people who had family. He'd told himself he was alone, no family left, but that wasn't true. Indignant anger took control of him when Auralie announced her marriage to Colton. Shame filled him when he remembered telling her she was no longer his sister.

The memory poured hot coals of remorse over him. Pastor Shuford was right. Refusing to reconcile with Auralie had robbed both of them of the joys of family.

The congregation finished the first hymn and began singing a second, and Auralie and Colton had still not appeared. They rarely missed church, even with their two little ones. Auralie and Colton had repeatedly told him they'd been praying for him and hoped he'd choose to be part of their family, but he'd refused. He raked his hands through his hair. He didn't have family because he'd turned his back on them. What a fool he'd been. He'd been a fool about a lot of things. He looked up the road again, but no wagon appeared around the bend.

With his head in his hands, Dale wondered for the thousandth time why the black soldier bothered to save his life. Dale had seen the scars on the man's back when he took his shirt off and used it to bind Dale's wounds. How could a man who'd been beaten and forced into slavery by white men, sent to fight in a war that could have resulted in continued slavery if the South had won, show such compassion for a white man?

"God, why did he do that? *How* could he do that?"

There was only one way—the way Pastor Shuford had been telling him for six years. The only way he would ever reconcile with Auralie, or understand what motivated that soldier to do what he did, or break free of the invisible shackles that bound him was by letting God have control. He pressed his lips tightly together. Could he find the courage to take such a step?

He blew out a stiff breath and looked for Auralie and Colton's wagon one more time. Clearly, they weren't coming to church this morning, and Dale feared the reason. He rose and walked as fast as his limp would allow down the street to the livery to borrow a horse. He had to ride out there. He had to know. He had to tell Auralie how sorry he was and ask her and Colton to forgive him.

As he walked, he lifted his voice to heaven. "God, I pray that Barnabas is all right, but somebody somewhere is grieving for the man who was lynched. I've been so stiff-necked and hard-hearted, Lord. Please forgive me."

When he reached the stable, the hostler told him to pick out a mount and saddle it himself. Dale pulled a gelding from his stall and tossed a saddle on his back. The horse snorted in protest at being taken away from his feed bin. Dale patted his neck.

"Sorry, fella, but this is one mission I don't intend to fail."

❧

Charity peeked from the corner of her eye during the singing to see if Dale had come in. She'd seen him in church the first three Sundays that she'd been in Juniper Springs. A prick of concern poked her, but she immediately dismissed it. There were a dozen possible reasons he wasn't there. But of all Sundays for him to miss, why this one?

After hearing the dreadful news about the black man they'd found hanging beside a burned cross, Charity wanted—no, she needed—to talk to Dale more than ever. She simply couldn't comprehend such a vile act. Could he?

In the light of the lynching, Dale's warnings to be careful rang in her head. At the time, she couldn't imagine anyone taking out their resentment of her as a Yankee in any way other than a frown and a snub. Now she wasn't so sure. But she couldn't quit, not now.

She still had her articles to write, and what she'd learned since coming here shed a whole new light on the slant of her stories. Her editor expected the first article on his desk before the end of October, and she'd not disappoint him.

But her dogged determination sent agitation swirling through her stomach. She was no closer to finding Wylie or learning what became of her father than she was when she first arrived. Every person with whom she'd spoken, every place she looked, she kept running into dead ends. The tenacity that drove her made the nerve endings in her scalp tingle. She *would not* give up.

The preacher's voice rose and fell with emotion as he grasped the sides of the pulpit and leaned forward. "The news of this lynching is on everyone's lips, but I wonder how many of those talking about it view it as a tragedy—just as tragic as the war. For four and a half years the destruction and the death toll made us gasp. It was more than we could comprehend."

He pounded his fist on the pulpit. "Well, I say that the lynching of this man is every bit as wicked and depraved as any of the atrocities of war, maybe even more so."

Charity blinked and held her breath. Since yesterday, she'd tried not to think about the unspeakable possibility of the murdered man being Wylie. Another wave of nausea crashed over her, and she bit her lip.

The pastor moved to the side of the pulpit and stepped down from the platform, walked down the aisle, beseeching the people to listen. "Don't you see? In a war, we're told there is an enemy who means us harm, and the soldiers go out and put their lives in danger to protect their homeland from that enemy."

He backed up slowly, turning from side to side and looking into the faces of those seated on the wooden benches. "That man who was hung wasn't an enemy. He didn't mean anyone any harm. The soldiers weren't called up to go out and hunt him down. The men who committed this ungodly act didn't put their own lives in danger. In fact, they hid behind hooded masks like cowards!" With every declaration, the volume and intensity of the preacher's voice increased until he was shouting.

A trembling began in the pit of Charity's stomach. The preacher was declaring the same sentiments she felt. Tears pricked her eyes.

"God's Word instructs us to put away malice, and he who sheds innocent blood will himself be condemned."

Charity poised on the edge of the bench, every muscle tensed in anticipation.

The pastor stood facing the silent congregation with his arms stretched out to his side like a loving parent encouraging his children to come. "Hasn't there been enough death? The animosity must cease." His voice broke as he began to weep. "Search your hearts. Put away the hatred. Let go of the bitterness and its poison."

His voice fell to almost a whisper, and Charity had to strain to hear him.

"And what do you put in the place of that hatred?" He turned his palms up and held his arms out. "Forgiveness, my friends. Yes, I can see in the eyes of many here this morning that you think I'm asking too much of you. But I'm not the one doing the asking." He held up his Bible. "God is."

Charity squirmed in her seat. How could she forgive the people who took her father from her?

With tears streaming down his face, Pastor Shuford's next words arrested her heart.

"Jesus said, 'Father, forgive them; for they know not what they do.'"

Brokenness rendered her weak with guilt and regret.

Precious Lord Jesus, help me forgive.

Chapter 11

Humbling himself never came easy for Dale, and finding the words to express a heartfelt apology tested his resolve, but God birthed a seed of fortitude within him and smoothed the way. The expression on Auralie's face when she opened the door to his knock would linger with Dale for as long as he drew breath. Relying on God's strength to carry out his purpose, Dale tasted the sweetness of His promise when he embraced his sister and shook his brother-in-law's hand.

Learning that their reason for missing church had nothing to do with Barnabas rendered Dale weak with relief. Both of the children were down with the croup. A slight moan shuddered through him at the sound of their coughing, but the little ones would be fine in a few days.

His private meeting with Barnabas had started out awkwardly, but he managed to tell the man how much it meant to him, knowing his sister wasn't alone during those awful months. Expressing his thanks to the former slave felt odd, to be sure, but his heart smiled when Barnabas got over the shock and finally responded with upturned lips and a slight nod of his head.

Despite the shortness of the visit, Dale savored the reconciliation with his sister. Auralie had urged him to stay for dinner, but he'd begged off, promising to return another day. Dale reined the gelding around and raised his hand in farewell. Auralie stood beside her husband on the front porch, waving and wiping tears away.

He nudged the horse into a canter down the road. The sun climbed above the treetops, chasing the morning chill into hiding as Dale headed back to town. Gratefulness hung around his shoulders like a cloak with the assurance of the restored family connection, but a dark cloud followed him. The lynching drew a sinister curtain around the community, and Dale's concern for Charity grew. Even though he'd already warned Tate and his friends to leave her alone, in light of the news on everyone's lips, he couldn't be sure of her safety. Perhaps it was time for another talk with her.

When he passed the sign that proclaimed WELCOME TO JUNIPER SPRINGS, he left the horse at the livery, paid his twenty-five cents for the loan of the animal, and turned his feet in the direction of the boardinghouse. He let himself in through the white picket gate in the front, but before he reached the porch steps, he spied Charity in the side yard, sitting on a small garden bench amid a swirl of autumn leaves.

He rounded the corner of the house, and she looked up. The scowl around her eyes immediately softened, and she rose to greet him.

"I looked for you in church this morning."

"There was something I had to do." Dale gestured toward the back porch. "Can we sit back here where we can talk?"

They climbed the three steps to the back porch, and Dale noticed the wicker chairs that had mysteriously disappeared last Sunday were back in place. He smothered a tiny chuckle. Hannah Sparrow had a mischievous streak.

The chairs offered to put distance between him and Charity, but today he had a choice. He crossed to the swing.

"Shall we?"

Despite the small smile that graced Charity's lips, unease creased her brow. A momentary question stung him. Was her angst due to the word around town of the lynching, or did the prospect of sitting close to him cause her discomfort?

She gathered her shawl around her and settled onto the swing. He lowered himself beside her, turning slightly to face her.

"I'm sure you've heard what happened." Distress laced her voice. "The whole town is talking about it."

Dale nodded. "Yes. That's why I wanted to talk with you."

She interlaced her fingers and clung to the corners of her shawl until her knuckles were white. A visible shiver coursed through her, but Dale suspected she wasn't chilled.

"How can anyone do such a horrible thing, Dale?"

Painful memories lanced him. "Thousands of horrible things were committed in the name of war for over four years."

She clutched his arm. "But the war is over. Like the preacher said this morning, that man didn't mean anyone any harm." She shook her head. "I don't understand the mentality of a person who could do something like that. One of the things I'm trying to clarify for my articles is the attitudes and opinions of people, and how they affect the Reconstruction."

Dale frowned. "I'd hoped you would write with a more positive slant. Not everyone in the South is as ignorant as the ones who hung that man."

She shot back a retort. "I know that." She released a sigh. "I'm sorry. I didn't mean to snap at you. This is obviously not your fault, but it's stirred some very powerful feelings in a lot of people."

He pressed his lips together tightly. He hoped she'd not take exception to what he needed to say. "My point exactly. Charity, whoever did this isn't likely to be put off by the fact that you're a woman." The words he overheard Tate say at the sawmill echoed in his mind.

"*. . .oughta be an example to everyone in the county. The message is clear.*"

A cold chill gripped him, followed in its wake by anger. But this anger was different from the heavy burden he'd dragged around for years. His gaze traced the outline of the stubborn set of her jaw.

"Why hasn't the sheriff done anything?" She leaned closer and dropped the volume of her voice. "I think Tate Ridley knows something about it. You should have seen the smug look on his face at dinner today."

He worked to keep his tone quiet and calming. "Miles Flint can't arrest anyone for the crime until he has solid proof. Tate said he was playing cards Friday night, and his friends are backing up his story. Unfortunately, a smug look on his face isn't enough to build a case against the man."

A tiny growl of frustration emerged from her lips. "You sound just like the rest of them. Dale, a horrible crime has been committed, and all anyone is doing about it is talking."

She rose from the swing and paced the length of the porch and returned. He let her spout her vexation. She stopped and extended her arms, palms up in entreaty.

"Did this man have family? Will they know what happened to him? What if no one is ever punished for his murder?" Her voice broke, and she covered her face with her hands. Her muffled words defined her dread. "Dale, what if that man was Wylie? How could I ever tell Essie that her son—"

Dale fairly leaped from the swing and was at her side in two strides. He captured her wrists and gave them a gentle tug. "Charity, I've asked myself those very same questions, and I agree with you. It *was* a horrible crime. Hatred is so deeply ingrained in some people they can't see past it." He cupped her chin and tipped her face up. "You and I can't change what happened—not the murder two nights ago, and not the death and destruction of war. All we can control is the way we respond to it."

She drew in a deep breath and let it out slowly. "I know."

He cocked his head at her. "I don't suppose you'd listen if I asked you to discontinue your search."

She arched an eyebrow and set her jaw in a stubborn posture that was becoming familiar.

He wanted to argue with her but knew it to be futile. "I didn't think so."

She adjusted her shawl and returned to the swing. "I looked for you this morning in church. When you weren't there, I grew concerned."

Dale sat beside her. "I went out to visit my sister and brother-in-law. There was something I needed to do that I'd put off far too long."

❧

Charity stood and pushed back the desk chair. Stretching her stiff legs felt good. Trying to put articles together to please Mr. Peabody and the readership of the *Keystone* put every journalistic skill she had to the test. Nothing she'd written this morning rang true. Just when she knew the angle with which she wanted to address these articles, the news of the lynching set her off balance. Perhaps she needed a brisk walk in the crisp fall air to clear her head.

She grabbed her shawl and hurried down the stairs. She found Hannah rattling around in the kitchen.

"I'm going for a walk. Is there anything you need from the store?"

"Oh yes." Hannah wiped her hands on her apron. "You would save me a trip if you could pick up a couple of fat stewing hens at the butcher." She stepped over to a shelf in the corner and pulled down a crock. She withdrew a few coins and deposited them into Charity's hand. "That should cover it. Be sure to get some nice plump ones."

Charity slipped the coins into her reticule. "I won't be long." She stepped out the back door and breathed deeply of the spicy scent of autumn leaves and wood smoke. A squirrel scolded her for interrupting his acorn-gathering. She grinned at him.

"All right, I'm leaving." The leaf-strewn pathway around the side of the house crunched beneath her feet.

She crossed the street and set out down the boardwalk. She smiled and said hello to several people she recognized from seeing them in church. Some returned the greeting while others narrowed their eyes in suspicion and passed by without so much as a nod.

The bell over the door of the butcher sang cheerfully as she entered. A stout man in a soiled apron gave her a gap-toothed smile.

"*Vat es* do you need today, *Fräulein?*" His German accent tickled her ears after hearing so much Southern dialect over the past month.

"Mrs. Sparrow at the boardinghouse wants two plump stewing hens." She dug Hannah's money from her reticule and held it out to the man. He bobbed his head and deposited the coins. She waited while he wrapped the birds in paper.

With the promise of Hannah's chicken and dumplings in her arms,

Charity headed back to the boardinghouse. As she passed by the saloon, two men nearly collided with her as they exited.

"Well now, who do we have here?" One of the men blocked her way.

"This here is that Yankee writer lady. Wonder what all she's writin' 'bout us poor ign'rant Southern folks."

Charity sucked in a breath and clutched the chickens tighter. She attempted to step around the men, but they bumped her into the alley between the saloon and the hotel. One of the men grabbed her wrist, causing her to drop the hens in the dirt. He leaned close and hissed in her face.

"You best watch your step if you know what's good for you."

The second man, who looked vaguely familiar, took up where the first one left off. Both men reeked of sour mash whiskey. "You keep askin' a lot of nosy questions about things that don't concern you, maybe you'll find yourself up to your neck in more trouble than you bargained for, missy."

Charity's heart pounded, but she refused to cower. She lifted her chin and drew herself up as tall as she could. "Take your hands off me. How dare you threaten me? You two are nothing but unprincipled reprobates with nothing better to do than harass a woman." She yanked her wrist free. "Furthermore, I suspect that you likely had something to do with murdering that poor man last week, and I hope you get everything that's coming to you."

The first man hooted in derision. "Whoever done that was just clearin' out the vermin."

Charity's lungs heaved with indignation. "I'm sure the sheriff will be very interested in your opinion."

The second man snarled and grasped her upper arm in a vise grip, digging his fingers into her flesh until she winced. His breath turned her stomach. "You better not go makin' any accusations you can't prove."

Before she could swing her foot back to give the bully a hard kick, Dale stomped across the boardwalk and knocked the man on his backside. Had the situation not been so tense, she'd have thrown her arms around his neck.

❧

Dale glared down at the man lying in the dirt between two rubbish cans and pointed his finger in the heathen's face. "You're lucky I can control my temper." He kicked the man's leg. "Get up."

He jerked his gaze to Jude Farley standing a few feet away. "Jude, I warned you and the others at the sawmill to leave Miss Galbraith alone.

Now I'm telling you, if you even look at her sideways, you'll have me to deal with. You understand?"

Jude muttered under his breath.

Dale eyed the first man who dusted off his trousers. "What's your name?"

The stranger sneered. "None of your business."

Dale nodded. "That's all right, you don't have to tell me, because I'm making it my business to find out."

He turned to Charity whose expression was a mixture of outrage and cussed stubbornness. "Are you all right?"

She answered through gritted teeth. "I'm fine."

Two chickens lay at Charity's feet, unrolled from their paper wrapping and now coated with dirt. He pointed at the two hapless birds. "How much did these cost?"

Charity told him, and he held his palm out to the men. "Pay up."

Both men dug in their pockets and tossed a few coins in Dale's hand. He in turn handed the money to Charity. She gave the pair of miscreants one last glare before turning on her heel and marching down the boardwalk toward the butcher.

Dale backed the two weasels up against the wall. "If you ever touch Miss Galbraith again, I will personally drag what's left of you to the sheriff's office and throw your worthless hides in jail."

The two skulked away, muttering oaths. Dale clenched his fists as he watched them go, trying to control his rage at seeing Charity accosted.

She returned a few minutes later with a bundle wrapped in butcher paper. Dale relieved her of the package. "I'll walk you home."

"Thank you, Dale. Those two made me so mad, but I wasn't any match for them."

His anger fought for expression, but he held it in check. "What did they say to you?"

"Nothing too much. They just don't like the fact that I'm a Yankee and I'm writing about the Reconstruction."

He shot a glance her way. Why did he feel she wasn't telling him everything?

"I didn't know that one man, but I'll deal with Jude at the sawmill." He paused. "You will tell me if anyone bothers you again, won't you."

She slipped her hand through the crook of his elbow. "I'm sure they won't."

"Charity. . ."

She pointed to a boy tacking up a notice on a post. "What's that?"

They stopped to read the poster over the boy's shoulder. The young towheaded fellow looked up at them. "Preacher is payin' me fifteen cents to hang these all over town."

Dale grinned down at him. "Fifteen cents? That'll buy a lot of candy."

The youngster grinned back. "I'm partial to peppermint." He tipped his cap to Charity. "I best get goin'. I got work to do."

Charity read the large headline aloud. "A Unity Rally?"

The notice proclaimed that Pastor Shuford called for everyone in town to attend church this upcoming Sunday because he was going to set forth a challenge to every person to put aside their malice and take a stand against the recent violence and come together in unity.

A tiny scowl dipped Charity's brow. "I'm glad somebody is doing something."

Dale released a soft snort. "Miles Flint better be there because things are likely to get pretty heated."

They continued to the boardinghouse. Dale handed Charity the paper-wrapped package and opened the door for her. "Charity, may I escort you to church this Sunday?"

She cocked her head. "Yes, you may."

He managed a tight smile and bid her a good afternoon. His temper still simmered as he walked to the mercantile. What was he thinking? Was it possible for a Yankee and a Rebel to worship together?

A smirk tilted his mouth. "I suppose we'll find out."

Chapter 12

The little church filled quickly, and Charity was glad Dale suggested they arrive early. Men stood to give ladies their seats, and by the time Pastor Shuford led in the singing of "Guide Me, O Thou Great Jehovah," the chapel was packed. As the hymn died away and people settled in, the preacher began by asking those who had lost someone in the war to raise their hands.

Charity turned in her seat and swept a glance across the room. Almost every hand went up. The pastor walked up and down the center aisle counting. He began whittling down the focus with more specific questions, demonstrating how some had lost sons or fathers, brothers or cousins, husbands or sweethearts. Some lost multiple loved ones, while others admitted to nightmares or periods of melancholia. Some lost land or business or fortune.

People all over the room murmured in response. A muffled sob sounded from the far right while others cleared their throats, fighting off tears.

Pastor Shuford returned to the front and held his arms out wide. "Do you see what we've shown here this morning? From the looks of it, almost the entire town is here today, and there isn't a person in this room who hasn't lost someone or something. True, some have lost more than others, but that should only serve to encourage us to be more compassionate, more Christlike."

Charity leaned slightly forward in her seat, hanging on every word. The picture he so eloquently painted was exactly the portrait she'd been trying to capture in her articles—this war affected everyone.

"Most of the folks here are Southern-born." The preacher cast his hand in a wide, encompassing arc. "But not all."

A hush fell over the crowd. Charity lowered her gaze to her lap. She'd experienced enough disdain over the past month to know several in the congregation stared at her. Hadn't the preacher shown, though, that everyone had suffered loss?

He stepped up onto the platform, and his booming voice carried to every corner. "South or North. Rich or poor. Learned or illiterate. Man or woman. Free or bond." He lowered his voice and sent a hard look across the packed pews. "And yes, white or black." He opened his Bible.

"In the tenth chapter of Acts, the apostle Peter preached that God is no respecter of persons. Brothers and sisters, listen to me. *Every* man who loves and fears God is himself a work of righteousness, because our Lord and Savior Jesus Christ is Lord of ALL!"

A man leaped to his feet two rows in front of Charity and Dale.

"That ain't so, preacher. Ain't no colored equal to a white man."

The preacher held his Bible aloft. "These aren't my words, Floyd. This is God's Word." He gestured to all assembled. "And Juniper Springs is a community. You and your family are part of this community, just like every other person in this room."

Another man stood. "I don't see no coloreds in this room."

A few others called out their agreement in ugly terms unfit for women and children's ears.

"Friends, please." Pastor Shuford held up his hands. "We must come together. Half of the word *community* is 'unity.' Violence has no place here. If we are to live as children of God, then we must acknowledge that we are *all* a family."

Two men toward the rear began arguing, and Charity tucked her bottom lip between her teeth. Squabbling only served to widen the gap separating the different persuasions. Above the angry shouts, the preacher's pleading voice called for attention.

"Listen to what God says. 'God so loved the *world*, that he gave his only begotten Son, that *whosoever* believeth in him should not perish, but have everlasting life.' Friends, neighbors, I tell you, the persecution and acts of violence are an abomination in God's eyes."

"What about violence done against us, preacher?"

"Them darkies is to blame. It's 'cause of them that war came down on us."

"Oh hush, Jess. You don't know what you're talking about."

A couple of women rose and ushered their children out the door.

Dale bent his head low and muttered. "This isn't right. God, help me." He stood and held up his hand for quiet.

Charity caught her breath, and her pulse tripped faster. She raised her eyes to the determined set to his jaw.

"Most of you here know me. You know who I am and what I was before the war. My family was wealthy and powerful. Now I work at the sawmill and the general store."

Comments buzzed all around them, but Dale didn't appear affected by anyone's opinions. He spoke up with confidence and conviction.

"I want to tell you about a man I met during the war. I'd been wounded—in my side and my leg. I tried to crawl for cover, but I couldn't move. Artillery exploded all around me. Rifle fire whistled on every side. I was a doomed man."

Tears burned Charity's eyes, and her throat tightened. She prayed silently for God's strength for Dale to say what needed to be said, and for those around to listen, not just with their ears but with their hearts.

"A man I did not know crawled over to me and told me I was going to be all right. He carried me into the woods, and hid me where I'd be safe until the battle was over. Then he tore his own shirt to wrap around my wounds. He gave me water and took care of me. When it was safe to move, he carried me. For two days we traveled until he brought me to a regiment that had a doctor. All during that time, this man prayed for me. He prayed for strength to carry me, and he prayed for God to let me live."

Charity dabbed tears from her eyes and glanced around the room. Every face turned toward Dale, every eye riveted on him.

"This man put his own life in danger to save me. He didn't have to do that. He didn't even know me. But he knew Someone else. He knew Jesus. I could tell by the way he kept up a continuous conversation, not with me, but with the Lord."

Dale shook his head and his voice broke. "I've asked myself a thousand times why that man did what he did. There is only one answer. He let Jesus do it through him."

The man two rows ahead spoke up. "I suppose you're gonna tell us he was a Yankee."

Dale turned his head. "No, Floyd. He wasn't a Yankee. He was a slave."

A gasp rippled through the crowd. Dale sat down, and Charity risked a sideways glance at him. How hard was it for a once-wealthy, influential man to stand before the town and relate the story he'd hidden in his heart for six years?

Pastor Shuford stepped down from the platform. "Dale, did you tell this man you couldn't accept his help because he was black?"

Dale shook his head. "No, sir."

The preacher scanned the room. "It's a good thing God isn't bigoted against sinners, for we'd surely all be as doomed as Dale was on that battlefield. Had it not been for the compassion shown by that man, Dale wouldn't be here today to tell us about it." He gestured toward Dale. "When a man acts in a Christlike way, does God ask about the color of his skin to determine whether or not the act is acceptable in His sight?"

A handful of men stood and made some uncouth remarks, walking out one after the other. Charity recognized two as the ones who'd accosted her in the alley.

Weariness evidenced itself in the preacher's voice and face as he addressed those remaining. "Brothers and sisters, instead of a closing hymn, I'd like for us to have a time of silent prayer, and each of us search our hearts for those prejudices God would have us remove."

Heads bowed and peace reigned. As each one finished praying, feet shuffled and hushed whispers accompanied them as people quietly got up and left. Charity raised her head to find Dale watching her. He rose and held out his hand.

She placed her fingers within the safety of his grasp and joined him tiptoeing out of the church.

Pastor Shuford stood by the door. "Thank you for what you said, Dale. You never told me that before."

Charity peered up and watched Dale's jaw twitch. She doubted that she'd ever know how much his speech cost him.

Low, gray clouds hung above the treetops and swallowed the sun as Dale walked her to the boardinghouse in silence, his limp barely perceptible. A chilly breeze shook leaves loose from their tethers and blew them across the road, tumbling with the ones that had fallen before them. No matter how long the leaves clung to the branches, eventually they'd all join the seasonal dance in a patchwork of colors.

They climbed the porch steps at the boardinghouse, and Dale reached for the door. Charity put out her hand to stop him. "I really admire what you did today. Relating your experience in front of everybody, especially those you knew would scorn it, took great fortitude."

His lips pressed together, and he lowered his gaze. "I'm not the man I once was."

She touched his hand. "No, you aren't. You're better."

&

Charity crumpled another sheet of paper and tossed it in the corner with the rest. She propped her elbows on the desk and laid her head in her hands. Not a single attempt at writing the first article satisfied her. She stood and paced the small bedroom between the door and the single window, muttering to herself.

"Something's missing." Agitation climbed her frame as she glared at the pile of discarded beginnings of her writing. "It lacks cohesiveness." She crossed to the window and pushed the filmy white curtain aside with her fingertips. "How do I capture what I can't define?"

A folded piece of paper taunted her from the corner of the desk. She picked up the telegram and opened it, even though she could quote it word for word.

MUST HAVE FIRST ARTICLE BY NOV 1.

That was it. No wasted words. But she read between the brevity and the signature. If she couldn't produce the first article on time, she might as well not bother writing the rest, and she couldn't afford to lose this assignment.

She slid one finger over her lips and contemplated informing Mr. Peabody of her two other missions. Couldn't she tie a search for a former slave and a Union officer into her other articles? Her editor might find it intriguing enough to warrant an additional article and grant her more time. On the other hand, catering to the readership was always foremost in the man's mind. No doubt he'd remind her that the people of prominence and affluence who subscribed to *Keystone* likely wouldn't be interested in a lowly dressmaker wanting to reunite with her long lost son.

She returned to the desk and pulled out a fresh sheet of paper, its vast emptiness looming before her. In order to keep her job, she had to draw a portrait with words in a way to captivate her audience. The trouble was the issues that captivated her were very different from the ones that would appeal to a Northern aristocrat.

Frost sugarcoated the ground when Dale stepped out the door of his house. He pulled his collar up around his ears and thrust his hands into his pockets. Dawn had barely broken, and he didn't know if the Ferguson ladies' bakery would be open yet, but he figured if he tapped on the door, they'd let him in.

His boots crunched through the leaves as the town awoke around him. A rooster crowed, a dog barked, the aroma of fresh coffee boiling on somebody's stove tantalized his senses, and muted sunlight filtered through the trees along the top of the mountain east of town.

He'd been awake for hours, unsettled thoughts causing sleep to remain out of his reach. People still talked of the lynching, but the past two days, the topic of most conversations was Pastor Shuford's unorthodox church service. Many folks stated adamantly that they never intended to forget or forgive. Others revealed hearts laced with bigotry. Had it not been for God sending that black soldier to save his life, he feared he'd be among them. He couldn't expect people to see things from his point of view if they hadn't experienced what he had. Still, he prayed a work of grace to be done within those who still viewed the former slaves the way Tate Ridley did.

Margaret Ferguson was just unlocking the front door of the bakery when Dale arrived. She gave him a syrupy smile while she wrapped up the apple fritters he selected, and batted her eyelashes at him when he paid her and bid her a polite good morning.

As soon as he left the bakery, his thoughts returned to those ponderings that had kept him awake most of the night. The "brotherhood," as Tate Ridley referred to it, tended to protect each other, so Dale wasn't surprised that some of Tate's cronies swore they'd all been playing cards the night the man was lynched. Tate's suggestion that perhaps Dale should join them, coupled with the comments he overheard, weren't enough to make an accusation, but they certainly raised Dale's suspicions.

Smoke curled from the stovepipe emerging from the sawmill office when Dale crossed the bridge. Hopefully Simon had brewed a fresh pot of coffee rather than warming up yesterday's leftovers. When Dale walked in, Simon looked over his shoulder at him. "You're early."

Dale shrugged. "Couldn't sleep. Figured I might as well get an early start." He laid one of the apple fritters on Simon's desk. "Brought you some breakfast."

"Thanks."

Dale poured two cups of coffee and handed one to Simon.

Simon took a noisy slurp. "I'm real pleased with the way you've kept things going here while I was at the logging camp."

Dale gave him a nod of appreciation.

"I'm leaving for the camp again today. Should be back early next week." Simon took a bite of his fritter. "But there's something I wanted to talk to you about."

Simon's tone caught Dale's attention. "Something wrong?"

"Not sure." Simon took another slurp of coffee. "In the light of what happened a week and a half ago, I'd like you to keep an extra close eye on Tate." Simon shook his head. "That one's a troublemaker. I hope I'm wrong, but I think he might have had something to do with that lynching."

Dale shot a hard look at his boss. He hadn't said anything Dale didn't already suspect, but he wanted to know why Simon thought so.

Dale sat across from Simon. "I've heard a few things he's said. A few weeks ago he suggested I attend a meeting of their brotherhood—that's what he called it, but you and I both know who they are."

"Hmph. The Klan. I thought as much." Simon finished off his fritter and licked his fingers. "I was coming back from the logging camp that Friday. It was getting late, and I knew I'd never make it before nightfall, so I made camp in the woods out by the Athens road. I'd already turned in when I heard voices. Three or four men. Couldn't really see them, but one of them was Tate. I recognized his voice."

"Did you hear what they said?"

"Just bits and pieces. There was a wind blowing that night. That's why I didn't keep the campfire going."

Dale set his coffee mug down and waited for Simon to go on.

"I heard something that sounded like, 'He ain't gonna have no more need of it,' or something like that. They moved on pretty quick."

"They didn't see you?"

Simon shook his head. "Don't think so."

Dale rubbed his hand across his face. "Have you talked to Miles Flint about this?"

"No. There's enough hard feelings around here toward anyone from the North. Didn't figure the word of a Yankee would be worth much."

Dale finished off his coffee. "There are some who don't think my word is worth much either."

Chapter 13

Charity stepped back to allow a young mother with two children to enter the general store ahead of her. The little ones, a girl and a boy, looked enough alike to be twins, but the difference in their height indicated the girl was a couple of years older. Before they were a half-dozen steps inside the store, the little boy dashed to the glass case that displayed the candy.

Saturday morning business was brisk, and Charity scooted past a few folks to pick up another package of writing paper. A wave of guilt pricked her when she thought of the number of sheets she'd wasted, but this time she knew exactly what she was going to write. At least, she hoped she knew.

She moved toward the counter and found herself standing behind the young mother again. Listening to the children's chatter brought a smile to Charity's heart. She'd hoped to have a family one day, but most men didn't want a woman who had a career.

The little boy turned around and peered up at her. "Hi, lady. Whatcha buyin'?"

His mother gave his shoulder a gentle tap. "Timothy! That's not polite." She turned and gave Charity an apologetic look. "I'm sorry. He just says whatever is on his mind."

Charity smiled. "It's all right. Both of your children are adorable."

The woman blushed. "Thank you. We haven't been introduced, but I've seen you at church. I'm Auralie Danfield, and this is my daughter, Rose, and my son, Timothy."

"Papa hadta go to the freight depot," Timothy piped up. "He said he'd be back in two shakes of a lamb's tail."

Charity chuckled, and Auralie placed her hand atop Timothy's head. "You're Miss Galbraith, aren't you? My brother mentioned you were here on assignment from your magazine."

"Your brother?"

"Dale Covington is my brother."

Charity nodded with understanding. "I should have seen the resemblance. Dale told me he had a sister, and I do recall seeing you and your family in church, but I didn't make the connection. It's nice to meet you."

The storekeeper finished Mrs. Danfield's order, and she stepped aside so Charity could pay for her paper. She sneaked a peek at the children, both of whom had their noses pressed against the glass case, gazing with longing at the selection of candy. Charity leaned toward their mother and whispered. "May they each have a peppermint stick?"

Her new friend smiled and nodded. "I suppose one peppermint stick won't spoil them too badly."

Rose and Timothy chorused a "thank you, ma'am" and scampered outside with their treat, while Charity became better acquainted with Dale's sister. The two women strolled out to the boardwalk together. The previous day's chill had mellowed into a milder, sunny day, providing a pleasant moment for visiting while they waited for Mr. Danfield to return for his family.

"I'm glad I finally got to meet you, Miss Galbraith."

"Please, call me Charity."

"Only if you will call me Auralie." She set her market basket down and turned to check on the children before continuing. "Are you going to write about last Sunday's church service in your articles?"

Charity tilted her head. "I hope to include many angles in the articles, but I must admit last Sunday's service was different."

Auralie's eyes misted. "I didn't know about that black soldier who saved my brother's life."

"Dale said he hadn't told people about that, but why didn't he tell you?"

Tiny lines appeared between Auralie's brows. "Dale and I have been estranged for the past ten years. He didn't approve of me marrying Colton. When the war started and Colton fought for the North, Dale was outraged. He refused to have anything to do with us. He even made it clear that we weren't welcome at his wedding."

"His—" Charity's breath caught. "His wedding? I didn't know he was married."

"Oh dear. Perhaps I shouldn't have said anything." Auralie touched her lips with her fingertips. "My brother has always guarded his privacy, but I didn't realize he'd not told you he'd been married."

The revelation spun in Charity's mind. "I don't believe I've seen his wife."

"Oh no." Auralie shook her head. "She died six years ago."

"I see." Uncertainty rattled her. Perhaps his wife's death was something he didn't wish to discuss. She tucked the information away for future consideration and steered the conversation in another direction that piqued her interest. "You said your husband fought for the North."

"It's a very sore spot with many people, but Colton did what he believed was right." Auralie's voice rang with pride for her husband.

"I can imagine. Dale has told me a little about his time during the war." A tiny light of understanding emerged in Charity's mind. She suddenly felt very privileged that Dale had shared with her as much as he had. "When I first met your brother, it was to ask him about a former slave I'm seeking. He is my friend's son. His name is Wylie, and he belonged to Covington Plantation from the time he was thirteen, but Dale didn't remember him."

"Wylie?" Auralie put one finger to her chin. "When I was a young girl, I used to sneak down to the slave quarters to visit with some of the children. I taught a few of them to read until my father found out. But I don't remember anyone named Wylie. I'm sorry."

Admiration for her new friend filled Charity. "It must have taken a great deal of courage to teach slave children to read when you were only a child yourself."

"My father called me rebellious, not courageous." A rueful smile wobbled across Auralie's face. "Maybe Barnabas knows him. Barnabas was a slave before Colton bought him and freed him. He lives by us and works with Colton. I'll ask him when we get home."

"Meanwhile I'll keep looking." Charity shifted her package of paper to her other hand. "I'm also searching for information about my father. He was an officer in the Union army, but he never came home from the war."

Sympathy etched lines across Auralie's brow. "I'm so sorry."

Charity acknowledged the woman's compassion with a slight nod. "I'm hoping to find some records that might tell me what became of him after he was wounded and captured."

Auralie pointed down the street. "Here comes Colton. He might be able to give you some information."

A wagon driven by a handsome man wearing a black coat pulled up in front of the general store.

"Papa! We got peppermint sticks!" Rose and Timothy clambered into their father's arms the moment he alighted from the wagon. He ruffled Timothy's hair and caressed his daughter's cheek.

Auralie reached for her husband's arm. "Colton, this is Miss Charity Galbraith. She and I have become friends."

Colton pulled his hat off. "Miss Charity. I've been hearing about you. It's nice to meet you."

"Likewise, Mr. Danfield."

His wife slipped her arm through his. "Colton, Charity's father was an officer with the Union army, and she is looking for information about him. I wondered if you could help her."

"If I can." Colton looked from Auralie to Charity. "What is it you're trying to find?"

Charity's heart accelerated with hopeful anticipation. "My father was Major Charles Hampton Galbraith, and he served under Major General Oliver Howard with the Fourth Army Corps. The last my mother and I heard was that he'd been wounded and taken prisoner at a place called Pickett's Mill."

A flicker of recognition lit Colton's eyes. "I started out with General George Thomas and the Army of the Cumberland, but I was briefly with the Fourth Army Corps in May of 1864. I was returned to Tennessee just before the battle at Pickett's Mill."

Charity's heart soared, and her breath quickened. "So you might have known my father?" A tremble ran through her.

"Major Galbraith?" Colton frowned in concentration. "I seem to remember a Galbraith. Tall, dark hair with gray streaks in it, thick mustache, soft spoken."

Tears of joy and anguish intertwined and gave Charity's heart a release of its long pent-up ache. She covered a tiny sob with her fingers. "Yes, that sounds like my father. He always said people would listen more closely if one spoke quietly."

Auralie touched Charity's arm.

A thread of caution laced Colton's tone. "I didn't really know him. I only remember him briefly. The battles at New Hope Church and Pickett's Mill occurred after I was sent back to the Army of the Cumberland, so I'm afraid I can't tell you what happened after that."

While a drop of disappointment trickled through her, the joy of speaking with someone who remembered her father—even for a short time—sent encouragement coursing through her veins.

"Perhaps you can tell me where I might find the prisoner of war records."

Colton pressed his lips together. "Hmm. I know the records for the Federal Army are kept in Washington, but the Confederate records aren't there. They might be in Milledgeville, but I'm not sure. I wish I could be of more help."

"Just speaking with someone who knew Father means so much to me." Tears burned the back of her throat. "Thank you for that."

Auralie reached over and squeezed Charity's hand. "I'm so glad we met, and I wish we could stay and chat, but we really must be going."

Charity returned the squeeze. "Will I see you tomorrow at church?"

"We'll be there." Colton picked up his wife's basket and deposited it behind the wagon seat, and then swung the youngsters into the back. He held his wife's hand while she climbed aboard then turned to tip his hat to Charity. "It was nice to meet you, Miss Galbraith. Good day to you."

Charity hugged the package of paper tightly against her and waved as the Danfield family wagon rolled down the street. Emotions tumbled within her. Dale's sister was a dear person, her children adorable, and her husband a man of character. His description of her father sang in her ears. But the thing that tugged for her attention was learning that Dale had been married. Why did it bother her that he hadn't told her?

ᴥ

Dale locked the office door and descended the stairs. He always welcomed the end of a long work week, but never more so than this one. Tate Ridley had done his best to antagonize him for the past three days—ever since Simon left for the logging camp. Even though Dale had a half day of making deliveries for the general store ahead of him, he looked forward to a day and a half without having to deal with Ridley.

Some additional paperwork had kept him a few extra minutes, and Clyde was probably wondering where he was. He hurried to the bottom of the steps, but before he went ten feet, a shiny glint caught his eye. He stopped and bent to take a closer look.

A silver chain lay in the dirt. Dale picked it up and examined it. He couldn't remember if Simon wore a silver watch chain. This one had an oval fob with an oak leaf carved into it. Made sense, he supposed, that a man who worked in the timber business would have a watch fob with an oak leaf, but Dale simply hadn't noticed it before. It had to be Simon's. He'd never seen anyone else around the lumberyard with something like that. Strange, he hadn't noticed it lying on the ground before now, but he'd been busy the past couple of days, and had much on his mind.

He was already late getting to the general store, so rather than climb the stairs and lock the chain in the desk, Dale slipped it into his pocket. Simon wouldn't be back until next week anyway. Dale figured to tuck the chain into the desk drawer first thing Monday morning.

He hastened across the bridge and decided to cut through the trees and the alley that ran between the bank and the post office to save time. Halfway down the alley, an unwelcomed voice hailed him.

"Covington."

Dale groaned. Couldn't he just pretend he didn't hear and keep going? He heaved a sigh and turned. "What is it, Tate?"

Ridley came sauntering up to him. Had the man been following him? "I hear tell you and that Yankee reporter been goin' to church together." He grinned at his companion, the same man who had harassed Charity a week and a half earlier. "Mighty holier-than-thou if you ask me."

"Is there a point to this, Ridley? I need to get to the mercantile."

Ridley lifted his shoulders and held out his hands. "Just appears like she's settlin' in to stay. Thought by now you'd be tryin' to get shed of her. 'Course maybe you got yourself other reasons for keepin' her close." Ridley and his friend guffawed.

Dale stiffened and curled his fingers into fists. "You better watch your mouth, Ridley." Acid crawled up Dale's throat at Ridley's insinuations.

"I ain't sayin' nothin' that ain't so." Ridley waggled his eyebrows. "She ain't too bad to look at. The two of you got ya a cozy arrangement goin' on?"

Dale growled from the pit of his stomach and connected his fist with Ridley's jaw. The man sprawled in the dirt holding his hand to his mouth.

Dale spread his feet and braced himself, waiting for Ridley to get up.

Ridley pulled himself to his feet and spit blood. "C'mon. You think you're better'n me?"

Arms gripped Dale from behind and Ridley rammed his fist into Dale's middle. A moment later the two men were throwing punches high and low. Dale bellowed with rage, putting every ounce of strength he had into a right hook.

Ridley ducked and Dale fell off balance. Ridley leaped onto Dale and began driving punches into Dale's face. Dale rolled and shoved Ridley into the dirt, the two of them wrestling for control.

A steel-like grip dug fingers into Dale's shoulder and pulled him off Ridley, depositing him on his backside up against the building. Miles Flint then yanked Ridley up by his shirt.

"What's going on here?" The sheriff's gruff demand rang through the alley.

Dale rubbed his jaw and stood gingerly, holding his ribs. "He just needs to learn some manners."

"That ain't so, sheriff," Ridley yelled, pointing at Dale. "He stole my watch chain. Look in his pocket."

"What?" Dale stared at Ridley, momentarily speechless. He shook his head, trying to dislodge the cobwebs. Surely he didn't hear correctly.

Miles tossed Dale a look over his shoulder. "You have his watch chain in your pocket?"

Dale tried to straighten, but the pain in his ribs grabbed him. "How did he know I had that watch chain in my pocket?"

Miles turned halfway around and nailed Dale with a hard stare. "You mean you *do* have his watch chain?"

"Yes, but—I mean, no. I didn't know it was—I found it." Dale groped to put the pieces together in his mind.

Miles checked Dale's pockets and extracted the silver chain.

"See there, I told you, sheriff." Ridley fairly crowed. "He stole my watch chain, and I was just tryin' to get it back."

Dale pointed at Ridley. "Miles, surely you don't believe I'd steal a watch chain or anything else. I found it lying in the dirt over at the sawmill. I thought it was Simon's. I was going to lock it up in the office, but I was already late getting to the mercantile."

Miles looked from Dale to Ridley and back to Dale. He slipped the chain into his vest pocket and took hold of Dale's arm. "Come on, Dale."

"What? Miles, you know me better than that."

"Dale, I got no choice. Tate, here, says you stole his watch chain. The watch chain is in your pocket. Until I can untangle this mess, I'm going to have to lock you up."

As Dale walked up the alley toward the jail with Miles, Ridley's evil laugh followed him.

Chapter 14

"Arrested!"

Charity blurted the word as if it tasted bad on her tongue. Surely Hannah must be mistaken. The distress in her land-lady's voice said otherwise.

"Yes." Hannah stood in the doorway of Charity's room, wringing the corner of her apron between her fingers. "Dale and Tate got into a fight, and Tate said Dale stole his watch. Miles arrested Dale."

Charity grabbed her shawl and bonnet. "This is preposterous. Dale would never do such a thing." She yanked her bonnet on and tossed the shawl around her shoulders.

Hannah followed her down the stairs, and Charity paused by the front door. "I'll be back as soon as I can. Try not to worry."

Charity marched out the door and lengthened her strides once past the gate. She placed one hand on her head to keep her bonnet from blowing off in her haste. Minutes later, she stepped in the door of the sheriff's office.

"Mr. Flint, what is the meaning of this? Have you lost your mind? How could you possibly believe Dale is guilty of stealing a watch? This is the most ridiculous, absurd, outrageous—"

The sheriff rose from his desk and held up his hand. "Whoa." He pulled an extra chair out from behind a cabinet and positioned it opposite his. "Have a seat."

Charity plunked both fists on her hips. "I don't feel like sitting. I demand you release Dale at once."

Flint heaved a loud sigh. " 'Fraid I can't do that just yet." He pointed to the chair. "Have a seat."

She narrowed her eyes at the man. "I don't want to sit."

Flint placed his hands on the desk and leaned forward. "I didn't ask you if you *wanted* to sit. Have a seat."

Steaming, Charity gathered her skirts and plopped into the chair, her arms folded across her chest and one foot tapping on the floor.

Flint sat at his desk and picked up a stubby pencil. "First of all, Dale didn't steal a watch. Tate Ridley said he stole his watch chain. Secondly, if it's any comfort to you, you're not the first person who's come in here in the past hour *demandin'* that I release him. I thought Clyde Sawyer was gonna climb over my desk and grab my keys, and I almost had to arrest his wife! The preacher clucked his tongue at me. The Ferguson ladies were pert near in tears, and Miss Hannah—" He shook his head. "I won't be surprised if she throws me out of the boardinghouse on my ear. I might have to sleep in the jail tonight, myself!"

Charity harrumphed. "Shouldn't that tell you something? If all those people believe Dale is innocent, how can you possibly keep him in jail?"

Flint leaned back in his chair. "Because the watch chain was in Dale's pocket." He tossed the pencil on the desk. "I can let you see him as soon as Doc Greenway is finished—"

Charity leaped from her chair. "Doctor? What's the matter with Dale?"

The old, gray-haired doctor Charity remembered interviewing a couple of weeks ago stepped through the door that led to the cells. "Afternoon, Miss Galbraith." He set his shabby black bag on the chair Charity had vacated. "I bandaged him up, Miles. He has a couple of cracked ribs, and some cuts and bruises. I've seen worse."

Charity's breath seemed to escape involuntarily. "But how—"

"He and Tate were goin' at it in the alley when I come up on them," Flint explained. "Doc, how much do I owe you?"

Doctor Greenway waved his hand. "Not a thing. Dale's a fine man. If you want my opinion, Miles Flint, I think you're a lunatic for keeping him in jail." He gave a snort and a sharp nod of his head to punctuate his statement, snatched his bag, and stomped out the door.

Flint rolled his eyes and sighed. "I suppose you'll be wantin' to see him now?"

Charity didn't answer but marched toward the inner door, tossing a look over her shoulder at the sheriff to make sure he followed.

Dale lay on a narrow cot in the small cell. Charity gasped when she caught a glimpse of his swollen eye, bruised face, and cut lip. Her stomach turned over at the sight of the bandages swathed around his ribs. Her heart thudded in her chest like a sledgehammer.

"Dale, I came as soon as I heard. Oh my soul, are you all right?" She couldn't keep her voice steady.

Dale released a muffled groan as he sat up. "I'm all right. Just a little sore." His cut lip slightly distorted his speech.

A basin of water and a cloth sat on the floor beside the cot. Charity turned to Flint. "Can you let me in there?"

The sheriff smirked and grasped one iron bar of the door. It swung open without benefit of Flint's key. "Take as long as you want." He turned back toward his office. "I'll just leave this here door open for propriety's sake."

Charity slipped into the cell, a shudder rattling through her middle. She hesitated. Despite the open door, it wasn't seemly to sit beside Dale on the cot. The sheriff read her mind.

"Thought you might want this chair." He carried the chair Charity had used in the outer office through the cell door and placed it opposite the cot.

Dale tilted his head, a painful grimace on his face. "Thanks, Miles."

Charity sat and scooted the chair a bit closer to him. "Dale, I don't understand. How in the world did this happen?"

"I'm still trying to figure that out myself." He shifted position and winced. "I already told Miles my side of the story."

"Would you mind telling me?" She took the cloth, dipped it in the basin of water, and gently placed it against Dale's swollen eye. "You don't have to if you don't want to, but I'd like to hear it from you. I promise I won't put it in my articles."

Dale tried to chuckle but instead held his hand to his ribs. "Ooh." He took a few shallow breaths. "I was finished for the day at the sawmill. I'd run a little late because there was some paperwork I needed to finish. I locked the office door and went down the steps. Not far from the stairs I saw something glinting in the sunlight. I picked it up. It was a watch chain and fob."

She blotted his cut lip and rinsed the cloth again while Dale went on.

"I don't remember seeing it before, but I figured it must belong to Simon. I thought it was strange, though, because Simon left for the logging camp a couple of days ago. If he dropped it, I should have seen it lying there before today. Guess I just had too much on my mind and didn't notice it."

"How did Tate come to accuse you of stealing it?" She tenderly laid the cool rag on his face again.

"That's another thing I can't figure out." He gave an almost imperceptible shake of his head. "Because I was late, I cut through a couple of yards and alleys to save time. It's not the way I normally go, but Tate came up behind me, almost like he was following me. That man who accosted you the other day was with him. Tate started saying some rude things. I told him to watch his mouth, but he kept on, making some very crass and insulting remarks, so I punched him in the mouth and knocked him down. Next thing I know, that other fellow grabbed me from behind, and Tate and I were fighting. When Miles showed up, Tate started yelling about me stealing his watch chain."

Charity pulled the cloth back. "He didn't mention the chain when he first approached you?"

"No."

"Did you tell the sheriff about this?"

Miles Flint's voice reached her from the front room. "Every word. I got it wrote down."

Charity sat back in her chair. "This doesn't make sense."

"It doesn't make sense to me, either, but Miles says he has to keep me here until he can untangle the facts."

She rose and set the basin down. "You need to rest. I'll be back later." She turned her head toward the door and raised her voice a tad. "If the sheriff will let me."

"I'll let you," Flint called out. "In fact, I might need you to bring us both something to eat from Maybelle's if Miss Hannah refuses to feed me."

She paused at the cell door and then returned to the chair. She leaned forward and lowered her voice to nearly a whisper. "Dale, may I ask you something?"

"Anything."

"Why didn't you tell me you were married?"

≈

Dale lay on the cot with one hand tucked behind his head. Why didn't he tell Charity about Gwendolyn? The only reason that kept prodding him was he'd also have to tell her—

"Dale, you want another cup of coffee?"

Dale groaned. Two nights of sleeping on the lumpy cot and drinking Miles's coffee hadn't improved his mood. He called back to Miles. "Is it Maybelle's coffee or yours?"

"You gettin' picky?"

Dale leaned against the wall of his cell. "I just don't like coffee that I have to chew."

The front door of the office opened. The legs of Miles's chair scraped against the floor. "Mornin', Simon. Guess I know why you're here."

Dale pulled himself up from the cot and came out of the cell that Miles hadn't bothered to lock. He'd wondered for the past two days how he was going to tell Simon about this.

Simon pulled his hat off and scratched his head. "When I got to the mill this morning and there wasn't anyone there, I knew something was wrong. Ran into Ned Caldwell, and he told me you and Tate got in a fight and you got arrested." He peered closer at Dale's face. "I sure hope you made him look worse."

Dale gave him a tiny smirk. "I threw the first punch."

Simon grinned. "Good for you." He looked at Miles. "You must not consider him too desperate a criminal if you're leaving his cell unlocked."

Miles poured coffee into a tin mug and pushed it across the desk toward Simon. "Sit down. I'll tell you all about it."

Miles pulled the watch chain out of the drawer and laid it on the desk. "You ever seen this before?"

Simon took at look at the chain and fob. "No."

Dale poured himself a half cup of coffee and grimaced at the first sip. "I found it in the dirt. I thought it was yours."

Simon shook his head. "Not mine. Miles, this is the worst coffee I ever tasted."

Dale watched Simon's face as he related his side of the story. Other than a raised eyebrow or two, his boss didn't seem at all surprised.

Simon set his coffee mug on the desk and turned to the sheriff. "I guess it's time I tell you what I saw three Friday nights ago."

Dale sat on the edge of the desk while Simon told Miles about hearing a commotion by the Athens road the night of the lynching. "I recognized Tate's voice."

Miles tilted backward in his chair. "What were you doing out there at that time of night?"

"I was going home, and my horse threw a shoe. Pulled up lame. I couldn't ride him, and I knew I'd never make it to town before dark walking, so I made camp."

Dale watched Miles roll the story over in his mind.

"Hmm. I believe you, but that doesn't prove Dale's innocent."

"How long you going to keep my foreman in jail?"

Dale looked at the sheriff, very interested to know the answer to that question.

"Unless I can find proof that Dale didn't steal the chain, I'm gonna have to keep him here till the circuit judge comes around again." Miles sent Dale an apologetic look. "That won't be for another two weeks."

"Two weeks!" Dale slid off the corner of the desk and thrust his arms out at his sides, immediately regretting the action. He rubbed his sore ribs.

Simon stood and nodded at Dale. "Appears like you need to rest up anyway." He picked up his hat. "Can I bring you anything?"

Dale snorted. "Some decent coffee."

❧

Dale sat across the desk from Miles, concentrating on the chessboard and munching on the sugar cookies Charity had brought earlier. "I hope you don't have plans for this queen." He slid his bishop diagonally and captured the sheriff's key piece.

Miles blew out through pursed lips. "Can't you let me win just one game?"

Dale grinned. "I will if you let me out of here."

"I might just lock that cell and—"

The office door creaked open, and a thin black woman tapped on the doorframe. "All right iffen I come in?"

Miles eyed her. "Come on in. What do you need?"

Her hair was covered by a kerchief, and her blue dress was faded and patched, but clean. "I hear'd about two men gittin' in a fight, and one of 'em stole'd a silver watch chain."

Miles frowned and narrowed his eyes at her. "Where'd you hear that?"

She lowered her eyes and shrugged. "Talk gits around, even out in Crow Town. Come to see fo' myself."

Miles pointed at her. "Aren't you the wife of the man. . ."

"Yes, suh." Her voice broke, but she lifted her chin slightly. "I be Annie Jarrell. My man, Henry, be the one that them no account drunkards lynched."

Dale stood and offered Mrs. Jarrell his chair, but she shook her head.

The sheriff's tone softened. "What is it you're askin', Miz Jarrell?"

She drew in a deep breath, as if what she was about to say was going to cost her dearly. "The night they came and dragged my Henry away, I followed, so's I can see where they take him. But I got lost. I listen hard, but all I hear'd was wind howlin' like a mournful thing. A while later I see a cross burnin', and I know. . .I know what they done to my Henry." She wiped tears away with her fists.

"When our men went and cut Henry down from that tree, and they's gittin' him ready for buryin', I looked through his pockets. His daddy's watch chain was missin'. Henry's daddy was Eli Jarrell. Eli's massah set him free befo' the war, and the massah give Eli his old watch chain. Eli, he never had no watch to hang from it, but he be mighty proud o' that chain. When Eli died, Henry took the chain, and he carry wid him all th' time, 'cause it be the onliest thing he have to remind him o' his daddy."

Grief strained her voice. "When they hang my Henry, whoever done it stole his daddy's watch chain." The set of her jaw defined her anger.

"Mm-hmm. Then I hear'd tell 'bout a watch chain turnin' up here."

Dale and Miles exchanged looks, and Miles rubbed his chin. "Miz Jarrell, can you describe the watch chain for me?"

" 'Course I can. It be the color of moonlight, and it be as long as from the tip o' my pointer finger to my elbow. The piece a-danglin' from one end have a oak leaf on it, and there be a li'l nick near the tip o' the leaf. The seventh link in the chain is crooked where it broke one time and Henry do the best he can to fix it."

Miles reached in the desk drawer and pulled out the chain. Mrs. Jarrell covered her mouth as she gave a little joyful cry. Miles stretched it out on the desk and counted the links. The seventh link had a slightly odd shape and the oak leaf fob had a tiny nick at the tip.

Dale reached over and scooped up the chain, picked up Mrs. Jarrell's hand, and laid the chain in her palm. She raised tear-filled eyes to him. "Thank ya kindly, suh."

Miles walked her to the door. "Be careful goin' home, Miz Jarrell."

Dale stared at the door after Miles closed it. "Is that enough proof?"

Miles crossed to the desk. "That you're innocent?"

Dale turned and locked eyes with the sheriff. "That Tate is guilty."

Chapter 15

C harity sipped her coffee. "Hannah, how well do you know Dale?"
Her landlady stirred a few drops of cream into her cup. "I know him
better now than I did before the war."

"Did you know he was married?"

Hannah raised her cup to her lips and looked at Charity over the rim.
"Yes."

Charity shoved aside her mild annoyance that nobody had bothered
to mention Dale's marriage. Why should they? Dale's personal life was
none of her business, and Hannah wasn't one to gossip. However, the
older woman must have detected Charity's unsettled chafing because she
lowered her cup and reached across the kitchen table to cover Charity's
hand.

"It wasn't my place to say anything." Hannah's gentle tone stroked
Charity's heart. "He was married just before the war. There was a notice in
the *Sentinel*. The wedding didn't take place here in town. They were a very
wealthy family and had no use for our little church." No cynicism laced
her voice. "The town folk simply didn't know a great deal about his wife
other than her name—Gwendolyn. She very rarely came into town and
didn't have contact with the 'common people,' if you know what I mean.
I think her family was from the Athens area.

"I remember seeing Dale from time to time during the war, but
like most, he was gone for long periods. You remember I told you that
scavengers looted and burned the manor house at Covington Plantation.
Nobody here in town knows for sure what happened, but I think
Gwendolyn died around that time. Dale doesn't talk about it."

Charity's stomach turned over, imagining the grief Dale experienced.
No wonder he was withdrawn. A new ache—a different ache—kindled
within her. But this pain wasn't born of anger toward the Rebels. It was
saturated with sympathy for one Rebel—one who had quietly, softly,
become very dear to her. When she'd asked him a few days ago why he'd
never told her about his marriage, she'd thought it a reasonable question
until she saw the haunted look in his eyes. Now the memory of it struck
her, and she regretted having put that expression of pain on his face.

Hannah didn't appear to notice Charity's discomfiture as she traced
the rim of her coffee cup with her finger. "When Dale came home, he'd

been wounded. The first time I saw him at the end of the war, he was like a broken thing—a mere shadow of the man he'd been. Within months, carpetbaggers came through the area and began buying up land cheap. He lost everything."

The front door opened, and Charity recognized Miles Flint's voice. "Miss Hannah?"

Hannah pressed her lips together and sent a look of exasperation to Charity. "That man! I'm still perturbed at him for putting Dale in jail." She called out, "In the kitchen."

Miles, hat in hand, poked his head through the kitchen door. "Got a man here who could use a cup of coffee. He doesn't like mine." Dale's face came into view behind Miles.

Charity's heart fluttered as Dale's gaze locked onto hers. Something unspoken bridged the space between them, and she rose from her chair. If he was angry that she'd asked about his wife, it didn't show. He looked straight at her, as if there were no one else in the room. She couldn't have torn her gaze away if she wanted to—and she didn't want to.

❧

Dale's pulse accelerated when Charity's gaze connected with his. His concern for her safety defied definition. He'd been aware for a couple of weeks that he cared about her, but with the confirmation of Tate's involvement with the lynching, coupled with the remarks he'd made about "that Yankee woman," sweet relief swept over his heart at seeing her at Miss Hannah's kitchen table.

Her lips parted. Did she want to say something? Apparently deciding this wasn't the time or place, she pressed her lips together into the tiniest of smiles.

Miss Hannah plunked her hands on her hips and glowered at Miles. "So you finally found your common sense and let him out." She crossed the cupboard and pulled out two coffee mugs.

"Miss Hannah, have you seen Tate Ridley?"

Hannah paused in midmotion pouring coffee into the mugs. "Why, no. He wasn't at breakfast, but I just assumed he left early."

Miles and Dale exchanged a look. "We already checked at the mill. He's not there, and Simon hasn't seen him either."

Miles scowled and pursed his lips. "Miss Hannah, could I trouble you to go up and check Tate's room?"

"Of course, but what am I looking for?"

"I'll come with you." He followed Hannah from the room.

Charity stepped over to the stove and finished pouring the coffee. She handed a brimming cup to Dale. "Peace offering?"

Dale accepted the steaming, fragrant brew. "For what?"

Charity's hands fidgeted at her waist. "Dale, I'm sorry. Asking about your wife was none of my business. I should have known better, and I didn't mean to offend you."

He gave a slight shrug. "You didn't. I should have told you sooner." He lifted the mug close to his lips and inhaled the bracing aroma. "Not talking about it won't change what happened."

She returned to the table and reclaimed her seat. "At least you can go to the cemetery and put flowers on the graves of your parents and your wife. That must be some comfort to you."

A chill raced through him, and an involuntary tremble shook the coffee in his cup so that it nearly sloshed over the rim.

Charity's gentle words carried a thread of sorrow. "I wish I knew where my father was buried. I've assumed for a long time that he's dead, but if I could just visit his grave and lay some flowers there, it would be like telling him good-bye."

He found his voice, but couldn't push much more than a mumble past his lips. "My. . .family—" He swallowed the lump of bitterness in his throat. "They aren't buried in the cemetery. They're buried at Covington Plantation, or at least what used to be Covington Plantation, on land I no longer own."

He couldn't look at her because he was afraid the sympathy he'd surely see in her eyes would be his undoing. Instead, he studied the black liquid in his cup and took a deep breath, as if coaxing the aroma to his nostrils.

Hannah bustled into the kitchen followed by Miles. Dale looked up at the sheriff. A frown troubled the man's brow.

"It's as I feared. All Tate's things are gone. He probably cleared out during the night."

The events of the past hour tumbled through Dale's mind, and he shot a pointed look at Miles. "Are you thinking what I'm thinking?"

"Mrs. Jarrell?"

"You think she's safe?"

Miles grabbed his hat. "Only one way to find out."

Dale set his cup down. "Do you want me to come with you?"

Miles hesitated a moment. "No." His gaze slid briefly to Charity. "It's probably best that you stay in town." He strode out the door.

Charity and Hannah exchanged a glance. "Who is Mrs. Jarrell?"

Dale held out his coffee cup. "If I can have more of that magnificent coffee, I'll tell you about it."

By the time he finished telling Charity and Hannah about the woman and her story of the watch chain, their coffee was cold and there were tears in Charity's eyes.

"What an incredibly brave woman."

Dale nodded, but he looked with new eyes into Charity's heart and saw a woman of similar courage. She'd undertaken a task many men would avoid and had not flinched when her mission took her into dangerous territory. And the feeling he had for her went far beyond admiration.

❧

Charity heaved a sigh of relief at supper when Miles told her he'd caught up with Mrs. Jarrell and escorted her the rest of the way to Crow Town. Speculation skittered around the table over Tate Ridley's disappearance.

Arch Wheeler smirked. "I knew he was trouble the first time I laid eyes on him." His tone suggested everyone present should compliment him on his discernment. Instead, the sheriff cautioned all the boarders to rein in their imaginations and not start any rumors.

The Ferguson ladies helped with dessert and coffee while Charity carried dishes into the kitchen for Hannah. The landlady scraped thin peels of lye soap into the dishpan and added steaming water from the stove. Suds began to form and suddenly Hannah gasped.

"Oh, Charity! I just thought of something. Oh, why didn't I think of this earlier? I'm getting to be so cloudy-headed. That's what happens when a body starts getting old. I'm so sorry, dear."

Had it not been for the distress on Hannah's face, Charity might have laughed. "What are you sorry for?"

Hannah grabbed a towel and wiped her hands. "The laundress at the hotel. Her name is Ivy. You should talk to her."

Charity stared at her, wondering if the dear soul had been working too hard. "The laundress?"

Hannah caught Charity's hands. "She is a former slave, and she's been in these parts a long time. I know it's an awfully slim chance, but maybe she knows something about the man you're looking for."

A tiny flame of hope kindled in her heart, and Charity cautioned herself not to fan it into a bonfire, at least not yet.

She excused herself and scurried upstairs to work on her articles, but unable to concentrate, she sat by the small window and looked out at the winking stars. "Heavenly Father, is this woman, Ivy, the one who will lead me to Wylie?" The heavens didn't reply, but the hope in her heart wasn't quenched. She snuffed out the lamp and tried to close her eyes. The images that formed were of Essie embracing her son.

After fighting with the bedcovers most of the night, Charity turned down sausage and eggs for breakfast. Her stomach couldn't handle much more than a piece of bread and cup of coffee. She chided herself again with the warning that this woman might turn out to be one more dead end.

Charity could barely restrain her feet to a ladylike pace. Each purposeful step carried her closer to the hotel. "Please, Lord, I pray this woman will be able to open the door to finding Wylie."

Instead of entering the hotel lobby where the desk clerk would, no doubt, discourage her from seeking the laundress, she cut down the alley between the hotel and the saloon. Behind the hotel, Charity discovered a half-dozen clotheslines stretched between the building and the broad back fence. Freshly washed sheets flapped from two of the lines. A Negro woman with gray frizzy hair peeking out from beneath a blue kerchief stood at the third line. She pulled a sparkling white sheet from the basket at her feet and began pinning it to the line. While she worked, she hummed a tune around the clothespins stuck in her mouth.

"Excuse me, ma'am."

The woman spun around and grabbed the clothespins from her mouth. She cast a distrustful gaze at Charity.

"Is your name Ivy?"

The woman didn't answer but glanced around warily before directing her eyes back at Charity.

Charity offered her a smile and approached easily. "I don't mean you any harm. Are you Ivy?"

The laundress nodded slowly.

"My name is Charity, and Mrs. Sparrow at the boardinghouse suggested I might come and talk with you. Would you mind?"

Ivy's eyes read like a book. She clearly didn't trust anyone with white skin.

Noise from the saloon next door spilled out every time the door opened, and Charity had to raise her voice. "Please, Miss Ivy?"

A glimmer of confusion, followed by a hint of amusement, flickered across the woman's face, and Charity wondered when was the last time anyone said *please* to her.

"I hope you can help me. I live in Pennsylvania—a long way from here, and I have a friend there. She used to be a slave, and she was at the Talbot Plantation. Her name is Essie."

A brief glint of recognition lit Ivy's eyes, and she nodded slowly. "I 'member Essie."

Joy flooded Charity's heart, and she clasped her hands at her chest. "You do?" She drew closer to Ivy. "Do you happen to remember she had a son?"

Ivy dropped her gaze to the basket of wet laundry and then looked toward the hotel. "I has work I gots to do."

"Of course." Charity tried to keep her excitement in check. "Let me help you."

Ivy's mouth dropped open and her eyes widened. "Oh no, missy. I cain't let you do that."

"Nonsense, I've hung plenty of laundry, and I don't want you to get into trouble." She took a wet sheet from the basket and shook it out. "Essie is my dear friend, and she hasn't seen her son for more than eleven years." She pinned the sheet securely to the line. "By any chance do you remember her son? His name—"

"His name was Wylie."

Charity almost dropped the clothespins in her hand. "Yes! Yes, you remember him?"

Ivy's voice took on a pensive tone and her eyes, a faraway look. "I 'member when Essie first come to Talbot. She weren't but twelve years old, and the massah put her in the kitchen."

Laughter and bawdy music from the saloon made it difficult to hear Ivy, as soft-spoken as she was. Charity moved closer to her and hung on her every word.

"Essie work in the kitchen, and when she get older, dey teach her to sew. When she was. . .maybe eighteen or nineteen, one o' the field hands catch her eye. His name be Abe, and he and Essie, dey fall in love right off." Ivy moved to the next clothesline and Charity moved with her, unwilling to miss a single word.

"Essie and Abe, dey jump de broom, but the massah, he don't know. Dey keep the secret. The other slaves, dey know, but nobody tell the massah. Essie and Abe, dey be together when dey can, but the massah say he be the one who decide which slave he breed.

"Essie come up in the family way. She try to hide it, but dey ain't no hidin' sumpin' like dat fo' long. Massah, he get real angry, and he whip Essie, even though her time gettin' close. But he don' whip Abe, no. He sell

Abe so dey cain't be together no mo'.'"

Tears burned Charity's eyes, and she gripped the clothespins so tightly they dug into her flesh.

Ivy pinned another sheet up before continuing. "Essie's baby come, and it be a li'l boy chile. I 'member she name him Wylie. Some o' us ask why she don't name him Abe after his daddy, and she say she 'fraid if she name him Abe, massah will sell him, too. Massah let Essie keep her boy till he be thirteen year, and old 'nough to work in da field." She shook her head. "Mmm-mm."

The tears Charity tried to blink back escaped down her cheeks.

Ivy's voice tightened. "Massah send dat boy to a slave auction. Essie— her heart near break, even mo' than when massah sell Abe. I thought she gonna grieve herself nigh unto death. She hear'd later Wylie sold to Covington Plantation."

Charity wiped the tears from her face and sniffed. Poor Essie. What cruel heartache she'd suffered.

"Do you know where Wylie is now?"

Ivy dipped her chin and shook her head. "He meybe be sold again, or meybe he run off when the war started. Some went North. Some massahs send their slaves to fight in the war, so lots of dem probably in da grave by now. Dere's some colored folk live out by Athens road, a place called Crow Town." She halted and turned abruptly to face Charity. "But you don' go out dere, missy. No, Crow Town ain't no place fo' the likes o' you." Ivy reached out bony fingers and grasped Charity's hand. "You promise ole Ivy, you don' go out dere."

A chill slithered through Charity's middle, but it wasn't from Ivy's cold hands.

Chapter 16

C harity couldn't resist the urge to enfold Ivy in a hug. The woman widened her eyes in astonishment as Charity released her.

"Thank you so much, Ivy. You'll never know how much this means to me."

Ivy lowered her eyes. "I hope Essie get to see her boy again."

A prick of wonderment held Charity in place for an extra moment. Had Ivy suffered a similar loss? Charity didn't want to pry. Instead, she squeezed Ivy's hand.

"I promise you, Ivy, I'm going to do everything I can to see that happen."

When Ivy looked up at her, a small light sparked to life in the woman's eyes. "I be prayin' the good Lawd go wid you."

Charity hurried down the alley between the hotel and the saloon, her feet pounding out the rhythm of the tinny piano music. She couldn't wait until the workday was over to tell Dale her news.

She snatched both corners of her shawl as she set her course for the sawmill. Dale was certain to be as excited as—

Charity skidded to a halt. The same two men who had harassed her before stood near the entrance of the alley, their arms folded across their chests. She drew in a shaky breath and proceeded forward with sure strides.

The man on the right spoke first. "We want to talk to you, lady."

"Well, I don't have time to talk to you, right now, so if you'll excuse me, please."

The man on the left moved to block her path. "You don't need to talk. All you gotta do is listen."

Her heart galloped and moisture popped out on her brow despite the cool air. "Don't you two have anything better to do than bully women?"

The first man scowled at her. "You didn't listen too good the first time we talked, so we're gonna make real sure you hear us this time." He pulled out a pocket knife and toyed with it. "You been doin' lots of talkin' all over town, and we don't like it. You think you're so high and mighty, comin' down here and writin' for your fancy Yankee magazine, stirrin' up the darkies with your questions." He reached out and grabbed the corner of her shawl.

Charity's breath caught and her throat strangled, as if the man gripped her by the neck. The sun glinted off the blade as he slit a six inch gash in

378

her shawl. "If we don't got your attention, Miss Galbraith, we got other ways to do it. So you best listen good, 'cause this here is the last warnin' you're gonna get. We don't like your kind around here. Whatever business you had in Georgia is finished. It's time for you to go home." He held up his knife, turning it first one way and then twisting it around.

The second man took a step closer to her, and the stench of liquor permeated him. A wave of nausea threatened to turn her stomach inside out, but her anger vanquished her fear. She yanked her shawl from the first man's hand and pushed with all her might against his chest. He stumbled backward, whether from the force of her shove or the effect of the drink, it didn't matter.

She barged past both the men and turned to face them once she reached the boardwalk. "Intimidation only makes me more determined than ever."

She spun on her heel and marched across the street where she would be closer to the sheriff's office if needed.

Her insides trembled with each footfall, but she breathed a prayer of thanks for God's protection and kept walking toward the sawmill. She wanted to cast a glance over her shoulder to see if the pair followed, but she refused to allow them to think they'd succeeded. After weeks of searching for someone who could tell her something, anything, about Wylie, she wouldn't let two drunken ruffians steal her joy. She could inform Miles Flint later about the confrontation.

She reached the bridge that crossed to the sawmill and paused, sending her glance scanning the lumberyard in search of Dale. The rhythmic clackety-clacking of the mill kept time with her pulse. Two men loaded lumber onto a wagon and two more worked at cutting what appeared to be fence posts, but none of them were Dale. She shaded her eyes and squinted across to the far side of the yard.

"Charity!"

She turned and saw Dale descending the stairs at the side of the mill. She tucked the damaged corner of her shawl into the thick folds and hurried toward him, but he raised his hand, indicating for her to wait. But she couldn't wait. Her excitement spilled over with giddy enthusiasm.

"I was going to ask if something was wrong, but you look too happy for that," Dale shouted over the racket of the machinery. He nudged her back the way she came. "Let's go across the bridge and talk where it's quieter."

He placed his hand on her back and gently guided her toward a cluster of pines near the edge of Juniper Creek. The thick foliage muted the noise from the sawmill.

"Charity, I don't think it's safe for you to be out alone at this end of town. Miles hasn't found Tate yet, so I'd feel much better if you'd stay closer to the middle of town where there are more people."

She bit her lip. Telling him that the same two men who'd accosted her before had confronted her again would only cause him undue concern. Sticking closer to town wouldn't guarantee safety. The hotel was right in the middle of town. Granted, they'd cornered her in the alley where no one could see them, but calling their bluff rendered their threats hollow.

Dale cupped both her forearms, and his eyes bore deeply into hers. "I wish you wouldn't go out alone, even in the daytime. Not until Miles can track down Tate."

His concern sent warmth spiraling through her, but the urge to share her news with him took priority over his admonition for caution. "Dale, I have something to tell you, and I couldn't wait. I spoke with a woman this morning." She clutched his sleeves. "She remembers Essie and Wylie."

Genuine happiness lit his eyes. "That's wonderful. Who is she? Where did you meet her?" Every bit of the mutual enthusiasm she hoped she'd see and hear in his response was there.

"She works at the hotel. Her name is Ivy, and she's a former slave." She interlaced her fingers to restrain them from flapping with glee. "She was at Talbot Plantation with Essie and remembers when Wylie was born."

Dale took his chin between his thumb and forefinger and his eyebrows dipped in concentration. "Talbot? I served with a Colonel Jerome Talbot in sixty-four. I recall he sometimes kept two or three slaves at some of the encampments. I remember a woman named Ivy. Small, thin. She did laundry and mending for several of the officers."

Charity could barely keep from jumping up and down. "That must be her. She works as a laundress."

Dale pointed to his forehead. "Did she have a little scar right here?"

"Yes, she did." She clasped her hands over her chest. Her heart tripped wildly within her rib cage.

Dale nodded. "Yes, I remember her. She was with the encampment at Ringold Gap and came with us when we moved south to Resaca. Then in May, the colonel sent her and the others to the rear when the fighting took place at New Hope Church and Pickett's Mill. After Kennesaw, we—"

The rest of Dale's words were lost in a fog of shock. Paralysis gripped her, and she forgot how to breathe. A shudder rattled through her, and she began trembling uncontrollably. A rush of heat filled her face and then drained away into the pit of her stomach.

"Charity? What is it? Are you ill? You're as pale a ghost." Dale reached for her, but every nerve ending in her body suddenly found life, and she backed away.

She willed her lips to move. "Pickett's Mill?" Her voice was a hoarse whisper.

"I can't hear you." He moved closer and took her arm. Alarm crept into his voice. "Charity, you look like you're about to faint. Let me help you sit—"

She yanked her arm away. "Pickett's Mill?" The impact of realization that nearly knocked her off her feet moments ago rolled through her again and took root deep in the recesses of her being, growing and heightening until a wave of rage crashed over her. *"Pickett's Mill?"* Her emotions became a runaway locomotive. "You fought at Pickett's Mill?"

Dale's pallor took on the color of a Confederate uniform. His jaw muscles twitched and his chest rose and fell as if he'd just come from the battlefield. "Yes. I was at Pickett's Mill."

She took another step backward, and then another. "You...why didn't you...my father...Pickett's Mill was where he..."

"Charity—"

He reached for her again, and the very motion of his outstretched hand sparked the tinderbox of emotion combusting within her. All the tears and agony she'd bottled up for six years came spewing forth unrestrained.

"How could you? You...you didn't tell me anything...all the times I talked about searching for some scrap of information about my father, and you... All this time, you knew." A storm of rage boiled within her. Every dark, private corner of her heart emptied in a rush of accusation. "You killed him."

Dale's features hardened into a frightful mask of mortal, stunned fury. His fingers curled into tight fists and then stiffened out straight, each appendage taking on the appearance of a weapon. He paled for several long moments. Then the blood surged back into his countenance.

When Dale finally spoke, his voice was a strained hiss. "I was at Pickett's Mill. Many men died there. Some of them from my hands." His chest heaved, and his eyes darkened with aversion. "You don't have any idea... the horror, the nightmares—" He grabbed his head in both hands and a guttural groan emerged from his twisted lips. "The screams of dying men, their pleas for someone to come and end their misery. The blur of wishing I would die and at the same time wanting to live. I had to live. Days of pain and fever wondering if I'd survive to see..."

He bent forward and his knees buckled, as though some unseen force crushed him. "The letter. She sent a letter. I read it over and over. 'Dear Dale, You have a son.'" An excruciating sob wrenched from his throat. "My son. . .my newborn son. All I wanted was to go home so I could see my son."

He raised his head. His eyes flamed with a pain so brutal, it loomed into a tangible thing between them. Charity held her breath, dreading the words she knew were coming.

"Yankee scavengers didn't just burn my house. They killed my wife and son." The sobs moaned from him like his very lifeblood oozing away. "My son. I never even got to hold him."

The comprehension of the war's evils ravaged the deepest part of Charity's spirit, and her grieving heart splintered and shattered. Each shard bore the name of a loved one who died—some woman's husband, some daughter's father, some father's son. How many arms ached with the longing to hold that one who now lay in a cold, silent grave? A dawning of understanding slowly emerged in her consciousness. Dale's infant son never wore a gray uniform or a blue uniform.

Hot tears coursed down Charity's face, and her feet moved of their own volition. One step, then another. Refuge, was there refuge to hide her from the evil? Faster, *faster*. With no destination or purpose, she simply ran. Through the woods and the hills, she ran. Underbrush reached out long tentacles to snag her skirt and trip her steps, but she pushed forward, not knowing or caring where she went. Was there a place anywhere on this earth where sorrow and pain didn't exist?

Sweat mingled with tears stinging her eyes and leaving salty moisture on her lips. With her heart screaming within her, she kept running. Her lungs nearly burst with the exertion, but as long as the tears flowed, she allowed her feet to carry her.

"God, please hide me under the shadow of Your wings."

Reaching out in front of her, she grasped rocks and saplings, straining to pull herself to the crest of an overlook. Below, the town of Juniper Springs nestled into the valley in idyllic serenity. The tiny houses and miniature structures looked so tranquil and undisturbed from where she stood. Her energy spent, she collapsed onto a bed of fallen leaves and soaked them with her tears, while the presence of God and the music of the wind through the pines whispered peace to her soul.

ૐ

Dale stumbled through his tasks the rest of the afternoon until Simon finally planted his hands on his hips and glared at him.

"What's got into you, boy? You're acting like you're in love or something."

The idea had occurred to Dale, but hearing someone else say it drove the ramifications home. *Yes, I love her, but she thinks I killed her father.*

Dale mumbled to Simon that he'd see him in the morning and headed across the bridge. The boardinghouse loomed ahead of him. After Charity ran off, he assumed she'd go back to the boardinghouse. What if she was packing to leave? He couldn't let her do that without talking to her again. His raw outburst had nothing to do with her, and there was no way of ever knowing if it was his minié ball that struck down her father.

Somehow giving expression to his deepest, hidden pain was reminiscent of the surgery that repaired his wounds—painful, but cleansing. The festering infection of bitterness released from its prison. Now the healing could begin.

But only if Charity stayed.

Just as Dale reached the boardinghouse, Miles Flint hailed him. The sheriff strode toward him with a grim expression.

"Dale, I just got word that those white-hooded thugs who think it's their duty to rid the South of anyone they consider undesirable are plannin' another get-together tonight." Disgust laced his tone. "I'm gonna ride out to Crow Town and warn everyone to stay inside and bar their doors. You think you could come with me?"

Dale sent a glance in the direction of the boardinghouse. "I have to check on Charity, Miles." He studied the toes of his boots and sucked in a deep breath. "I just want to make sure she came back to the boardinghouse. Once I know she's with Miss Hannah, I'll come with you."

Miles nodded. "I'll be back here in ten minutes with a horse saddled for you."

Dale climbed the front steps of the boardinghouse, and Hannah opened the door to his knock.

"Dale, come in." Tiny lines creased her brow. "Charity isn't here. I was hoping you'd seen her."

Dale's stomach clenched. "How long has she been gone?"

"Since this morning." Hannah picked up the corner of her apron and fidgeted with it. "I told her about the woman who does the laundry at the hotel, and Charity went over there to talk to her, but that was hours ago. I'm beginning to get worried."

Worry wasn't a broad enough term to describe the turmoil in Dale's gut. "If she comes back, you keep her here. I'm going looking for her."

Chapter 17

Dale stuffed extra ammunition into his coat pocket. He filled the reservoir of the lantern with coal oil and patted his shirt pocket to confirm he had a few lucifers tucked there. He picked up his rifle and headed out the door.

Good sense told him the best place to start looking was the spot where he and Charity had spoken earlier that day—the place where she'd accused him of killing her father and where he'd finally relinquished his grip on the pain that had held him captive for six years.

Dale turned the corner and strode toward the boardinghouse where Miles Flint waited.

"You ready to go?"

Dale shook his head. "Charity is missing. We. . .had words earlier, and she ran off into the woods."

"Somethin' upset her today?"

Dale shrugged into his coat. "That's one way of putting it. I'm sorry I can't go with you, but I have to find Charity."

Miles mounted his horse. "Ned Caldwell said he'd go with me. What direction you goin'?"

Dale pointed up the wooded slope. "She ran toward the mountain that way, but there's no telling where she is now."

The sheriff shaded his eyes and looked out across the mountains to the west. "It'll be gettin' dark in another hour. I don't know where those hooligans are goin' either, so you take care." He reined his horse around and headed east toward Crow Town.

Dale leaned the rifle against his shoulder. He returned to the spot where he and Charity had talked earlier and found the place where she'd fled away in tears. As long as he had a bit of daylight, he followed her trail where the underbrush and fallen leaves had been disturbed.

Judging by her direction, she was headed for some wild country. Dale squinted into the glare of the descending sun. Charity had no idea of the danger that lurked on the mountainside, especially after dark. He paused to study her trail. Dismay filled him as he realized she was headed farther away from town. Dale whispered a prayer for her safety and trudged up the steep incline.

Since he didn't know for sure if the "brotherhood" was indeed headed to Crow Town or lurking in the vicinity, he didn't take the chance on calling out Charity's name as he searched.

Shadows gathered like a shroud, cloaking the countryside in veiled mystery. Twilight's brush painted the sky lavender and gold. Casting a wide look across the ridge through the trees revealed no sign of Charity. Dale knew these hills as well as he knew his own name. Charity didn't, and the waning light would disappear all together in another twenty minutes.

He stopped beside a rock outcropping and set the lantern down. He fished a lucifer from his shirt pocket and lit the lantern. It spilled friendly light in a halo around him, but it also marked his location to anyone else roaming about.

Fading light created spooky silhouettes of the bare trees. The promise of frost hung in the air. He looked up into the darkening sky. No clouds hid the stars. He pressed on, lowering the lantern from time to time searching for evidence of Charity's trail.

A rustling noise just ahead stopped him in his tracks. He held the lantern aloft.

"Charity?" His hushed voice echoed like a battle cry through the trees. He flinched and cast a glance around him. "Charity? It's Dale."

"Dale, I'm here."

He swung the lantern to the right and the light danced over her. Her shawl was torn and one of her hands bore some scratches, but she was otherwise all right. He breathed a prayer of thanks. "Charity." He laid his rifle down and set the lantern beside it. "Thank God you're safe." He pulled off his coat and wrapped it around her.

"I'm all right."

He angled his head to peer at her face and tipped her chin up with his fingers. "Are you sure?"

She nodded. "I just ran and ran until I couldn't go any farther, and I lay down in the leaves and cried. I guess I fell asleep."

Dale took hold of her shoulders and gently pulled her to him. "I'm so sorry for the way I blurted all those things at you today. None of that was your fault. I just couldn't seem to stop the words from coming out."

She laid her head on his chest. Having her in his arms sent an ardent shiver through him, and he immediately decided he never wished to let her go.

"I know. While I was up here today, I did a lot of praying." Her voice caught. "Dale, I'm sorry for the horrible things I said to you. Every aspect of the war was so despicable, and it reached far beyond the battlefield."

She raised her head and tipped it back to look up at him. The lantern light glimmered off the tear in the corner of her eye. "I had no comprehension of the battle you fought alone, inside you."

He wiped her tear away with his thumb. "We should get back to town."

She tugged at his sleeve. "Can't we stay awhile? It's so peaceful here."

They sat in the leaves side by side and looked out over the valley below. Tiny pinpoints of light speckled here and there showed where the town settled in for the night. Dale laid the rifle beside his leg and set the lantern at their feet.

"Dale, do you mind telling me about your wife?"

Strange. As much as he'd wanted to avoid the subject in weeks past, in the light of what he'd uttered today, sharing the rest no longer seemed repulsive.

"Her name was Gwendolyn. She was. . .delicate. Shortly after the wedding, my mother died. Then the war broke out, and I went to serve with the state militia. My father took ill, and Gwendolyn couldn't deal with the adversity. She went through periods of melancholia, so the servants told me. She wrote letters begging me to come home. At first I thought it was simply because she'd been overly sheltered all her life.

"I was able to get leave a few times when my unit was close to this area. Each time I went home, she became more and more selfish in her demands until she finally told me if I left her again to 'go back to the war,' that I'd find her gone the next time I came home." He shook his head. "I believe she needed medical supervision, but it was beyond my control at the time."

Charity touched his arm. "Perhaps she was frightened of being alone."

"No." Dale sighed. "I don't think it was that. Many of the house slaves were still here, and she held tea parties and went to Athens regularly. At least that's what I was told, so she wasn't alone. The war hadn't really affected this area too much at that point."

The sequence of events drifted through his head as it had in a thousand nightmares, but this time the pain was dulled. Was it because he'd finally been able to free it from the shackles that kept it bound to his spirit, or because he felt so comfortable sitting here with Charity watching the stars?

"Then I got the letter telling me she was. . .in the family way. The letter was dated in late December, but I didn't get it until February. I tried to get a leave to go see her then, but I couldn't. Sherman's forces had launched a campaign trying to take control of the railroad, and General Johnston and his troops were sent to help reinforce the area around Dalton."

He gave the memory tentative free rein and was surprised that it didn't hurt as much as it once had.

"In that letter she said she hated the thought of bearing a son. She wanted a daughter, because girls didn't go off to war." His voice dropped off, and they sat in silence. Charity slipped her hand under his arm.

He reached into his inside vest pocket and withdrew his wallet. His fingers found the folded paper tucked under a hidden flap. The creases were so worn the paper nearly fell apart in his hands, but he carefully unfolded it and held it close to the lantern. "This letter caught up with me in early June that year."

Charity leaned forward to examine it. Her voice quavered slightly as she read it. "Dear Dale. You have a son. He was born April eleventh. I have named him Bradley James."

She glanced back at Dale, and the lantern light outlined the puzzlement in her brow. "*You* have a son. Not *we* have a son." She leaned to look at it again. "She didn't even sign it."

Dale drew in a slow, even breath and blew it out, letting it turn to a frosty cloud and dissipate into the night. "No. It's her handwriting, but she didn't sign it." He folded the scrap of paper and slipped it back into his wallet. "All I could think about was getting home to see my son."

Charity's soft voice blended with the murmur of the wind in the pines. "How long—until you. . ."

Dale stared at one of the pinpoints of light in the distance. "I was wounded at Peachtree Creek. That was in July. You already know that part of the story. It was early September, I think, that an old man with a mule cart took me as far as Mount Yonah. I walked the rest of the way."

"Oh, Dale. Your leg. Walking so far. How did you ever do it?"

The lights in the distance seemed to waver as moisture burned his eyes. "I had to see my son. He was why I didn't give up. Just the thought of holding him in my arms kept me going." He paused and swallowed hard, forcing the tightness in his throat to retreat. "I remember walking down the road that led to Covington Plantation. There was an odor hanging in the air. Stale smoke. The iron gates at the front of the drive were torn from their posts. I went up the drive—you couldn't see the house from the road because of the magnolia trees. When I rounded the bend—"

Charity's fingers tightened around his arm. "You don't have to say any more."

Dale shook his head and patted her hand. "The house was still smoldering. I walked around the ruins looking for some sign that Gwendolyn had gotten my son out. Two of the slaves, the only two who hadn't run off, came out of the bushes when they saw me. They told me when the scavengers came and started looting the place, Gwendolyn took the baby and hid in the root cellar under the kitchen."

Charity released a tiny gasp, and she whispered, "They burned the house." She covered her mouth, but a muffled sob escaped anyway. She leaned her head against his shoulder, and they sat in silence.

Unmeasured minutes passed before Dale trusted himself to speak again. "Charity, I have something else to tell you."

She lifted her head. "What is it?"

He shifted his position and turned so he could look straight into her face. "I'm afraid you're going to be very angry with me, but please know that I didn't want to see you hurt any more than you already are."

"What are you talking about?"

Looking away from her when he said what was on his mind would be easier, but he refused to allow himself comfort if his words inflicted more pain. He held her gaze. "As an officer in the Confederate army, I had access to the military records. I know where the prisoner of war records were kept."

Her expression crumbled, and even in the pale glow of the lantern, he saw her wince. Was she angry or hurt that he'd withheld the information?

"You probably feel that I've betrayed you, but please listen. Because I was there and witnessed what usually happened, I feared that finding out the truth about your father would only increase your pain rather than relieve it."

The lantern light flickered off the tears that clung to her lashes. Her chin quivered. "I still need to know for sure." One tear left a glimmering trail of moisture down her cheek. "And if at all possible, I want to put flowers on his grave. To say good-bye."

Dale didn't bother reminding her most of the flowers had been killed off by the recent frost. Perhaps they could cut some magnolia branches or cedar boughs instead. How he longed to kiss away her tears.

He was about to tell her he knew which office to contact when a tiny movement caught his eye. He jerked his head around to stare hard at the lights from town. But they were no longer down in the valley. These lights—a small cluster of them—moved just below the ridge. Dale grabbed the lantern and extinguished it.

"Dale, what's wrong?"

He jumped to his feet and helped Charity up. "Shh. We need to go. Now."

"But—"

"Don't argue. Just don't let go of my arm. I know every inch of these hills, even in the dark. We'll be back at the boardinghouse before you know it." He bent and groped through the blackness until he found the rifle.

"Come on." He tugged her close to him and steered her in the opposite direction of the moving lights. If it was what—or who—he suspected, they were in grave danger.

Chapter 18

Dale hefted the third crate of grocery items on the Juniper Springs Hotel's order and carried it through the side door to the hotel kitchen. The cook signed the slip, and Dale tipped his hat, eager to head to his last delivery of the day. He saved Miss Hannah's place for last, hoping to take a few extra minutes to speak to Charity.

The entire time he'd led her down the mountain in the dark last night, he relished holding her hand—just so she wouldn't stumble, of course. He'd prayed with each step that the cluster of torches he'd seen moving toward them was only a figment of his imagination. But when they'd arrived at the boardinghouse and Hannah met them at the door with the news that some of the Klan members had burned three houses out in Crow Town, he sent a prayer of gratitude to heaven's throne for their safe descent through the inky blackness.

He climbed aboard the seat of Clyde's buckboard and released the brake. The team moved forward with little urging. Steering the horses in the direction of the boardinghouse, he rehearsed his planned speech one more time. The memory of Charity's wounded expression when he'd told her he had knowledge of military records still hovered in his mind. He'd wrestled all night with a possible way to make it up to her. If only he could be sure. . . .

He pulled the buckboard around to the side of the boardinghouse and hoisted the loaded crate in his arms. A tantalizing aroma of something sweet met his nostrils even before he knocked on the back door.

Miss Hannah peeked out the door. "Oh, Dale, come in. Set that inside the pantry. Charity and I were just having coffee. Won't you join us?"

Dale set down the crate and straightened. Charity stood by the stove with the coffeepot in her hand. Was that a blush on her cheeks, or was it a reflection of the heat from the stove?

He pulled off his hat. "Charity." A smile stretched across his face. "I'd love some coffee."

She retrieved another cup from the shelf and poured the steaming brew. When she handed it to him, his fingers overlapped hers for an extra moment, causing a burst of hope to invade his heart. Oh, how he prayed he was doing the right thing.

Hannah cleared her throat, reminding Dale she was in the room. "We heard that Miles arrested Tate last night. Is that true?"

He released Charity's fingers and tore his gaze away from hers. "Yes. Didn't Miles tell you this morning?"

Hannah nudged a plate of fragrant molasses cookies toward him. "He wasn't here this morning. Sometimes he has to stay at the jail all night."

Dale took a warm cookie and bit into its spicy goodness. "Mmm." He nodded. "I saw Miles this morning. He said he caught Tate and another man last night as they were setting fire to some of the houses over in Crow Town. A few others got away." He turned toward Charity again. "I suspect the torches we saw last night belonged to those reprobates."

A tiny smile graced her lips. "I'm just glad you came up the mountain and found me when you did." She dipped her chin and lifted one shoulder. "I'm also glad we had the chance to talk last night."

Dale shot a quick glance at Miss Hannah, who took the hint.

"I have a few things to do upstairs." She bustled out of the kitchen, leaving Dale standing there begging God to smooth the way for what he wanted to ask Charity. They sat together at Hannah's worktable with their coffee. He slid his chair close enough to reach out and touch her hand.

He drew in a fortifying breath. "Charity, I want to apologize again for not telling you sooner that I had knowledge of military records. Every time you spoke of your father, I could see the pain in your eyes and hear it in your voice." He dropped his gaze, knowing he might hurt her with his words and hating himself for doing so. "At first, before I got to really know you, I tried to justify withholding the information because you're a Yankee. I still harbored such ill will toward anyone from the North, I couldn't bring myself to help you in any way." He forced himself to glance up at her.

Charity quirked an eyebrow at him. "And now?"

Dale ran his finger around the rim of his cup. "My concern isn't for myself any longer. I don't want you to be hurt any more than you already have been."

Her gaze grew intense and determined. "Dale, I have to know." The plea in her voice nearly unraveled him. How could he have thought she wasn't strong enough to handle any possible result from what he was about to suggest?

"I know. That's why I'm asking your permission to wire a man I know in Atlanta. He works in the federal courthouse in the office of records. He may be able to find the information you seek."

She gasped. "Oh, Dale." Her breathy response told him everything he needed to know. "Yes, of course you have my permission."

He reached past their coffee cups and took both her hands. A slight tremble danced through her fingers all the way to his heart.

ॐ

Charity leaned back away from the small desk and stretched her arms over her head, turning her neck this way and that trying to relieve the kinks. Mr. Peabody expected these articles on his desk in a week. As much as she'd struggled and fought for the words and wasted paper trying to find the right angle for each of the four articles, now she had a grasp of that elusive element, the unique twist she sought.

After two days of barely leaving her room, three articles lay at the corner of the desk, completed. Dear Hannah had slipped in and out bringing coffee or a sandwich, offering encouragement and admonishing her to rest.

Charity stood and walked the four steps to the window and looked out across the peaceful town. Everything looked so normal. People came and went, doing their jobs, running errands, greeting friends and neighbors. On the surface, nothing seemed amiss. But Charity knew better.

Tate Ridley sat in jail, charged with the burning of three houses and the lynching of Henry Jarrell. What kind of hate drove a man to commit such heinous acts? Hannah, whom Charity could hear singing off-key downstairs, had lost both her sons in the awful war that nearly destroyed the country. Dale had once been a wealthy landowner, and the war stripped him of his family, his home, and every material thing. There were still those people who cast distrustful glances Charity's way, simply because she was from the North. One couldn't detect by simply looking at another person, what motivated or strengthened them, nor what fueled their passion, be it love or hate.

She looked at the paper lying on the desk and the muddled fog she'd battled for weeks lifted. A clear picture painted itself in her mind. Why hadn't she caught it before? Pastor Shuford had preached it. God had certainly whispered it to her soul. North or South, Yankee or Rebel, it made no difference. True Reconstruction didn't end at readmitting states to the Union, nor was it limited to the election of a state assembly, ratifying constitutional amendments, or adherence to federal requirements. It was as if God lit the wick of understanding and held up the lamp to shed light into all those dark and wounded places of her spirit. She sat and picked up her pen. She *knew.*

The missing piece of the puzzle had been right there all along.

Her exposé on the Reconstruction could not, *must not,* exclude the emotional and spiritual reconstruction that had to take place if the political Reconstruction was to have any true purpose. Her own battle with resentment and bitterness defined what needed to happen within the heart of every person in the country. She dipped the nib of her pen into the pot of ink and, bent over her desk, began writing as fast as God gave her the words.

Harbored bitterness was as destructive as artillery. Hatred inflicted wounds as grievous as a bullet. Rancor provided a place for those wounds to fester. Animosity took captives and malice spread poison. How could true Reconstruction take place without restoration? Restoration couldn't happen without forgiveness. The only way people could forgive each other was to know God's mercy and forgiveness for themselves.

Charity wrote feverishly, barely taking a few seconds to replenish her pen. The words poured from her soul. Her editor may very well reject her point of view, but it was what God gave her. Finally, she set her pen aside and held up the page. It was done. "Thank You, Lord. Breathe on these words, heavenly Father. Use them to change hearts."

A soft tap on her door drew her attention. Hannah poked her head in. "I'm sorry to disturb you, dear, but Dale is downstairs in the parlor."

Charity rose from her desk and smoothed her skirt. "Tell him I'll be right down." She took a quick peek at her reflection in the small mirror over the washstand and pushed a wayward curl into place. Exiting her room, she forced her feet to maintain a sedate pace down the stairs.

Dale stood when she entered the parlor, and Charity's pulse tapped out an accelerated rhythm. Could he hear it? He tossed his hat on a chair and moved to the settee. "Can we sit down for a few minutes? I hope I'm not disturbing your writing time."

She beamed and sat beside him. "Not at all. I just finished the last article."

"I knew you could do it." His smile warmed her all the way to her toes.

She dipped her head as a rush of heat filled her face. "What brings you over here in the middle of the afternoon?"

The grin that had accompanied his congratulatory words a moment ago faded. Unease traced creases in his brow, and his eyes darkened. He reached for her hand. "I got a reply to my telegram."

Charity's stomach tensed, and her breath caught. She braced herself for the expected answer to her search.

"The man I wired works in the records office, as I told you. He looked up the casualty lists from the battles at New Hope Church and

Pickett's Mill, since they were so close to each other and happened almost simultaneously." He paused, his lips in a tight, thin line. "He found your father listed under those wounded and taken prisoner. Major C. H. Galbraith was included with a company of Union soldiers who were being marched to the railroad. Their destination was the prisoner of war camp at Andersonville."

Charity clenched her fists. Such horrible things she'd read about that place. And to think her father—

Dale's voice was quiet and even. "Your father died before they reached the railroad. He was buried somewhere along the roadside in an unmarked grave. I'm sorry, Charity. I know you wanted to pay your respects at his final resting place."

She squeezed her eyes shut against the sharp pain that stabbed her middle. A burning lump formed in her throat, and she slipped her hands up to cover her face. The tears won the battle and escaped down her cheeks. Dale's arms enfolded her against his chest, and he simply held her while she quietly wept.

After several minutes, Dale pulled a handkerchief from his pocket and blotted her face. "I wish it could have been different. I'm truly sorry."

She pulled in as deep a breath as she could manage and sniffed. She didn't know if her grief would ever come to closure, but one thing she knew. Her father loved the Lord. Their separation was temporary. She'd see him in heaven one day.

Dale placed two fingers under her chin. "Are you sure you're all right?"

She forced a smile and nodded. "Thank you for sending that telegram. It wasn't what I wanted to hear, but I think it's what I suspected all along. His final resting place isn't an unmarked grave. He is in the presence of Jesus."

Dale nodded and took her hands, giving her fingers a squeeze. "I'm asking Simon for the day off tomorrow. You're finished with your articles. I'd like to come by and pick you up right after breakfast."

Charity blotted the rest of the dampness from her eyes. "Where are we going?"

He looked straight into her eyes with an expression so tender, she nearly forgot to breathe. He brushed the tops of her fingers with his thumbs.

"It's a secret."

Chapter 19

C harity took a deep breath of the crisp morning air. Light frost still encrusted the grass and rooftops, awaiting the sun's warming rays to melt it away. She snuggled into her shawl and tucked the corners around her arms.

She glanced sideways at Dale as he drove the rented carriage down the lane where the last of the autumn leaves relinquished their hold on the tree branches and drifted lazily earthward. He sat tall and strong and held the reins with easy confidence. As if he could feel her eyes upon him, he slid his gaze to her and winked.

"Why won't you tell me where we're going?" She tried to sound petulant but failed. In truth, she relished the excitement of Dale's planning a surprise.

A boyish grin that made Charity's heart turn over tilted the corners of Dale's mouth.

"Be patient a little longer. We're almost there."

She'd not been down this road before, and the scenery passed like a continuous painted landscape. Even the stark barrenness of the trees bore its own beauty against the cornflower blue sky. Through the trees she spied a few rooftops. She pointed in their direction.

"What is that over there?"

"That's Crow Town."

Ivy, the hotel laundress, had warned her against coming out here, but the reassurance of Dale's company chased away any apprehension. She scooted a tad closer to him.

"Is that where we're going?"

"No."

She waited for him tell her where they *were* going, and when he didn't, she blew out an exasperated sigh and leaned back against the carriage seat. She could have sworn she heard Dale chuckle.

Wood smoke spiced the air with its pungent aroma as they rounded a bend in the road. A river came into view, sunlight sparkling off the water as it tumbled over the rocks.

"What river is that?"

Dale grinned. "Do all journalists ask so many questions?"

Charity cocked an eyebrow at him and planted one hand on her hip. "It's my job to ask questions. And then I write about the answers I find." She pursed her lips. "Maybe I'll write about an obnoxious Southern gentleman who thinks it's great sport to irritate visiting journalists."

He laughed. "It's the Chestatee River."

Dale snapped the reins and encouraged the horse to pick up the pace. Less than a half mile down the road, Dale slowed the carriage. An odd-looking structure loomed just ahead. It appeared constructed of brick with openings here and there along the sides. A dome-shaped hole yawned on one end. At least a dozen men labored at various tasks. Dale steered the horse up the rutted drive toward the activity.

"Dale, what is this place?"

He pulled the horse to a halt and set the brake. "It's a brick foundry. That structure there is a large kiln where they bake the bricks." He hopped down and strode around the other side. "Come on."

She hadn't planned on a lesson in brick making, but Dale's obvious excitement teased her senses. She took his hand as he solicitously helped her step down. They stood for a moment while Dale scanned the work yard. The workers gave them little notice. He captured her hand and tucked it securely within the crook of his arm.

"This way."

She noticed that he measured his strides to match hers, but what she suddenly realized was the absence of his limp. Had God healed Dale's leg, or had He healed his soul? A smile warmed Charity from the inside.

They walked up to a man holding a clipboard, and Dale addressed him. "Mr. Burnett."

The man looked up. "Ah, Mr. Covington. Good morning." He shook Dale's hand. "This must be Miss Galbraith."

Dale made the introduction. "Mr. William Burnett. Miss Charity Galbraith."

He tipped his hat. "Miss."

"Mr. Burnett and I spoke yesterday at the sawmill when he stopped in to see if we could give him any scrap wood for the kiln."

Mr. Burnett tucked the clipboard under his arm. "I understand you're here from Pennsylvania."

"Yes, I am." Charity gave him a polite nod. "I write for *Keystone Magazine*. I've just finished a series of articles."

"But Mr. Covington here tells me that's not the only reason for your visit." Mr. Burnett glanced back at Dale and pointed across the yard. "Right over there. The man in the gray overalls unloading the firewood."

Charity looked in the direction Mr. Burnett pointed. A young black man, perhaps twenty-five years of age, dragged pieces of scrap lumber off a wagon and stacked them near the kiln. She clutched Dale's arm and drew in a sharp breath. "Dale, is that who I think it is?"

He placed his hand over hers. "We're about to find out."

Hope sprang up in her heart. *Oh, God, please let it be him.*

The young man looked up as they approached, and Charity gasped. He had his mother's eyes. The hope within her burst into joy.

Dale greeted him. "Good morning. You might not remember me. You worked on the plantation owned by my family for a time. I'm Dale Covington."

The fellow lowered his eyes. "Yes, suh, ah 'members you."

Charity couldn't restrain herself a moment longer. "Wylie?"

He yanked his gaze up, alarm etching his face.

Tears burned Charity's eyes, and her throat tightened. "I'm so glad I found you. Your mother, Essie Carver, is one of my dear friends."

The uneasiness fled from Wylie's expression, and his eyes widened. "My mama is still alive?"

Charity brushed a tear away, and a glorious shiver ran through her. "She is. She lives in Harrisburg, Pennsylvania, and she works as a dressmaker. The greatest desire of her heart is to find you."

Elation spread across Wylie's face. "Oh, praise de Lawd, my mama. . . my mama is alive and safe."

Delight danced through Charity's midsection. She could hardly wait to take the news back to Essie and watch the expression on the mother's face as Charity told of meeting her son.

Dale stepped forward and pulled out his wallet. "Wylie, I took the liberty of checking into the cost of a train ticket to Harrisburg." He peeled off several bills and folded them. He reached for Wylie's hand and slipped the bills to him as the two men shook hands.

Overwhelmed with Dale's act of compassion and generosity, Charity could barely contain her jubilation.

Wylie shook his head. "Oh, no, suh. I cain't take this."

"Yes, you can." Reassurance rang in Dale's voice. "Please." He enclosed Wylie's hand between both of his. "Miss Galbraith here can give you your mother's address."

Disbelief sagged Wylie's jaw. "I can really go see my mama?" He stared at the money in his hands.

"Anytime you want."

He raised his eyes first to Dale, then to Charity. "How do a man say thank you fo' sump'in' like this?" Moisture shimmered in his eyes. "Seein' my mama again is a dream I made myself fo'get."

Giddiness tickled Charity's middle. "I know how much it will mean to Essie."

Wylie thanked both of them again and again, his voice wobbly. They said their good-byes, and Charity took Dale's arm as they returned to the carriage.

Just as they reached the conveyance, Dale halted abruptly. Charity glanced to see what had caught his attention. A black man leaned on a shovel beside a large trough where they mixed clay soil with straw. The man appeared to be studying them intently. Apprehension snagged Charity's stomach. Why was he staring at them?

❧

Memories stirred in Dale's subconscious and drew him back in time. The face that was forever etched in his mind stood before him. Was he dreaming? Could it be?

Dale slowly released Charity's hand and turned to fully face the man, who now approached them slowly. The man's face took on an ethereal reflection, and he raised his eyes and his hands heavenward.

"Oh, thank You, sweet Lawd Jesus. I'd been prayin' fo' this day, and You gived it to me. You's the God who answers prayer."

The man's words of praise threw open the floodgates in Dale's heart. He knew that voice. He especially recognized the way the man spoke to Jesus. "It's you. You're the man who saved my life."

"An' yo' be the man I prayed fo' all these here years. I prayed fo' you to live, and I prayed fo' God to let me see you ag'in."

God's mercy and grace rained down. Dale took two strides and embraced the man, clapping him on the back.

When they finally released each other, Dale brushed a hand across his eyes. "All these years, I never forgot the sound of your voice as you prayed. Thank you. Thank you for what you did."

An exuberant smile broke across the man's face. "Ah jus' done what the Lawd whisper in my ear."

Dale pulled out his handkerchief and blew his nose. "I've asked myself a thousand times why you put yourself in danger to save me. I know the answer now. But there is one question I've regretted not asking. What is your name?"

"I be John."

Dale gripped his hand. "Thank you, John, for carrying me, praying for me, for saving my life. You are an incredible man."

"I didn' do nuthin'. Lawd Jesus, He done it all. All the glory go to Him."

They parted with a vow to stay in touch. Dale helped Charity into the carriage and set the horse in motion. He reined in at the entrance to the brick mill to look back. John and Wylie were both waving.

Once they were underway back toward town, Charity slipped her arm through Dale's. "Thank you, Dale. I dreaded going home and telling Essie I'd failed."

Her touch made him ache with the longing to hold her in his arms. "I've been meaning to talk to you about that."

"About what? Telling Essie I couldn't find Wylie?"

"No." He pulled the horse to a halt and turned in his seat. "About going home."

The glow on her face lost a bit of its luster. "Now that the articles are finished and mailed, I suppose I'll be leaving at the end of the week."

The ache in his chest spiked. "Do you have to?"

Confusion etched its mark across her brow. "What do you mean?"

"I mean. . ." He took both her hands. "You've put in many hours of research since you arrived here, and I'd like your opinion. Do you think a Yankee and Rebel can find love for each other?"

A blush painted her cheeks, and she drew in a soft gasp. An exquisite light brightened her eyes. "No. Not a Yankee and a Rebel. But a man and a woman whose lives have been forever changed by God can."

He cradled her face in both hands and lowered his lips, hovering an inch away from hers. "I love you, Charity Galbraith."

Her breath caressed his face. "And I love you, Dale Covington."

He pressed his lips to hers, and his heart danced.

Connie Stevens lives with her husband of forty-plus years in north Georgia, within sight of her beloved mountains. She and her husband are both active in a variety of ministries at their church. A lifelong reader, Connie began creating stories by the time she was ten. Her office manager and writing muse is a cat, but she's never more than a phone call or email away from her critique partners. She enjoys gardening and quilting, but one of her favorite pastimes is browsing antique shops where story ideas often take root in her imagination. Connie has been a member of American Christian Fiction Writers since 2000.